DEATH
TAKES
A
BATH

DEATH TAKES A BATH

A COTSWOLD CRIMES MYSTERY

SHARON LYNN

LEVEL
BEST BOOKS

First edition

ISBN: 978-1-68512-242-3

Cover art by Level Best Designs

This book was professionally typeset on Reedsy.
Find out more at reedsy.com

For Jade and Kim - I couldn't have done it without you.

Praise for Death Takes a Bath

"A whale of a read! Dip your toe into *Death Takes a Bath* and you won't come out until you've reached 'the end." A highly recommended page-turner with archaeology, intrigue, an intrepid heroine, a dishy policeman, and…a rabbit."—Molly MacRae, The Highland Bookshop Mystery Series

Chapter One: The First Discovery

"What's nine-one-one in England?" I squeaked at my cell. Black dots dancing before my eyes, I stabbed at the mic icon on the phone and repeated the question.

"I found one number for emergency services in Great Britain," the soothing electronic voice informed me. "Nine-nine-nine."

My fingers trembled, and the phone smacked to the ground. As I reached to retrieve it, Roddy, the cottage's fluffy black-and-white rabbit, hopped to inspect the object.

Jaw clenched in a death grip, my vision getting cloudy, I forced myself to stand still and count slowly to five. The world stopped spinning, allowing me to reach for the phone.

"Don't eat that," I warned Roddy in a passing imitation of my mother. I scooped him up for comfort and maneuvered my cell so I could see the screen.

"Okay. Here we go." I pushed the numbers as I said them. "Nine, nine, nine."

"What service do you require?" a voice on the other end inquired. "Ambulance, police, fire, or Coast Guard?"

"Um." *Coast Guard?* My brain short-circuited on the unfamiliar option. If there was one thing you never needed in the Arizona desert, it was the Coast Guard. My body swayed unsteadily as I contemplated the question.

"Are you able to speak?" the voice prompted.

Emergency. I needed to tell them. "Ear," I stuttered, unable to form a sentence around the horror of the situation.

"You're here, yes. If you are unable to speak, tap twice if you are in imminent danger."

The professional but concerned voice had its intended effect of calming me. Shaking my head, I changed tactics. Instead of discussing the details of what I'd found, I asked for the police.

After a complicated exchange that gave me time to form my response, a male police officer asked my emergency.

Shuddering, I said, "Hi. My name is Madeline McGuire. I'm an exchange student from America, and I found an ear." The words tumbled from my mouth. "A human ear. A freshly severed human ear."

Saying it out loud made it real. Bunny in arm, I sunk to the floor, clinging to fluffy comfort. The image of the blood-stained ear spilling out of the salt-packed box loomed in my mind, stirring the acids in my stomach.

The voice of the officer broke through my thoughts. "You did the right thing to call. Do you have the address of your location?"

"Ash Tree cottage on Greenway Lane, Bath, England."

"I'll stay on the line until a constable arrives," he told me.

Teeth chattering, I nodded robotically.

"Miss?"

"Yeah. Okay. I'll be fine. Fine," I said, not sounding even a little fine. "I'll make coffee. This seems like a coffee moment."

"I've found that tea is quite soothing in difficult situations," the officer offered.

Ignoring the suggestion, I treaded into the kitchen, Roddy clutched to my chest, the phone pressed to my ear.

"I could have done without your discovery, Roddy," I muttered. When I brought the rabbit in from the pouring rain, I let him roam free long enough for him to chew a hole through the cardboard of a newly delivered package.

"What was that, miss?" the policeman on the line asked.

"Oh, sorry. Talking to my rabbit."

"Miss?"

"Nothing. I'm fine."

I hadn't blinked in a long time. A tremor rippled through me as I set the rabbit on the kitchen floor. With a weird detachment, I noted that Roddy's black-and-white fur matched the checkerboard tile. The pattern became mesmerizing, a safe place for my mind until I collapsed against the counter.

Catching myself, I said, "Coffee. Coffee is good." Filling the electric kettle, I flickered the "On" switch, then retrieved the French press. A mostly empty bag of stale coffee sat behind the press.

Dumping the ground beans into the glass cylinder, I filled the press with hot water.

It was a mundane task that I had done hundreds of times. I wondered, *could I make coffee without my ear?*

As I pushed the plunger to infuse the water with grounds, I almost shoved the contraption onto the floor. Catching it just in time, I shakily poured myself a cup. Ignoring the scalding heat, I gulped.

Caffeine coursed through my system, making me jumpy as I thought about the consequences of receiving a body part. An ear in the mail would make a little sense back in Chicago, where I was getting my archaeology degree. Mobsters still controlled parts of the city, and the paper always mentioned grizzly retribution crimes.

As I took another sip, I imagined finding the package while at college. The dorm would buzz with gossip, wondering what the intended recipient had done. And I would know it wasn't meant for me.

I had only been in Bath for two days. I didn't know anyone in England, especially not well enough to offend them.

Did that mean the homeowners where I had a room were being warned? My stomach curdled at the thought. I hadn't met them yet, but I considered them friends after the year of emails we exchanged. Bad people wouldn't own a bunny, would they?

Losing control, I hunched over, retching dry heaves.

I leaned my back against the pantry door and slid to the floor. Roddy hopped in my lap, comforting me.

"Miss?"

I yelped, causing the rabbit to bound off of me, his powerful legs digging into my jeans. I'd forgotten the phone.

"Hello?"

"Constable Bailey is on your street. His collar number is 16941."

"There's a pull chain to open the latch on the gate. The box is in the mudroom. Tell him to come in."

"Mudroom?" For the first time, my dispatcher sounded unsure.

The unreal feeling associated with jetlag and finding a monstrosity had me flustered. Explaining Americanisms grounded my thoughts, and I spewed out an architectural description. "It's the small room in the front of the house where you can knock mud off your shoes." The room at Ash Tree Cottage was glassed in, protecting a deep, white-washed bench, and cast iron white bistro table with two matching chairs.

"Ah!" The operator sounded pleased to learn something. "We call that the boot room," he informed me. With a more serious tone, he added, "The constable will be there momentarily."

Without another word, the connection severed.

My fingertips tingled with pins and needles. What if a constable wasn't at my door but a knife-wielding ear-maniac, instead?

Closing Roddy into the kitchen, I snuck to the front window and pulled aside one of the ivory linen curtains, barely far enough to peek through.

Beyond the massive ash tree, stepping stones lined with red, purple, and yellow flowers led up to the gate at street level. A fairy-tale setting at odds with body parts. The white-painted wood swung open with a gust of wind, revealing a constable.

To my relief, the policeman appeared in an official blue uniform. Plastic covered the hat, which topped a man of medium height and build covered by a clear rain poncho. He must have noticed the swish of the curtain because when he saw me, a lopsided grin graced his features.

I groaned, letting the cover fall into place over the window.

The overbearing clod I'd met in a pub last night rang the doorbell.

The previous day I called my mom to let her know I arrived safe and sound in England. She insisted I could not nap the day away or I would never get over jet lag. After I was sure she could no longer hear me, I huffed. "Fine," I said aloud. "If you want me to go out, I'm going to a pub." Pulling on my favorite pair of worn jeans and a blue flannel shirt, I gathered my hair into a long ponytail and set out.

After a couple of missteps, I found the Cellar Bar, and just as I was settling in with a local pint, this guy waltzes in like he owns the place and invites me to leave with him.

Now, that very clod who had caused me to scamper away from my first legally purchased beer like a frightened squirrel stood outside my door.

Chapter Two: The Overbearing Clod

A pushy guy was a situation I knew how to handle. Shoving all thoughts of severed ears from my brain, I set myself for a fight. Secretly pleased I had something to focus on, I answered the door, setting my stance wide, hands-on-hips. "You have got to be kidding me," I greeted him.

The corner of his mouth tugged up. "Did you meet Van Gogh after you snuck out of the pub last night?"

I rolled my eyes and responded, "I made quite an impression."

Constable Bailey laughed.

My annoyance with him broke as I smiled, and for a brief moment, I felt normal. Clinging to the humor, I managed to keep the friendly expression in place. The police were here and would figure everything out.

"And I didn't sneak," I clarified. "I escaped."

The bar I found required descending a flight of stairs, where I discovered a low-ceilinged pub pumping out classic rock.

The menu, written on a chalkboard behind the bar, listed local ales. Taking a stool, I ordered a pint and scanned the room. The cellar walls were unfinished and must have been rough once, but now they were smoothed and almost glossy. Posters of concerts and flyers for local bands hung everywhere.

There was an added wall at the end of the bar where I was sitting, covered in posters. It wasn't lined up with the others. Slightly under three feet square, and I wondered what secrets lay behind the area.

It turned out to be a stairwell and my salvation from what I thought had been a threat. Constable Bailey needed to work on his PR skills.

A gust of wind whipped rain against the windows before he could respond. I wrapped my oversized gray sweater more tightly around my body.

Bailey observed my reaction. "You can wait inside. Have some tea. I'll secure the evidence and ring the bell when I'm done."

"Don't bother ringing," I told him. The doorbell had taken on supernatural dimensions in this house. In two days, I'd been awoken by two bizarre objects. "Just come in."

I went to the living room and cuddled in the big armchair, surrounded by royal blue pillows and the fluffy pink afghan. The better part of an hour passed, and a deep chill settled on me.

Finally, I couldn't stand it anymore. Throwing off the covers, I went to the mudroom, or boot room, and peeked at Constable Bailey.

He glanced around, his expression softening as he saw me. A latex-gloved hand waved.

I waved back and returned to my chair.

Another eternity passed. My mom would tell me not to exaggerate. I would say to her I'm not used to ears arriving in the mail.

"Ding, dong." Bailey opened the door a crack. His rain coverings were off, and he moved stiffly in his silver-buttoned jacket.

I attempted a smile. "Over here."

"Brrr." He rubbed his arms. "It's freezing in here." He strode to the white marble fireplace and leaned on the black button beside the mantle. Flames burst into the little grate, chasing away the cold.

The Priestlys, the couple who rented me a room for the semester, left me a note explaining how to turn on the fire. I'd been afraid that I would start a gas leak and the house would explode, so I hadn't tried it. My childhood home in Arizona didn't have a fireplace inside. We had a flagstone fire pit by our pool, but my mom always lit the propane.

I missed my old house so much. Warm, big, and full of love. Well, not anymore.

A rustling of paper made me look up. The constable pulled out a notepad.

Reality crashed around me as I gazed at Bailey. "Was it, you know... real?"

I asked, sinking back into my protective nest of pillows.

"Question time. Brilliant." He sat on the white damask Queen Anne-style couch across from me and opened the notepad.

"We'll need your information."

"Madeline McGuire, from Tempe, Arizona. You can call me Maddie." I handed him my driver's license, and he copied my vitals. "But I'm going to college in Chicago."

"College or university?"

I shrugged. "Same thing."

"What brings you to Bath, England, Madeline McGuire?" He returned my ID.

"I'm starting an internship in archaeology at the Roman Baths. So, was it?" It seemed gruesome to keep asking, but, well, *ear*.

"How long will you be in the country?"

"I'm hoping to stay a full year, but if things don't go as planned, as little as four months." I approached the subject from a different angle as I needed answers. Strange country, far from home, and a very disturbing warning sign turned me from curious to panicked. "Has anyone reported a missing body part?"

His lips twitched as he struggled not to smile. Ruining the moment, he asked, "Do you know of any person who would send this?"

My stomach lurched. "Me? No! I've only been in the country for two days!" Adrenaline flooded through me, switching panic to anger. I slammed a throw pillow on the coffee table. "What kind of country are you people running? Yesterday a strange man woke me up with a fish at my door. A fish! And today, I get this? The package wasn't even addressed to me! Why would you ask me that?"

"Slow down," Constable Bailey suggested in an overly soothing tone. "Start from the beginning."

Grabbing the discarded pillow, I balled my fists and counted slowly to five. To my credit, my counts have gotten much shorter during the course of my life. My nerves still jangled, but that wasn't the constable's fault. "Sorry." I cast about for a peace offering. "Do you want hot tea?"

"Tea? Very much. Allow me."

He rose and strode through the swinging door to the kitchen.

The warmth of the fire spread through the room, driving away the gloom. The pretty flames dancing in the grate distracted my muddled thoughts. I curled my legs under me.

Constable Bailey returned with two steaming cups and a plate piled high with thick slabs of toast, which he set in front of me.

"Were you aware of the rabbit in your kitchen?" he asked, unable to mask the amusement in his eyes.

My shoulders relaxed. "Roderick the Rabbit, Roddy to his friends."

"I couldn't help but notice definite signs of nibbling on your box." He gestured toward the boot room where the box with an ear crouched.

A full-body shudder shook my frame. "Not my box," I interjected.

He ignored my words but attempted to lighten the mood. "I may be thinking above my station here, but I'm willing to bet that Roddy, if I may, got hold of the box?"

He emphasized the word 'the.'

Cupping the mug in my hands, I uncurled and leaned toward him. I took a sip before answering. He had added something to the tea, a hint of sweetness, and a dollop of milk.

"This is delicious," I admitted. "How did you do that?"

He winked by way of answering. "Scotsman's magic," he said with a thick Scottish burr.

Taking another sip, I explained, "The rain." I gestured to the water-splattered windows with my cup. "I felt bad for Roddy, so I brought him in."

As he wrote, I eyed the toast the constable brought to me, noting a distinctive dark brown swatch of goo where butter should live. I sniffed and wrinkled my nose. "What is that?"

"Toast." His eyebrows narrowed. "How long has the package been here?"

I checked the time. "A couple of hours, I suppose. The doorbell jarred me awake, and yesterday when I had tried to ignore the bell, it kept ringing and ringing. I finally answered, and a man in a lab coat held out a gaping fish for me. Up until today, that was the most disturbing thing that I had ever encountered."

"Cornish Fishmongers?" he offered as if bringing fish to jetlagged Americans was an acceptable thing to do.

Nodding, I continued, "I told him the Priestlys were out, but he took some convincing to make him take it away. The fish kept staring at me with its silvery eye."

"Only the one eye?" he asked, grin flashing.

"Anyway," I went on. "This morning, I knew better than to ignore the ringing. No one was around when I came out, but the box sat there, lurking under the eaves like a troll." I gestured to a white, wrought iron garden table visible through the window. "I brought it into the mud, or boot room, and set it on the table."

My throat constricted as I saw the table. I didn't want to think about it, or the box, or my rationalization in finishing what Roddy started. If I had just left it alone, I could have gone on with my life.

Turning back to the toast, I said, "And I meant the brown goo. It looks… suspicious."

"Marmite. Try a bite." His friendly expression darkened as he scanned his notes. "Did you say the package wasn't addressed to you?"

Examining my toast, I took a tentative bite. Salty and sharp. Odd, but not bad. Suddenly starved, I gobbled the bread, then finished my tea. Aiming for some restraint, I avoided licking the crumbs from the plate.

When I looked at him, Bailey's gaze bore into mine. "Why did you open the package if it wasn't addressed to you?"

I plonked my empty teacup on the table. "It wasn't addressed to anyone. The address just said Ash Tree Cottage." I didn't want to admit how much time I spent poking at the box before deciding that since the rabbit had started it, I might as well finish. Curiosity got the better of me. "Besides, Roddy opened it, as you deduced."

"Does he live inside the house?"

"I'm fairly certain taking residence in the garden gives Roddy the right to open mail addressed to Ash Tree Cottage," I answered, evading the question.

Truthfully, I wasn't sure if the rabbit was allowed inside. But the rain had been coming down in buckets, so after I brought in the box, I rescued Roddy from his garden hutch and left him in the boot room. He made a beeline for the cardboard and chewed a hole. Now, he was settled into the kitchen, and I hoped the Priestlys wouldn't find out that I'd given him the run of the place. "It was raining, so I brought him in."

"Did you say you told the fishmonger you were alone here?"

When he put it like that, it sounded like a stupid thing to do. "He was far more interested in the fish than me," I huffed.

"Fair enough," the constable continued ignoring my increasing agitation. "Who else have you spoken to since you arrived?"

"No one."

He placed his pen on the table and turned his head to the side. "I am an actual eyewitness to the fact that you were out," he stated. "And speaking to people."

"Fine," I said, recalling the last forty-eight hours. "Day one. My arrival. I spoke with a cute flight attendant who refused to serve me a mimosa, making him decidedly less cute. A short, round man in the airport who helped me find my coach, and a local bus driver who insisted I pronounced Devonshire wrong."

"You're nineteen." He jumped back to the beginning and to what I considered the most irrelevant part of my list.

"I know. The drinking age is eighteen here."

He focused on me, making sure he had my attention. "But not on the plane." He made the statement like he was an ancient sage instead of being roughly my age. Probably a couple of years older.

Rolling my eyes, I explained, "It was worth a shot. He didn't serve me."

Nodding, presumably with approval of my mimosa denial, he pressed for details. "You didn't speak with anyone else at the airport?"

"I called my dad in Chicago and thanked him for upgrading me to first class."

Bailey's eyebrows shot up, I guessed because of the extravagance.

"I earned the money for my ticket," I added, a touch defensively.

As if he knew I was thinking of him, my dad sent a message, announced with a loud ding. Looking out of reflex, I regretted drawing attention to the text.

Bailey stood, peeking at the screen, so I clicked it off.

"May I see that?" To his credit, he asked very politely.

Handing him my phone, I sighed. My dad had used his pet name for me. It read, "Take the castle by storm, Pumpkin!" and included an Easter Island head emoji.

"Why is there an Easter Island head?" The constable asked.

I shook my head with a fond smirk. Talking about my dad had a soothing effect on me. He was a high-powered businessman, but also a dork. A world that produced that man couldn't be all that scary. "He probably just discovered them and wanted to use it."

"Not a hidden message?"

He was treating my dad's goofy text like a clue.

Only, Dad was involved with executives all over Chicagoland. What if this ear was a mob threat that had to do with him? If it was, they picked the wrong family. No way would I tell my dad about this, or he would have me in a sales job in ten seconds flat.

"Well?" Bailey prompted.

I confirmed, "Absolutely not. I thanked him for the flight, and the phone, and the international calling plan." I groaned inwardly at how spoiled I sounded. How was I supposed to be independent if I depended on my dad for everything?

"If I told him I'd found an ear, he'd have a ticket waiting for me at the gate for the next flight home."

In fact, Dad probably already had his secretary book me an emergency return ticket when he upgraded my flight. He wanted to be supportive, and he was super sweet, and I loved him. A warm feeling spread through me. There was no way he could be involved in anything criminal. He was just too, well, Dad.

He didn't understand how important this internship was to me and that I had to succeed on my own. Still, he wouldn't ever do anything to jeopardize my future. Including getting sucked into the mob, I assured myself as a rope tightened in my gut.

"No one overheard your conversation?" Bailey leaned forward, trying to focus my attention.

The weight of my situation and this interview must have telegraphed across my face as annoyance. The constable's shoulders tightened, he sat straighter, and his expression smoothed over.

"Who else?"

"No one," I spat, tired of being grilled. As the victim, I shouldn't be questioned like a suspect. "I hadn't even met the rabbit yet."

Unrelenting, he continued. "Day two began with the fishmonger whom you told you were alone."

I'm not sure if he meant his statement to sound like an insult, but it came out as such. "Listen, officer 16941, I'm the one who got the ear in the mail. I'm in a strange country where you'd think I'd understand the language, but your exit signs say, Way Out, I don't know how to respond to Y'alright and I'm tired of looking like an idiot when I ask which coin is a shilling versus twenty-five pence. And someone mailed me an ear!" I repeated for emphasis.

Instead of reacting to my outburst, he glanced at the number on his uniform's shoulder. "How could you see this from over there?"

Confused, I squinted at him. "I can't."

"How did you know my collar number?"

I slumped toward him, trying to read his mood. "The operator told me."

"You remembered?"

I shrugged. "They're perfect squares backward. You must have noticed."

His eyebrows knit together. "Six doesn't have a square." He glanced at me. "Does it?"

Shaking my head, I explained. "Sixteen has a square of four, nine of three, and four of two. I'm not sure if math experts count one as a square or not, but it fits the pattern."

Without a change of expression, he asked, "How did you say Devonshire before?"

"Devon-shy-er. Not Dvnshr, like it doesn't have any vowels."

He smiled at my description of the pronunciation, and I regretted both my outburst and my paranoia.

Somehow sensing I was ready to start back to the interview, he asked, "Day two? Who after the fishmonger? Think carefully. Did you encounter anyone unsavory?"

Chapter Three: The Second Discovery

Fish incident aside, none of my adventures of the previous day were essential to the situation at hand. Answering Constable Bailey's question, I recalled, "A little lady at the Abbey, and a server at Sally Lunn's. My biggest discovery was that Roddy likes to chew on cardboard." I lifted both my palms. "That's it."

He tapped his pen against his notebook like he wanted to press for details, but he moved on. "What can you tell me about the people who live here?"

Oh no. I wasn't about to pin this awful business on the lovely family that let me stay in their top floor studio. The ear couldn't be their fault. They were on a Mediterranean cruise.

"They're still out." Not a lie. "Most of our relationship has been through correspondence. They rent their upstairs room out every year to a student. They're very nice." I nodded for emphasis. "Very."

"I'll need to speak to them."

Uh oh. "There may be some difficulty with that."

His eyes narrowed in suspicion. "What do you mean?"

I stood and paced around the room. I didn't want to make it sound like this family that had opened their home to me fled the country on a whim. But they had.

"Miss McGuire?"

"Maddie, please."

"In that case, call me Edward when you answer my question."

On the other hand, what if the Priestly's house held dark secrets? Or body parts? I froze, blood chilling to my toes.

15

I hadn't explored the cottage. After a long bus ride from the airport, I collapsed onto the living room couch. When I awoke in the middle of the night, I snooped around only long enough to find the kitchen and a breadbox perched on top of the butcher block island. After making toast from the loaf of nutty, homemade bread, I made my way back to the couch and fell asleep.

What if my ears were next on the list? Former student residents might be stuffed into a hidden passageway at this very moment. A high buzzing sounded in my ears.

"Are you alright?"

I couldn't move, couldn't blink.

The tinkling of a teacup set on wood infiltrated my brain. A creak of a spring in the couch.

Edward touched my shoulder. "Maddie?" he asked, clearly concerned.

I turned to face him. "Can you make sure all the other students who lived here are alive?" I swallowed hard. "Ears intact?"

Alarm intensified across his face. "Where are the owners of the house?" he repeated, this time with steel in his voice.

"Greece, or Italy. They left on a cruise before I got here. Is that suspicious? Why would they do that?"

His manner was reassuring, but his expression hadn't mellowed. "Did they get a cracking price? My sergeant took off on a last-minute deal a couple of weeks ago." Despite the words, he gave the impression that something coiled and dangerous hid under his exterior.

"Well, their note implied a cheap trip."

Edward straightened. "What note?"

When I got off the bus at the Devonshire Arms, I'd trekked up the very steep but very beautiful ivy-lined hill indicated by the coach driver. The little wheels of my suitcase had complained on the cobbled streets, and I thought that little annoyance would be my biggest problem.

Greenway Lane's tall, gray stone walls gave way on the left to a riot of ivy. Breaks in the foliage revealed a large, open park beyond. I gazed transfixed, trudging ever upward.

Reaching the apex of the hill, I turned. The view opened over the city. Steep, peaked rooftops, curving streets, and honest to goodness fairy tale cottages met my gaze. The towers of the Bath Abbey reached for the sky. I gaped, opened mouthed.

Names of each property were carved into iron gates or wooden doors. Ever since reading Little Women as a child, I wanted my home to have a name like Jo March's Orchard House.

Ash Tree Cottage on Greenway Lane was ideal, perched halfway along the road. "When I arrived," I explained, "I found a note stuck to the house number, with "Madeline McGuire" written in cursive. There were notes everywhere welcoming me."

The first one described how to open the gate. That was it. I flipped the note over to make sure, but there were no further instructions.

I had been so enamored of the view when I opened the gate, I didn't worry about it. The huge ash tree, colorful flowers, and verdant foliage that swooped across to a ravine lay past the low garden wall took my breath away.

The house was nestled below, white with black shutters and decorative putlogs. Rising three stories, the attic loft overlooked the lane.

"Another envelope hung on the front screen when I got to it." Pulling the hefty old-fashioned key from my pocket, I handed it to Edward. "The key was in the second one, and the explanation of why they weren't there."

Turning the key over in his hand, Edward's body leaned toward mine, taught with tension. "Was that it?"

"They left me three notes," I explained. "One by the gate, another on the front door with the key. The final one told me to help myself to the food along with care instructions for Roddy."

"I'll need to collect those."

My head nodded so violently that my brain rattled.

His eyes bore into mine. "Why didn't they email you, do you think?"

I took a tiny step toward him, suddenly wanting shelter from this strange house. "Well, they did, but it didn't come in until after I'd arrived when my data plans kicked in."

"Stay here and have another cuppa. I'll start on the second story." He strode toward the stairwell at the front of the house.

"Why don't we start at the top?" I asked, following. The third floor attic loft overlooking the street and garden was where I was staying.

Not that I wanted a man in my bedroom, but I needed the reassurance that it wasn't hiding secrets.

He glanced back. "That's what I said."

Perhaps he was confused about the height of the house. It was built into the side of a hill, so one floor was hidden. "Top is the third story," I clarified. "Ground, second, third."

"You forgot the first," he told me as we ascended to the bedroom level. "This is the first floor."

I narrowed my eyes at him, not sure if he was teasing me or if I was missing something. "No. This is the second floor. Don't you count the ground level as a floor?"

"Zero," he said. He turned at the top of the landing, where a bathroom anchored short halls that branched out. With a wave, he continued up the steep and narrow flight of stairs to my studio.

As he swung the dark blue door open to reveal the bedroom, I couldn't help a sigh at its loveliness. My own princess tower.

A plush, quilt covered, built-in bed was surrounded on three sides by overflowing bookshelves. Lace curtains floated over a picture window opposite the door.

Edward flicked them open. He checked the lock on the window and flung open the sash. A fierce wind whipped in, blowing papers off of a delicate, white desk. He deftly pulled the window closed as I gathered the notes the Priestlys had left for me. Rain streaked across the window, obscuring the view of the ash tree and Roddy's hutch.

"On a sunny day, you could sit out there," he commented as I handed him the notes.

I hoped that someday I would feel safe enough to relax that much.

After searching inside the wardrobe, behind the pedestal sink, and moving a few books, Edward gave my bedroom the all-clear.

A small knot in my shoulders released, and my breathing started to deepen. Maybe everything would be okay. But we had a lot of house to go through.

Clinging to the handrail, we descended to the next level and checked out the four bedrooms and two bathrooms. The baths were back-to-back, with two bedrooms on either side of each forming a Y.

"Zero doesn't count," I continued our argument as I examined the hall with the larger bedroom. Keeping the mood light kept me from running to the next plane home. "You start counting at one."

The teasing died in my throat as I noticed an architectural inconsistency. Not visible from the hallway or once inside the room, I could see the misalignment from where I stood in the doorway.

"Look at this." I stood sideways on the threshold and pointed. "The wall in the master bedroom doesn't align with the one in the room opposite."

My heart rate ratcheted up a notch, the knot in my shoulders wrenching tight again. I discovered a hidden passageway.

Edward stood in the doorway, head swiveling back and forth until he saw what I was talking about. "You're right," he said. "Let's see about this."

He moved a dresser out of his way, bent, and pulled a flashlight out of his belt.

Shuffling sounds made me picture a wall decorated with ears, rats scuttling over them. My stomach flopped as I fought down the urge to wretch again. "What is it?" A tremble shook my voice.

"Access panel," his muffled voice returned.

Metal snapped into place, and he emerged. "My guess is indoor plumbing was added after the house was built. All the pipes run through that wall."

He nodded at me. "I wouldn't have seen that. Sharp, you are." The lopsided grin flashed briefly, and relief flooded me.

Plumbing. That made sense. Thank God.

Preening a little at Edward's praise, I told him, "I love ancient Roman architecture. Hidey-holes were built by the wealthy to conceal valuables. Spotting inconsistencies in dimensions of a room is easy when you practice."

His face relaxed for the first time in a while. He seemed genuinely interested. "Is that how you managed to sneak out of the Cellar Bar? Did you find something no one else sees?"

I beamed at him. "A stairwell to the Huntsman."

"Impressive." Pausing, he asked, "Why did you sneak out?"

His voice had been friendly, and when I said 'hi,' I thought he was kind of cute. Brown hair cut short but with a little curl around the ears, brown eyes, and a slightly lopsided smile greeted me. He noticed that I was American, and we enjoyed a couple of minutes of pleasant conversation.

Then, he had the nerve to invite me to leave, and walked off like I would follow. Annoyance at the presumption bubbled up. "That was the worst pickup line ever, is why. What kind of jerk flirts for two minutes and then assumes the woman will follow him home?"

His face looked boyish for the first time. "I wasn't," he began. "I wouldn't do that," he said, embarrassed. "That bar gets a rough crowd at night. I always do a sweep to get unsuspecting women out of there."

Skepticism warred with finding him sweet. "That," I made a vague gesture with my hand to indicate the previous night, "was supposed to be protecting me?"

Striding past me, he said, "Right. Zero story, next."

"First," I corrected, feeling better. I'd spent most of my time on this level. In addition to the glassed-in porch, living room, dining room, and kitchen, there was a pantry or larder.

The rollercoaster of emotion I'd been experiencing all morning threw me for another loop. Inside the larder lay a hidden door tucked at the back with an oddly ornate doorknob.

"There's a secret door in the kitchen." I rushed to the pantry, wanting to be done with this expedition. The crystal knob gleamed like it protected a goblin's lair. Reaching for the ornate globe, I hoped it would be locked, but the crystal turned easily.

I yanked the door open.

A dark cavern lay beyond, smelling musty. I yelped, surprised by Edward's sudden appearance behind me. Peering into the gloom revealed what looked like a perfect place for stowing unsuspecting college students.

Edward's arm reached around my shoulder, and I had a sudden image of him pushing me, the door slamming shut with the snick of a key in the lock.

An overhead light blinked on, illuminating stairs.

Or, OR, he could be doing his job. I dropped my head for a second, collecting myself.

"I'll go first," he stepped around me, pressing close. "Don't push me down and lock the door," he warned, echoing my thoughts.

A nervous titter escaped me. "No way. You're the closest thing to a knight in shining armor I have at this point."

"Stay here," he cautioned.

After a moment's hesitation, I followed him. The worn, sturdy wooden stairs squeaked under our weight.

Plaster walls gave way to rough stone beyond the first two steps. Dewy moss grew in dark crevasses. With each descending step, my mood turned darker. Cold sweat coated my palms.

When Edward finally reached the bottom, he flicked the switch on the wall and plunged us into darkness. He immediately switched it on again. "Sorry. I thought more lights would come on." He scanned the chamber and located a pull chain. "Aha!" Pulling it, another feeble bulb flicked to life.

I'd never understood the term 'chased away the shadows' until now. "Not exactly the friendliest of spaces," I observed. "At least it's not filled with... you know."

"Body parts?"

He read my mind again. I rolled my shoulders, working away more of the tension.

He pointed to a contraption. "Boiler for the radiator. The exposed stone allows the damp in. You couldn't store anything down here."

I inched off the bottom stair. I'd been treating the stairway as a safety zone, and I didn't want to stray far. The rest of the basement came into view. Exposed old blocks formed three walls, but the fourth had been left natural. Limestone boulders, solid and impenetrable, also formed the floor. There couldn't be anything buried under there.

I tapped on a few stones, listening for a hollow sound. "What if someone is sealed behind here?"

He laughed. "You're thinking Poe. He's American."

"So, I should be thinking Sherlock Holmes, you're saying? No evidence of *The Hound of the Baskerville,* either."

"No mysterious trap doors or exotic snakes." He added.

My eyes crinkled in surprise. "I remember that one."

He opened his mouth to give me the title, but I held out a hand. "No, don't tell me." I scrunched my nose, concentrating. *"The Speckled Band!"* I announced, triumphant.

"Good to know they're giving you a proper education in the Colonies."

I arched an eyebrow, my emotions settling. "I'll have you know that my mother is a Shakespeare professor. My education in the literature of England was more than proper. And I've read all of Conan Doyle."

I trailed off as a memory of a story edged its way into my mind. "Wait," I said and charged up the stairs to my phone and the internet.

Edward didn't follow.

I poked my head through the pantry door. "I didn't mean actually wait. I meant, I thought of something."

"Something sinister?"

I checked if he was teasing me, confirmed it, and started my search. I typed, 'Sherlock ear story.' *The Adventure of The Cardboard* Box resulted.

"I knew it!" I read the synopsis of The Cardboard Box from Wikipedia to Edward. "And I quote, 'she received in the post two severed human ears packed in coarse salt.'"

My triumphant grin faded as I took in his expression of intense concentration.

"What?" I asked.

"This may be rather important." He reached for my phone, scanning the page. "Hmm."

"How does the story end?" I couldn't remember.

"The box was sent to the wrong house. The ears were meant for the woman's sister." He glanced at me. "Do you have a sister?"

I shook my head no. "Meryl Priestly might, though."

Our eyes met as he handed me the phone, his fingers lingering on mine.

"I'll check on it. Make sure to keep your phone with you at all times. Take my number as well."

I handed the cell back, and he input his contact information. I texted him so he could log my number.

Edward nodded when my message arrived. "If you get lonely in this big place, call me."

The more he emphasized staying in contact, the more frightened I became. My eyes must have grown huge because he assured me, "I'm sure you're safe. I believe I've seen the name Priestly on a church sign across from the station."

My head rattled quickly in ascent. "Reverend Priestly. You don't think he's a crazy religious zealot?"

"You'll be alright."

But then the concerned, probing look returned. "Do you want me to stay?"

Considering it, I looked around the bright kitchen with the fluffy bunny. I needed to unpack my clothes, and after all the stress of the morning, I wanted a bath. Finally, I shook my head no. "Sending the cop away is how someone dies in every horror movie ever, but no." I stood still for a moment, feeling the energy of the place. "I'm okay."

I held out my hand to shake. "Thank you, Edward."

"Call me." He smiled, the somber facade dropping away. "Anytime."

As inviting as the offer was, I hoped I'd never need to.

Chapter Four: Sherlock Holmes

I checked the time difference to Arizona and decided it was close enough for a call. I opened the chat app on my computer and punched in the number of my best friend.

"Be there, be there," I chanted.

"Hey, world traveler!" Tori Gonzalez's expressive dark eyes filled my screen. "How's jolly Olde England? And just so you know, I put an e at the end of olde when I said it."

All of the tension, jetlag, and weirdness ebbed away as I laughed.

"Beautiful. I didn't expect everything to be so different. I'm pretty sure I'm gonna get hit by a car. That whole driving on the wrong side of the road thing is hard to remember. How are you? How's Scott?"

Scott was Tori's high school sweetheart. I say sweetheart, but he was actually her high school weight around her neck.

I half-listened to what she was saying. Scott was always in some sort of crisis. "I can't stand to see him so blue. When he gets this way, he doesn't want to be alone."

In my mind I said, he wants you to be at his beck and call and do his bidding. Out loud, I mumbled, "Yeah, poor guy."

I once suggested that Tori leave Scott in the dust where he belonged. She didn't talk to me for three months. I kept my mouth shut now.

When Scott's woes came to a close, I mentioned, "I met a guy. Edward Bailey of the local constabulary. At least I think that's what you call the cops here."

"What? Where? How? What's he look like?"

I started with the last question, shrugging. "Normal, I guess. Brown hair, brown eyes. We're about the same height. I tower over most of the girls here."

"You are freakishly tall," she pointed out.

"No." I corrected, falling into our old banter. At five-foot-nine inches, I stood out if I wore heels. Tori, on the other hand, barely scratched five-foot even. "You are la camarón."

"I regret ever teaching you that," referring to the Spanish word for shrimp. "How did you meet a cop?"

I relayed the ear incident.

"What the hell, Maddie? Don't go all *Taken* on me. I don't think your dad has those particular skills."

"He could sell them something," I offered. Dad was great, but not an action hero. "Why did we watch that movie before I left? It was your idea."

Nodding, she said, "Of course. It is required viewing for every young woman traveling abroad. You're welcome." She paused, then asked, "Did you say you're alone?"

"No," I'd forgotten to tell her about Roderick. "I have a rabbit!"

"What? A bunny! I wish you hadn't forsaken social media. I want pictures."

She had a point. Staying connected is easier when you can show everyone what you're doing. But, after a bad breakup in high school, I deleted my accounts. Besides, I preferred face-to-face connections. "Absolutely not worth it."

"Fine." We'd had the conversation enough times that she didn't try to convince me to start posting now. "Email me pics of the rabbit."

"Will do. You look ready to burst. What's up?"

"So, my big news." She faltered. "Well, it's silly compared to an ear on your doorstep. I'm going to have to do something drastic to catch up, aren't I?"

"I don't recommend it."

"Noted. Okay, here goes."

"The anticipation is killing me," I told her, yawning.

"I'm changing my major to religious studies."

"No," I argued.

"No? You sound like my mom."

"Your mom is a wise lady. You need a degree in something that will land you a job. Notice the major isn't even a job title. It's a school subject."

Tori laughed. "Says the girl pursuing an archaeology degree."

"Point taken." I conceded though I bristled. No one thought I would make it as an archeologist. My mom was completely supportive of my bachelor's degree, except for her habit of mentioning I could use the degree to get any job. This internship was my chance to show them all.

"You okay?" Tori's voice cut into my thoughts.

"Yeah, just thinking that you take classes in religious studies and stay with a more employable degree. Do you want to be a religious studier for a living?"

"Point to you. Because that's not a thing. Frankly, my first two classes in the subject are already convincing me to go back to poly-sci. But, Abuela Gonzalez—"

"Your scary grandmother who wears all black and can see into your soul?"

"Got it in one. She's paying for my apartment this semester and will continue to do so as long as she is pleased with me."

I understood. "And as someone who attends mass twice a week," I began.

"My new major will make her happy," she finished.

"And lying about religious studies to your sainted grandmother is probably off the table?"

Tori chose not to respond to the suggestion.

I tried again. "You could double major."

Her eyes brightened. "Hey, yeah! Thanks."

We chatted a while longer before Tori's tone grew somber.

"Seriously, though, Maddie. What's up with the ear? I mean, is that super creepy, or what?"

I covered my face with my hand. "Right? Think about it. Someone out there is without an ear. It makes me want to vomit. And let's not even go into who was supposed to be the recipient of that box." I pulled my knees to my chest and sat in a little ball.

"What are you going to do?"

"Cowering under the covers was my first plan. I might find out if I can start my internship early to get me out of the house." Showing up early would also show my commitment to the job, I thought hopefully. Unless it made me look pushy.

"How will that help you find the one-eared man?"

I tilted the laptop toward my face and glared at the app icon. "Why would I want to do that? Are you crazy? I plan to hide, then forget, in that order. I've already sent the policeman away. Which, in retrospect, seems ill-advised. I'm hoping this was like that Sherlock Holmes story, and the box was sent to the wrong house."

"What stor—"

A flash of insight interrupted my thoughts. "Tori, wait. What if the ear has nothing to do with me at all, and the maniac sent it to Ash Tree on purpose to get the attention of the police? The whole ordeal has nothing to do with me or the Priestlys! The ear sender would know that in the story, the ear goes to the wrong house. I repeat *the wrong house*. I'm not in any danger at all."

I stopped when Tori's delicate laugh drowned me out.

"You're a horrible best friend, and I love you dearly," I told her.

"Of course you do. Now, go back. What story? What's that have to do with anything?"

My legs dropped back to the floor, and I sat straight. "I didn't tell you? I discovered a real-live police clue. In Sherlock Holmes' *The Adventure of the Cardboard Box,* a woman gets mailed a box with two severed human ears packed in salt."

"Gross," Tori commented. "Also, bizarre. What happened to the woman?"

"She's safe. The box was sent to the wrong house." I smiled at the laptop, clinging to the idea.

Tori was quiet a beat too long.

"What?"

"Well, part of your rant was correct. If the person mailing the ear was following Sherlock Holmes, they would not want to make the same mistake

27

of mailing it to the wrong house, would they?"

I shook my head, clearing away the muddled thoughts. "Think about it, though. If an ear-wielding psycho is using this story, they'd want it to be the same."

"Except, didn't you say that the story had two ears?"

My knee jostled nervously. Maybe this didn't have anything to do with the Holmes investigation.

"Although," Tori continued, her voice slowing. "What better way to cause a stir in the neighborhood than to have the police casing the street? I think you're right. The box was sent to the wrong house on purpose."

"You think?"

"Definitely. Tell you what. I'm going to read the story and research. Okay?"

"You're the best," I told her.

"Yep." She paused, then added, "Stay safe. Okay, Maddie?"

When we disconnected, my stomach growled.

Remembering I had a container of bunnies from Sally Lunn's, I padded downstairs to the kitchen. Roddy greeted me by standing on his hind legs and twitching his nose.

"Roderick! How could I forget you?" I hoisted him for a hug. "Such a sweet rabbit." Setting him on the floor again, I went to the pantry door and found bowls of his food and water set out. A newspaper lay in the corner, with unmistakable evidence of rabbit poop.

Constable Edward must have set this out while making tea and toast. My estimation of the man went up quite a few notches.

Making a sandwich with one of the famous bunns, I was careful to eat slowly. Still a little delicate, I didn't want to push my luck and get ambushed by my emotions upsetting my stomach. Feeling steady, I headed upstairs, fixed my hair, and found a presentable shirt. I decided to ask the Roman Baths to start my internship early.

As I trotted along the hill leading into town, thoughts of a one-eared man floated away.

Chapter Five: The Roman Baths

I stood in the Abbey square, indecisive. On the one hand, I hadn't seen the Roman Baths yet, and there were over two thousand years of history there. On the other, the Abbey still held more to explore.

I'd seen it on my first day, which had been glorious and ear-free.

Still reeling from the morning I'd had, I aimed for the familiarity of the Abbey. The first king of England had been crowned here over 1,000 years ago, the father of King Lear.

As I studied the weathered stone carving on the bell tower, sunshine broke through the clouds illuminating one of the many limestone figures. The carving appeared to be falling off a ladder, and for some reason, I shuddered.

A cold breeze swept me to the gift shop door. Opening it, I strode in like I knew what I was doing. No one stopped me.

I made my way to the organ and soaked in the beauty of the pipes, arranged like a cascading waterfall.

"You came back," a quavery voice stated.

Smiling, I turned to greet Ella, the docent who had shown me around the day before. The organ pipes were her favorite. Her outfit looked identical to yesterday's, only in tan, pearl-buttoned gloves matched her shoes.

"I needed sanctuary," I admitted.

Brows furrowed, she wrung her hands, allowing her cane to rest against her body.

"Is everything okay?" I asked, stepping closer and reaching my hand toward her shoulder.

She straightened and lifted her chin, lips compressing.

"The Abbey is quiet today," I covered my faux pas, shifting away from her to create space between us. I needed to practice being less demonstrative in this country. "Peaceful and calm."

Nodding, she gave me a tentative, distracted smile.

She cleared her throat. "Young people don't usually come back." She thrust her chin in the direction of the nave. "Is there something else you'd like to see?"

Tall stone columns the color of butter lead my eye toward the heavens, revealing a flower pattern spread across the ceiling like a field of daisies.

"What can you tell me about the ceiling? The flower pattern reminds me of fan vaulting."

"Well done, my dear. The fan vault is visually representative of the beauty of heaven. It is architecturally self-supporting. The interlocking petals of the fan distribute weight evenly, allowing for longer expanses without support columns. The buttresses on the outside of the abbey also support the towers."

"The design is so delicate and beautiful," I said, hoping to sound reverential.

"The inspiration of the stonemasons seems to have come straight from God, actually. There is one piece of stone for every six pieces of glass in the Abbey. Miraculous." She nodded at me.

Her face relaxed back to her regular serene expression.

Just as I was about to ask about the rose window, she checked her tiny silver wristwatch and declared, "Oh dear. I need to help Deacon Michael."

I said goodbye to Ella and promised to visit again. "Don't be surprised when I return," I warned her with a smile.

She tilted her head, giving the impression of a curious bird. It wasn't the worst reaction I could have gotten, but it wasn't as welcoming as I'd hoped.

Outside the Abbey, I lifted my face to the misty rain. Refreshed by the beauty of the abbey, my confidence returned. The police were handling the...incident, and I was the brilliant student who landed the sought-after internship at the Roman Baths.

With the air of someone who knew where she was going, I strode toward the Georgian Pump House that resided atop the Bath Museum.

A sign announced a tour beginning in twenty minutes. I added my name to the list, smiling at the perfect timing. Good luck was already washing away the horrors of the morning.

While waiting, I drank in the exhibits. Carved stone, mosaic tile, and statues lined the 2,000-year-old walls. My mood ticked up another notch as I looked around with a possessive eye. Ancient Rome would be mine for months.

As the tour time drew closer, I milled about near a gathering group. A boy around my age with a clench-jawed accent announced himself as the guide. The owner of the voice was tall and blonde with watery blue eyes. He would have been handsome if he tried smiling. Although, he seemed to prefer looking down his thin nose at us.

I wondered if he interned here as well and if this would be one of my duties. The job description wasn't detailed, but the office I'd be working for coordinated tours.

"My name is Simon Pacok. Please, now, follow me."

Excitement tingled my fingers, far more wonderful than anything I'd felt that morning. Moving to the front of the crowd, I began to introduce myself. "Hello, Sim—"

He turned from me and walked at a brisk pace through an arch. "If you have any questions, please hold them until the end."

He was a bit off-putting, but I reminded myself he didn't know I'd be working with him. For now, I would be content enjoying his knowledge.

The tour started in the very spot that made me declare archaeology as a major.

"You see before you the 2,000-year-old Roman baths, the Georgian Pump Room circa 1779, and the Bath Abbey, which was rebuilt in 1611." Simon recounted. Our tour group murmured appreciatively, but I wanted to dig deeper. Pun totally intended.

I opened my mouth to ask a probing question regarding the chemical compounds in the water, but he cut me off.

"Right then," he continued. "Here, we diverge from the self-guided tour to explore a few of the more exciting aspects of the Baths."

Despite Simon sounding not at all excited, I was thrilled. Going through the exclusive parts of this active dig site got me bouncing on my toes.

"As we go by this original arch," he continued, "note the keystone in the center. This example of the founding principle of arch construction is one of the finest in the country."

I ached to pull on a pair of gloves and touch the brick and mortar. But that would have to wait. Everything I saw sparked the need in me to work, to dig, to uncover ancient mysteries.

"We're quite sure the Baths continue for at least another 100 meters beyond this point." Simon stopped in front of a solid wall of stone. "Too bad they won't let us knock over the Abbey to have a look."

The group broke into laughter, and I joined in, amused. The tour concluded, and Simon answered every question that came his way. Until mine. Before I could ask anything, he marched away. My raised hand fell away. "Oh…well."

I wanted to introduce myself to the powers that hired me, and if Simon wasn't going to hang around for me to talk to, I would have to find the offices on my own.

Scanning the domed entrance hall, I focused on signs that sounded administrative rather than exciting. Despite my quest, I stopped at a window that opened into one of the Baths and quickly became lost in daydreams of Romans coming here for healing.

With a lightness to my step that belied the morning I'd had, I turned and located an understated sign that read, "Oversight Office." It sounded promising, so I straightened my polo shirt and tapped on the door. Fighting the urge to turn and run, my mind spun in unhelpful directions. What if this wasn't the right office, or what if they didn't want to see me for another week, and I was being pushy again?

The next thing I heard was an exasperated voice berating me in a thick Irish accent. "What are you waiting for, girl? Go on in. Set everything on my desk."

Hesitantly, I smoothed my hair behind my ears, turned the brass knob, and pushed my way in.

A short pixie of a woman brushed past me, her flaming orange hair cut short around her ears. Despite my bewilderment at what I was supposed to be setting on the desk, I sneaked a peek to see if her ears were pointed. I couldn't tell, but elven radiated from her.

"I swear this fundraiser will be the death of me, it will," she remarked as she fluttered into her chair and finally looked at me.

"You're not Lily," she accused me. "What have you done with Lily, girl?"

So far, nothing about this day was going like I wanted. Seriously considering turning tail and running, I instead made a stunning first impression by saying, "Uh."

Saved from further embarrassment, the door swung open, and a girl about my age, with my hair color, wearing a polo shirt, entered the room.

"I'm sorry for the mither, Ms. Niven," she said, her slightly nasal accent one that I couldn't place. "Here's your tea. You must be gaggin' for it."

Smashing myself against the wall to give her room, I deduced that this was Lily.

"Would you look at that?" Ms. Niven declared. "You could be sisters."

Lily and I turned to regard each other. After scanning me up and down, she said, "If I were a foot taller and a lot prettier, maybe."

I laughed. "Or if I had the most hauntingly beautiful blue eyes on earth," I countered. Lily could stop a rugby team with one look.

"You're American!"

She seemed genuinely pleased by the fact, and the knotted-up muscles in my back released. The suspicion that everyone I encountered was judging me took its toll. To have someone excited by my nationality lifted my spirits.

Sticking my hand out, I introduced myself. "Maddie McGuire. All the way from Arizona."

Pumping my hand like a car jack, she grinned. "Oh, I've always wanted to go to Hollywood. Are you near there?"

Before I could answer, Ms. Niven broke in with her Irish brogue. "Madeline McGuire, is it? My intern come all the way from across the world?"

33

Samatha Niven! How could I forget the name on the email that offered me the position? Turning all my attention to her, I tried to regain some sense of formality.

"Hello." I used my professional voice. "Yes, I'm scheduled to begin next week."

I had a lot more to say planned out, but she stopped me.

"A good Irish name you have there. And with those green eyes and touch of red in your hair, you look the part. Welcome, welcome!" She stood and came around her desk to shake my hand, which Lily had finally released.

She, too, gave the impression that she was happy to see me. The knots uncoiled a bit more.

"I'm so happy to meet you," I reached to shake with both hands, remembered to curb my enthusiasm, and took a step back. Stiff upper lip and all that. I ran my fingers over a strand of hair, racking my brain to find a way to ask her if I could begin work a week early.

"I don't suppose you'd be willing to start tomorrow, now, would you?" Ms. Niven asked.

My head shot up, and I'm sure my eyes bulged. Sometimes things work out. "Honestly?" I squeaked.

"Aye," she confirmed in her delightful accent. "Our last intern got a wee bit too excited about his position in Wells. He bolted without giving us so much as a by your leave. Since you're here, we could use you."

"I would love to, Ms. Niven. Thank you." I responded in a reserved, not overly American tone of voice.

"What? Are you not happy, girl? A lot of folks vied for this post!" she chastised, only with a smile to take out the sting. "Call me Sam."

"Yes!" Bouncing a little, I let loose. "I'm thrilled. I can't believe I'm here! Everything is a wonderland research project. The house I'm staying in, Ash Tree Cottage, was built over 200 years ago. I think all of the houses on Greenway Lane are that old. My state back home is half that! My whole country is barely older. I finished a guided tour of the Baths and have a million questions. One of which is, by the way, will I be giving tours myself? Because I'm willing to do anything." I paused for breath. "And I go by

Maddie."

Sam sat, chuckling at my enthusiasm.

"Better." She indicated a chair for me to take. "We could use a bit of energy around here. Was it Simon who gave your tour? Dry as dust, that one."

"I miss Cliff," Lily interjected.

That feeling you get when you're sure this is the place for you? I had that.

"Simon's group did laugh," I volunteered on behalf of my new workmate.

Before I explained, Sam interjected, "With the quip about not letting us knock over the Abbey?"

She waited for my nod before continuing. "Thought so. That was Cliff Whitley's line. Simon got a wee bit jealous that Cliff's groups gave better reviews than his."

My eyebrows rose. Reviews? Of an American girl giving a tour in a British institution? How was that going to go? I'm sure I would question a non-local tour guide's knowledge.

Sam misread my concern as confusion and explained. "Cliff was the last intern. The one that run off. Charmer, that one." A fond grin played around her lips.

"Dead charming," Lily agreed. "Hey," she said, getting my attention. "I get off at four. Do you want to grab a brew?" She tilted her head toward the outdoors. "Show you around a bit?"

"Absolutely," I agreed, snapping up the offer. "Where should I meet you?"

Lily worked at the Pump Room café attached to the Baths. I would meet her outside when she finished her shift.

Lily took her leave, and I turned to Ms. Niven. Sam.

Taking a sip of tea, she rummaged through the papers on her desk. "Here you are." She handed me a sheaf of forms to fill out.

As I completed each sheet, I wondered how anyone could leave a prestigious internship like this. Cliff must have been crazy.

Perhaps he had been taken to be sold into slavery, like in the movies. Or lying in a ditch somewhere, and no one had bothered to search for him.

Blowing out a puff of air, I exiled such dark thoughts from my brain. But not before one more haunting image; that of Cliff Whitely, bleeding from an earless hole in his head.

Contrastingly too hot then too cold, I let my head flop forward to keep the dizziness at bay.

"Alrighty," I said, far too loudly, trying to get blood back into my brain.

Sam grinned. "Excited, then, are ya?"

Yes, I realized. Roiling emotions aside, the thought of starting the next day sent tingles all the way to my toes. Far more excited than scared. I was going to be an archeologist.

After I passed the papers back, she shook my hand. For the first time since my arrival, I felt secure.

The door opened, and Simon strode in. I turned, hand extended.

"You were on the tour," he remarked flatly.

Not to be deterred, I smiled. "Yes. I enjoyed every single thing you explained. Your knowledge is vast."

He sneered.

No, no, I thought. *Not a sneer.* Maybe I was reading him wrong.

"It should be. I'm the most qualified person in the building."

Was he? I sent a glance at Sam, who didn't look remotely offended. Wondering why he didn't have the supervisor's job if he was more qualified, I said, "I'm the new intern."

He finally took my hand with a fishy shake. "Simon Pacok."

Or, no, maybe not fishy. He did that thing where he took my fingers instead of crushing my hand. Perhaps it was a gentleman thing. "Maddie McGuire. Pleased to meet you." My smile received nothing but a blank stare as Simon stepped past me to talk with Sam.

"Ms. Niven," he addressed her formally. "When can I expect the new schedule?"

"I'll be putting that out tomorrow. If you'd like to come in first thing, you can show Maddie here around," Sam suggested.

Simon glared at me.

I may not be the best at understanding social signals in a foreign country, but this much was certain, Simon Pacok did not like me.

Chapter Six: An Omen

At 3:55 p.m., I lingered in front of the Pump Room, waiting for Lily. She bounced down the stairs with a wave and a shout.

"Maddie! You made it!" She laced her arm through mine and guided me around the square. Stopping in front of a plaque outside the Roman Baths, she said, "Sulis Minerva. Why we're all here."

Before I could read what it said, she spun me around in a gentle arc and pointed to the front of the abbey. The clock face sitting between two towers hung over the huge arched double doors. "Towers of St. Peter and St. Paul with the angels climbing up to heaven."

Just as I was about to ask about them, Lily dragged me out of the square.

"Wait, wait, wait," I insisted, spinning her around, in turn, to look at the church. "See that one carving?" I pointed to the ladder on the right tower. The statue that the sun illuminated for me the day before. "It looks like it's upside down."

Standing tall, she rubbed her freckled nose and considered. "That it does," she commented before pulling me out of the square.

"But, what does it mean?"

Lily shrugged. "Lucifer, probably."

With a series of blinks, I took in the information. The carving depicted the angels' ascent to heaven. It made sense that the upside-down one was falling. Lucifer, the fallen angel.

Silently hoping that Lucifer being highlighted the day before wasn't an omen for my whole trip, I told Lily, "It's so obvious when you point it out. You're brilliant!"

Lily snorted with laughter. "No one's ever called me that before," she said as we arrived in front of a familiar blue building with white mullioned windows and a colorful riot of flowers in boxes.

"Sally Lunn's," Lily declared proudly. "The oldest house in Bath," she explained as she grabbed a small honey oak table for two.

Confused, I doubled checked the menu. Definitely not a pub.

My expression must have been off because Lily asked, "What's wrong? Don't Americans do afternoon tea?"

Smiling, I answered, "As a matter of fact, no, but I love the idea." Pointing at the menu, I explained, "When you said 'brew,' I thought you meant beer."

Rubbing her nose again, she said, "I suppose you do brew beer, don't you?" With a lift of her shoulders, she reasoned, "Not as often as you brew tea, though."

"Excellent point," I conceded with a grin.

The same bored looking server I had the previous day approached the table. Lily ordered a cream tea with Earl Grey.

"Same for me," I added.

"Oh, it's you," the server said, the bored expression dropping away. "I asked my manager about delivering Lunn Bunns to your house on Greenway Lane, and he said it would be no problem."

"Thank you!" I told her, touched that she asked, and remembered me. "I still have some from yesterday, but I'll let you know when I need more."

When she left us, Lily's gaze scrutinized me. "You're staying on Greenway Lane?"

Nodding, I told her. "Yes, at Ash Tree Cottage. I'm renting a room from a couple, although they're out of the country right now."

A sudden jolt shocked my mouth shut. Remembering Constable Bailey's words from that morning, I realized I must have told the server my address yesterday. Now her manager knew, and my new friend knew, and I wondered how many other people I told. I was so charmed by the house having a name I may have let it slip more than I intended.

Tempted to tell Lily about the ear, I decided instead to put the incident behind me. I didn't want to scare her off, and I definitely did not want to relive the horror.

"Have you been to the Devonshire Arms yet?" she asked, a sly expression on her face.

I wagged my finger at her until I noticed how much it made me look like my mom. "I have. It was," I paused, searching for the right word. "An adventure."

The Devonshire Arms lay at the end of Greenway Lane. The local bus had dropped me off there when I first arrived in Bath. The ivy-covered entrance hinted at a cozy interior, so when I needed a pub last night, it was my first choice.

However, when I pushed on the oak door, chaos confronted me. Several large, muscular men were gathered around the bar, drinking and toasting each other. Their blue and yellow shirts matched, so it seemed likely that they were a sports team.

"It was my first stop, and it lasted about sixty seconds," I told Lily.

Her giggle was infectious, and I joined it. "What are we laughing at?" I wanted to know.

"Did you find a rugby team?"

When our tea arrived, Lily spread the clotted cream on her scone, followed by a dollop of jam.

Following her lead, I did the same. Although I poked at the cream, a little unsure. It had a weird texture, more like butter than anything. Clotted, I supposed.

"I did indeed," I told her. "One of the men caught sight of me and held his beer stein in my direction. When his friends turned and joined in the invitation with a cheer, how could I say 'no?'"

Lily shook her head. "Minute. Why did it only last a minute?"

"Well, as the door closed behind me, a different man called, 'Hey! This one's quite fit for a ginger!'"

Eyes going flat, Lily growled. "No he didn't."

"I turned on my heel, yanked the door open, and stalked out."

"Good for you! We strawberry blondes need to stick together," she proclaimed, flipping her ponytail over her shoulder proudly. "Not," she emphasized, "gingers."

Holding up a teacup, I agreed. "Exactly

"Cheers!" Lily clinked her mug to mine and said, "Anyway, The Arms isn't a place you should go in unless you want a pint spilled on you."

"Noted."

As I was about to ask where I should go, since the Cellar Bar was also off the table, Lily wondered what else I had been up to. "How long have you been in town?"

Hesitating, I pushed the thought of the ear incident away. "Two days. I'm starting my internship at the Baths tomorrow."

"Are you going to uni?" she asked.

Nodding, I answered, "In Chicago. Archaeology."

"Is that in Arizona? I don't know how your states work. You've got so many of them."

With a laugh, I said, "That we do. Chicago is in Illinois. It's, let's see, how far is London to Edinburgh?"

"650 kilometers or so," she said.

Doing the mental math, I converted kilometers to miles then divided. "It is about four times as long as that from where I grew up in Arizona to where I'm going to school."

Lily's mouth dropped open. "I've never even been to Scotland. That's crazy."

As a world traveler, I was feeling very exotic. "How about you? Are you going to school?"

"Me? Nah, not the brains for it."

"Rubbish," I disagreed. "You've said at least three brainy things since we met."

Preening, she held her cup out again. "Cheers."

After chatting happily about nothing and enjoying our scones, I steered the conversation to Simon.

"Yeah." She nodded. "He probably hates you. Nothing personal. It's because you're not his kind."

Chapter Seven: Lost

The following morning, I arrived at the Baths an hour before opening. Sam hadn't exactly said when to start, but I figured 'first thing' meant early. Simon waited by the entrance, watching me approach. I waved at him. He crossed his arms across his chest.

I hadn't had time to do anything to him, so maybe this was a "guilty until proven innocent" moment.

"Good morning!" *Cheerful, I am.*

Simon uncrossed his arms and turned his back. "You're late," he snarled before unlocking the double doors.

My first day, and I'm late and have a hostile co-worker. This was worth flying 5,000 miles for. I liked my failures international in scope.

"Oh? Sam," I used her first name since Simon hadn't yesterday. "Didn't mention a specific time. Is she here yet?"

Without answering, he stomped inside. Following him, I got my answer. The empty office proved that if I showed up sooner, I couldn't have gotten in anyway.

Maybe if I became oblivious to his offensiveness, he would relent.

"How long have you been working here?"

He slammed a clipboard onto Sam's desk. "I don't work here." He spat out the word work as though it tasted sour in his mouth. That, with the way he always appeared to be smelling something awful, was a stellar combination.

We've been together five minutes, and my patience was already wafer-thin. I wondered at what Lily meant when she said I wasn't his kind. *American? Female? Student instead of graduate?*

41

Whatever it was, my existence annoyed him.

"I live and breathe here," he continued with an eye roll, insinuating my student status meant nothing. "Ms. Niven is in charge of interns." He sighed before continuing, "That Cliff Whitley couldn't dig his way out of a paper sack, let alone an archaeology site."

I laughed despite myself.

Turning to me, his face relaxed. He looked handsome.

I doubted many appreciated his humor. I smiled in response. Which was a mistake, apparently. He scowled so swiftly daggers swished past me.

Which got me thinking about Simon's jealousy that Cliff got better reviews.

Before my thoughts could spin out of control, the door opened, and in ambled Sam.

"Bright and early as the morning sun." She beamed at me.

That smile was all it took to make me realize all my suppositions were misguided. My boss liked me for me.

I moved aside, giving her room.

"Simon," she continued. "Give Maddie here the deluxe tour before we open."

"Of course, Ms. Niven."

I wondered if she requested that he call her by her title or if formality was second nature to him. She didn't seem to care one way or the other.

The door yanked open, almost hitting me. Simon smirked, his hand on the doorknob. "Thank you." I attempted not to drip with sarcasm. "How sweet of you."

"Try to keep up. You'll probably want to take notes."

Well, I probably did. I liked notes. They were useful. The act of writing information cemented it into my mind. But was I going to take notes after Sir Simon Sneers-A-Lot suggested it? No way. Not this girl. At least not while he could see me.

"I'll be fine," I muttered to his back. Scampering to match his long strides, I noted he was only an inch or so taller than me.

He abandoned trying to lose me and instead flooded me with information.

Fortunately for me, the Baths were fascinating. I absorbed every tidbit. My lunch break would provide plenty of time to scribble notes, unobserved.

At the *Calidarium*, Simon pointed to the wooden clogs that kept the Romans from burning their feet on the heated tile. Natural hot springs fed the baths, and there were different spaces for various stages of relaxation. The chamber we were in resembled a modern steam room, only tiled and heated from below.

A single piece of the ceramic floor still existed, but the rest of the excavation revealed the cross-section of the room, including underneath floor level.

"During the day, there are projections that fill in the missing bits," Simon told me.

"I saw them yesterday before your tour. The projections are so lifelike," I let him know. "The Poseidon Pediment is unbelievable. I sat on the steps and watched it for about thirty minutes." Most of Poseidon's face and about half of the archway exist. The projectors slowly faded in the missing pieces so that the entryway appeared intact.

After a few minutes of seeing the area complete, color projections transformed the pediment again. The whitewash of the building shone bright, contrasting with the deep green of Poseidon's hair. "The color was a great touch."

Simon sniffed and turned away.

"I also visited a display that depicted Romans using the room. Does the projection at the *Calidarium* do that?"

Not waiting for Simon to answer, I retrieved my phone, snapping multiple pictures, including the wooden shoes. Dangerous, especially considering how slippery the surface would be when wet.

Opening my mouth to tell Simon as much, I discovered that he had left me.

"Simon?" There were two different paths, and I didn't know which one he took. Each route was cloaked in dark shadows.

I chose the right-hand hall, its walkway ending in a T.

"Simon?"

The path got darker the further I went. Something shuffled.

"Simon? Is that you?"

Water droplets echoed off the low stone walls. I crept along, keenly aware that it might be the wrong thing to do. On the other hand, it was a functioning museum. How dangerous could the area be?

I had no idea.

Venturing forward, the pavement crumbled under my feet, with only ambient light filtering in. This path couldn't be the correct one. I turned around, planning to go back the way I came.

It seemed to take forever to find the T. The narrow hallway grew darker, and the wall curved in a way I didn't remember.

My head flopped back in disbelief. I must have passed the fork in the road, and now I was poking around an entirely new section. So much information crammed into my brain must have short-circuited my sense of direction.

Something brushed by my foot, and I stifled a scream.

"Are there rats in here?" I asked out loud.

The scratching sound of tiny claws answered me.

Turning around yet again, I felt against the damp wall, hoping to find the original fork I had lost.

Suddenly blinded, I stumbled, falling to my knees. This time when something touched my shoulder, I flat out screamed.

"Do be quiet. What are you doing?" Simon sounded as though he caught me drinking margaritas.

"Simon." Relief coursed through me until the blinding light returned. I batted away his flashlight. "Thank goodness," I continued.

Shining the light on the floor, he huffed, "And be careful, would you?"

Sympathetic to the core, he was.

"Come on." He walked away without helping me. "The Baths open in five minutes' time."

Scrambling to my feet, I caught up with him, panting. "We got separated somehow," I commented neutrally. Not at all accusing him of ditching me, which is precisely what he did. Even now, I practically trotted to keep pace.

As we approached the Oversight office, I smoothed out my shirt and ran my fingers through my hair, hoping for a put-together appearance. A quick once over, unfortunately, reported red dirt stains on my khaki slacks where I'd fallen onto my knees.

"Hey, Simon?"

He didn't slow.

"Where is the Ladies' Room?"

His pointing finger shot out so fast he narrowly missed my jaw.

"Thank you!" I called, turning in that direction. I think I showed remarkable restraint by not adding, *You insufferable jerk.*

The restroom allowed me time to put myself together. After dusting off the blue polo that all tour guides wore, I took out my ponytail, smoothed my hair back, and retied it. "Let's do this," I whispered.

Chin held high, I strode to Sam's office door, knuckles poised to knock.

"Really, Sam, she's quite impossible." Simon's words came through.

Now she was Sam and not Ms. Niven.

Sam's lilting voice took over. I leaned in.

"...first day." She sounded exasperated.

With Simon, I hoped, and not me.

Simon continued. "Which she was late to. Not to mention that she entered a restricted tunnel, damaging the floor. We'll have to ask Sir Henry to take care of it."

My jaw clenched as tears forced their way into my eyes. *He ditched me! On purpose!* I wanted to scream.

My chest caved in as I hunched over myself, wondering if it was too late to book a flight back home today. I didn't want to see any of these people ever again. Awful, horrible, judging me without even giving me a chance.

Swiping at the tears that had spilled, I balled my fists and counted to five. Then ten. Teeth grinding, I knocked.

"Come in," Sam offered.

The best defense is a strong offense, my dad always said. I intended to use his advice in my own career, not one of his choosing.

Squaring my shoulders, I forced my fingers to relax. I would not give anyone a chance to fire me. Opening the door, I went on the verbal attack.

"Wow, this place is amazing. Simon here was especially helpful," I laser-locked eyes with him. "Thank you so much for the tour. Your knowledge is endless. You must know every inch of this place." I forced a tight smile.

I turned to Sam. "Ms. Niven, I am ready to help you in any way." I noted the massive stack of papers topping every surface of the office. "Filing? Organizing your correspondence? Updating the blog? Your wish is my command." Despite the grinding of my teeth, I think I pulled off enthusiastic.

Simon, disgusted, stood and strode out without saying another word.

I didn't move, a manic grin plastered on my face.

"I could use a bit of help with these documents," she said doubtfully.

A foot in the door was all I needed. "Okay! Do you have a system? Do you want them by subject and date?"

A glint came into her eyes. "Three piles, if you please. Donations, tax documents, and thank you letters. By date." The electric kettle on her desk went off, and she made us each a cup of tea.

"And please, do call me Sam."

I plopped into a chair and began sorting, reveling in my small success. I hadn't been fired.

Sam took her tea and informed me that she would be back in a couple of hours.

I continued to sort.

My success crashed to an end fairly quickly as filing proved to be mind-numbingly dull. Jetlag made my head weigh more than it usually did, and it kept drooping. I let my eyes fall closed. Just for a minute. Not a big deal. Just resting.

An ear-splitting snore erupted from my mouth, snapping me awake.

Sam's chair remained unoccupied.

A snort of derision sounded behind me. Simon peered down his nose.

I thought about explaining jetlag, but I doubted he cared.

He picked up one of my completed piles, shuffling through each paper. He laughed.

"What?" I spat at him.

"You may want to file the donations by date processed, not the expiration date of the credit card." With that, he tossed the sheets onto the desk, knocking into another pile. The two paper towers teetered before cascading onto the floor.

Simon smirked and left.

As I gathered the documents, Sam returned.

"Right then," she said. "Is the filing done yet?"

* * *

Impressing absolutely no one, I finished my first day and slunk away. At least I hadn't been deported.

Lingering in front of the Pump Room restaurant, I searched for Lily. She hadn't said she was working, but I hoped to see a friendly face.

A different server ran up to me, but his expression fell when he saw me up close, realizing I wasn't Lily, probably. He scampered off before I could ask about her.

When I got back to Ash Tree Cottage, I called my mom.

"What's wrong?" She asked in a voice so filled with concern that I almost sobbed.

"Nothing."

"Nothing, nothing? Or something nothing?" she prompted. "Maddie, are you okay?"

"I'm okay." A partial lie. I wanted to tell her about the ear, the Priestlys being gone, and that I didn't know what I was doing. And I was lonely. But I couldn't make her worry about something she couldn't fix. "It's just," I swallowed. "Everybody hates me."

When she next spoke, I could hear the smile in her voice. "No one hates you."

"Simon does." I sounded like a little kid. "He tried to get me fired."

"Fired? Did you start work already? What are the ruins like?"

"Awful. The last intern left without notice because he got a job at Stonehenge, I think. I stepped in. My boss is friendly, but the other tour guide has it out for me. Honestly, I have no idea what I did to him."

"I'm sure it was nothing. Perhaps the English have a different way of expressing themselves."

I relaxed a little. "You have no idea. My social skills suck."

"Madeline."

"Well, they do."

"I'm sorry," she said in a superior tone. "Is this the sophomore who was awarded an international internship reserved for students in their final year of college? The woman whose skill and charm could be felt across an ocean?"

I snuggled into my chair. "But—"

"No buts. Stiff upper lip, don't you know. You shall persevere and be brilliant. Yes?

"Thanks, Mom."

"If you want to change our calling deal," she began. "We can check in every evening."

The warm hug of my mom's voice was so tempting that I was about to say 'yes,' when a text from Edward derailed my response.

Edward's message asked, "Hungry?"

Suddenly, everything seemed okay. "No, Mom. I'm sorry I panicked. I'm good now. Once a week."

"If you're sure?"

"Yep! Love you!"

After disconnecting, I focused on Edward. I didn't want to sound like I wanted to go on a date, but I needed someone to talk with.

I responded, "Always! What did you have in mind?"

Without answering directly, he texted, "I'll pick you up."

It seemed like several steps were missing from the conversation. Still, dinner with Edward sounded more fun than eating alone.

The clouds had lifted, making the flowering garden a perfect place to wait. As the sun dipped below the horizon, the garden lamps blinked on. They were like gas lamps I'd seen in old movies. Tall with three globes branching out, each light capped with a wrought iron fleur-de-lis.

When the roar of Edward's motorcycle rumbled, I popped up to the gate and leaned out.

"I'm not riding on that deathtrap," I informed him, my mom's voice still in my head.

He took the helmet off, mussing his short hair ever so slightly.

"Walking it is," he said.

Looking away to keep my pleased expression from him, I closed the gate.

"To where are we walking?" I asked.

He cocked an eyebrow. "Do all Yanks talk like you?"

I couldn't tell if he thought I was charming or annoying. "What do you think we're doing in the States? Riding around on horseback shooting guns?"

Nodding, he said. "That's about right."

A bubble of laughter came out of me, and he joined in.

"Well," I admitted. "I can ride a horse. My mom took me to a stable where I had lessons. I started when I was five."

He raised his eyebrows. A look I now associated with astonishment on his part.

"Yep," I confirmed. "I usually rode a brown and black bay named Boots. I'd brush her after every ride and pick rocks out of her shoes. By the time I was in middle school, I had even learned to barrel race and breakaway rope."

"That sounds frightfully like something from a Western movie," he commented while seeming suitably impressed at my skills.

"It is. Big oil barrels are set in a pattern, and you have to maneuver the horse around them in a time trial." I wasn't very good at it or roping, so I gave up horses and focused on more interesting extracurricular activities.

"Tell me about Arizona," he offered.

The little pang of homesickness crept back into my chest. "Picture the opposite of here. Everything is tan. You can see forever like the sky is bigger there. There is a lot more space. Not as many people. The roads are wider, the cars oversized," I said, stepping off the curb to avoid a light pole.

A Mini Cooper flew down the street, coming within inches of my arm before Edward pulled me onto the sidewalk.

49

Wide-eyed and heart pumping, I said, "And we drive on the right side of the road."

He settled his arm around my waist. I let it stay there for a long moment before switching sides. I did not come all the way from America to become distracted by a boy. Or to become dependent on one to save me. This relationship was strictly in the friend zone.

"Have you always lived in Bath?" I asked, wanting to shift the conversation off of my life.

He shook his head. "I came three years ago to do my police internship."

I'd never heard of such a thing. "Do you know if the internship is like the academy in the US?"

"Not sure. I'm a full constable, but I take classes at uni, too."

I nodded. "My internship counts toward my university credits, but I'm not enrolled in any other courses right now." If I could wrangle full-time work out of the Roman Baths, I could finish my degree online.

"Where were you before you moved?" His accent sounded just like Simon's, so I figured he was local.

He had guided me into town. "Have you seen Pulteney Bridge yet?" he asked without answering.

Shops and cafes crowded together on both sides of the street. "No. Where is it?"

He took me into a pub called The Boater, which was blasting rock music. We walked past the seating area and a long bar to the tall, narrow windows which opened out over the water. I leaned out the sill, watching the river flow underneath us.

Glancing to the side, I saw walls with windows. The shops were on the bridge. Turning to face Edward, I bounced a little. "This is like the Ponte Vecchio in Italy, isn't it? The bridge is disguised like a regular street until you get inside one of the buildings."

He squinted at me. "Did you not notice the Avon as we walked by the park? Where did you think it went?"

My shoulders pumped up and down. "I tend to get lost easily," I confessed.

"But you can tell if a room has a hidden passageway with just one glance?

That doesn't make sense."

I faced him, putting my hands on my hips. "Of course, it does. Rooms are small and have to abide by certain rules, or they'll fall apart. Streets can go anywhere." Besides which, I don't have a sense of direction, but he didn't need to know that.

Turning back to the window, I soaked in the view. "Those aren't natural," I observed, pointing at the cascade in the Avon River created by three horseshoe-shaped steps cut into its center.

"Weirs," he answered.

"Oh, okay." I'd research weirs later. "Beautiful."

He cocked his head to the side, looking. "It's alright."

A crooked smile let me know he was teasing.

Going to the bar, we ordered, then took our dark ales down the stairs through the restaurant to the beer garden by the water. Tables made of thick wooden slats created narrow walkways. After brushing leaves from a tall oak tree off of our seats, we sat. Meat-stuffed pies in shortcrust soon arrived.

"This smells wonderful." I took in the aroma. "I hope this isn't like *Sweeney Todd*," I mentioned, digging in.

"What's that?"

I stared. Everyone knows *Sweeney Todd*. I mean, even if you don't go to Broadway shows, they made it into a movie. With Johnny Depp. Not possible to ignore.

"Meat pies? Below the barbershop?" I asked in an attempt to jog his memory. "Slice the patrons' throats during their shave and use the dead bodies for, well, meat?"

His face scrunched up. "That's disgusting."

He had me there. I nodded happily. "The movie version is awesome, though. We should watch it."

"Absolutely. It's a date."

My foot kicked back and forth under the table. "Speaking of meat pies, did you get the ear DNA tested?"

He shook his head, either at my choice of dinner conversation or in response to my question. I couldn't tell.

"Since there isn't an apparent victim, the ear goes to the bottom of the list. We share our forensics lab with the whole South West, so other tests take priority."

"Southwest?" The term sounded so alien in this environment that it threw me for a loop. Images of brilliant red and orange sunsets spreading across the desert flooded my mind.

Edward didn't pause in his explanation or change his expression to show that he noticed my mood change. Still, he lay his hand across the table onto my forearm as he answered. Casual, comforting, no big deal. "Avon and Somerset, Devon and Cornwall, Gloucestershire, Dorset, and Wiltshire. The South West of England. We're not a big crime area, so the staff is small."

"But I found a human ear!" I sat back, pulling my arm away.

"A human without an ear would jump to the front of the queue."

I bobbed my head around. "Point," I said. "but," I trailed off, not knowing what I wanted. "I'm glad I didn't find the body, but I need to know what we do next?"

He lifted a beer for a toast. "Have a drink."

I couldn't argue with that.

After dinner, we strolled along the paved footpath by the river. Manicured grass grew along the riverbanks, and the moon shone through the scudding clouds.

I sighed. "I feel like I've stepped into a watercolor painting."

"All I see are places for thieves to hide."

He seemed to be kidding, but it broke the mood enough for a random thought to strike me. "Can the ear be sent to Scotland Yard? They must have a ton of resources, right?"

Before answering, he stopped and leveled a glance at me. We were definitely the same height.

"I hate to disappoint you, lass, but DNA testing and human body parts are above my pay grade," a Scottish burr surfacing.

"I acknowledge that. But I'm in Bath for an important internship, and I can't be distracted." Either by an ear or a constable. "This whole ordeal needs to be taken care of so that I can clear out my head and focus."

I spun on my heel and marched ahead of him. As he approached, he said, "Consider it taken care of. The police are handling the situation." His fingers touched my upper arm, gently lingering, before sliding away. "Alright?"

He was right. I needed to let it go. "Alright," I said, turning back to the view.

Three picturesque narrowboats bobbed on the water.

I rummaged through my purse for my phone. "Stand right there." I maneuvered him in front of the longboat, framing the shot.

He stepped forward, hand in front of my phone's camera. "The department frowns on pictures and any type of social media for their officers."

My shoulders went up a bit. "I don't post."

Skepticism spread across his face, speaking volumes about whether or not he believed me. "Especially when they involve beguiling foreign women."

I gave him a flat stare. "At least move out of the shot, then."

He stepped aside but gave me a shoulder bump as I snapped the picture. In retaliation, I aimed the camera at him and held the button into a burst.

"Hey!" He called in mock protest.

"Don't mess with me," I warned with a silly grin before we returned to our stroll.

Edward played tour guide as we made our way back to Ash Tree Cottage. His knowledge of local pubs included reviews of three that we passed on our walk home. If I could manage to stay here, I wouldn't be at a loss for entertainment.

On the street outside my gate, I asked. "Can I take a picture of your bike?"

His eyebrows raised, questioning.

"Proof that I know someone cool," I joked. Besides, the bike gleamed in the mist and moonlight. I snapped a few pictures from different angles. "And come on. Let me take a normal one of you. Not to post."

His eyes narrowed, and I rolled mine. "Otherwise, I won't delete the," I checked the photo-burst count. "Nineteen goofy ones."

Without a word, he did the classic guy leaning on a cool bike pose, muscular arms folded across his chest.

After stowing my phone, I leaned against the bike next to him. I wasn't going to invite him in. Although at that moment, I thought that maybe a little romance wouldn't be too big a distraction.

Looking into his face, I shifted closer so that his arm automatically went around to keep me from slipping off the seat.

His eyes locked onto mine.

A car rumbled by. Neither of us reacted.

He leaned in, our breath mingling. His hand lifted to mine, and our fingers intertwined. Closing his eyes, he brought my palm to his lips and settled a gentle kiss in the center.

Electricity shot to my toes. Maybe I'd at least let him through the gate.

Our eyes opened at the same time, and I fell into his gaze, turning to him. His expression switched to something like panic. He stood.

Kissing the top of my head like, I don't know, a grandfather, he grabbed his helmet from the back of his motorcycle and rammed it over his face. He moved so fast that I almost fell off the bike.

"I have to go." He swung his leg over the seat. Flipping the visor up on his helmet so that all I could see were his eyes, he winked. "Call me?" The eyeshade returned to its place.

Without waiting for an answer, the engine roared, drowning out the slam of the gate as I darted inside. No way would I let him catch my dumbfounded expression staring after him.

"What?"

The garden didn't answer.

Shaking my head, I stomped along the stepping stones to the front door. "This is exactly why I didn't want to get involved with a boy," I complained. They are impossible and annoying. All of them.

I eyed the clock, calculating the time in Arizona. It was way too early to disturb Tori.

With a puff of air, I silently berated myself for not getting Lily's number. She would be able to help me understand what just happened.

Instead, I called Tori despite the time.

"Hola. You're up early. Or late. Which is it?" Sleepy but coherent, Tori's voice greeted me.

"Late."

I heard rustling sounds as she adjusted. "I'm glad you called. I have a homework thing I need your help with."

"Mine?"

Tori somehow understood school. She never struggled with tests and loved going to classes. I preferred a hands-on approach. Which is probably why I chose a career that involved digging.

"Well, your mom's, more accurately."

My head bobbed. "That makes more sense. What are you working on?"

I shifted the computer, remembering why I called.

"Wait, no. I had a date. I think."

"A date?" she squealed like this was groundbreaking news. "You've been there like, what, a day? When did you meet him? What's he look like? Wait." She paused dramatically. "The constable?"

"Ding, ding, ding."

"Ooooh, awesome! It's a pretty good bet he's not a serial killer."

I nodded again. "Yeah, that's what I was thinking. They probably screen for stuff like that."

"So, tell me everything."

My fingers wrapped around a strand of my hair that I methodically smoothed. "Things seemed great at first, but I don't know, ended oddly."

"Oddly, as in he showed you his collection of deadly spiders that roam freely around his apartment?"

I laughed. "No. Okay, wrong word." I paused for a moment. "Unsatisfying?"

"As in, he's a bad kisser?" Tori asked sympathetically.

"As in, I don't know." My hands moved to a different piece of hair, smoothing.

"Well, so not much of a date?"

This is why I called Tori. She knows the right thing to say. Always.

"So," she continued. "Let's explore this. Logically."

The second reason Tori is my best friend is that she doesn't pity for long.

"Does he know your deep, dark secret?" she asked.

"I don't see how he could," I answered. "Or why he would care," I reasoned. "So that's out."

Tori moved on. "There isn't a gentle way of asking this. Are you sure it was a date? Did he invite you out, or did you call him?"

"I thought of that, too. He texted me."

"Good start."

"He didn't specifically ask me out in so many words," I confessed.

"How many?"

I tilted my head to the side, recalling our conversation. "I don't know. Five?"

"Which five? Did they include date or dinner?"

I read her the three short lines of our exchange.

"Could he be any more vague?"

"Right?" I agreed. "He's a man of few words. Which is actually okay. I'm not looking for a relationship. I honestly just wanted to hang out with a friend. But when we got back here." I paused, searching for a way to express what had changed. "I don't know." I pulled my hair back into a ponytail. "It seemed the kiss would happen, and I was okay with it."

"I definitely think it was a date. How did he not find you irresistible?"

I gnawed at my lip, again, not one hundred percent sure that I wanted that kind of attention. Settling further into my chair, I propped my feet on the desk.

"Maybe he was being terribly British?" Tori continued. "Perhaps he's too proper to show affection."

I glanced up, thinking. "Maybe."

"So, did he give you an awkward hug?"

My exhale of breath was so loud and long that Tori snorted.

"Worse," I told her. "He kissed me on the forehead." *Right when I was ready to invite him into the garden,* I didn't add.

She burst out laughing, which got me going, too.

"I know, right? What is up with that?"

"Okay, sorry." She tried to control her laughter. "That is so cute!" More giggling.

"Yeah, great."

"Okay, okay. Do you think he wanted to kiss you?"

The memory of our eyes locking onto each other caused my heart to skip a beat, despite my insistence that the evening wasn't a big deal. "Yeah, I think so."

"Clearly, he's trying not to fall head over heels for you. As, of course, any guy in his right mind would do." Tori's eyes flitted, and I knew she was checking her logic. She confirmed, "You're good."

What I couldn't decide was what I actually wanted. "Now, the problem is that I'm not sure I'm interested in a relationship."

"Nothing new there. On to me."

I laughed at the abrupt change of subject. "Tally-ho."

"For Religion in Government class—"

"Wait. Weren't you changing majors?"

Tori rolled her eyes. "Abuela, remember? I got Poly-Sci added as a dual major. Best of both worlds."

"An employable degree and a grandmother funded apartment. I get it. Carry on," I suggested.

"I need a subversive pop-culture example."

"Um…" I had no idea.

Tori knew that. "I remembered Heather told me about nursery rhymes and English politics. Could you ask her for me?"

My mom has all kinds of arcane knowledge, specifically during the time frame of Shakespeare's life. Fortunately for Tori, I knew this one. "No need. I got you. Mary, Mary, Quite Contrary is the religious one. Bloody Mary tried to turn England Catholic again after Henry VIII made the country Protestant."

"Look at you! Paying attention to your mom."

"Don't tell her. She'll be insufferable."

Tori muttered the nursery rhyme under her breath. "What's a cockleshell?"

"Not sure."

"Could you ask your mom?"

"Won't Google know?"

"Obviously, but professors love it when you reference an actual person."

Ella's fount of knowledge suddenly struck me. "I have someone even better. I met a docent at the Bath Abbey. She'll know, and you can quote a professional religious person."

"Perfect," Tori agreed.

A yawn shook me so thoroughly my jaw popped.

"It's the middle of the night there, isn't it?"

I stretched. "I'm done. Thanks for being you."

"Call when you find stuff out!"

The connection broke, and I padded upstairs. After showering, setting my alarm, and settling into bed, I closed my eyes with a wish: that I wake up without anything ghastly on my doorstep.

Chapter Eight: Silver Bells and Cockleshells

My alarm went off. The sun shone behind big, fluffy clouds. I opened my window and crawled out onto the roof, examining the garden area below. No packages or strange deliveries awaited me. Excellent.

Hoping to impress my new employers, I arrived at the Baths early.

The doors were locked tight.

Giving Simon the benefit of the doubt that he wasn't late merely to annoy me, I used the opportunity to explore the areas Lily had blown by. The area surrounding the Baths had so many placards explaining historical sites that the square was like an outdoor museum.

One read: Hundreds of years before the Romans, the Celts built a shrine here paying tribute to Sulis, a mother-goddess, which the Romans adopted in their temple. Sulis, in addition to being nourishing, also cursed people.

You go, ancient girl.

I saw Simon out of the corner of my eye, unlocking the door to the Baths. I scampered to join him, ready to start my day. His eyebrows knit together at my approach. Willing my body to remain relaxed, I greeted him. I would charm him if it was the last thing I did.

"You're late," he admonished.

My eyes must have bulged out of my head. Or maybe he could hear my teeth grinding together because he allowed the door to close in my face before I could point out that, no, I wasn't late. Early, in fact.

Hoping my glare would melt his insides, I followed him to the Oversight office. My commitment to friendliness lasted for precisely one statement from him.

Counting to five, I willed myself to let go of tension. If I couldn't win Simon over, at least I was determined to keep him from ruining my mood. "Where's Sam today?"

"Traffic. Some bus accident. She won't be in." Uninterested, he continued, "After, she'll be traveling." Pointing to a new stack of documents, he added, "File," slamming the door as he left.

Pressing my hands to my temples, I turned my scowl to the papers. How had they gotten there? I had finished Sam's documents yesterday.

I sorted, wondering if Simon had emptied a file drawer and left them for me to refile as a practical joke.

"Relax," I told myself, releasing the stiffness from around my eyes.

Glancing at a sheet, I searched for a telltale date. When I found it, I sighed. Yesterday. These were indeed new papers.

"How come so many people donated in one night?" I asked aloud.

The desk helpfully provided an answer in the form of a flyer that drew my attention. There had been a fundraiser the night before.

A slight pang of disappointment that I hadn't been invited to the event crept into my thoughts, and my sorting got erratic. Boredom tried to drag me into sleep. Standing, I took a few pictures of the office. Because there was literally nothing else to do.

Except play a game on my phone. Competitive trivia distracted me for twenty minutes before my conscience forced me back to my task.

At 12:15 p.m., I figured an official break was in order.

I scribbled a note about going to lunch. Not that Simon cared, but in case Sam came in.

The fluffy white clouds from this morning had turned gray, closing in around the square, but the fresh air renewed my spirit. The Abbey's giant wooden doors remained closed, but the gift shop door stood open, beckoning me.

As I approached, running footsteps clattered behind me. A female voice called, "Lily, thank God!"

Confused by our matching ponytails, someone else had mistaken me for my new friend. I turned to greet the woman my own age, but she burst into tears when she saw me.

Instinctively, I hugged her, and she clung to me for a few brief sobs.

Panicked, I needed to find out what happened to my new friend. Tears welling in my own eyes, I gave the girl a long squeeze before she pulled herself together.

"Sorry," she sniffed, pulling away. "I thought you were someone else."

Before she could turn to go, I stopped her. "No, I know Lily. What's happened?"

Knitting her brows together, she considered me. "You're that American she told me about." With a nod, she reached out to give me another quick hug before saying, "I'm sorry. I was hoping it was a joke when I saw you. Traffic accident this morning. They flew her back to hospital in Manchester. Her parents are there."

Stunned, I watched wordlessly as the woman left, heading toward the Pump Room.

A dark pit opened in my stomach. Lily had been so much fun, and I was looking forward to pub crawling with her. I couldn't even send a supportive text since I didn't get her phone number or last name.

Unconscious of getting inside, I found myself at the Abbey's welcome table. No one was there, so I drifted about, reading gravestones and stories etched in colorful windows. The rose window, a big, round, stained glass above the altar, sparkled. I smiled briefly, glad that the sun came out at that moment.

"You've come back," a familiar voice came from behind me.

I pivoted on my heel to face Ella. She must not have expected such a sudden movement because her face turned thunderous at first. Her brow furrowed, and mouth pinched before her usual grandmotherly expression returned.

Tempted to tell her about my friend's accident, I instead kept to a more professional script. Despite the calming atmosphere of the Abbey, Ella's demeanor screamed efficiency.

"Ella, I'm glad you're here."

She looked expectantly at me, blinking quickly, like a sparrow.

"My friend is doing research on the rhyme Mary, Mary Quite Contrary. She, my friend, wanted to know what cockleshells were. I thought you might know since you are so knowledgeable…." I let the compliment dangle as Ella fiddled with the top button on her sweater.

"Bloody Mary, you know," she murmured. Her hand hung in mid-air, index finger bouncing back and forth.

My head bobbed to her rhythm as I recited the words to myself. Mary, Mary, quite contrary/how does your garden grow?/With silver bells and cockleshells and little maids all in a row.

"Little maids are nuns, but that part is easy," she murmured.

I perked up. "What? I didn't know that."

"Silver bells and cockleshells are torture devices. Let me see." As she spoke, Ella retrieved a fallen gum wrapper, probably dropped by tourists.

I stooped to help, but there wasn't anything else to retrieve.

"Torture?" I straightened. "Tortured who?" Or was it whom? I could never remember.

"Protestants," Ella turned to me, serene but shaking her head. "Not a very popular queen, I'm afraid."

Torture was more than I could handle at that moment, but Tori would insist I find out everything. "I thought silver bells were a reference to church music."

"Thumbscrews," she corrected, dashing my childhood innocence to the ground. "They tended to be metal, although not silver, I imagine. And cockleshells." She paused, eyes darting around to make sure no one overheard us. She put her gloved hand to her mouth and whispered, "Went on the genitals."

Yep, I was right. I did not want that information. My stomach churned uncomfortably.

"Thank you," I said, adding, "I think," under my breath. "I can see why she wasn't everyone's cup of tea."

Ella shook her head in a bird-like movement. "Her father, Henry VIII, you see, caused so many problems in the church that there was bound to be unrest. He even damaged this abbey when he took all the church lands."

Gazing at the beautiful proportions of the tower, I commented, "But it's so lovely."

Ella nodded, pleased at my response. "The devoted rebuilt it in the 1600s, and again in 1850."

We stopped our conversation as a group of people came in. "I should check on them," she told me as she strode off, tapping her cane with every step. I wondered why she had it. Her feet never faltered on the familiar stone slabs of the Abbey.

Drawing strength from her example, I straightened my spine and headed out. Visions of silver bells and cockleshells haunted me as I left.

Chapter Nine: The Third Discovery

Outside, the Abbey clock tower chimed 1:00. Time to go back to work.

Inside my cave of an office, nothing had changed. Except Lily was hospitalized, making it even harder to concentrate.

Since I knew it wouldn't take the rest of the day to finish, I pulled out my cell and figured out how to set up my email on my international plan. After deleting the spam, I emailed Tori with my gruesome findings while they were still fresh in my mind. I would tell her about Lily later, pushing my feelings to the back of my mind.

Dad had sent two emails which I read before finishing the filing.

The first one was sweet. Dad told me he was there for me if I got into a tight spot. I'd never make him understand that I needed to do this on my own, but I appreciated his support.

The second email, though, set my teeth on edge as I read:

I talked to Bobby about you today. You remember him—head of acquisitions. Anyway, he says he can set you up in a paid internship as soon as you're back from your adventure. Hugs and kisses, Pumpkin!

I didn't even know what the conglomerate my dad worked for did. The company touted enterprise software solutions, which I could not have cared less about. He just assumed I would work there when I graduated. Everyone did.

I gently set my forehead on the desk and groaned.

Sitting upright, guilt at goofing off inspiring me, I claimed, "I'm going to file these papers better than anyone on earth. That'll show him."

One of the final few pages of the pile halted my progress. The paper felt different under my fingers. I lifted the sheet on top of it and pulled it out. Printed on thick parchment, it read:

The path to the Roman most grand private bath awaits you and is filled with treasures no person who is a friend and generous supporter to us should miss.

God Save the Queen.

I squinted in concentration, reading again. It didn't make sense.

Setting the note aside, I grabbed the next page to file and yelped out loud after scanning the amount. "Oh my god!" Someone named Sir Henry Gilliam donated 20,000 pounds at the fundraiser the previous night.

I snatched the parchment and reread the message. It suggested a route to the largest bath in the museum, and once there, a treasure awaited. Maybe the note had been intended as a special thank you to Sir Henry. Or is it Sir Gilliam?

Had he followed the route leaving the note behind? The directions weren't complicated as far as treasure maps went. Basically, go to the grandest private bath. There was no reason to take the letter along.

But what if he never got the thank you? If there was a special gift waiting for Sir Henry Gilliam, he should have it.

I took a picture of the note in case I was wrong about the directions and checked the time. 4:00 p.m. Plenty of time before the museum closed for a bit of exploring.

After carefully filing the last of the donations and double-checking a few to make sure the dates were correct, I wrote a note to Simon. "Hi! I hope you had a nice day." When I wasn't confronted with his brusqueness, I still hoped we could get along. If not, the sentiment would bug him. A win either way. "Since I don't have keys, I am going to look for you as my duties for the day are complete." That sounded formal enough, even by his standards.

Firmly closing the door, I went in search of the grandest pool, per the note. The largest bath was the one in the courtyard, but it wasn't private. I had noticed a private bath when Simon tried to lose me on his tour. The King's Bath was under restoration and counted as both massive and secluded. Down a side hall and around a corner sat a temporary wooden door set into the stone wall.

I tugged, expecting it to be locked. The door swung out so easily that it bashed into my forehead.

"Ow."

Entering, I blew a stray piece of hair out of my face. The chamber was illuminated by the filtered sunshine reflecting off the water. The effect created an illusion of firelight dancing across the ornately carved walls.

I sucked in my breath, awed.

Being in the room was treasure enough for me, but I still hunted for signs of a gift left behind for a big donor. The note said, "filled with treasure." I leaned down, touching the stones which were warmed by the natural hot springs. They were flat and solid. Nothing could be buried.

My eyes raked the room. As I straightened, I caught sight of something dark in the murky, green liquid. Unlike the crystal-clear water in most of the Baths, sunshine turned the lead-lined pools opaque and green. Stretching out, my fingers hovered over the pool. Clenching my jaw, I plunged my hand in, grabbing the dark mass.

My first thought was corn silk, but that didn't make sense.

Hair. It felt like hair floating around a human head.

I yanked out my hand.

My brain went fuzzy, and I couldn't feel my legs.

The head bobbed in the ripples caused by my disturbance. A face rolled toward the surface before receding.

"Help." My face mouthed the word, but nothing came out.

"Hhhhh." A keening whine. I couldn't force a sound.

My hands windmilled around. "Help." Barely a whisper.

"What the devil do you think you're doing?" a voice demanded. "You'll ruin everything. Leave at once!"

"Ahhh!" My shriek, once released, echoed, multiplying my horror.

Turning blindly, I stumbled toward the speaker.

Arms akimbo, Simon peered down on me. "Do be quiet, would you?"

I rushed at him, throwing my arms around his neck. "Simon! Oh, god!"

He pulled away, shocked. "Bloody hell!"

"De..." I couldn't get out the words. "He's... Oh, god." I gasped for breath, not able to take in enough air.

Simon turned me around and lowered me to the ground with a single firm shake.

I hugged my knees into my chest, rocking.

"Right, now. Head down." He pushed my face toward my bent legs.

I didn't understand his words. "What?" My voice muffled.

"We don't want any hyperventilating now, do we?"

Tears blurred my vision. At last, my voice returned. "Dead." My hand shook as I pointed to the pool. "He's dead."

Chapter Ten: The Dead Man

"What are you talking about? Who's dead?" Simon demanded.

Sniffing, I wiped my face on my shirtsleeve, pointing again. I wanted to say that I might have been wrong. That I've never seen a dead body, so how would I know? That it could have been something else.

But I couldn't. When that face came to the surface of the pool, every part of me knew that it was a human male. Even bloated and splotchy, it was undeniable.

The black spots clouding my vision returned. I set my forehead on my knees. Stable breathing helped. I didn't want to see the face ever again, but a splashing sound snapped my head toward the bath and Simon. Legs spread in a firm stance, he leaned over the edge, both hands in the pool. He rotated the body so its full face cleared the eerie, green surface.

"Good God!" he exclaimed, pulling the body onto the stone floor. "Sir Henry!" After gently settling Henry on the floor, Simon whirled. "What have you done?"

Honestly?

Nerves and absurdity collided in my head. My breath came in gasps, and my focus narrowed to a tiny circle. A sound kept repeating. I heard myself saying, "Oh god, oh god, oh god," but I couldn't stop.

Simon approached, probably to give me another shake. The threat alone had the right effect, and I froze.

"I'm fine," I declared in an odd squeak.

My mind cast about for something else to think about and landed on thumbscrews and cockleshells. Fortunately, thinking about the implements of torture helped stabilize my breathing.

Simon blinked down at me, then offered a hand. I pictured corpse water dripping off of his fingers.

A gasp shuddered through me, but I shook it off and gave Simon my hand. With his help, I got to my feet. Back tall, stance firm, I took charge of myself without looking back into the chamber. Not that I needed to. The image of the body had already been seared into my brain.

Appraising me, Simon must have decided that I wouldn't lose it again. "You stay here. I'll call the police."

He opened the door, and I followed him out.

"I'll stand guard outside."

Simon's lip curled critically, but before he said anything, I added, "So we don't contaminate the crime scene."

Nodding, he walked away.

"Wait!"

He turned.

"You can use my cell phone to call nine-nine-nine."

He sneered. "We can't call emergency services. Henry Gilliam is," he paused. "Was a knight. The Baths can't have ugly publicity. There's a number in the office for emergencies. Ms. Niven must be informed."

Striding away, he called, "Do not touch anything."

"Do not touch anything," I mimicked.

I didn't want to touch anything anyway.

But with nothing to do, my mind started to spin. What if the standard police procedure was to haul me in since I had found the body? How would I explain what I was doing in that room? If I told anyone I was following a treasure map, they would think I was crazy. It sounded fake even to me.

Wishing that Lily were here to make me laugh, I instead felt sobs threatening. "No. Do not cry," I commanded, picturing Simon's stern gaze.

With nothing to focus on, I looked back at the door, the image of the body bobbing up on the other side.

"Not helpful," I chastised, searching my brain for a useful subject. The police would be here soon. What would that be like? I only knew how American cops did from tv. I needed a cheat sheet for British police.

My head flopped back, and I stamped my foot. "Edward. Duh."

Pulling out my phone, I stared at the screen. *What do I say? Hey, I found a DB, and what's up with the kiss on the forehead?*

No.

Instead, I went with simple and said, "Hi, Edward. Something bad happened at the Baths. The police are being called in. Join them if you can?"

He texted back before I put my phone away. "So, you're causing the kerfuffle? They're not taking my lot. I'm off in fifteen."

My fingers poised over a response while I interpreted his messages. The station must be gathering forces while keeping the murder quiet. That made sense, except that the last part confounded me. Was Edward coming once he got off in fifteen minutes, or letting me know he won't be coming because he'll be off the clock?

Edward made me feel like I needed a class in how to text British. I'd rather be in any classroom than where I currently was.

I stowed my phone without responding, not wanting to add to my confusion.

The shuffling of feet came near. I instinctively ducked into a shadow. Which I realized appeared suspicious and stepped in front of the door again. The feet crept by without noticing my hallway.

Silence. Loud, thick, and ominous quiet.

The solitude ate at my nerves. I pulled out my phone and stared at it some more, but my mind refused to work.

Stowing my cell again, I swayed from one foot to the other, feeling my weight. Once centered, I bounced a couple of times.

"Okay," I whispered. "Get it together, Madeline."

I always thought of myself as calm under stress. Today was as intense of a situation as I've ever been in, and I wasn't impressed with my fortitude. So far, Simon had seen me stumble, screech, and pretty much lose it. My reactions were justified, but Simon hadn't shown a hint of distress.

If he could be tough, so could I.

I stood resolute, guarding the door until a detective arrived. A short, thin man in a raincoat flashed his badge at me.

"Alright, miss. You may go."

A caution light blinked in my head. Something didn't feel right. He showed his badge so quickly that there was no way to read his name, almost like someone trying to scam his way in with fake credentials.

I did not move aside. "I'm sorry. I didn't see the department you were with. May I see your badge again?"

His answering exhale took forever, indicating his annoyance.

I put my hands on my hips.

"I don't have time for this," he informed me.

I tilted my head to the side, appraising him. Time for what? It took longer for him to exhale than it would have to show me his badge.

I crossed my arms across my chest in an attempt to appear impenetrable. The movement had an effect on him.

Sighing, he patted his jacket and trouser pockets like he couldn't remember where he put the badge that he showed me not one minute ago.

Voices echoed through the hallway, sounding authoritative. The man in front of me stopped making a show of finding misplaced credentials. His eyes bugged out, and he side-stepped me, speed-walking the opposite direction of the newcomers.

Simon, following an impeccably dressed woman, marched toward me. The muted pink jacquard of her dress screamed money and class. She caught sight of the retreating man and barked out, "Jeffery."

He halted.

"Am I to have no peace?"

Jeffery returned to us with an expression that can only be described as smarmy.

"My Lady! I didn't see you. You and the family well, I hope?"

The decision not to let him into the room was looking better and better.

"Simon." Another bark from the lady. "Please escort Jeffery from The

Daily Times out."

Simon nodded once, employed his sneer to surpassing effect, and guided the reporter, apparently, to the exit.

"Aw, come on, Simon," the man, Jeffery, complained. "You know I'll do right by ya. I'm with the city newspaper, thanks to you and her ladyship." His voice continued to whine as Simon led him out.

The lady in question turned her intense dark blue eyes on me. I had to fight every fiber of my being not to run away. A ridiculous need to curtsey took me. I refrained.

Clearing my throat to make sure I could speak, I said, "I'm Maddie. That man tried to dismiss me, but I asked to look at his badge to make sure he was legit...imate. Legitimate." When under scrutiny by an honest to goodness lady, one should probably use proper grammar.

She nodded. "Very good."

Simon returned to us.

"Ah, Simon. There you are," she said as though he had run off without her knowledge. "Introduce me to this resourceful young woman."

I almost looked for someone else but caught myself in time. Resourceful and collected, that's me.

Simon, to his credit, did not point and laugh. Instead, he transformed into the most polite host I'd ever seen. Especially considering he had never said a kind word to me. And we were standing near a dead man in a hall where I wasn't supposed to be.

"May I present Miss Madeline McGuire of Tempe, Arizona. Maddie, Vivian Pacok, the Dowager Countess of Comer. My aunt."

My mouth almost fell open. First off, Simon was an aristocrat. Second, he knew my name. And where I'm from. More was going on than I could take in.

However, I managed to stop gaping, bowed my head a little to defeat the urge to curtsey again, and held out my hand. "Your Ladyship." I hoped Jeffery, the reporter, used the proper term of address and that adding "ship" to the end was a thing.

A nod from the countess. Perhaps her approval of me?

"Vivian," she offered.

I took it to mean I should call her by her first name. I decided to not address her at all if I could help it.

"And if I may call you Maddie?"

Bobbing my head, I chanced a peek at Simon, who smiled briefly. I think I did okay in the eyes of his aunt.

"Quite right. Simon, which Detective Chief Inspector is coming?"

"DCI William Bray. His cousin used to hunt with Uncle, and he came a few times. You'll remember him from the bit of trouble we had before. He can be counted on."

Lady Vivian smiled. "Of course. Make sure you're included in every aspect."

Simon stood taller, capable of taking on the world.

"Something will need to be done about Jeffery," Vivian continued.

She sounded a little like she wanted the reporter thrown to the wolves. What if I had let Jeffery in to see Sir Henry's body? Would she want me in a dungeon? What kind of people arranged which police officers came to examine a death? Who had that kind of power?

A buzzing sound muffled my ears. I was way out of my depth. Shaking my head, I tried to listen.

"And you'll be coming to dinner on Sunday?"

I panicked when I thought she meant me, but Simon answered, "Of course, Aunt Viv."

Vivian spoke as though she dealt with bodies regularly. So did Simon. How were they so calm? This was the most relaxed I'd seen him. It was creepy.

Vivian's head cocked to one side, listening.

"Here they come."

She and Simon stood on either side of me, effectively sealing off the entrance to the pool.

A well-dressed man strode into the hall, giving instructions to those around him. He pulled up short at the sight of Vivian.

"Dowager Countess. How nice to see you again."

"Detective Chief Inspector Bray. We do miss having your family at the house for the hunt. Perhaps you'll come this year?"

"Very kind of you. Cousin Algie misses the Earl very much."

"As do we all."

I strained to understand what was going on with the aristocracy.

My breathing became shallow, and I shook myself, focusing on the people around me. Vivian was married to an earl who had died. Algie is the DCI's cousin, so he, too, must come from an aristocratic family. This was like an upper class looking after each other club.

So far, Vivian seemed to be including me in the ranks, and it had a strange effect on me. I silently pledged not to disappoint her.

"Is this the American who found the body?" DCI Bray addressed Lady Vivian, not me, which was oddly comforting.

Curt nod. "Yes. My nephew will accompany her to the interview for support."

It sounded like she meant support for the victim and not for me. But a familiar face was better than nothing.

Simon stepped forward and lifted an arm to indicate I should come with him. "We'll use the Oversight room," he said, taking charge.

He and an investigator named Parikh led me to Sam's office. We entered, finding Sam stuffing something quickly into a drawer.

"Ms. Niven," Simon said. "Detective Inspector Parikh will be taking Ms. McGuire's statement."

Sam leaped out of her chair. "Of course, Detective Inspector. Whatever you need." She gazed at Simon with a thankful expression, then practically ran out of the office.

I couldn't tell if it was the police or the countess that had set her off. Either way, I vowed not to let Sam's nerves further rattle my own.

"Tell me what happened," Parikh suggested, pulling a small notebook from his tweed jacket. Adjusting his wire-rimmed glasses, he peered at me.

I wracked my brain thinking of a way to avoid mentioning that I had been following a treasure map, especially in front of Simon.

"I finished my duties for the day, so I wrote my co-worker a note letting him know I was looking for him to lock the office."

DI Parikh nodded for me to go on.

So far, so good. "After looking at the main tour routes and not finding him, I checked the less traveled halls that he had shown me on my first day." Which sounded like a perfectly valid excuse for me to go to the King's Bath. "I tried the door, and it swung open. Something floated in the water, which seemed odd, so I reached in to retrieve…." Trying to sound official, I groped for a phrase.

Instead, a full-body shudder shook me. My fists balled up, but I soldiered on. No breaking down now. The countess thought I was resourceful. "Simon came in," my voice croaked. "He hauled the body out and identified it. Him. It."

Detective Inspector Parikh's pen hovered above his notebook as he stared at me over his glasses.

I said nothing, holding my natural tendency to babble in check.

Parikh blinked a couple of times.

The words "treasure map" clawed their way up to the tip of my tongue. Keeping things from the police had to be a bad idea. They needed to know absolutely everything to solve a crime. On the other hand, the note may not have anything to do with the drowning, and Simon would use it against me. Also, the death was probably an accident. No crime at all. I shouldn't let a little embarrassment keep me from doing the right thing. Of course, it could be a distraction and send them on the wrong path for no reason. Still—

A sharp knock halted my internal debate, my hand flying to my neck at the sound. No screaming, though, and not a full-on jump. I picked a strand of my hair and smoothed it with both hands, using the rhythm to calm me.

"Yes," Parikh called.

Edward stuck his head in. I almost leaped out of the chair to hug him. Instead, I avoided eye contact and hoped that my reaction hadn't been visible to everyone.

"Bailey," Parikh continued. "What are you doing here?"

Edward stepped all the way in and stood tall. "I spoke with the DCI, sir.

I'm to escort Ms. McGuire home when you're finished, as we are acquainted with one another."

DI Parikh finally closed his pen and took off the reading glasses. Pinching his nose, his gaze went from me to Simon. "May as well take her now." His attention turned back to me. "Right. Call me at once if you remember anything else."

My head bobbed enough to rattle my brain. I didn't trust myself to say anything out loud. Repressing the impulse to wave bye-bye in Simon's direction, I instead gave a formal nod. It seemed like the right thing to do because he responded with a slight head bow of his own.

Edward held the door open for me, and I kept my pace dignified as I walked through. I did the head nod thing at Edward, suppressing a flood of tears. "Officer Bailey."

Once the door closed, he wrapped his arm around my shoulders in a comforting side hug. "What have you gotten yourself into, lassie?"

Chapter Eleven: Fleeing Through The Park

Edward's accent, thickly Scottish, came out once clear of DI Parikh. I gazed into his brown eyes, trying to erase the memory of what I'd seen.

"I'm normally very, well, normal," I insisted. "Trouble has it out for me here."

We strolled to the exit for a few steps before his arm dropped away. With another stride, we were outside in the thick of several police officers. He exchanged greetings with a few but didn't slow.

One of the plainclothes officers started our way, then abruptly turned around. I lingered, focusing on him.

"Hey," I tapped on Edward's arm. I pointed at the man. "I think he's a reporter. He looks like the man who tried to get past me to see the body. The countess called him Jeffery."

Edward scanned the area, spotted a bench, and indicated that I should sit there. "Don't move. And don't get into any trouble," he warned.

The problem with treating me like a child is that I want to react like one. I showed great restraint in not sticking my tongue out at him as he marched back to his colleagues.

"Hello," a familiar voice said to me. Ella stood before me, wearing an awful tweed coat, a carpetbag purse looped over her cane arm.

"Ella!" I smiled at her. "Thank you again for the information on the nursery rhymes."

"My pleasure." She took in the crowd of officials near the Baths. "Oh my. What on earth is going on?"

As soon as she asked, my fortitude crumbled. If I told someone that I found a drowned man, the words would make it real. Right now, I was coasting along in denial. Also, I wasn't supposed to tell. No one said that to me, but I could imagine Vivian's disappointment if I gave out private information.

My hands trembled, so I stuffed them under my legs and stared at my feet. "I'm not sure," I lied. "I only file." The little truth felt better.

"Are the police there?" Ella pushed for information.

I glanced over my shoulder. Edward was nowhere in sight, but I needed to escape from this well-meaning but nosy woman.

With very little grace, I rose to leave. "Wow. What a long day. I have to go." Groan. I couldn't have sounded less sincere if I tried.

Ella, to her credit, didn't call me out. "Of course. Goodbye."

I smiled at her and crossed my arms, pinning my shaking hands to my sides. My head dropped as I willed my feet forward.

One foot, then the other. Left, right, left, right. I squeezed my eyes shut, forced them open to focus on my shoes. Still moving. Good. The way to Greenway Lane was familiar already, like going home.

When I got to the stairs that crossed behind the busy road, my head tilted to the top. It looked so far away, miles away, but I forced my legs to keep moving.

The sounds of birds and insects that delighted me during the day sounded ominous and threatening at night. My pace quickened.

As I mounted the final step in the park, a motorcycle roared along on the ivy-lined street at the top. Edward raised his visor. "Do all Americans fail to follow directions?" he chastised.

I wanted to say something witty, but I wound up sitting on the ground instead, shaking uncontrollably. Gorge rose in my throat.

Edward hopped off his bike and was at my side. He rubbed my arms and helped me to stand. "Let's get you home, shall we?"

"K." I couldn't manage more. He put me on the bike first, sitting behind me. Removing his helmet, he gently placed it on my head. His hand went to the handlebars pinning me upright.

"Hang on," he instructed.

"K." My hands flopped uselessly.

"I'm serious, Ms. McGuire."

Nodding, I clung to Edward's legs.

I had never been on a motorcycle before, and by the time we got to the gate at Ash Tree Cottage, I couldn't remember anything about the ride.

My stomach roiled with nausea. Edward got me past the stepping-stone walkway and into the living room before I bolted the stairs to the bathroom. What little food had been in me was now out.

Peeking out the door, I hoped for an empty hallway. As much as I wanted company, I didn't want to appear so weak.

Edward leaned against the wall, jacket off and a snifter of amber liquid in hand. He held the glass in my direction. "Come along, lassie. A little brandy to calm your nerves."

I held up a finger, ducked back into the bathroom to splash my face with water. When I emerged, I told him, "I don't like brandy."

"Just a sip." He handed me the glass.

The sweet but rich and warming liquid filled the dark void in my stomach. "It's not bad," I said as he steered me along the narrow stairs to my room.

By the time we were at the top, I had finished the snifter, and the waves of panic had subsided.

"Where did you go?" I asked him.

He put his hands on his hips and tilted his head. "I should be asking you that question. I got back to the bench, and you were gone."

My hands went to my face, swiping at the mental cobwebs. I gathered my hair in both hands and twisted it into a ponytail. It fanned across my shoulders as I let go. "The docent from the Abbey asked me what was going on. I had to get away from her."

"You didn't tell her, did you?"

Shaking my head, I wrapped my arms around myself tightly. He squeezed me in another side hug, and my trembling stopped. "I'll be back in five minutes."

"I've heard that before." I secured the door before changing into an oversized t-shirt and wrapping myself in my robe. Sitting on the bed, my eyes fluttered. I caught myself swaying.

A knock brought me back. Rising, I let Edward in. He held another glass of brandy.

"Oh, no. I'm already feeling it."

His smile flashed, and I became aware that the only place to sit in the room was the bed. I stumbled to the window and perched on the sill.

Edward's smile returned as he approached. "Here," he handed me the glass.

I sipped slowly this time. Definitely calming. My eyelids got heavy. Strong arms supported me as I moved to the bed, my head lowering to the pillow. Covers got tucked around me as I tumbled into sleep.

"Goodnight, Maddie McGuire. Dream of Scotland," he said in a thick accent.

And he kissed me on the forehead.

Chapter Twelve: Bending Rules

I bolted upright in bed, heart pounding, not recognizing my surroundings through the darkness.

"England." The sound of my voice grounded me, but only slightly. "I'm in England, and everything is amazing. Except for one dead body and a random ear." Hoping she would be okay, I added, "And Lily."

I considered calling my dad and asking him to arrange for transportation home. No one would blame me after what I'd been through.

Except... I sighed. Except depending on him to fix my problems was precisely what he expected. Not that he thought I would fail, but that he would need to rescue me. Once he provided the ticket, I'd be trapped, working in a giant skyscraper, my dreams crushed.

If I called my mom, the situation wouldn't be much different. She'd want me to go to her university, close by, so we could have lunch every day. Supportive, loving, but still a trap. Every so often, she'd give me helpful advice about getting a job that didn't involve archaeology.

Wide awake, I searched for my phone to check the time. Pawing around woke me up even more. I squinted, picturing where I set the cell before falling asleep.

When I remembered that Edward helped me to bed, I leaned back, bonking my head on the bookshelf that served as a headboard. Between shock and brandy, I'd had no control. Thank goodness he was a gentleman.

"Okay," I asked the room. "Where would Edward have put my phone?" The desk seemed the most likely place, so I swung my feet to the floor and padded over.

5:00 a.m.

On the bright side, my jetlag was improving. Also, Tori was awake. I turned on my laptop and connected.

"Ello, love!" Tori said with a spot-on English accent.

"How come your accent is better than mine?"

"I've spoken two languages since birth."

"Showoff."

"Anyway, I'm so glad you called. I have, like, three more hours before I have to turn this paper in. I need more info on the nursery rhyme stuff you sent."

"Okay, but—"

"Yes!" Tori all but shouted. "You are the absolute best."

"I have to tell you something." I squared my laptop in an attempt to look important.

"Of course you do! You're a world traveler. But let me get the notes first. Tell me the name of my source."

"Ella something."

"I can't use that!" Tori protested.

"Okay, okay. Hold on. Let me think." I scrunched up my face, recalling an image of her name tag. "Thomas."

"Perfecto."

"From the Bath Abbey. And who knew that silver bells and cockleshells are implements of torture?" I thought emphasizing this bombshell would shake her into listening to me.

"Yeah, I know. Gross, huh?"

"If you knew, then why did I have to find out for you?"

Tori laughed. "I could hardly use wiki as a source. This is far more impressive."

I rolled my eyes at the screen. "You want to know what's really impressive? Edward, the constable, got me drunk and carried me to bed."

A sharp intake of breath from Tori's end. "No," she whispered.

Tempting as it was to string her along, I needed help. I confessed, "Nothing exciting there. He kissed me on the forehead. Again."

I jumped at the bark of her laughter. "How did you let him get you drunk?"

I giggled along with her, which gave me the courage to say what I needed to. My stomach churned at the memory. I considered changing the subject.

"Well?" Tori prompted.

I balled up my fists. I couldn't say it outright. "Something bad happened at the Baths, Tori."

"Oh, no. Are you okay? What kind of bad?"

Tears stung my eyes. I knew that all I needed to do was say the word, and she'd be on the next flight to London.

"I found a dr...." I gulped the excess saliva that filled my mouth. "Drowned man."

"What in the hell have you gotten yourself into?" Tori demanded. "You've been gone less than a week! I swear you need a guardian."

"I know, right? The brochures failed to mention the dark side of Bath. Mostly they said everyone must visit this lovely tourist spot." I picked a strand of hair and twisted it around my finger. "Why is this happening?"

"You got me there. Was your body missing an ear?"

Unable to blink, I grew still.

"Maddie? You okay?"

I nodded, rocking gently from side to side. "Tori, you are so smart. I don't know. It was submerged in one of the baths when I found it. Him. It. What are you supposed to say?"

"It, I believe. So, a full complement of ears?"

"Like I said, I don't know. Simon pulled him, it, out of the water. I didn't look. But you've got me thinking."

"The mystery would wrap up perfectly. It'd be less creepy to have one earless body than a dead guy and a one-eared guy."

"Yeah, I agree." I continued to rock, thinking. "Remember that one Sherlock Holmes adventure with the ears?"

"I was thinking the same thing. How did Holmes and Watson find the bodies in that one?" she asked.

"I don't think they did. Holmes pronounced his solution, and the killer confessed. Maybe this is tied to a different story."

The clicking of Tori's keyboard came through our connection as loud pops. "I'm looking up drowning mysteries." The typing stopped.

"What?"

"Huh. There's like, fan-fiction, but nothing by Doyle shows up."

A ghost of a memory teased me but faded away. "I don't know."

"You're saying that a lot today."

"You try finding a body and see how eloquent you are."

Tori busted up, and I felt the tension release out of my jaw.

"Anyway," I said to recapture her attention. "I feel like there's something I should remember, but I can't grab hold of it," I told her.

"Well, what else do you know?"

"I don't know."

"See?"

"Nothing. There's nothing that I know. I found him, it. Freaked out."

"And Edward got you drunk?"

Groaning, I picked up the laptop and moved to the bed so I could explain in comfort. "Not technically. Shock, a little brandy, and I was out like a high school sophomore."

"Aww," she cooed. "He's a gentleman. A proper English gentleman, he is!" Her accent returned.

My lips curled into a smile. "Yeah. He kinda is, isn't he? I wonder if he has a girlfriend. Maybe that's his problem."

"There are worse things."

"Serial killers, for example," I offered.

"That," she agreed.

A tinkling of chimes came through the line, which I knew was Tori's alarm. "Oh, crap. I have a class. Gotta go. You stay safe. Okay? Promise me?"

"Yeah. No kidding."

"Call me any time. I mean it."

"You're the best. Love you!"

Disconnecting felt like severing a physical connection. The tension crept back in. Nothing for it but companionship.

Snatching a pair of shoes and a thick robe, I padded down both flights of stairs, out the front door, and confronted the dawn. The sun attempted to lighten the dense mass of clouds. The air didn't smell like rain, but the clouds were so low that they scudded across the garden.

Roddy's enclosure radiated a storybook charm that counteracted my gloom. I opened his hutch. "Roderick! Come here, bunny, bunny!"

He hopped out, came to me, and put a front paw on my leg, stretching toward my face. "You're such a good boy. Do you want to hang out in the kitchen with me?"

Nose twitch.

"Alright." I picked him up and went inside. Closing off the kitchen, I refilled his dishes and set out a new paper.

"I admit I've had a rough start, but from here on out, things are going to be normal. Right?"

Roderick hopped across the checkered floor in three long bounds toward his food.

"Hop and a skip." I smiled at him, petting his soft fur.

That niggling at the back of my mind returned. "Skip, skipping." I hoped saying the words out loud would trigger something, but nothing materialized.

"It may be," I told Roddy. "That finding a dead body is playing tricks on my mind. It's a distinct possibility."

The rabbit offered no opinion.

I made crispy fried eggs and ate them with the last of my Sally Lunn bunns. With my nerves under control, I was ready to go to the Baths.

I expected some sign of the previous day's chaos, but the square bustled along like normal. Opening the Georgian double doors of the Roman Baths, nothing was out of place. Until Simon charged out of the Oversight office.

I braced for a nasty remark.

"Ah, Maddie. Good morning." Simon smiled.

I almost dropped my purse. My jaw snapped shut as I returned the gesture. Setting my things on Sam's unoccupied desk, I bit back the impulse to ask him if Sir Henry had both of his ears.

"Did Ms. Niven leave any filing for me?"

"Sam was feeling a bit under the weather today," he answered, his hand closed, thumb and pinky out, tipping toward his mouth in the universal gesture of drinking.

My eyes grew wider. So many questions filled my head. How did he know? Did she come in drunk, or did she call? Had this happened before? Did her bosses think she drank on the job? Did Sir Henry want her fired? Or had he known? Was she suspected of negligence in Sir Henry's death?

I let every query go unasked. Partly because it was expected of me and partly because I didn't want to talk about it.

"Oh?" I arched an eyebrow.

Simon opened Sam's top drawer and pulled out a beautifully filigreed silver hip flask. He waggled it back and forth.

Simon's jovial mood was a pleasant change of pace, and I didn't want to derail him. "Ah. I see," I offered, sounding nonplussed. It did the trick as Simon continued to treat me courteously.

He stowed the flask, closing the drawer. "Do you think you can handle a couple of tours? I want to get things straight on this end."

Plopping into a chair, I stared at him. His jaw was relaxed, the pinched expression disappeared. Combine a handsome face with an open, friendliness, and I had a great work companion. But seriously, Simon had to be involved in a death before he lightened up? That fact didn't sit well. I shook my head.

Was I skilled enough to do a tour? I memorized all the maps before I got on the plane to England, but my relationship with directions is tenuous. Also, what if someone asked me a question that a senior-level student should know? On the other hand, what would the countess say if I didn't step up? "Of course," I smiled at Simon. Not too big. "Is there a list of facts that I need to cover?"

He handed me a pamphlet. I groaned inwardly. Anyone could pick up the same brochure when they entered the Baths. Why listen to me?

"My notes are in blue, and it shows where to depart for the private tours. Copy those to your own map."

Relief washed over me like a warm shower on a cold day. Simon provided me inside information. I would sound like an expert. The first tour began at 11:00 a.m., which gave me an hour and a half to review the route and facts.

As Simon behaved far better when in a position of authority, I asked permission. "Do you mind if I run through it on my own before the first tour begins?"

His thoughtful nod seemed so cordial that I had a hard time believing he was the same man who had slammed a door in my face. Twice.

"Thanks." I grabbed my map and speed-walked through the tour. Fortunately, the route was pretty obvious when I read Simon's notes. Memorizing lines was second nature , and I could now easily fake my way through this first tour. I silently thanked my mother for making me take acting as a child.

At 10:45 a.m., nervous butterflies fluttered into my stomach. Willing them away, I held my head high and strode to a corner of the murky green water of the Great Bath.

A face bobbed up and turned toward me, but I shook the mirage away.

The comforting sight of the Abbey's gothic tower soared up behind the Georgian pump house. Double-checking Simon's notes, I confirmed my next step.

"Guided tour starting in fifteen minutes," I shouted to the visitors. A group formed around me as I stood there, looking official.

A small, gloved hand raised from the back of the pack. Peeking through the crowd, I caught sight of Ella.

I stepped to her. "Hello!" Too expressive. I curbed my enthusiasm, echoing the DCI's words to the countess. "How nice to see you. I didn't think you liked it here."

She sniffed as she examined the entrance to the Baths. "No. Rather not, really," she said, shaking her head. "We have a new display at the Abbey. I thought you might like to visit it, so I came here." Her eyes raked the area as though she were looking for something.

"Yes, please." My tone remained reserved. "I'll have time later."

A quick check of my phone showed three minutes before the tour would begin. A familiar face in the audience would be a bonus, so I risked an invitation of my own. "Would you like to join my tour?"

"Of course." She gave me a tepid smile.

I beamed at her in return. Suddenly, I felt like the most qualified person in the world to guide this group through the Roman Baths.

As we entered the East Bath, warm, moist air enveloped us.

"Were the hot springs always here?" a middle-aged man wearing white socks with sandals asked in a clipped German accent.

"As long as people have been around. The Celts used the springs crediting the Goddess Sulis with their control. They believed she had healing powers, partly due to the minerals in the waters. The Romans put their temple on the same site." I sounded like I knew what I was talking about. Thoughts of running home faded away.

"How hot are they?"

"About 115 degrees," I replied confidently.

The crowd turned to one another, confused. Oh, yeah, Fahrenheit.

"Or around 45 degrees Celsius," I amended. The furrowed brows relaxed in comprehension. Simplifying the formula in my head made it fast for me to convert. I may have been off a degree or two, but it was close.

This time a hand went up.

"Yes?"

A polite elderly man looked around to make sure I indicated him. "How did they lift these rocks?"

Fortunately for him, ancient architecture fascinated me. "The Greeks invented tongs, but holes had to be drilled into the rocks for them. Since you can't see any damage to the stones, these Roman builders probably used a *holivela*. They took a chunk out of the top of the rock, inserted the *holivela*, which is a wood and metal object that looks kind of like an ankh. When they lifted it, the bottom would spread out. The heavier the rock, the greater the outward pressure. The only downside with this method was that the stone was weakened from the hole. The upside is that since the hole was on the top of each block, the fault was hidden." I beamed at him.

He tilted his head to the side. "But," he coughed like he was embarrassed on my behalf. "How did they do the lifting?"

Oops. I left that part out. "Block-and-tackle. A basic pulley system. There is a display on the upper floor. We still use the block-and-tackle here in the museum to move heavy objects without damaging them."

"Like on a ship?"

I nodded.

"Thank you, miss."

A little girl wearing a long blue ribbon in her brown hair wiggled her fingers in a little wave, too shy to attract my attention any other way.

I crouched to her level. "Did you have a question?"

She nodded.

"What is it?"

"Why is...?" She whispered between embarrassed giggles.

I glanced at her mother for help. "Why is the water hot?" her mom translated.

"It's geothermal. Which means," I explained to the girl, "the water goes deep into the Earth and touches hot rocks."

"Brilliant." She nodded vigorously.

Success.

I tore through the rest of the tour, adding bits of humor here and there to Simon's knowledge. His notes were invaluable, but I'd finally found an activity where I could show off my expertise. I even threw in Simon's joke, borrowed from Cliff, the intern, before me, about not letting us knock over the Abbey to excavate more.

A huge laugh ensued, but I realized that I might have offended Ella. Searching for her, I discovered she was nowhere to be found. I hoped she'd left the tour before my closing remark.

Floating on air, I returned to the office.

Simon greeted me cheerily. His change from the previous day was so significant that I almost thought this guy had to be a twin. Was he nice because his aunt approved of me or because Sam was out of his way? Or maybe a death at work was right up his alley.

Cliff, the previous intern, invaded my thoughts. What if he hadn't simply run off? What if he had disappeared? Could Simon have been involved?

"How did it go?"

I shook my head, banishing the scenario. "Quite well, actually," I said, trying out a British phrasing.

He grinned, looking boyishly cute. I hoped the smiling version of my colleague stayed around. "Did you use the joke at the end?"

I noted he didn't admit that the crack about knocking over the Abbey came from Cliff. "Yeah," I smiled back. "It went great."

"Well done. Two more for today, and you will be a seasoned professional."

Somewhere in the back of my mind, I hoped he would say "jolly good," but "well done" would do. "Thank you, Simon. That means a lot to me."

The rest of the day flew by with two successful tours. Sam never showed up, but Simon remained in charge and charming.

Exceedingly charming. Odd.

After work, I headed across the bustling square toward the Abbey to check out the exhibit Ella mentioned. I practically skipped to the entrance. My foot hovered at the threshold.

Skipping. There was something significant about skipping, but it wouldn't come to me.

Shaking my head, I entered the Abbey. A burly security man with a friendly face told me that the church would be closing in five minutes unless I was going to services. With a shrug, I headed home, a light drizzle dampening my hair but not my mood.

Chapter Thirteen: The Note

After a hot shower, I settled in with drinking chocolate, toast, and the company of Roddy. The only thing that would have made the day better would have been a companion to chat with. I pulled out my phone to text Edward and invite him to celebrate the success of my day.

When my phone dinged with a message from Edward, I tapped my feet in a happy dance. Perfect!

"Busy?" he asked.

"Reveling in my day. Want to help celebrate?"

"Be there in ten."

Putting my phone away, I went to the mirror to touch up my hair. Fortunately, its length keeps my natural curls soft and wavy, so I settled for taking it out of the ponytail and brushing. I quickly applied a peachy pink blush and a swipe of mascara.

As I added lip gloss, I wondered if Edward knew where I was. I could have still been at work. Retrieving my phone to text him, a loud ding sounded. I almost dropped my cell in surprise.

A new message from Edward. "You're home, yes?"

Smiling, replied, "Yeah."

Making my way to the living room, I caught myself humming. "Hey, Roddy! Time for the hutch."

In the kitchen, I found the bunny napping by the fan of the refrigerator vent. "Hey, are you cold?"

Closing his eyes, he snuggled closer to the warm air. "Well, I can hardly take you out into the rain now, can I?" I squinted at him, suspicious. "Doesn't your fuzzy fur coat keep you warm?"

No response.

"Fine, you can stay in the kitchen. Don't tell the Priestlys that I spoiled you when they get back."

Ear twitch.

A clever rabbit, Roddy was.

The doorbell rang in the other room. I ran my fingers through my hair one more time and went to answer it.

Throwing open the door, I greeted Edward, his wavy hair mussed, wearing a leather jacket, jeans, and boots. Maybe riding a motorcycle wouldn't be too deadly. The wind rush would give me an excellent excuse to buy a leather jacket.

"Hey," I greeted him, shrugging into my fleece-lined coat. "Any suggestions?"

"Want to grab a drink at the Devonshire Arms?"

His voice sounded steady and smooth without a trace of brusque Scottishness. British men are harder to read than Americans. I had no idea where he stood as to whether or not this was a date.

"Sure." I gave up trying to figure it out. At least I had entertaining company. I strode past him into the garden.

Edward caught up and managed to reach around me to open the gate. He made sure to walk on the street side of me, keeping me from accidentally straying into traffic.

"Have you been there before?" I asked.

"I thought you had. Isn't this where you learned to pronounce Devonshire properly?"

As I answered, his hand brushed against mine, lingering.

What was with this guy? He seemed to like me, but the forehead kisses indicated something else. Maybe I'm not used to proper manners. Or perhaps he's not into me. Most boys are more straightforward than this. Why couldn't he be normal?

"This way," he said, tugging my hand as I turned the wrong way to get to the pub. I was so wrapped up in figuring him out that I hadn't noticed our arrival.

A quick flash of annoyance at the rugby player who called me a ginger crossed my mind. "The night we met, I came here first, but it was too busy."

The ivy that covered the front of the stone exterior enchanted the entrance. He dropped my hand to open the door for me.

I braced, expecting that same chaos. But wood floors, a half-timbered ceiling, and a cheery fireplace with the massive brick mantel creating a cozy retreat welcomed us. None of these things caught my attention the first time.

"It's so," I paused, not wanting to be obvious, but I couldn't think of what else to say. "So English."

Edward's lips quirked up.

"In you go, then." He indicated a table near the fire where we sat facing each other.

As we entered, the storybook charm illusion faltered. The oak tables were scared, the carpet discolored, and the curtains threadbare. The place smelled of stale beer and old grease. "Should we get food?" I asked skeptically.

He shook his head, and I nodded mine in agreement. Edward popped to the bar and ordered two pints from the pimple-faced bartender, who looked younger than me.

Wanting nothing more than to forget every awful thing that happened to me this week, I asked, "Are you still involved in the death, or is it above your pay grade?" Sometimes my mouth doesn't consult my brain.

He raised his eyebrows in response.

Since I'd already ruined the mood, I rolled with it. "Because I've had a hell of a week and need answers."

The eyebrows lowered to a furrow.

"Need. Seriously. Did Sir Henry have both his ears, for example? And don't raise your eyebrows at me."

He did, smiling, the edges of his eyes crinkling.

"Well?" I asked, not dissuaded.

Finally, he nodded. "Yes, both ears."

Relief seeped into me, loosening its grip on my stomach. This death didn't relate to me at all. "So, a bizarre accident, but nothing more sinister than that. I can live with that."

I waited for confirmation, but Edward's smile faded, and his jaw tensed. "What?"

"What, what?"

"Something's wrong. What is it? And don't say, "what," again."

He cocked his head to the side. "Right to the point, aren't you?"

Nodding, I used my hands in a hurry-up motion. "Yeah. So, tell me."

"It seems that the death wasn't an accident. The bruising on the back of his head couldn't have been from a fall."

I gripped the edge of the table. Tension knotted my back, yanking the muscles tight. "Murder?" I whispered.

Edward's hand reached across the table, and he laced his fingers through mine.

If I hadn't been quietly panicking at the thought of finding a murder victim, it would have been confusing. Under the circumstances, I pulled comfort from his touch.

"As far as my pay grade knows. I've been tasked with looking up all violent crimes and seeing if they relate to any Conan Doyle stories because of your ear."

"Not mine," I insisted. I leaned closer to the roaring fire.

"And if not," he continued, "any 19th Century British short stories, which are really quite tedious."

I squeezed his fingers, drawing in his calming aura. "Tedious? Are you crazy? That sounds like the best job ever. I love reading. Although my friend and I already checked. There are no drowning or water-related Sherlock Holmes stories."

Simultaneously, he put his beer on the table and removed his other hand from mine. "What do you mean, your friend checked?"

He had that look people get when they're going to scold you for something, and I wasn't in the mood to hear it. "My friend, Tori. I mean, I found a fricking dead body and a human ear my first week in a foreign county, which I obviously can't tell either parent about, because they'd fly over here, take me home, and sentence me to a life of corporate sales, but I need to talk to someone, or I may bail and jet out of here anyway, and my only local friend got in a car accident and had to go to the hospital." I glared into his eyes in a silent dare.

"What car accident?" Edward seemed genuinely perplexed like people didn't drive like maniacs on cobblestoned streets designed for horses, not cars.

Shaking my head, I amended my story. "Well, I don't know her last name, but I really enjoyed spending time with her. All I heard was that her car hit a bus, and they took her back home."

Compassion filled his eyes as he gathered my hands in his. "The bus accident was with a pedestrian, not a car."

My fingers turned cold, robbing Edward of his warmth. Flashes of Lily lying in the street under the wheels of a two-decker bus strobed in my mind. Gripping Edward's hands tighter, I sent Lily healing thoughts.

"I'll see if I can get an update on her condition."

Touched, I gave his fingers one last squeeze and let go of his warmth. "Thank you," I said, meaning it.

His eyes refocused, and he looked away. "I hate to bring it up, but you must respect an active homicide investigation. You shouldn't be talking to strangers."

He could have said it to keep me from slipping into sadness, or he could be an insensitive jerk. Either way, my temper flared.

"First off, no one told me not to talk." Although yes, in my brain, I knew I shouldn't. I mean, I watch tv. But I wasn't in the mood for concession. "Second, I didn't know it was a murder, did I?"

His hands went up in a stop motion.

Sitting back, I crossed my arms over my chest. My fists balled up so tight that my nails dug into my palms. I counted to five, then ten. Puffing out air, I sat up and leaned across the table. "I'm a little freaked out."

"Me, too," Edward admitted. "Things like murder don't happen in Bath. Or even accidents, for that matter." He paused, then added, "It's a test for

95

me, isn't it? They're seeing what I can handle."

"Can I talk to you about my ideas? Since I can't talk to Tori?"

He hesitated a little too long, and I knew he wouldn't be the support I needed for this. Which was fine, but that meant I'd talk to someone else.

Since he brought up his new responsibility, I confirmed, "There aren't any drowning Conan Doyle plots, right?"

"No. There's one about a missing horse. No good. Another is an aristocratic ritual disguised as a treasure map. Not helpful, is it? In another, someone drops dead for no cause after reading a random note. Not related—what on earth is wrong?"

Sometimes my big eyes flash my thoughts like a cartoon character. I work to control it. My expressions used to land me in a lot of trouble, especially in high school, when adults would say something idiotic, and they knew I thought so.

In this case, the secret message I had followed to Sir Henry's body burst its way into my mind and flared across my face. Edward mentioned a random note as unimportant to the case, but that was because I hadn't told the police what I'd found. And now it was a murder investigation. *Dammit.*

I didn't want to hear what Edward would say if I confessed to not giving the police evidence, especially after criticizing me for talking to a friend. Leaning forward and placing a finger on my lip to bide time, I scrambled for a way to provide him with the information without incriminating myself. "I remember something." Which was true.

"Having to do with Sir Henry?" He lowered his voice despite being alone in the pub.

"Maybe?"

His gaze felt like a cage encasing me, making it hard to think. The tension in the air around us crackled, and not in a fun way.

I slammed my hand on the table, and he startled. "Give me some breathing room here," I insisted.

He jerked forward lightning-fast, but his face returned to a neutral expression. The impression I had when I first met him, of a coiled snake under a pleasant exterior, returned. "Please," he gestured with an arm, leaning back. "Carry on."

Better. I could deal with this. "I filed donations all day from the fundraiser the previous evening."

His lips twitched.

I nodded. "Yeah, I know. Thrilling stuff. Today was fun. I gave tours."

"Filing?" He encouraged me to get back on track.

"I noticed Sir Henry's donation, and the amount was so big that I paid closer attention to it than the others."

A slight crease formed between his brows. I knew disapproval when I saw it. He might not have cartoon features, but his poker face needed work.

I turned toward the blazing fire, arms crossed again.

"Was there something on the donation?" he prompted gently.

Annoyed as I was, I didn't want a murderer running around, so I continued. "There was a personalized message next to the donation. I thought the note might be for Sir Henry's, so I read it. It sounded like a thank you poem or something."

Out of the corner of my eye, I saw Edward whip out his phone and either text someone or log a reminder for himself.

I turned to face him again. "You think it might be important?" I asked.

"Possibly."

I give him a case-breaking clue, and all I get is, "possibly?"

My annoyance must have shown in my expression because he covered my hand with his. "It could be a clue, couldn't it? Pulling his hand away, he grabbed his beer and raised it in a toast. "You're brilliant."

I clicked my pint mug to his. "It could. You would be the one who brings a new clue and gets the credit. And that could be a plus for your career."

"It could." His lopsided grin appeared but fell away just as quickly.

"I should go to the station and report." His eyes drilled into mine, daring me to look away. "This is important, Maddie. Do not talk to anyone." His official countenance took over.

Sigh. I liked the smile better.

Chapter Fourteen: The Exception

I n the comfort and safety of Ash Tree Cottage, I researched the twelve stories in *The Memoirs of Sherlock Holmes* online. *The Adventure of the Cardboard Box* had come from that collection. A shudder ran through me. The fact that an ear arrived at my doorstep surprised me sometimes. I forged ahead, reading through plot summaries.

Holmes and Watson had tried to find a lost horse, which Edward mentioned. I scanned the synopsis, but no note. In the next adventure, the duo helped a stockbroker understand a predicament. No random messages.

I needed an extra set of eyes on the problem. Tori was the obvious choice because she already knew about the body. I wouldn't tell her anything more, like the murder part, until Edward okayed it. A rationalization, perhaps, but whatever.

Tori answered my call right away, quipping, "Do not tell me any horror stories about your day. I dare you."

I slumped forward onto the table, relaxing. "Actually, the most shocking thing that happened was that Simon was civil to me."

"Looking down his nose guy? What did you do to win him over?"

"All it took was finding a murdered earl. Easy, eh?" Okay, so I failed in not telling her. In fact, I didn't hold back at all. But I needed help.

A sharp intake of breath came out of her, but Tori didn't freak out. "You're such a flirt."

"I'm not sure Simon is the flirting type," I mused but realized that subject would take a whole lot of time I didn't have to unpack. "That's not important right now. Here's the deal. As an official murder, I'm not supposed to talk to anyone about the investigation."

"Except me."

"Except you. Edward is looking through the Sherlock Holmes stories on the chance my ear and the murder are connected."

"Which is foul," she interjected.

"Totally. Anyway, he mentioned something about a story with a seemingly senseless letter, and I need help finding it because I found an odd note."

Her eyes drifted to another part of the screen as she typed, muttering. "Here's one. Wait."

I waited, watching the low quality of our video connection pixelate.

"Tori?"

"Give me a second. I'm gonna call you back."

"Thanks."

I knew I'd get a response, but I didn't know what to do with myself since I gave her my task. I considered calling my mom while I waited for Tori to get back to me. I wouldn't have to tell Mom about the murder. In fact, I'd been ordered not to. But she would wonder why I was calling early.

On the other hand, I didn't want her stumbling across the news. If my parents could find out about the murder online, they should hear it from me, and that wouldn't be breaking any rules. I couldn't imagine what my mom would do if she read about a body at my internship.

Nope, scratch that. I could totally imagine it. Mom would fly on the next plane, wrap me in a blanket and carry me home like I was five years old. Sweet, but she'd do her best to arrange for me to have a desk job and a more "sensible" major.

I searched "news at the Roman Baths, England." The only thing displayed about Sir Henry was the fundraiser. Wow. Simon's Aunt Vivian had a lot of pull with the press.

If my mom kept tabs on my workplace, at least she wouldn't hear anything wrong about Sir Henry.

Before I could think of something else to worry about, Tori called back.

"Success!"

"Tell me!"

"*The Adventure of the Gloria Scott*, noteworthy as Holmes relates the tale to Watson, instead of the good doctor telling the public directly."

"Tori," I said in a warning tone. Tori loved drawing out a story, but I needed answers now.

"Oh, come on! I found it, didn't I?"

I sighed at her but smiled to myself. She loved her trivia, too. "Okay. What other fun facts did you discover?"

"There are only two stories told by Holmes instead of Watson, so it actually is a big deal."

"Does that have anything to do with the note?"

"No," she admitted. "Here's the thing. This old school chum—"

"Chum?" I laughed.

"Would you prefer chap?"

Laughing more, I tried it out. "Tori is an old school chap of mine."

"Your accent is appalling. You know that, right?"

"I know. You should hear Edward. He has this neutral accent, almost like Simon's, but he goes all Scottish when he relaxes. I love it."

"Yet, you defy his orders and call me?"

"Damn straight. I'm not the kind of girl to swoon at an accent," I assured her despite the number of times I've swooned when anyone calls me 'love.'

"Yes, you are," Tori pointed out.

"Fine," I conceded. "But the accent and right are two different things."

I picked up my computer and carefully made my way down the steep staircase to the kitchen. This conversation desperately needed toast and hot cocoa.

"You're out of sight and making weird sounds," Tori complained.

I set the computer on the butcher block island and leaned over to pet Roddy. "I got hungry."

"Are you eating the keyboard? Because that's what it sounds like."

"The story?" I prompted.

"So, this jolly old school chum of Holmes invites him out to his jolly old estate to find out why his jolly old dad—"

"Ahem," I said, not wanting to encourage her.

After slipping the bread into the toaster, I retrieved the porcelain pot, set it on the stove, and splashed in milk.

"Right-o." Her voice went up on the 'o' as if punctuating a point. She continued in a normal tone. "He, the dad, had a stroke after getting a letter. Holmes figures out a skip code."

"Wait," I stopped her.

Silence.

I cast my mind about, remembering this story. "The note looks like a normal message, but you skip over words to get the real meaning. Right?"

"Exactly. So, in the book, the note said, 'The supply of game for London is going steadily up. Head keeper Hudson, we believe, has been now told to receive all orders for fly-paper and for preservation of your hen pheasant's life.'

"Okay, I see why Edward described the wording as a random note. What's it really say?"

"Every third word is, 'The game is up. Hudson has told all. Fly for your life.'"

"Incredible."

"I know, right? So, do you remember the wording on your treasure map?"

Whisking the chocolate into the milk with one hand, I pulled out my phone with the other. "Even better, I took a picture." Once the powdery bits were stirred in, I turned off the heat.

"The full message reads, 'The path to the Roman most grand private bath awaits you and is filled with treasures no person who is friend and generous supporter to us should miss. God Save the Queen.'"

Tori let out a low whistle. "I would have followed it too."

The toast popped. I considered butter but changed my mind and rummaged around for the marmite. Finding it in the larder, I spread a thin layer on the toast, then poured cocoa into a thick ceramic mug.

"Um," I looked at my phone as I gathered my goodies. "Every third word is, 'The the grand awaits is treasures who and to miss the.'"

Tori's laughter bubbled from the computer speaker. "That's a big no. Try every other."

I took a sip of my cocoa, savoring the dark chocolate before sampling the nutty, salty bread. Through a mouth full of toast, I read, "'The to Roman grand bath you is with no who friend generous to should god the.' Also, a no."

"I think you owe me a favor to pay for my research, even though this is not the brilliant deduction I expected."

I crunched into the bread, shaking my head. "You're right. On the bright side, if the murder doesn't have anything to do with Sherlock Holmes, the severed ear was randomly sent to the house, which is a plus."

Tori nodded her agreement. "Definitely. Except, ew. Are you sure you're okay out there?"

I took a moment to think about my situation. I liked doing the tours, and I proved my capability. Sometimes I'd turn cold when a murky green memory surfaced, but I could deal with it.

"Yeah, I think so. Thanks for asking."

"Okay, so, does the Bath Abbey have a green man?"

I typed the search into Google. An image of a carving from the Abbey of a face surrounded by leaves displayed.

I glared at the computer. "You know it does," I accused her.

"Of course, I know. I want to know what your docent thinks." She paused before saying, "And don't glare at me."

I grinned. "What's a green man? He's brown in the picture. The carving looks more like a monkey." I turned my head. "Or maybe a fox."

"He's usually made of stone. A lot of early Christian motifs were adopted from existing rites. The green man dates back to Roman times and before. The early Celts, for example, thought the soul resided in the head, but they also worshipped trees."

"Why are you looking at this already? Won't the nursery rhymes keep your professor busy for a while?"

"Different class."

"Oh yeah. The price you pay for a grandmother funded apartment. Totally worth it. Okay. I'll ask Ella. Thanks for your help."

After disconnecting, I went to store my phone, and the picture of the letter caught my eye. What if I strung together every fourth word?

Mumbling out loud, I read, "The Roman Bath is no friend to God." A shiver shot through me. "Yikes," I said, this time much louder.

Every fourth word sounded like a threat.

Chapter Fifteen: The Rain, Rain, Rain

Weak sunshine streamed through my windows, awakening me gently. After a long stretch, I bounded out of bed to greet the day, pushing away the gloom that followed me. Low clouds held the promise of more rain, so I made a cup of strong tea, started a fire, and settled into a bit of research before work.

I took the whole fourth letter skip code phrase I uncovered in Sir Henry's letter and plugged it into the search bar. The results included a sermon and a lot of stuff on the Roman Baths, but the phrase itself didn't find anything specific.

The sermon told the Bible story of a Centurion who built a synagogue for the people of his town. The search result made sense but wasn't terribly helpful.

Sighing, I closed the laptop and got ready for work. Roddy received an extra carrot to keep him happy during the impending rainstorm. As I closed the gate, a little pitter-patter of drops began. Opening the sturdy, polka-dotted umbrella, I made my way to the Abbey to ask Ella her thoughts on green men.

The rain remained a steady drip, keeping me company as I strolled. "The rain, rain, rain, came down, down, down," I sang, followed by humming through the rest of the tune because I couldn't remember the rest of the words. Suddenly, it hit me that *Winnie the Pooh* was English. The rainstorm that washed away the 100 Acre Wood could have started like this one. I still couldn't believe England was my home.

A floating face peeked out of my memory as I passed a puddle. The happy rain song died away in my throat.

I stomped in the water to chase the gloom away. A single spray of mud hit my face.

Wiping away the muck, I marched to the Abbey. As I approached, a gust of wind grabbed hold of my umbrella and gave me a shove. The sky opened, and a wall of water flew at me.

Fighting the umbrella, I backed into the Abbey door and flung myself inside. Right into a priest.

"Oh, my God! I'm so sorry!" I apologized, reaching to steady him.

His hostile gaze pinned me to the ground as my arm fell to my side. That's when it hit me. Phrases that shouldn't be used in front of a priest include, "Oh my God." Also, avoid bashing into them when you're soaking wet.

"I apologize," I tried again. "The rain," I explained.

"No harm done," he said with a curt nod that made it seem like I had, in fact, caused grievous harm.

I didn't think more groveling would do any good, so I moved on. "Is Ella here?" I asked.

His expression didn't change. The glare made it impossible for me to turn away. "Sir?" I added.

"I'm not a sir. Deacon Michael. What do you want with Ella?'

"Oh. Sorry, Deacon Michael." How many times was I going to have to apologize to this man?

"You may address me as Father."

The admonishment made me feel about two inches tall.

"Yes, father," I said in a quiet voice. "I'm sorry." One more time. I turned to go.

"Young woman," his icy voice froze me one step from the door.

I turned. I kept my eyes on the floor.

"What did you want with Ella?"

Maybe if I asked him about the green man, he would relax. Asking questions always worked to make Ella chatty. "I'm interested to learn about the Abbey's green man."

I figured it would carry more weight if I wanted the information instead of a friend. I thought wrong. His eyes blazed as he answered.

"We don't do green men here. This is a place of worship, not a tourist attraction." He straightened.

The stand of tourist pamphlets stood directly behind him. I willed myself not to point it out.

"My apologies, father," I interrupted, not sounding sorry at all now. This guy, man of the cloth or no, managed to irk me. "I need the information for a class. If you're not willing to talk to me directly, I'll find a different cathedral."

"Abbey," he corrected.

My eyes narrowed.

"Technically," he continued, either oblivious or enjoying my discomfort. "We are a parish church." Smiling, he looked at the lovely building appreciatively.

I continued to glare.

He didn't react to my expression, but he finally answered. "Many early stonemasons were pagan worshippers, so they included the green man to pay tribute to nature. It was their way of ensuring that their souls were covered no matter which religion turned out to be correct." He checked his watch. "Now, if you'll excuse me." He stalked away.

"Now, if you'll excuse me," I repeated, but very quietly because I didn't want the deacon to come back and yell at me more.

I stomped around the Abbey, pausing to check out anything wooden because the green man I'd found online had been brown. Each pew displayed a different carving and resembled that one. Going along the center aisle, my head swiveled back and forth, looking for the image I'd seen in my research.

The green man was carved into a wooden pew that sat across from the gift shop. I snapped a picture for Tori and included the father's curt description.

Errand completed, I darted into the rain, not bothering to open my umbrella for the short dash to the Roman Baths.

Braving the weather had been a mistake. Once at the Oversight office, I wrung water from my hair.

Simon burst into laughter at the dribbling sight of me.

"What?" I demanded, not in the mood to be looked down on in the slightest.

"Caught in the rain, were you?" He pulled out a silk handkerchief and tossed it in my direction.

Simon belonged to a world that wasn't real to me. A world I didn't comprehend. One where gentlemen offered silk handkerchiefs to women in distress. A world that could keep grisly murders of prominent men out of the news.

I blotted my face, wrapped the handkerchief around my hair, pulled it into a swirl, and squeezed. I gave the soaking silk square back to him. "Thanks. What am I doing today?"

Taking the dripping cloth with his fingertips, his eyes flicked from it to me. "If you can manage to make yourself presentable before the first tour, you may play guide again today." He held the handkerchief by its edge, watching water drip.

"Pardon me," I said, turning to go.

He laughed.

My temper flared, as I had been spoiling for a fight since I left the church. "What?" I spat.

Still smiling, he came around the desk, standing close to me.

"Nothing at all," he grinned.

I hadn't noticed his dimples before today.

"Then, what?" I snapped.

He shook his head.

"Honestly?" I confessed, "I'm never going to get the hang of this country."

Simon patted me on the shoulder in a fond way. "You're doing fine." He offered a smile.

I felt better. Who knew that Simon would make a decent manager?

I opened the door. "Well. I'll be right back."

The restroom mirror reflected a muddy, drowned rat. I washed the dirt from my face, pulled my hair to the side, braided, and secured the ponytail with a scrunch from my purse. I nodded. Presentable.

Racing back to the tour area, I saw Simon striding toward a group. I passed him, whispering, "Too slow."

To my surprise, he saluted and left me to be the guide for the day.

* * *

At the end of my shift, I was exhausted but happy. I gave a fantastic tour and knowing that meant I would always be able to secure a job in a museum. And that was the first line of defense against my dad's well-meaning, but soul-crushing offers of employment. Smiling, I stumble-skipped to the Oversight office at the end of my shift.

Simon's voice carried through the drab, wooden door. "No, I'm in charge," he said with finality.

My hand fell away from the doorknob, and I leaned in closer, listening.

"Of course, it worked. Do you take me for a fool? My planning was perfect."

He couldn't sound more like a melodrama villain if he tried. I shook the thought away. Simon could be a jackass, but I couldn't see him plotting to get his boss fired.

After a quick tap-tap on the door, I entered.

Guilt was written all over Simon's face.

Chapter Sixteen: Wookey Not Wookiee

Ding-dong.

The front doorbell awoke me with a start. Today was my first day off, and I did not want it to begin with a stranger. Or anything strange, for that matter.

"Not again," I prayed.

Pulling a nearby sweatshirt over my oversized tee, I rolled out of bed and stumbled to the window. Fresh, cool air pushed into the room. There wasn't a cloud in the sky.

Ding-dong.

"Hello?" I called.

A dark figure stepped back and waved at me. Edward, lopsided grin in place, held out a white paper bag. "I brought breakfast," he said with a smile.

"Um." Sometimes my eloquence is overwhelming. "Be right there. Give me a sec."

I splashed water on my face, brushed my teeth, and scooped my hair into a bun on the top of my head. By the time I let Edward in, I was ready for company and food.

"What did you bring?"

"Croissants, raspberries, and espresso."

Nailed it. Being woken from deep sleep is okay if raspberries are delivered by a sweet guy. However, I didn't want this behavior to become a habit. "I'm not crazy about surprises. Just so you know."

"Everyone loves surprises," he answered with a smile.

I jerked my head toward the dining room and walked away without waiting to see if he followed.

He didn't.

Shrugging, I grabbed a couple of plates and set them on the table. The screen door in the mudroom banged shut. I found placemats and napkins for the table. The screen door screeched open. A moment later, it and the front door closed.

As I searched in a drawer for spoons, the cupboard in front of me opened into the kitchen.

"Ack!" I yelped at the unexpected movement. "What?"

Edward stood in the kitchen with a rabbit in his arms.

"Here." He handed me the bags with breakfast into the dining room and set Roderick on the kitchen's tiled floor. He disappeared from view as he left through the kitchen door, reappearing in the dining room.

"This way, we can keep an eye on the wee scoundrel," he explained with a wink, gesturing to the window disguised as a cabinet.

"I thought it was a cupboard," I admitted.

"It's a passthrough, so you can hand food from the kitchen into the dining room." His lips twitched. "Handy."

"Yeah. The dining room in the house I grew up in was attached to the living room, not the kitchen."

The mischievous expression playing around his eyes kept me from explaining further. He was up to something.

I took a bite of food. The croissant melted deliciously on my tongue. "Mmmmm."

"Would you like to go on an adventure?" he blurted out, unable to contain himself.

"No!" The word popped out of my mouth unbidden, and my hand flew to stifle the response. "I mean, yes. I mean..." I didn't know what I meant, but my confusion caused Edward to laugh out loud. "What?" I demanded.

"A wee bit flustered, are you?" He reached across the table, squeezing my hand. "Let me rephrase. Would you care to accompany me on a drive through the country?"

"No dead bodies or related parts?" I wanted to be clear on this. If he wanted to take me on official business, I needed a lot more prep time. Like a year or two.

"None."

I squeezed his fingers before letting go to tear another flaky morsel off of the croissant. "Awesome. When?"

"As soon as you're ready."

I popped a raspberry into my mouth and hopped up. "Give me ten minutes."

Taking my hair down, I brushed thoroughly, pulled it into a ponytail, and threw on jeans, a sweater, and boots.

I burst into the dining room, ready to go, in time to rescue the last few berries from his grasp. "Bringing me breakfast isn't as sweet if you eat all the yummy stuff yourself," I pointed out.

"But they're really quite good," he commented, snatching one back from me.

I went to the kitchen and spoke to Roddy. "You behave, okay, bunny?"

By way of answer, he hopped to me and rested his head on my foot.

Edward waited by the front door, smiling. "You'll want a jacket," he remarked.

If we were riding a motorcycle, I would get cold, so I pulled out a heavy raincoat and white cotton scarf from the mudroom before locking the house.

Excitement tingled through my fingers as we moved through the garden. I still believed motorcycles were dangerous but zipping through the countryside sounded like a grand adventure.

Edward reached over me and pulled open the gate. I scanned the lane. A white SmartCar and a powder blue boxy sedan were the only vehicles.

No motorcycle.

"Your chariot awaits, m'lady."

There are few things on earth as mesmerizing as a Brit saying, "m'lady."

Unfortunately, the chariot in question served as a cold splash of water to the face. He opened the door of the SmartCar, holding his hand out. Inviting.

My fault, I suppose, for calling his bike a deathtrap. I thoroughly appreciated his thoughtfulness in finding a different kind of transportation. But honestly, what is less cool than a tiny two-seater that looks like a soap dispenser?

He got in.

"No bike?" Disappointment seeped out of me despite my best efforts.

His lips twitched. Turning the key, the tiny engine squeaked to life. "Feel the power," he said as we laughed.

"My chum lent it to me for the day." He patted the dashboard.

I had refrained thus far, but restraint isn't my forte. "Any breaks in the case?" *Subtle.*

Edward checked his watch. "A record," he commented.

"Well, since we're talking about it anyway," I pressed on. "I overheard something yesterday I thought someone on the police force should be told," I offered.

He added an eyebrow crook to his smile.

"Let me begin by saying—"

"Uh, oh."

"What now?"

"Any time someone starts a sentence with, "let me begin," he started.

"They're going to say something you don't want to hear," I finished. "Exactly!" I continued. "You wouldn't want to hear that I was eavesdropping, and that's my point. I wasn't. I walked into my own office, and the opportunity fell into my lap."

"The person in question was fully aware that you were there?" Edward countered.

I bobbled my head around in a vague gesture. "Not fully. However, the office is semi-public, so it is perfectly acceptable for me to be there. And to listen."

He frowned.

Turning toward the window with a shrug, I said, "It's okay with me if you don't want to know."

Pitch-roofed houses made of limestone, little front gardens filled with flowers, and long granite fences stretched before me. As we pulled out of the city, I got my first real view of the countryside in its patchwork of green. After a few miles, we turned onto a narrow, winding road by a sign declaring Mendip Hills.

"I guess the other clues I've provided weren't helpful to you." I dangled the bait in front of him.

Sighing dramatically, Edward said. "You have been very helpful. I appreciate your insights."

I smiled but didn't turn.

In the Scottish burr, "Now, tell me what you heard, lassie."

I relented. "Simon was on the phone, and he sounded annoyed."

"More annoyed than usual?"

"Right?" I laughed. "But no. He's been in a much better mood since being put in charge. He claimed that his plan was coming together perfectly."

I gave a firm nod of my head and went back to soaking in the scenery. The road cut through stunning, grass-covered cliffs that bloomed with little pink flowers.

"This is amazing. Where are we going?" I tore my eyes away from the road and was met with Edward's skeptical stare.

"And?" he asked.

"And? And he had a plan. A plan that might get Sam in trouble so that he could take over."

"Why did he sound annoyed?"

I scowled. "You have an irritating logical streak."

"Wookey Hole," he said incongruously.

I wasn't ready to concede. "You have to see how amicable Simon's been since the murder. Something is going on there," I insisted. "And what does Chewbacca have to do with anything?"

"No, not Wookiee, Wookey."

"I... you lost me." The quality of light changed, and I gazed out the window, transfixed. A long line of trees on either side of the road grew together overhead, creating a tunnel of green bramble. Dappled sunshine sparkled through. No wonder people believed in fairies.

"W-o-o-k-e-y," he spelled as I gaped. "A tourist spot, but more for locals. Part of the Cheddar Gorge caves. Nothing to do with giant teddy bears."

"Got it. How is Cheddar spelled?"

"Like the cheese."

"So, how do you think the cheese got the same spelling?"

"Because they make it here. The cheese is aged in the Cheddar Gorge."

Huh. Who knew?

We pulled up to an old, three-story brick building. I got out and strolled toward the entrance. Even the parking lots in England were bursting with plant life.

A light blue car zoomed behind me, and I leaped out of the way. "Jeez!"

Edward scowled at the departing bumper but gave me a reassuring smile. "Alright, then?" he asked, Scottish accent settled in.

Nodding, I said, "There are a lot of those kinds of cars, aren't there?"

His eyes followed it, a slight crease between them. "Citroens," he commented. "Very popular."

Edward purchased tickets while I managed to restrain myself from running into the park. Taking my elbow, he guided me to a path that followed a still stream. We ambled slowly because I kept stopping to gawk.

The trail led to a stone cliff-face with a giant opening where the stream spilled in. Grass and trees topped the area, and moss grew around its crevasses. A warm light glowed from inside. We entered Wookey Hole.

The cave mouth was low compared to the inside of the cavern. Yellow lamps shone at different angles illuminating stalagmites, stalactites, and the water's mirrored surface below. A rickety metal fence kept people on the right path.

My teeth chattered, and I wrapped the scarf around my neck as we fell into a tour group.

"Where's your coat?" Edward asked, rubbing my arms.

"In the car. I didn't realize we'd be exploring a cave."

He pulled me close to his side, sharing his body heat.

"It won't get any colder," he assured me. "The temperature is always the same inside."

114

"Cool," I said.

"But not cold," he quipped.

I poked a finger into his ribs and found a ticklish spot. He jerked away. Both of his hands came up to my shoulders to keep me in front of him. "Behave," he muttered.

We lagged to the very back of the tour, Edward giving me a private experience. "There's a witch, turned to stone," he whispered in my ear, pointing to a misshapen blob of rock.

"What happened to her?"

"The local villagers called in a monk to exorcise her. Turns out, townsfolk aren't fond of witches."

I nodded. "Did she curse the cave?"

He crooked an eyebrow. "Haven't you had enough going on without adding curses to your list?"

The tour went around a bend, and we lagged further behind. A little aluminum rowboat bobbed on the still water at the bottom of the cave.

"Why is there a boat?"

"For the divers."

"You can dive in these waters? I mean, people do?" My foot slipped out from under me a little as I stepped from the path to peer into the black water. I caught hold of the shaky railing. "Shouldn't this fence be sturdier?" Three rusty rails, loosely screwed together at random intervals, didn't create much of a barrier. "A kid could climb over or under."

Edward shook his head. "Why would they? The water is frigid."

I hopped back onto the safety of the trail. "I've only scuba-dived where the water is warm and the sky sunny. Why would you want to swim in a cold, dark tomb?" I peered into the reflection of the boat in the water. "What's in there?"

"Oy!" The tour guide's voice echoed back to us. "Move along, there!"

"Stall him? I want to capture the way the light is playing." My pleading eyes found Edward's.

He snuggled my muffler closer around my neck. "Right. Duck." He nodded toward an outcropping.

I slipped behind the rock formation as he put on his official face and aimed for the unsuspecting guide.

Sure of my footing, I leaned against the rickety railing. Positioning my phone as far out as possible, I snapped the picture of the white and red boat, perfectly mirrored by the surface of the lake. I got two more, for good measure, until the drips and odd echoes of the chamber started to freak me out. I took off at a run to catch the group.

My shin hit something hard, and I crashed to the cold, slippery ground. Without something to grab hold of, I slid under the fence toward the wet darkness. Digging in with the toes of my shoes and my nails, I clung to the rock-face, determined not to fall into the icy water below. The buildup of slime caused one foot to slip, and my hands lost traction.

I made a desperate grab for the rail, but my fingertips barely brushed the solid metal surface before I fell. With my eyes squeezed shut, bracing for impact, I was pulled up short by my neck. My scarf had caught a rusty screw from the fence and held me dangling.

"Help!" I cried, but it came out as a faint rasp. Wheezing, I hung, arms flailing.

My hands got hold of the scarf, and I tugged, lifting myself to relieve the pressure on my throat. As I did, the muffler tore a little, dropping me another inch.

Slowly, I let go, letting the fabric strangle me. Inhaling as best I could, I reached above me to where the muffler attached to the rail. Between suffocation and icy water, I'd take the water. At least the splash would attract help.

I tugged.

Nothing happened.

"Let go," I rasped. Not a budge.

No. I would not be a victim of death by clothing accessory. I moved my toes back to the slime wall and steadied myself. Putting both hands on the scarf, I sucked in as much air as possible, but it wasn't enough.

Black spots danced in front of my eyes.

"Okay...go!" With the sound, I yanked with all of my might, rope climbing my scarf. The fabric tore, releasing me, but my hands made contact with the rusty rail.

Gulping in air with gasping frog sounds, my feet scrambled to push me up. I managed a stronger clutch on metal, but my body still dangled.

"One foot," I told myself. "Just one."

Clenching my hands around the fence with all my might, I brought a leg to the rim. Managing to put my shoe on a post, I closed my eyes and shifted my weight onto the ledge.

Something blocked the light source, and my eyelids flew open.

"Maddie," Edward cried, reaching to pull me the rest of the way up.

With both legs on the flat surface, I rolled once to move safely from the edge.

"I thought I'd check out cave diving, after all," I said, panting.

Chapter Seventeen: Bruised

"Come on. Let's get you out of here." Edward hustled me along, past some gorgeous geology that I didn't want to see at that particular moment. We reached the back of the group as the tour exited the cave.

And we walked into a circus. I expected a gift shop, but instead, I was met with dinosaurs and a giant gorilla. King Kong, to be exact. A pirate-themed mini-golf and a Victorian penny arcade lay further along the path. I didn't think I could recover from almost falling into the water so quickly, but this place did the trick.

As Edward caught my expression, he sniggered. "Brilliant, isn't it?"

Taking his arm for balance, I gawked in every direction. "Yes," I agreed. "But why is it here?"

He steered me toward the arcade. "No idea. There's also a paper mill, and you can try cave-aged cheddar if you like."

Without mentioning my fall, Edward became more protective. He opened doors wide, pulled out chairs, and skirted rowdy people. To tell the truth, it felt like a warm hug to have him around. At least I knew I wouldn't land in a well.

That enjoyment lasted about two hours. After Edward insisted on holding open the Ladies' Room door, I was done.

"Look," I told him in the parking lot. "I'm not a fragile flower. I can take care of myself."

He held the car door open for me.

I sighed but sat. When Edward got in on the other side, I resumed. "I'm serious."

"You could have been killed." His quiet voice softened me a little.

I rubbed his shoulder. "When I collided with a rock, I lost my balance. If you'd come ten minutes later, I would have been out, and you wouldn't have even known."

His eyes traveled up and down my slime-stained sweater.

I smiled. "Okay. Your expert police training may have spotted something amiss."

"May have?"

We rode in companionable silence through Mendip Hills, which described itself as an "Area of Outstanding Natural Beauty." I couldn't argue, finding every view enchanting.

My fingers ached from my misadventure, and I rubbed them absently. The winding roads and green vistas soothed me.

"What rock?" Edward asked, startling me.

I shook my head. "I don't know. If I had seen it, I wouldn't have run into it."

"The area was clear. I checked after you were on your feet."

Thinking back, I recreated the moment before my collision. My feet went two steps from the fence to the outcrop I'd hidden behind, and then I ran. But I definitely hit something, or I wouldn't have fallen that hard or been so off-balance as to slide under the rail.

I brought my foot to the seat and rolled my jeans up. A red lump, tender to the touch, was exposed.

"Well, my shin hit something." I pointed to the splotch.

"Ow." His voice was neutral, as if he didn't want to admit that his sweep of the area hadn't succeeded in finding anything.

I examined the bruise more closely. The lump on my shinbone rose in a horizontal line, a small deep-red ring in the center like I had been hit by a bat with a screw sticking out. I remembered the crack as my shin connected.

"Yeah." I didn't know what else to say. Lowering my jeans, I hugged my knee to my chest.

If nothing remained on the ground, whatever I tripped on had been removed.

Chapter Eighteen: Paperwork

Monday morning arrived bright and blue. The sun shone through the trees, but I didn't have time to enjoy it.

After feeding Roddy, I raced to get myself ready and to work before Simon. I arrived at the Baths fifteen minutes before my schedule. I waltzed into the Oversight office before stopping dead. Everything had changed. I backed out of the room, checked the door to make sure I was in the right spot, and stepped back in.

The office furniture had been rearranged. A tour host schedule, complete with handy tips, hung on a freshly installed corkboard. My old friends, the metal filing cabinets were gone, replaced by oak ones with brass knobs.

"Wow." I couldn't think of much else to say.

Sam must have been gone, and a new manager hired. I would miss her. She approved my internship, welcomed me in, and got me started. Now, I was more alone than ever.

Off-balance, I checked the schedule for tour guides. I wasn't on it for today. Maybe when they fired Sam, they'd found out my secret and were going to send me home. Dad would be waiting for me at the airport, corporate sales internship at the ready.

"Ah, good, you're here." Simon's voice preceded his footsteps into the room, so he didn't see me jump at the sound. "A lot of these files are molding, so we're going to scan them all."

By "we," I was sure he meant me. "Okay. No problem." I had a ton of questions, but I was so relieved at not being booted out of the country that I didn't say anything.

Simon hauled a banker's box full of papers onto the desk. "Start here," he directed.

But not rudely. Simon's sneering had dissipated. He treated me like a typical boss would. A little odd, considering we were about the same age, but this temperament was an improvement.

"Okay," I repeated as I removed my denim jacket, not trusting myself to talk much. I needed this internship, both for school and to keep my parents from running my life. Not to mention, I didn't want to live with either of them if I got sent home because neither had a permanent room for me. Just guest rooms.

So, if Simon wanted me to scan, I'd scan. After about ten sheets, I realized I couldn't leave the digital copies with the default name of a dozen random characters. I opened each file and renamed it. Scanning and naming took a little longer, but I got in the swing of things.

Until I realized that the computer desktop had icons covering every inch of the screen. Each document needed to be organized into folders. Filing. I was back to filing.

Why did they want a senior in the archaeology program if all an intern did was file?

My mind eventually drifted to dark thoughts, mostly centering on Simon because he was having fun giving tours, and I wasn't. I couldn't figure him out. Awful to nice to normal all in the space of a week. And the thing that changed? A murder.

A sheet of paper caught my eye, Simon Pacok's name jumped out at me. His application for the Oversight Manager was part of these files. Two years ago, he was passed over, and Sam hired. I flipped through the papers more carefully.

There was a second application from him for a paid intern position. His qualifications way outstripped mine. Probably Sam's, too. He's been after Sam's job here for two years. Now he had it.

Edward ignored my tip about Simon's impeccable planning, but this murder undoubtedly turned out well for him.

"Progressing, then?" Simon asked.

I jumped so spastically that five sheets of paper flew into the air. I leaped to gather them before Simon could see what I was looking at. I needed to find a way to put a bell on that guy.

"Yes. I've created a system of folders and grouped things by year within each." I'm sure my smile looked fake.

"I'll leave you to it, then."

Double-checking that he had indeed left, I examined his application more closely. Simon listed Sir Henry as a reference. Qualified and a recommendation by a major donor, who wouldn't want him?

Unless… I burrowed through the papers, searching for notes about why he hadn't been hired. Nothing.

Until I ran across my internship paperwork.

There were notes about my grade point average on my application, but the transcript section had a To Be Determined note. It appeared that Sam had never checked the number of credits I completed. I placed my application gently in the Already Scanned box.

Almost immediately, guilt took hold of me, and I snatched the damning evidence out again. The bottom of the To Be Scanned pile would at least delay anyone finding out that my class status had been overlooked. As I lifted the sheet, I noticed the references section on my application. A small box indicated they'd been checked with a plus sign, but nothing told who said what about me.

I went back to Simon's application. The reference box was checked. Not a plus sign, but a checkmark. Like they had talked to people, and reviews hadn't been glowing.

Searching for Sam's application took longer, but I found it. Her filing system definitely needed work. She didn't have Simon's administrative background, but her reference box also had a plus.

My mind spun a web as I mindlessly scanned the next few documents, organizing them automatically.

Were the references that important to getting hired here?

What if Sir Henry gave Simon a lousy review?

It made sense. Simon found out that Sir Henry blackballed his applications, so Simon got rid of Henry and made Sam appear incompetent in one fell swoop.

"Talk about killing two birds with one stone," I muttered.

I took a picture of Simon's and Sam's paperwork to show Edward, then stuffed all the papers into the Scanned pile.

By the time I got home, my conviction about Simon's guilt had faded. I mean, if I was honest, it didn't make much sense. People like Simon didn't commit murder to reach their goals. Connections like his would pay off eventually. He wouldn't need to do anything so stupid for a job.

I should call Tori to test my logic.

When I opened my computer, a flood of messages from my best friend affronted me. I connected right away, not even bothering to check the time difference. When Tori needed to talk, she never slept.

Her big brown doe eyes were puffy. She sniffed.

"What happened?" I asked.

A heavy sigh full of pain traveled from Arizona to England and seeped out of my computer. "I'm okay," she said. "I mean, I'm upset, but he apologized. It's more my stupid friends."

Translation, her boyfriend Scott had screwed up. Again. Usually, Tori's friends were right when it came to her relationship. But right now, she needed someone to vent with, not advice.

"Start from the beginning," I suggested. "What did he apologize for?"

"Kissing someone," she said in a flat tone.

"That's awful!" I blurted out but caught myself before explaining that he was a jerk, and she was too good for him and that she should dump him. "Are you okay?"

"Yeah. I'm fine. He'd been drinking and stuff."

"I'm sure he's sorry." True. I'm also sure she could do so much better. I needed a change of subject before I said something I'd regret. "My day included more filing and deciding that Simon killed Sir Henry."

Okay, honestly, it sounded ridiculous once I heard it. "I mean, my theory is still in the developmental stage. Not a lot of facts to go on."

"Just because you don't like a guy doesn't make him a murderer," she pointed out. Sure, she's all logical with me, but nothing would make her see sense when it came to her boyfriend.

She sighed loudly again.

Break up with him! I shouted in my mind. Out loud, I asked, "Do they want you to break up with him?" referring to her friends.

"Everyone says it! But they didn't see how sorry he was. He said I didn't deserve that kind of treatment."

"He is right about that."

She dropped her voice meaningfully. "He even cried"

"It sounds like he learned his lesson," I offered.

"Exactly!" Tori's voice filled with hope.

Simon would need to do something a whole lot more sinister to outstrip Scott's stupidity. And I could live without that.

Chapter Nineteen: Someone Else's Discovery

As I strolled to work the next day, I made a pact with myself to not accuse Simon of any more misdeeds. I would file, scan, organize and be friendly.

The Oversight office door stood open when I arrived. Odd.

Peeking in, I noted Simon's detailed schedule had been covered by a scrawled handwritten note which read, "Maddie - take all my tours today."

Awesome! Tours beat data entry any day of the week. I checked the schedule and saw that my first one started in an hour. I poked at the To Be Scanned papers and decided to take a refresher stroll around the Baths to make sure I remembered everything accurately.

A big commotion surrounded the Archway entrance. Three or four volunteers huddled together, whispering. A museum administrator I hadn't met directed people away from the public portal.

Adjusting my employee ID, I approached the group of volunteers.

"What happened?" I asked.

A woman scrutinized me, then gave me a smile so bright she lit the hall. "We've found another passage!"

I was so excited that the tops of my ears thrummed. "You're kidding! Where?"

In terms of things to come across during my internship, a significant discovery ranks at the top. Ears, murder, and even a friend getting hit by a bus could be tolerated. If they geared up for more excavation, I could wrangle a full-time job here! And then I could visit Lily if she didn't move back to Bath.

"In the Undercroft."

The Undercroft was a public discovery area about two stories beneath street level. The exhibit was the most recently opened at the museum. The level taught as much about archaeology as it did the Baths. The Undercroft was displayed as an active excavation site.

"How come they didn't see the passage before?" The site probably extended under the whole city. Even if a section wasn't open, it didn't mean that no one knew it was there.

"With the Undercroft open, we volunteers have started digging around in the back chambers." She beamed at the entrance to the Undercroft.

Her expression was so proud that a thought struck me. "Did you find it?" I asked her.

Speechless, she nodded vigorously, tears shining in her bright eyes.

A twinge of envy crept into my thoughts. Why did she, a volunteer, get to have this kind of glory while I filed papers?

Not that I cared about the glory, but I craved the thrill of the find. I have to admit that even with an administrative internship, I couldn't help but picture myself brushing off thousands of years of dirt to expose a new mosaic.

The volunteer started to fidget uncomfortably, and I realized that my face must have reflected my thoughts.

"Congratulations." I stuck out my hand. "You must be very proud." Which sounded silly once it came out of my mouth.

But the words had the right effect. "Thank you, but it's not about me. Everything is for the museum. The history is why we're here, isn't it?"

My jealousy faded. We were here because of the history. I should be thrilled that I'm this close to a find. I smiled, sincerely this time, and congratulated her again.

At that moment, Simon bustled out of the elevator, and I was not in the office where I should have been. My options for not getting caught included ducking into the center of volunteers and hoping they weren't horrified at my behavior or bolting through the exhibit. Since those weren't real options, I chose a direct approach and called his name.

"Ah, Madeline. Have you heard the news? Exciting. Very exciting." The restraint in his voice didn't hide the enthusiasm bubbling out of him. He looked like a kid in a candy shop. "I'll be busy with this for the next few days, but everyone has their marching orders. Continue with the filing and cover my tours. Good?"

I nodded.

"Good." He backed slowly away from me, clearly itching to get back to the site. "I wish we really could knock down the Abbey. We would go so much faster," he muttered.

For a quick moment, I wondered if he should be searched for explosives. Instead, I went about my day.

* * *

After finishing my tours and mindlessly scanning documents, I made my way to the Undercroft to experience 2000 years of history. I couldn't believe it.

My enthusiasm quelled as soon as I got to the Archway, and Simon announced the site closed.

"But come on!" I'm not above pleading when the stakes are high. "When else will I have a chance to see this? Please, Simon."

A sigh that rivaled Tori's theatrical flair emitted from his lips. His drooping shoulders let me know I had added the weight of the world to his load.

"Please?"

"Perhaps another day, Madeline." Simon walked off.

"When?" I followed, practically skipping.

He stopped short. "What?"

I bounced on my toe in excitement. "When can I see the mosaic? This is a once in a lifetime thing, and I want in. So, when?"

"Fine." Snapping around, he stalked to the entrance. He unlocked the private stairwell and led me into the dark.

"Could it be any creepier down here?" I asked, not expecting an answer.

The lighting wasn't designed for the public. Nothing warm or cozy lit our way. Instead, stark fluorescents flickered with a sickly blue tinge, throwing strange shadows onto the walls.

Down we went. Two stories are nothing normally, but in this setting, it felt like descending into another universe. Simon held keys to the elevator. I think he led me this way as mental warfare.

We emerged in the public area of the Undercroft, but again only emergency lights lit our path. At the far end of the display, we stepped over a rope and arrived at an ordinary wooden door.

Shining his phone light on the keyhole, Simon unlocked and opened it. He went in, grabbed something from a shelf, and marched out.

Curiosity propelled me into the room.

The door slammed, plunging me into darkness.

"Dammit!" I shouted, pounding on the door with my fist.

Nothing.

I stopped pounding and listened.

Silence.

I pulled out my phone using the light to discover a supply closet with minimal cell service. I typed to Simon, "I got locked in." How dorky did a person have to be to get locked in a closet?

Sighing, I hit send. A red exclamation point returned, telling me the text didn't deliver.

Fine, I'd find another way out. I turned on my phone's flashlight, searching for anything that would help. Freestanding shelves stood along the back wall, filled with brushes, sifters, and picks. The remainder of the room showed clear signs of recent construction. I hoped Simon hadn't already left the area, not realizing I was trapped.

With the thought came thirst. The last time I had anything to drink must have been at lunch. The dryness in my mouth became all-consuming. My throat ached. What if Simon knew where I was, didn't care, and I was stuck in here overnight? I didn't think I could stand it. I had to have water. "Wait."

Startled, I whispered. "My purse." I always carried a small bottle of water with me.

I searched frantically but came up short. Feeling betrayed, I gave one last search before remembering I removed the bottle at airport security.

My tongue felt overly large and stuck to the roof of my mouth.

What if Simon didn't care? The refrain echoed in my thoughts.

"This is stupid," I told myself. "I'm from the desert. I refuse to die of thirst in such a soggy place."

I used the flashlight to scan the room again, revealing nothing useful. "Where was a can of soda when you need one?" I muttered.

"Think!" And I surprised myself with an idea. I remembered learning in seventh grade that centuries ago, Native Americans would put a pebble in their mouth to force saliva to form. On the roughly poured cement floor, I found a smooth little stone and brushed off the dirt.

I grimaced.

Looking for alternatives, I dug through my purse again. A spray bottle of organic, all-natural disinfectant that I had gotten as an impulse buy at the store fell into my hand. I grabbed it, sprayed the pebble. I got the little rock into my mouth, but my fingers refused to let go. The rock quivered, suspended above my tongue.

"Nope," I told it, lowering my hand.

This situation did not have the power to make me suck rocks. Instead, I read the disinfectant ingredient list. Called thieves' oil, the spray had five essential oils and distilled water.

Opening my mouth, I gave myself a squirt. Surprisingly, it didn't taste half bad. As a bonus, my thirst abated. I could stay here all night, and Simon would have to explain what I was doing in here in the morning.

I used the phone flashlight to examine the tools again. Taking a fine-pointed excavation pick, I set to work at the mortar around the inset for the door latch. The area was old and crumbly, but not ancient, so it wasn't like I desecrated anything. If repairs had to be made, Simon would need to deal with that, too.

The snick, snick of the pick scratching the wall must have penetrated through because I heard the sound of a key slipping into the lock. I held the pick as Simon yanked the door open. Good timing since using my flashlight dropped the phone's battery to eighteen percent.

"What are you doing?" he demanded while trying not to laugh.

I narrowed my eyes at him.

Turning away to avoid whacking that expression off of his face, I placed the pick on the shelf, arranging it with precision. Leaving the room, I conjured as pleasant of an expression as possible.

"Excavating," I said breezily. "Did you forget where the passage is? I looked in there." I jerked a thumb at my prison closet. "No sign of it."

Smirking, Simon led me in the opposite direction, passing another "Private No Entry" blockade to a different door, which he held open for me.

Seriously?

"Please," I pointed into the inky-black passage. "After you."

His eye roll put mine to shame as he confidently strode by and faded into the darkness.

I followed at a safe distance to avoid any more traps.

The area we entered was a part of the Undercroft but not finished for the public. The real archaeology happened here. I was seeing history firsthand.

For a few moments, my annoyance with Simon battled with my curiosity.

"Why isn't this place on the website?" Curiosity won.

"Vandals." Simon spat the word.

I couldn't tell if he was mad at the vandals or me. Although I was the one locked in a closet and, therefore, had a right to be annoyed.

But I could fill in the rest for myself. The Baths didn't want a lot of security so that the public could feel comfortable roaming around. If there was an opportunity to explore where they shouldn't, some people would, and take stones or shards as souvenirs.

The scent of something spoiled crept into the air. "What's that smell?"

"Mildew," he answered like it was the most obvious thing on earth.

The desert doesn't develop mildew unless you do something ridiculous. Like the time I did a load of laundry when my mom was out of town and forgot about it for five hot days. The machine smelled pretty vile after that.

At that moment, I missed the clean, dry air of Arizona. Here, moisture was a part of the atmosphere, impossible to avoid. I couldn't get used to it or the stench in this part of the ruins.

We passed one passage covered with a large stone which Simon ignored. A block-and-tackle pulley system was suspended above the rock for easy removal. Why replace the rock if the archeologists were working in there? I examined the area.

Sawed-off putlogs left an indentation around the doorway. I touched one, communing with the ancient engineers.

"Isn't that it?" I asked, pointing to the pulleys. I don't know why I bothered asking. It's not like he was leaping at the opportunity to answer my questions.

"No."

He needed more questions. "What is it?"

"A chamber."

"A chamber for what? Does it go anywhere? Why do they have it closed off?"

"Storage."

"Storage for what? For us? Isn't that what the closet was for?"

No answer.

I mean, what was with him?

"Or is it an ancient storage facility? If ancient, why aren't the archeologists working in there?"

"Do be quiet," he said.

Snapping, I railed at him. "Of for god's sake, Simon. What is your problem? I am here to learn and work. I've done everything you and Sam have asked, and my tour reviews are awesome. I know because I looked when I had to scan the stupid things into the computer. You know what I'm not learning about? Archaeology. Because, yeah, I traveled across an entire ocean to do filing. But I've done it. And I'll keep doing it because I'm happy to be here, unlike you."

He started to say something, but I was on a roll, spurred on by his obvious enjoyment of the situation.

"I'm not finished," I said louder than before. "All you've done since I've been here is hassle me. No, of course, I don't know what I'm doing, so I ask questions. I'm new, and I'm a student. So, give me a flippin' break."

A gentle smile formed. "Maddie, I—"

"And," I said louder. "I discovered a murdered man. And while you seem fine with murder, I'm not. Stiff upper lip and all that, but I'm a little freaked out. We have emotions in America. So, if you could just… just… I don't know. Be nice or something." I ran out of steam.

He beamed in that way that made him look handsome and charming as opposed to a pompous jerk. "You finished?" He crossed his arms and leaned against a wall. If he made that same move in a bar, admirers would line up to talk to him.

I nodded, trying not to fall for his facade. Although he was much more appealing when he acted casual.

"Sorry." He cocked his head to the side. "I've had a long day. Have you not been here before?"

I shook my head.

"I thought Sam had shown you this area. Come along." His hushed tone set a mood of reverence, and I forgave him so that I could make room for concentration. This area was ancient and mostly untouched.

I followed with short steps, sheepish about my outburst.

We came to a roped-off area with floodlights set all around. Simon flicked them on, illuminating the past.

I sucked in my breath. The threshold was lined with tesserae, small square mosaic tiles.

Feeling the presence of something bigger than Simon and me, I bent close to see that a few of the tiles had inscriptions.

"This will lead further under the street, possibly to the Abbey foundation or its cemetery. The fastest way to excavate would be to have a shaft going straight to the surface. Or to build an elevator above the site, but we can't." Simon shook his head. "We'll have to take the dirt through the current exhibit to sift it." He sighed as though the Abbey had been put in place solely to vex him.

I wanted to run up the hall, grab a brush from the dreaded closet, and get to work.

"We should go."

I didn't want to leave. Maybe if I got locked in the closet again, I could sneak out later and excavate. Of course, without keys, that wouldn't work. I regarded Simon. "Thank you for showing this to me. I'm very grateful."

At this moment, it was hard to imagine why I thought he was a murderer.

* * *

Walking home alone didn't feel right. I wanted company.

A motorcycle zoomed by, and I admitted that what I really wanted was to talk with Edward.

I pulled out my phone and pressed Home. The screen came on, then went black. A red battery displaying One Percent flashed briefly.

Dammit, I thought as I stepped into the street.

A light blue sedan almost hit me, sending my heart rate skyrocketing.

"Look both ways," I admonished myself, leaping back onto the sidewalk. A conjured image of Lily's crumpled body in the street fouled my mood.

Maybe it was better to go home and sleep.

I'd call Edward tomorrow and tell him about the passage discovery. It'd be novel to not report a disaster.

Unless Simon decided to knock over the Abbey before morning.

Chapter Twenty: The Code

The next day I rolled over in bed and pulled my phone out of its charger. A text from Edward illuminated the screen.

Smiling, I opened it.

"Supper tonight?"

I frowned. The message had been from last night, and I'd never responded.

Texting back, I explained, "I was in the Undercroft. Flashlight drained my battery. How's it going?"

He responded instantly. "Undercroft—can't wait to hear about it."

"How about supper tonight?" I offered.

"7?"

"Perfect! See you!"

Grinning ear to ear as the sun broke through the clouds, I strolled to work. The air smelled sweet and held a hint of warmth. Optimism bubbled through me, quelling any leftover fears that Simon was a raging lunatic.

Simon sat behind the desk, re-organizing the boxes of files to be scanned. Again.

"Hey," I greeted him. "When are my tours today?"

The smile he flashed me absolutely glowed. His face transformed from pinched into dashing. I couldn't help but beam back.

"Sorry, but I've had to give you two extra today to cover for me. I'll be coordinating the volunteers on the Undercroft passage dig."

"That is so cool, dude," I said, caught up in the moment.

He guffawed.

Come to think of it, I hadn't heard anyone say "dude" since I'd arrived in England. And hardly ever at home. Too many repeat viewings of John Hughes movies affected my vocabulary sometimes.

"Um, American moment," I confessed. "Let's try. I think it's really, rather quite nice that you are coordinating volunteers on an important discovery." I grinned. "Actually," I added for good measure.

"Quite nice," he agreed, still laughing. "Well done." He stood, ushering me out of the office. "Your first tour starts soon."

I was finally beginning to win him over.

* * *

After a day of tours to exclusively school children, I was exhausted, and I needed to hurry home and get ready for my dinner date.

Stumbling into the empty office, I grabbed my purse and coat and combed the desk for paper to leave Simon a note.

Unlike when Sam was in charge, the office had become exasperatingly clean. I couldn't find notepaper anywhere, although the pens were neatly aligned at the top right corner of the solid oak desk. Sitting, I selected one.

Logically, the notepaper should be close to the pens. I opened the top right drawer of the desk, and there it lay. As I tore a sheet off the top of the pad, it shifted, revealing a handwritten letter underneath.

Sitting straight, I put on a poker face, glancing from side to side. I moved the notepad a little more while keeping up the appearance of writing.

Simon's handwriting. I'd recognize it anywhere since he wrote out the schedule. On the loose sheet, he had written, "THE path to the ROMAN most grand private BATH awaits you and…"

Ice water flooded into my veins. I slammed the drawer, and with a shaking hand, wrote to him. "Great day. Lots of school kids. —M"

Why did Simon have the words to the treasure map in his desk, skip code intact? Had he created the original note? If he did, had he intended for the message to lead to Sir Henry's death?

After carefully lining the pens together, I stood. Crumpling the note I'd written, I stuffed it into my bag. I didn't want Simon to discover I'd been in the drawer.

"Maddie. How were the tours?"

"Ack!" I threw my purse in the air at the sound of his voice. Sure that "guilty" screamed across my face, I said, "Sorry! Busy day. Super tired." I snatched my bag, hugging it to my chest.

"I was going to write you a note, but I couldn't find any paper." My hand snaked into my purse pocket, stuffing my note further in. I maneuvered around him, keeping my back to the wall.

"Lots of school kids today. I'll see you tomorrow," I muttered before fleeing the building.

Outside I took deep breaths, willing the dread away.

I could imagine Simon checking the desk drawer now, seeing the notepad out of alignment. He'd narrow his eyes, imagining my intrusion. He'd destroy the evidence. And any witnesses.

I started walking, stiff-legged, farther from the Baths and Simon.

"This is bad," I said to my feet. "Walk faster."

Simon had a handwritten note for the code. He could have figured out the code and printed it out on linen paper. Under that calm, snooty exterior, he could be boiling with rage at getting a negative reference.

I knew from firsthand experience that he could be petty without provocation. If he felt slighted, would he escalate?

Speed walking, I made my way to Greenway Lane in record time. I made sure everything was secured. Grateful for the view of the garden and gate from my bedroom, I confirmed no one could sneak up on me.

* * *

Getting ready to see Edward was slow going due to stopping every few minutes to check my bedroom window for invaders sneaking through the gate.

The roar of a motorcycle vibrated the windows before cutting off. I ran to the window to be sure. A hand reached over the gate, unlocking the latch. I held my breath until I saw Edward stride into the garden carrying a brown paper bag. The moonlight glinted off of his worn leather jacket, giving him a roguish appearance.

Suddenly thoughts of Simon seemed silly. Petty twit? Yes. Crazed maniac? Probably not. Worth thinking about tonight? Not at all.

Halfway to the garden path, Edward stopped in his tracks and zeroed in straight at me. His crooked smile spread across his features, and he lifted a hand in greeting.

I waved and scrambled downstairs to let him in.

"Hi!" I said with an American amount of enthusiasm.

The sack slipped to the ground as he moved toward me.

"Hey there, lassie," he murmured and moved like he was about to hug me but changed his mind.

"I'm going to need to change if we're riding your bike." I indicated the long skirt I'd chosen for the evening.

"Deathtrap, don't you mean?" Focusing his attention on the bag and not me, he picked it up and strode into the house.

"I'm willing to give it a try," I let him know, following. After locking the front door, I added, "If accompanied by an officer of the law."

"I've got other plans," he informed me, hefting what I now recognized as a grocery bag.

"What's in there?"

His lips twitched as he backed into the kitchen. Out of the bag came leeks, carrots, a can of chicken stock, barley, and something wrapped in butcher paper. "Cock-a-Leekie soup," he announced, the words sounding exotic in his Scottish accent. "Where's a stockpot?"

I pointed vaguely to the cupboards where pots and pans lived. Edward found what he was looking for and set to cooking while I hopped onto the black-and-white tiled counter to watch.

A comfortable silence fell between us. I wanted to tell him what I had learned about Simon and the note, but it didn't seem that important now that Edward was cooking in my kitchen.

I vowed to myself not to mention police business until he did.

"Why don't you always have a Scottish accent?" I wondered.

He froze for a few beats, his spoon poised over the sautéed vegetables in the pot. Then he went back to stirring.

"*Ah dinnae ken.*"

"What?"

"The Scotts use a lot of phrases that not even the English understand. If my accent is too strong, no one understands me."

"Well, I like it."

This time when he stopped stirring, his shoulders relaxed.

"Is there that big of a difference between the English and Scottish? I mean, aren't you all Brits at this point?"

He unwrapped the package of butcher paper, which held diced, cooked chicken. It went into the veggies.

His head went from side to side as he turned to me. "If you wanted to be president, could you?"

I nodded. "Of course. Well, I'd need money, but in concept, yes."

"I could never be king. My family isn't important. Socially, everything would be harder for me if I had a lower-class accent."

Thinking about it, I understood his point. If a boy used the word "ain't," I wouldn't consider dating him, but that was more about education than social position. Unless, that is, I discovered he was smart, and then it wouldn't matter.

With a shrug, I sniffed in the scent coming from the stove. "What's your unimportant family do for a living?" I asked, not accepting his point entirely, but not wanting to argue.

"Nothing," His face clouded. "Except my brothers, who cause trouble."

I wondered if he had a bad childhood but didn't want to pry. I skirted the subject. "Where were you raised?"

"Craigmillar." He didn't say it with any enthusiasm and paid too much attention to the barley as he measured.

"Where is that?"

"Edinburgh. The dodgy part."

I smiled. "Dodgy?"

He poured stock into the veggies and added the chicken and barley.

139

Walking to my perch, he asked, "What, don't you Yanks say dodgy?"

"Only in gangster movies from the 1930s." I sniffed the aromas coming from the pot. "That smells wonderful, by the way. When do we get to eat?"

"If you're starving, ten minutes, but it'll be better in thirty."

"Okay. I've only seen pictures of Edinburgh. It looks beautiful."

He blinked a couple of times, contemplating. "Parts of it. Not where I'm from." His head gestured to the door. "Let's check on the wee rabbit, shall we?"

The round globes of outdoor lamps bathed the garden in a soft glow.

"Allow me," Edward said.

He stepped over the short fence and opened Roddy's hutch. "*Wee bawties*," he coaxed.

"What did you call him?"

"Rabbit," he answered as Roddy hopped to him. Edward scooped the bunny up and kissed its fluffy head.

"*Bawdy?*" I attempted the pronunciation.

The twinkle in his eyes pointed out I wasn't close, but that wouldn't stop me from trying.

"Okay. How about *I dinna can?*" I failed at getting the words out like he said them in the kitchen.

He stepped closer to me, the short fence still between us. His fingers stroked Roddy's ears.

"Close. *Ah dinnae ken.* It means, 'I don't know.' My grandmother spoke Lallans and used the phrase whenever any of us complained that something was unfair. She was a tough old bird." His fond expression told me that we'd hit on a family member that he liked.

He didn't give me a chance to ask about her or anyone else. He pointed to Ash Tree Cottage. "Why do these old buildings have pieces of wood sticking out of them?"

I turned to appreciate the house that I was calling home. It must have been 200 years old, but it didn't possess the clean lines of the Royal Crescent or Pump Room. Its rough-hewn construction spoke of a more straightforward architectural style. "Those are probably fake, like half-timbers in new buildings," I explained.

I may not be as far along in my archaeology degree as I would like to be, but my Architecture Appreciation course taught me plenty. "In Roman times, they built logs into the buildings to attach the scaffolding. Real putlogs are cut off and plastered." I stepped over the fence and stroked Roddy's ears. "The Baths have them, too. I found them right after I got out of the closet."

I'd been trying to find a way to introduce my suspicions of Simon, and this segue fell right into place. On one hand, Simon ran the tours well and was very professional. But the fact that he had the skip code kept niggling at me. Did I think he was a murderer? No, but that wasn't for me to decide. The police should know about it.

"What closet?"

My stomach made an unladylike grumble. As I described the discovery, I touched Edward's arm to indicate that we should go back inside. "I can't believe I haven't told you already! A passage was uncovered by one of the volunteers at the Baths. They thought the passage was a dead-end off of the Undercroft."

Edward turned his face toward me to fully take in what I had said. "Brilliant!" He beamed. "What did it look like?"

"At this point, dirty. Simon is helping the lead archeologist, Dr. Daniels, coordinate volunteers in the excavation. I got a chance to see," I paused, recalling the tingling in my chest as I gazed at the discovery. "Beautiful. The Romans lined thresholds with little tiles." My fingers formed a one-inch square. "They were glazed, so the color holds up beautifully. These were blue and turquoise." Dropping my hands, my mouth came open, but words failed me. I settled for "Amazing."

Reaching toward me, he gave my shoulders a little squeeze before snatching his arm away. Sharing my excitement with someone doubled the pleasure. "A packed wall of dirt hides more rooms. These tiles wouldn't be there if there weren't more to the building. The soil will be removed, sifted, and cataloged, so the going is slow. I can't believe I'm here in England for the unearthing. I'm overwhelmed."

"Your logs were already exposed? Wouldn't those be an indicator of more building, too?"

"Putlogs," I corrected. "And no. They were located in a different part of the Undercroft. I saw those before the closet incident."

Edward sighed, somehow sensing that I was going to talk about closets and not architecture. He was right. "I asked Simon to take me to the dig site after the museum closed. Once we were in the Undercroft, he went into a closet, and I wanted to see what was in there. After he came out, I went in."

Edward's lips tightened. He probably thought I should have asked permission to go in. Sometimes his strict adherence to rules got in the way of a fun story.

"And I got locked in," I added, hoping to build sympathy. "It was pitch black, too. No light switch." I glanced at Edward's expression, and his face had gone blank, impossible to read. "Simon took an excessively long time to let me out."

Edward did not take the bait I'd dropped about Simon's behavior. Instead, he asked, "Doesn't your phone have a flashlight?"

Nodding, I said, "I used it to explore. I didn't have a signal, so I couldn't text Simon to come and open the door. But he should have noticed I wasn't with him. I mean, there were only the two of us."

Again, Edward chose to ignore my hint that Simon might be up to something… my mind cast back. Dodgy. He was up to something dodgy.

Edward suggested, "Turn off wifi and roaming when you're underground. The phone keeps trying to find a signal. That eats your battery faster than the flashlight."

Opening the door so Edward and the bunny could enter the house, I followed, nodding. "Okay. I'm hoping to be down there a lot, so I'll use airplane mode."

"Good."

Lifting his face, he sniffed. I did the same, taking in the rich, peppery scent of the stewpot wafting out the front door and across the garden.

After setting Roddy in the kitchen, Edward handed the soup to me in the dining room via the passthrough. We sat at one end of the dark, mahogany table. Placemats depicting scenes of Bath protected the surface from the heat of the steaming bowls.

The stew was delicious. Thick with barley but lightly scented with leeks.

I nodded in appreciation as we slurped. "This is fantastic soup. Thank you so much."

His lips twitched into a shy smile. "I have a favor to ask in return."

My eyebrows raised. "Yes?"

"Could you let me know when you're going dark on your phone?"

I tilted my head to the side, contemplating his request.

He hastened to add, "You've only been here a short time and have had a few rather nasty turns." His eyes found mine. "I'd feel better if I knew you were safe underground and not being kidnapped."

He looked away. "You don't have to, of course. It's really up to you."

I smiled and nodded. Given what I'd found, I appreciated the idea of someone in the world knowing my whereabouts.

He sighed, scraping the last of his soup from the bowl. "Anything for pudding?"

I blinked a couple of times before he clarified, "It doesn't have to be actual pudding. What do we have for afters?"

"Dessert? I have drinking chocolate. Will that do?"

"Brilliant," he remarked, collecting the bowls and spoons and taking them into the kitchen.

By the time I'd finished stowing the placemats and wiping off the table, Edward had the sink full of hot, soapy water. Sleeves rolled up, he was deep into washing.

Retrieving a large tea towel, I dried and put away. I was itching to rearrange the dishes in a more logical order. Why were plates in two different cupboards? But the Priestlys may not welcome the intrusion.

Retrieving my favorite pot, I set milk to simmer while Edward located two big mugs.

"Make lots," he suggested.

Adding another cup of milk to the pot emptied the glass bottle. As I opened the trash compactor to throw it out, Edward stopped me. "Leave the bottle out by the gate," he told me. "They'll collect it on delivery day."

I narrowed my eyes at him. "Honestly?"

He chuckled, went to the pantry, and pulled out a wire carrier. He slipped the bottle into one of the slots and held the basket for me to see. "You've had a fish delivered. Why would milk be a problem?"

"True." I shook my head. "We don't have that kind of thing in Arizona. Dairy would go bad, like, instantly. As would fish. If we had any place to get fish in the desert, which we don't."

As I whisked in the dark cocoa, Edward asked skeptically, "I heard the temperature once got to fifty degrees in Phoenix." The Scottish brogue returned as he relaxed.

In my head, I quickly did the calculation to Fahrenheit. "122. Yeah. It doesn't happen a lot, but 115, or, um," I reversed the conversion. "Forty-six is pretty common in July and August. The rest of the year is lovely, though," I added quickly as his eyes grew wide in horror.

Grabbing a blanket from the mudroom, we took our steaming mugs out to the garden. Rather than sitting at the wrought-iron garden table, a twin to the one in the mudroom, we scrunched together onto the ash tree's swinging bench. The ropes of the swing creaked as we gently swayed.

I felt completely safe.

"You've done yourself proud tonight, lassie."

I quietly agreed. "I didn't ask about the investigation once."

"A hint, but no questions. Which is just as well, as I don't know anything new."

I didn't want the moment to end. My body was relaxed, my mind content. But sometimes, I'm an idiot. "I think Simon had a grudge against Sir Henry."

The swing stopped, and Edward tensed.

"I'm not saying he had anything to do with the death, but somebody should check him out."

"That is a very grave accusation," he began. "Especially for one of his position."

I sprang up. "What position? He's my temporary boss. And he's only that because he got rid of Sam. I saw their applications. Simon is way more qualified, but I think Sir Henry must have given him a bad reference."

Edward's eyes rose skyward. I guessed that he was silently praying for me to stop. No such luck. I pulled out my phone and showed him the pictures I took of Simon's applications.

"Look. See how his Reference section has a checkmark?"

Edward nodded, taking the phone from me.

"Compare that to Sam's. Her section has a plus sign. My internship paperwork also had a plus sign. I think the plus sign means you got a positive review. Which means Simon got a bad one."

Edward swiped through my pictures. "This is a good one."

An image of the entrance to the Wookey Hole cave displayed on my phone. Clearly, he hadn't been floored by my logic.

"Well?"

He continued to swipe. "I like this one, too," showing me a picture taken of King Kong from our day trip.

"Nothing?" I insisted.

He froze. An expression I now knew meant something terrible was turning in his mind. Shaking his head slowly, he put the phone to sleep.

"You can't take pictures of official documents, Maddie," he admonished. "It's just not done."

He handed the phone to me, removed the blanket, and stood. "Thank you for a lovely evening."

The way the words came out, you'd have thought I kicked his grandmother.

Following him into the house, I tried to steer the conversation back to neutral ground. "Edward, I—"

"Goodnight," he called as he grabbed his jacket, draping it over his shoulder.

Stunned, I couldn't think of what to say to make him stop.

I opened the phone and saw the last picture he had swiped to; the photo of the note that led Sir Henry to his death.

Chapter Twenty-One: The Dig

A sheet of water hit the side of the house. Rain battered the window. I checked the time. After wrapping myself in a fluffy robe, I padded downstairs to make a strong cup of coffee, then went back to my tower room to turn on the computer and call Tori.

"What time is it there?" she asked.

"Way too early. I screwed up."

A muffled voice came through the connection. Male.

I face-planted onto the desk. Scott must be with her. "I'm sorry," I told her. "I can call back later."

More muffled sounds, followed by Tori's voice, loud and clear. "No, I'm okay. I'm in a different room now. Work or guy?"

"Probably both. Also, it's raining so hard I'm thinking of building an ark."

Tori snorted. "One thing at a time. First, what's the rain like? I'm picturing a garden tea party, a peal of thunder, and everyone scurrying inside in a very dignified manner."

Leave it to Tori to brighten my day, even in a massive storm. I turned to contemplate the pouring rain. "Probably pretty accurate. Although no thunder or lightning, as far as I can tell."

"That's odd."

I nodded. "Yeah, strange."

If the sky opened up like this back home, the storm would be electrical. Cold breezes from the clouds mixed with hot desert air caused sheet lightning to blaze across the sky every few minutes, booming thunder echoing all around. "No light show. A river of water is assaulting me."

"Sounds enchanting." She paused, saying more quietly, "You're my inspiration. I've put in applications for two internships. One in DC and the other in Peru. Keep your fingers crossed for me."

I gripped the edges of my computer and leaned in close. "You did?" I wondered if she was quiet so that Scott wouldn't hear her. "That is so cool! Peru would be such an adventure. Plus, you're already fluent in Spanish as a bonus."

"I'm sure the dialect is different in South America." Her voice returned to a regular volume.

I nodded my agreement. "Don't I know it. Did you know pudding meant dessert?"

"Everyone knows that," she informed me.

Ignoring her, I repeated, "So cool. Fingers and toes are all crossed."

"Why?" A male voice intruded on our conversation. Scott must have entered Tori's room.

"Ten more minutes," Tori's distant reply to her boyfriend to shoo him out of the way came through.

"Okay," she said, loud and clear.

As much as I wanted her to myself, I felt terrible that I was keeping her from her date. "Do you want to call me back?"

"He's good," she assured me. "He wanted to make sure that I wasn't talking to Mckayla."

"Why not?" McKayla was an archetypal mean girl, but Tori always hung out with her.

"She's a cow."

I burst out laughing. "True."

"Anyway," she changed the subject. "Tell me about your screwups."

I scrunched deeper into my chair, kicking my feet onto my desk. "I think Simon is a murderous psychopath."

"As you've said. Fresh evidence?"

"He locked me in a closet with no light for, like, an hour."

"What? Totally psycho! An hour?"

I screwed my face up. "Well... I don't even think he did it on purpose. I snuck into a room after he left, and the door locked behind me. But it took him a long time to rescue me."

"Wait. For an hour?" She paused. "How long is a long time in minutes?"

"Probably five." I knew where she was going with this, and I got defensive. "Maybe less," I admitted. "I still don't trust him."

"How long did my brother lock you in a closet our freshman year?"

Back when Tori and I thought we knew everything as we entered high school, her older brother put me in my place by locking me in their downstairs laundry room. "Forty-three minutes and sixteen seconds. I timed it." Tori had thought I'd gone back across the street to my house and hadn't bothered to look for me.

"So, two possibilities. One, Simon wasn't paying attention and didn't notice you weren't following him."

"Yeah, but he's not very polite."

"Or," Tori ignored my interruption. "Maybe he's just plain, old obnoxious."

"Okay," I dropped that point. "But there's one more thing. He had a handwritten note of the skip code."

"You mean the same one you have a picture of?"

I squinted at the computer. Tori was a lot more to the point when Scott was waiting for her. "Yes," I admitted.

"Well, there you go. If you have evidence, Simon can have it too. No need to worry about him. Okay?"

My head bobbed reluctantly. "Okay."

"Don't sound so disappointed."

I laughed. "That is an excellent point. Not having a psycho at work is a bonus. Obnoxious I can live with."

More muffled voices came through, but she came back as supportive as ever. "What else?"

My head flopped back. "Arg." I steadied myself and explained. "Edward came over and cooked me dinner. That I really did screw up."

"Are you kidding me? He cooked you dinner? He's like straight out of a rom-com."

Heat rose in my cheeks. "It's not like that. We're just friends." I thought about the quick hug he gave me. Also, the platonic forehead kiss. "I think. Anyway, I tried to accuse Simon of murder."

"Oh, no." Tori's voice held both sympathy and dread.

"I found paperwork that I think means Sir Henry gave Simon a bad reference, and I took pictures of it, which I showed Edward."

"Wait. You showed a cop you'd taken pictures of private human resource documents?"

"Yes." Recalling the blank expression that clouded his features when I explained my reasoning, I added, "He wasn't too pleased about that."

"Sometimes," she offered, "your relationship with rules is a bit casual."

Ignoring her admonishment, I continued. "The worst part was that Edward found the picture of the note that led me to Sir Henry."

"The same one you tried to use to accuse Simon?"

"Yeah. That. Edward must have been pissed that I had a picture of evidence."

"Well, yeah." She paused. "Not sure what to do about that one."

"Tori," Scott's strident voice cut through.

"I'll think about it. Gotta go. Bye!"

And she was gone.

As much as I complained, silently, about Scott, at least he was always there for her. Except when he was kissing someone else at a drunken party. I couldn't tell if I was jealous that her relationship was that solid or annoyed that she couldn't see that she deserved better. Probably both.

I peered out the rain-streaked window at the deluge.

Walking to work was out of the question. I'd need rain boots just to get through the garden, not to mention a coat and umbrella. I didn't have anything for my feet. Boots took up too much room in my suitcase. And I didn't own anything waterproof, anyway.

Edward was justifiably mad at me. Buckets of rain. Shoeless. Not the best start to a day.

On the bright side, Simon probably wasn't guilty of murder. And maybe I could make my way to the dig site again today.

Since I kept referring to the screened-in porch on the house as a mudroom,

I wondered if it might have been one. As I unlocked the front door to explore the area, the sound of the rain quadrupled. A waterfall pounded the roof.

"Jeez!" I shouted at the storm. "Calm the heck down."

It ignored me.

Padding lightly to a bench in the corner, I sang bits and pieces from childhood rain songs until noticing the bench seat had hinges. Opening the lid exposed boot storage. Voila!

I hoped Mrs. Priestly wouldn't mind me borrowing a pair of green overshoes. "Wellingtons" was stamped onto the soles.

Smiling, I slipped them on over my tennis shoes.

After gearing up, I ordered a ride-share car and waited inside the mudroom until the app on my phone beeped that the driver was close. I gave my jacket belt another tug and braved the storm.

Soaked to the bone before I got past the rope swing, rainwater seeped into every possible opening in my clothes and into my boots. I squelched with every step.

The car lights cut an anemic path through the water, its windshield wipers no match for the force of nature coming from the sky.

I slammed the door getting in, grateful for the warmth of the heater.

"A little wet out today, eh?" my driver quipped.

Water dripped from my hair onto his upholstery.

"A little," I agreed.

"What?" He couldn't hear me over the sound of the storm beating against the car roof.

I leaned forward and raised my voice. "Thank you for picking me up."

"Not from around here, are you?"

I forget that I'm the one with an accent. "No," I began, but the driver lost interest in my origins as he navigated the road. Because of the switchbacks, it took almost as long to drive to the Baths as it did to walk. But on a day like today, the ride was justified.

He pulled as close to the Baths' doors as possible, and I scampered at full speed up the steps. Squelch, squelch, squelch.

Slipping in a puddle of my own making, I threw open the door to the

Oversight office.

Simon burst into laughter at the sight of me.

I narrowed my eyes at him. "What?" I shook the rain off me like a dog and squelched to the coat rack. When I looked back, Simon had assumed an expression of patient benevolence.

"Why are you wearing men's Wellies?"

"Men's what?"

He indicated my boots.

I plopped soggily into a chair and struggled to pull one off.

"Carefully," he cautioned. "They'll tear. Start at the heel."

Doing as instructed, the boot popped off, taking my shoe with it.

"How are you not wet? Did you tunnel here? Is there a secret dryer you're keeping from me?" I asked as he smirked.

"Wellies. Wellingtons. They're not meant to be worn over other shoes." He smiled. "Besides, it wouldn't dare rain on me."

Smiled. At me. Like, a genuine friendly gesture. Which I didn't trust. Simon had shown me the dig site but took too long to get me out of the closet. I narrowed my eyes. "What's going on? Do I have an early tour or something?"

His grin widened as he opened his desk drawer and drew out an object. My first panicked reaction was that he pointed a knife, but I felt terrible once my brain took in what he held out to me.

He offered me a brush. A set excavation dust brush, to be exact.

I rose slowly and sloshed to him, afraid he would snatch his hand away. His little joke, like losing me the first day of work. But he didn't. "Does this mean what I think it does?"

Nodding, he said, "Your little rant last night made an impression. It's an awful job, but you can sift and brush everything they pull out at the site today."

My eyes grew big as my heart pounded out of my chest. Archaeology. "You mean it?" My voice shook.

"Try not to drip on things. Head to the Undercroft emergency stairwell. We have a small station there."

My feelings for Simon went up about seventy-fold. So, yes, he may or may not have enjoyed me getting locked in a closet, but right now, he was making my dreams come true. Tori's brother actually locked me in a closet on purpose, and he turned out okay.

Before entering the worksite, I texted Edward that I'd be underground, like he'd asked me to. I waited a couple of minutes for a response, but none came. He must have still been mad about my taking pictures of evidence. Which, worded like that, did sound like a bad idea. I'd apologize later.

I switched my phone settings to airplane mode and descended deep into the past.

The trained volunteers at the newly discovered portal carefully brushed away soil and rock under the supervision of archeologist Dr. Daniels. The dirt got collected in buckets that were passed to me. I conducted a second sift by pouring my bucket over a sieve and shaking, sort of like panning for gold.

When I was six years old, my grandparents took me to a museum with a gold mining exhibit, complete with a full-sized model stream and pans. I scooped the sand, shook, and methodically tapped my sieve until I saw a golden glint. A museum worker rang a bell, and everyone clapped at my success. The tiny nugget was weighed, then placed into a small glass vial for me to keep. I still had it. That day ignited my love for archaeology, although I didn't know what the career was called back then.

Today, I sifted and brushed at every piece of rock that didn't fall through the sieve. Unlike my first search for gold, it didn't yield much.

More precisely, nothing. After four hours, the novelty wore off. My mom's voice whispered in my head, "You could be out in the world advancing women's rights. Why do you want to hide in the dirt?"

I brushed more soil from an ordinary rock.

Unbidden, my dad chimed in. "Don't you want to own a big house? With me to guide you in sales, you could be making six figures a year out of college. You'll never get that digging."

Wiping a stray, still-moist strand of hair from my forehead, I willed their voices and my doubt away. Almost immediately, thoughts that I had permanently lost Edward as a friend invaded my mind. He was fun, smart, and a gentleman. Now I'd never find out if he could be more. How many times does an opportunity like that come along? Instead of enjoying myself, I sabotaged our friendship.

"You can't take pictures of official documents," I repeated Edward's admonishment when he'd been swiping through my pictures. True, but an ear was sent to my address, and I had found a dead body. I wanted the cases solved and didn't want to investigate. I was just trying to give the police the information they needed so they could catch the murderer.

When Simon was mean to me, I wanted him to be guilty. But not today. Today Simon was the man who gave me an excavation brush.

I made a resolution. No more interest in Sir Henry. Forget about the ear. All obsessing did was make me feel frightened and alone.

Instead, I would focus on the new Roman passageway, appreciate Simon more, and have fun with Edward. In that order. If Edward was still a possibility.

Pulling out my phone, I checked to see if Edward had responded to my "going dark" text. Then I realized, duh, I went dark, so I turned off airplane mode. One bar of connection. I reset it and went back to sifting.

"Maddie!" Simon's voice echoed into my station.

I stood and took a few steps in the direction of the dig site.

"Madeline!" More urgent.

Dropping my brush, I bolted down the hall to Simon and the rest of the team.

"Ah, good. You're here."

"Did you find something new?" I panted.

He blinked at me. "No, but we could murder for a cuppa. Would you pop over to The Bath Bun and grab us drinks?"

It was more of a statement than a question, so I couldn't say "no." Not that I would, but still.

Despite being grunt work, getting coffee for a team digging ancient Roman artifacts still felt like an honor. Taking the order and pound coins from Simon, I nodded. "Be right back."

When I walked outside, I welcomed the fresh air. A light drizzling rain fell, but as all my clothes were still wet from the deluge this morning, it didn't faze me. The damp, clean air smelled delightful. The dig site's strong mildew odor still wafted through the Undercroft. If Coffee Girl got to stroll around the square, Coffee Girl I'd be. Or, more specifically, Tea Girl.

The first thing I did once out in the open was to turn off airplane mode on my phone. Four happy bars dinged to life, but no message from Edward. Checking my phone was becoming tedious.

"You haven't been in for a while, have you?" a quavery voice accused. Behind me, Ella marched up, stamping her cane confidently across the uneven stones. Her step was so sure it didn't look like she needed the extra support. Edward's description of his grandmother came back to me. *Tough old bird.*

Remembering my decorum, I nodded to her politely. I wanted to hug the little woman, but, as she would say, that would never do.

"How lovely to see you, Ella."

She presented me with a flyer. "We're having an Ice Cream Social. Do come."

The event sounded so all-American that my eyebrows shot up in surprise. "We're making it from scratch."

I assumed she meant the ice cream.

"Father Michael heard about the idea at a museum conference he attended," Ella explained. "I've been experimenting with recipes for the last two weeks. Rather a ridiculous process, really."

She must have a self-cranked machine because she was too small to churn by hand. I remember trying it once when I was a kid at a block party on our street. One of the neighbors had an old-fashioned ice cream maker with a wooden bucket and red crank. Everyone tried turning the handle while the dads dumped in rock salt around the pail. Block parties and yard sales were the things I missed most about my old neighborhood.

Taking the flyer, I carefully folded it into my purse. "I certainly hope I can make it." I nodded again.

"I should hope so." She sounded awfully accusatory for a woman inviting me to ice cream.

We split ways as I arrived at the door of The Bath Bun, a postage-stamp-sized cafe nestled into a courtyard by a gigantic tree. Like, six feet across big. I stared, wondering how old it was.

As I gaped, a little man hobbled over to me and happily declared, "That there's the hangin' tree."

"What?"

He pointed to a long horizontal branch as thick around as my waist. "The rope went 'round there. People would crowd onto the street to watch the show."

I examined his face to see if he was kidding. Nope.

"Ta," he said cheerily with a wave.

"Okay. That was both cool and disturbing," I said, walking into the cafe.

Once inside the shop, the rich smell of brewing coffee triggered a flood of memories. Whenever my mom drove me to high school, we'd stop and get a caramel macchiato at the place by our house. On allowance days, Tori and I walked to the corner of our block and had deep conversations over iced coffees.

During one of those chats, I first told her that I wanted to be an archeologist. We made plans to walk to the shop after every year of college and discuss the progress of our dreams.

Except that the second I moved to the dorms, my mom sold our house. There's nothing like being pushed out of the nest to learn to fly, wings intact or not. I pictured myself flopping helplessly while a hungry cat licked its paws.

But fly, I did. Here I was, working at an actual dig site in the very place that cemented my decision to be in this field.

The steam rising from the mugs of tea was so enticing that I ordered one for me, too. I paid for my drink separately so I could account for Simon's cash properly.

"May I have a receipt, please?"

The barista blinked at me. Peering at her pile of paper orders, she found mine and wrote the total amount on it. "Here you go." She smiled, pleased at her ingenuity.

"Um, thanks." Gathering the wobbly crate of teas to go, I hoped Simon wasn't as concerned about accounting as I was.

Managing the drinks for the team was a tricky business. I never waited tables, so I didn't have the balance or grace of Tori when it came to carrying a tray of liquid. Thankfully, only a little sloshed onto my shoes by the time I got back to the Undercroft.

After delivering the goods as well as the makeshift receipt, my mood plummeted. Nostalgia edged with a sharp pain of my parents not believing in my dream, combined with the dark atmosphere and musty smell, weighed on me as I sifted.

Gray dust filtered through the screening sieve leaving small rocks on top of the mesh. I touched each with a brush. Definitely rocks.

Even as I concentrated on the task, the fact that I would need to give Edward a hefty apology kept creeping into mind. Tampering with Evidence didn't have a pretty ring to it, and cops tended to be rule followers. I needed to revise my plan.

More dust. More little stones.

Then a glint of white.

A rush of adrenaline jolted me as I brushed off the specimen. Bone or tooth? Or pottery? I could write my ticket to a job in the field with a find like that on my resume.

Only, the more I brushed, the more it looked like a white stone. A perfectly normal, non-resume-worthy rock.

I set 'definitely not an ancient artifact' aside anyway, noting the bin it had arrived in. The dig site was covered with a grid of numbered one-foot squares. Each square had a corresponding container. If any relics were found, they'd be cleaned, cataloged, and replaced in the grid where they'd been found.

At the end of the day, I couldn't help being discouraged by not finding anything but a white rock. On the other hand, if my eyes were sharp enough to pick out that, perhaps Dr. Daniels would be glad to have me search again tomorrow. Me, on a real dig. Unbelievable.

Standing, I stretched the stiffness that had settled in.

Squelch. My shoes were still wet. I wondered what awaited me outside. The teatime drizzle or another tempest?

Chapter Twenty-Two: Dinner With Simon

When I emerged into the main museum, I found the hall mostly deserted. I checked the time on my phone and realized that I hadn't gone back to airplane mode after my drink run, draining the battery to seven percent. I shook it a little to see if any messages from Edward jarred loose, but no such luck. It clicked to five percent.

"Hey! What happened to six?"

The phone responded by telling me it was going into battery-saving mode.

"A little late for that, don't you think?"

My hands trembled slightly, reminding me that I hadn't eaten enough today. I'd been so excited to be on a dig that I'd forgotten about lunch.

It wasn't a problem as I packed a snack with me wherever I went. Opening my purse, I pulled out the ham and tomato sandwich I'd made and wrapped in cling wrap before work. The plastic had filled with water from the storm this morning.

My stomach protested loudly.

"Shh," I told it as I listened to the quiet of the museum. No, not silent, white noise. A steady whoosh of sound filled the air.

Outside, the storm had returned with a vengeance.

"Fine. Be that way." I pulled out my phone to order a ride-share.

No battery.

Heat formed in the middle of my head, radiating out to all my limbs. With every passing moment, I could feel the energy abandon me. I dug through my purse, searching for any kind of food.

Three soggy cough drops. I popped the lozenges into my mouth and chewed frantically.

The tremors subsided. It was enough to keep me from passing out, but it didn't solve my problem of getting home.

Something hit my shoulder.

"Ack!!!" I screeched, snapping my head to the left. Nothing was there.

I heard laughing to my right.

Simon had tapped my left shoulder then darted to my right side. Maybe Tori was right. If I thought of him as an obnoxious big brother, I could deal with him.

"Does it always rain like this?"

He shook his head. "No, this is special. Do you need a ride?"

"Yes, please. Thank you. That'd be great." I was so thankful for dry transportation that I didn't care if yesterday I thought he was a murderer.

He drove one of those little cars that kept trying to run me over. "I see these everywhere. Usually, when I forget to look the right way crossing the street," I commented.

"Yes, the Citroen," he replied, patting the immaculately clean dash fondly. "They're a good car."

Through the water and dim street lamps, I couldn't tell the color, but the zippy engine came to life as we cornered. No wonder everyone who drove them sped. The heater worked great. Warm air circled around my soggy shoes and warmed my hands.

"Are you hungry?" Simon cut into my thoughts.

"Starving," I admitted.

He turned on an unfamiliar street, and it flashed in my mind that he could, at this very moment, be kidnapping me. It wasn't the first time I'd let my stomach lead me along a dubious path.

"There's a cracking place under the bridge."

My fears vanished. I cocked one eyebrow as I turned to face Simon. "Cracking?"

Through his smirk, he said, "Giving you the full English experience."

159

"The Boater?" The restaurant Edward took me to had also been under the bridge.

It was Simon's turn to raise an eyebrow. "Old hat. Right-o, then."

As we entered the restaurant, I found myself scanning the room for Edward. I mean, this restaurant was my first sort of date in England, so it was a natural reaction.

At least, that's what I told myself. In reality, I missed him, and the fear that I had permanently ruined our relationship before it even began weighed on me. Even when being his most charming, Simon was not a romantic substitute, especially as I was pretty sure his attentions lay in the opposite direction. It was also too easy to imagine that he was up to something.

I sat at a table in the middle of the bustling dining room. Music blared as Simon went to the long, mahogany bar to order an appetizer of zucchini fritters.

"You seem rather peckish," he explained, setting a half-pint in front of me.

I could hardly argue. "I forgot to eat lunch."

The steaming fritters arrived with the parchment menus, and I attacked the plate in the least lady-like way imaginable. Chewing, I flipped through the selections. Once nourishment hit my system, I perked up. "Thank you for this."

Simon appeared completely happy and relaxed. It was a good look for him.

"Did you have fun today?" His critical examination of my face made the question less friendly than I wanted.

In between bites, I nodded vigorously. "Oh yeah. I mean, for such a boring job, it's exhilarating. You know what I mean?"

"Absolutely."

"You do a great job coordinating the volunteers," I told him.

His head bowed as though acknowledging one of his subjects. "Actually, I wanted to talk to you."

My heart jumped. Simon sounded exactly like a teacher who caught me ditching class. It took all my willpower to not blurt out, "*Am I in trouble?*"

"You came all this way. I wanted you to have a good day."

He made this statement like one day was all I had. I swallowed.

"It turns out," he rested his elbows on the table and drummed his fingertips together like an evil overlord.

I still couldn't figure him out. He'd been so kind, and now he seemed to be toying with me.

"DCI Bray has a few concerns about your involvement with Sir Henry's death."

"What?" I practically shouted, but no one noticed over the roar of the music. Of the scenarios skittering around my head, my connection to the murder of Sir Henry wasn't on the list. "How? I couldn't possibly—"

Simon's hand came up in stop motion. "This isn't my decision, Madeline. I'm sorry, but I had to inform the police of your involvement."

No, no. No, no, no, no, no. "No," I finally got one out loud. "There is no involvement. I found him. That's it. What are you talking about?" The food I'd been stuffing into my mouth turned to stone in my stomach.

Simon reached across the table and took my hand, which had taken on a life of its own, gesturing madly.

As he did so, smiling that beautiful, hateful smile, someone knocked into our table. The retreating back fit Edward's description. Tousled hair, leather jacket, and shoulders tensed in anger. Definitely him.

On top of whatever Simon was talking about now, Edward probably thought I was on a date with another guy. If I got myself out of this mess with Simon, I'd have to make my way through multiple apologies. And why would Edward bother with me? At best, I'm in the country for a year. At worst, maybe a day.

I snatched my hand away from Simon. "What on earth are you talking about?"

"First, there is the fact that you are here under false pretenses."

Crap. Crap. Crap. "Wait, I—"

"I'm not finished," Simon continued. "The internship clearly calls for an upperclassman, and you are only in your first year."

The rock in my stomach flopped. I felt my face turning red. He knew, and there was nothing I could do about it. I stammered, but we both knew I'd barely started as a sophomore. The one and only aspect of the internship that I wasn't qualified for was that the Baths wanted a senior level student. Submitting the application without filling out the class section hadn't been a lie of omission. I figured they would check.

"Second, you willfully skipped entering your application into our database, presumably so that I wouldn't find out."

I froze. Had I forgotten? I remember toying with the idea. I was going to be kicked out of the country and sent home in disgrace. My parents were waiting to support me if something negative happened. I had told them I could do this on my own. But I couldn't.

"Simon, I can explain."

He turned and signaled to someone. "Perhaps, but I'm not the one you have to convince."

A small, tidy man in a suit appeared at our table. He looked familiar, but I couldn't place him.

"Ah, Detective Inspector Parikh," Simon addressed him.

Inspector. I groaned. DI Parikh had taken my statement at the Baths after Sir Henry's death.

The sick, sinking feeling I had fled as outright panic took over. I stood so abruptly my chair fell and clattered to the floor.

The inspector calmly set it upright. "Please, miss. Have a seat," he suggested putting a hand on my shoulder.

My fist cocked automatically as I pulled out of his reach.

"Please," he said more firmly.

"Get it together, McGuire," I whispered. This was no time to lose it. I needed to think.

I dropped into the chair. "I don't understand."

"There are things we need to clarify that were brought to our attention by Mr. Pacok."

I shot a death glare at Simon. He grinned like this was all a big joke to him. Why would he bring me all the way here? He could have had the police come to the Baths. The picture of Edward's retreating form came to me. Simon wanted my humiliation to be complete. I couldn't figure out how or why Simon invited Edward to witness my disgrace. Even if he hadn't, the result was the same.

"We'll just need to take you to Bridgewater for questioning."

My face froze. "Bridgewater?" Somehow the picturesque name tolled doom for me.

"Yes. If you wouldn't mind joining me, miss."

He placed his hand on my elbow, and I saw the glint of his badge under his raincoat.

I couldn't feel my fingers. Standing, I swayed unsteadily.

Chapter Twenty-Three: The Station

The inspector held me in a tight grip, steering me out of the lively bar and to his black car. The rain continued to pour, finding its way into the back of my jacket.

In the back seat, I shivered, my teeth chattering.

DI Parikh spoke, but his words didn't make sense. I wrapped my arms around myself and hunched. As fat drops pelted the car's windows, tears welled and spilled over my cheeks.

The car pulled to a stop, and a uniformed constable led me to what appeared to be an interrogation room. There was a camera in the corner and a guard posted outside. The room's sickly pale green walls made me queasy, and my breath came out in fast gasps.

A muscular block of a uniformed officer entered and handed me a steaming cup of sweet, lemony tea. The act of taking a sip settled me, and I managed not to hyperventilate. The sugar left a cloying film at the back of my throat. By the time I finished the tea, my breathing was under control, but I felt more nauseous than ever.

Standing, I paced the confines of the room. My shoes, still wet, continued their musical squeaking. I didn't know what was going on, but I wouldn't panic again. I wouldn't give Simon the satisfaction.

A second officer came in, this one gray-faced and lined with wrinkles.

"Flannel, miss?" He presented me with a hand towel after helping me out of my coat.

I rang out my hair to keep it from dripping onto my shirt. "Do you think I could have a cup of coffee?" I asked.

A curt nod was the only response, but the coffee arrived shortly. A little bitter, but the acid cut through all the sugar left behind by the sweet tea. The burst of caffeine helped me think.

Simon knew about my application but let me work at the dig site an entire day. He claimed he wanted to give me a single happy day, but I had a hard time believing that. Maybe, like me, he wanted the police to have all of the information available. But what information? I honestly did not have a single connection to Sir Henry.

Would Simon's pull with DCI Bray be enough to have me arrested on false pretenses? He probably got Edward to The Boater, too. Somehow. Although, how would Simon even be aware of Edward? If it had been a coincidence that he was at the pub, my luck was officially at rock bottom.

At that moment, DI Parikh entered, followed by the expansive, muscular guard who stood stony-faced, blocking the door. The scene looked so much like a cheesy crime show scene that I could have laughed if not for the coiling in my stomach.

"Can I have my phone call?" I asked, not sure who I'd call.

Parikh's expression darkened. He pulled out a recorder and flicked it on.

If this was a prank set up by Simon, no one else seemed to be in on it.

I leaned forward but failed to make eye contact. "I don't understand why I'm here."

Parikh took a pair of reading glasses from his jacket breast pocket, polished them on a cloth, and carefully perched them on the end of his thin nose to read. The small fabric was neatly folded and placed back in his pocket.

"Perverting the course of justice, to begin. Possibly murder."

I bolted out of my chair, and the guard shot forward, grabbed my shoulders, and pushed me back into it.

Oh god. I was in real trouble. And I couldn't ask Edward for help because the last thing he saw when we were together was evidence of the case on my phone.

The shivering returned.

"You said in your original statement that you had no connection to Sir Henry Gilliam."

I nodded mutely.

"If you wouldn't mind speaking for the voice recorder."

"No. No connection."

He opened the file. Again, it was a move that a cop on TV made when they knew a suspect was lying. But I wasn't.

He slid the paper across the desk. A ledger page listed donations to the Roman Bath Society. One column detailed the person who secured the pledge, another showed the donor and amount. I had created a similar list the day I discovered the body.

Parikh pointed to a name. Ed McGuire, 10,000 pounds sterling collected by Sir Henry Gilliam.

My insides went hollow. "I—"

"Do you recognize this name, miss?"

My head shook from side to side in disbelief.

"Speak into the recorder, please."

High-pitched buzzing filled my ears. "Um, that's my dad, but I didn't—"

The screech of his chair drowned me out as he stood.

"Wait!" I screamed, making a desperate grab for the folder. The contents scattered across the polished concrete floor. The guard returned, this time with handcuffs.

"No!" My flailing didn't impress either man.

Click.

One wrist in. I deflated, watching the other cuff slide into a ring on the table. Collapsing into the chair, I stared at my doom.

Click.

That was it. I was officially a prisoner in a foreign country. "I want..." Trailing off, I scanned my memory banks to see if I knew anything about British jails. The phone call request hadn't gotten much tread. I could try to talk to the American Embassy.

My forehead clunked onto the tabletop as I gave up. An embassy. Who was I to talk to an actual embassy? No one, that's who.

Ruined, I listened as the officer retrieved the papers I'd knocked to the ground. He set them on the table as I sat straight and chose my words carefully.

"I didn't know my dad, father, donated money. Or that he knew who Sir Henry was." There was only one criterion for the internship at the Roman Baths that I didn't meet. 'Must be a senior or in the last two semesters of the program.' And I wasn't. I'd just begun my sophomore year. I applied anyway and sort of failed to mention that I wasn't as far along in my program as I should be. I figured if it were vital, someone would check.

I thought no one had noticed that I was a fraud, not knowing nearly what I should about archaeology or Ancient Rome. Only that wasn't it. My dad had paid for my way in. I'd never see if I could make it on my own.

An evil voice in the back of my mind whispered, *mob money*. I shook the thought away, not wanting to think of the ear or its implications.

No, it wasn't the mob. It was my dad's way of being helpful. Defeated, I pleaded, "Honestly, I didn't know."

A tiny bit of pity must have surfaced because Parikh sat. He took off the glasses and gave me a once-over.

Choosing the ledger sheet, he used the temple of his glasses to point to my dad's entry. "Is this date familiar to you in any way?"

October of the previous year.

I shook my head no.

Flipping through the pages, he continued to push. "You're sure? Nothing in October?"

I cast back. October had been cold in Chicago, which was a first for me. All my childhood Halloweens in Arizona were warm. My mermaid costume was the hit of the party when I was a senior in high school. In the frigid Midwest, I dressed as a sexy snowman for Halloween, which was harder to do than it might seem. In between shopping for costumes, I filled out my application for…"The Roman Baths," I muttered. My head drooped, but I avoided smashing against the table again.

He reorganized file contents, apparently looking for a paper.

As he shuffled, a picture caught my attention. Pausing on the photograph, his eyes bored into me. "I'm sorry?"

"October is when I filled out my application for the internship," I confessed.

And oh, how it felt like a confession.

"Yes," he confirmed. "I have your inquiry here somewhere." The photo flashed by again.

"What's that?" I asked, pointing to the photograph of a green-blue straight line with a discolored circle in the center of something. My wrist caught on the restraints as I gestured. "Ow."

Parikh snapped the folder shut.

"No, wait. It looks like—" Again, I pointed and pulled up short on the metal cuffs. "Ow."

Setting my hands lightly on the table, I turned sideways in my chair and plopped my leg up. Wet jeans hindered the movement. "Oof." Folding in half put a lot of pressure on my bladder.

The guard leaped forward, making to knock my leg off of the table.

"Really, miss," DI Parikh complained.

"Wait, wait," I pleaded, turning the pant leg back a few folds to expose the bruise on my shin.

"Look." The bruise on my leg had blossomed greenish-purple since my trip to Wookey Hole. Its outline was distinct. A straight line with a small, darker round in the center. It matched the picture in Parikh's folder.

"See?" I said, gesturing to the dark circle on my leg, then to the closed folder. "They kind of match."

The skepticism fled the detective inspector's face. Opening the folder, he retrieved the photo I'd seen. He turned his head to one side, eyes flicking back and forth between the picture and my leg.

Without a word to me, he pulled out his phone and took multiple pictures of my shin. Snatching the folder, he stalked out of the room, followed by the guard.

The excitement of the bruise comparison ebbed. I was still handcuffed to the table, still wet and cold, and still out of luck. My leg flopped to the floor.

Fleetingly, I considered asking for more coffee to keep myself warm. But there was no one to ask, and I kind of needed to go to the bathroom.

Looking around, my eyes landed on the camera in the corner of the room. I lifted my hand to wave and possibly attract someone's attention, but the cuffs caught my hand six inches from the table, jostling against my wrist bone. "Ow."

Another bruise. Closing my eyes, I pictured the photo from the file, which wouldn't be in there if it weren't pertinent to the case.

My eyes twitched open so wide I could feel them dry out. Edward had mentioned that the bruise on Sir Henry's head couldn't have been caused by a fall. That fact led to the conclusion that Sir Henry had been murdered. The bruise that matched mine had caused a murder.

I rocked in my seat, unblinking. I'd seen a photo of the killing blow. "This is bad," I whispered.

The constant movement awoke the biological urge of the moment. My bladder sent a message to my head, asserting its needs over my panic. I required the bathroom.

Twisting from side to side, I couldn't see anything that could be used to get someone's attention. I aimed my face toward the camera. "Hello?" At first tentative, but I got louder as time ticked by. "Hey! Someone? Please?"

When I was officially escorted into this room, I thought I had hit rock bottom. The humiliation and consequences couldn't have been worse.

I was wrong. What would be worse would be a repeat of the time I peed my pants in second grade and had to run home at lunch before any of my classmates noticed my ruined jeans. The mortification of losing it, literally, here in Edward's police station with Simon in on every bit of news would be enough to send me fleeing from this country, admitting my failure to my dad's waiting arms.

"HELLO?"

At that moment, the expressionless guard came in with a pair of slippers and a blanket. He removed the cuffs and draped the afghan around my shoulders. Like everyone who has ever been handcuffed, I rubbed at the delicate bones of my wrist to make sure they were all intact.

Maybe everything would be okay. The slippers were a good sign. The police didn't want me to freeze to death. If they believed me, they'd let me go.

The guard didn't invite me out of the room when he turned to leave.

Clearing my throat, my voice went horse. I didn't want to ask. I squeezed my eyes shut then blurted out, "Would it be possible." My eyes popped open to stare at my shoes instead of looking at him. "To use the restroom?"

He stopped at the door, head turned to glance at me, and continued through without comment.

I sank further into my dismal abyss.

Peeling off my wet shoes and socks gave me a moment of comfort. The gray house shoes were fuzzy and warm. The contrast between my feet and my heavy, soggy jeans was appalling.

The pressure in my midsection turned to pain. As I considered using my shoe as a bucket, a stout, pretty female officer swiftly entered my little prison. Her dark hair was pulled back in a tight bun.

"Is it the toilet you want?"

Taken aback at the brusqueness of her question, I nodded meekly.

"This way, miss," she said without much sympathy.

Apparently, the slippers weren't a sign that I was off the hook. Otherwise, the constable would have just given me directions. I could barely stand straight as we walked the corridors to the loo.

At last, we arrived. She opened the door for me. A small but clean room with a toilet and a sink.

The officer followed me in and turned toward the door. Presumably to give me privacy.

The jeans squeezed muddy droplets on my legs as I wriggled them down. Sifting debris from the dig seemed like a million years ago.

I sat on the toilet, willing the pain in my mid-section to release.

It wouldn't.

I have never had to go to the bathroom so badly in all my life and I. Couldn't. Go.

The female officer shifted from one foot to the other, impatient.

Closing my eyes, I leaned forward. Still a no go.

The officer stamped her foot. "Do hurry up," she complained.

Long, slow exhale.

Nope.

"If you don't need to use the loo, then—"

"No!" I beg-shouted, which isn't a thing.

And the final step to humiliation. "Look," I explained. "I can't go with you just standing there."

"Well, I'm not leaving, mind you," she shot back.

I supposed it would have been asking a lot. "Could you make some noise or something?" I asked, feeling the full weight of the stupidity of my situation.

She pivoted on her heel, reached to the sink, and turned on the tap. The sound of rushing water filled the room.

Encouraged by the noise, my body finally released. Nothing ever felt so good or ever would.

When handcuffed to a table, do not ask for extra coffee after tea. Words of wisdom.

She accompanied me back to the interrogation room, and I crumpled into my familiar chair.

Detective Inspector Parikh ushered DCI William Bray into the room.

"Doing okay, then? Right," DCI Bray said without waiting for my answer. "Where did that nasty bruise come from?"

I straightened. "When Edward, um, my friend took me to Wookey Hole, I cracked my shin on something. The momentum caused me to slide under the railing, and I almost fell into the lake in the cave. When I looked around after, there was nothing there. No rocks or posts or anything that I could have fallen on." I shrugged. "I guess I could have tripped over my shoe, but I felt something whack my shin when I crashed. I have this bruise." I held out both hands, offering my story.

DCI Bray smiled at me. His eyes crinkled behind the thick, black-framed glasses.

Since he was the first friendly face I'd seen in hours, I asked about the photo. "Was that picture I saw," I swallowed. "Was it from Sir Henry?"

The Detective Chief Inspector clapped once. His big hands made a resounding pop, and I jumped in my chair.

"Astute," he observed. "Very astute."

He stood, turning to Parikh. "What do you say we get Ms. McGuire here back home, shall we? Who's free? Bailey? He's proved handy." Striding out of the room, he left Parikh in his wake to deal with me.

I pulled the blanket around my shoulders. I didn't want to get my hopes up, but it sounded like they were releasing me. Plus, giving me a ride home.

Picking up my shoes, I pulled out the rumpled socks. Muddy and cold.

The socks went into the trash. Reluctantly, I removed my feet from the soft comfort of the slippers and wriggled my toes into the runners. The leather was too stiff to allow my feet the rest of the way in, so I flattened the heel into a makeshift mule. They were hard and uncomfortable but a step closer to getting me home.

"Step. Shoes." I laughed at my silly joke.

I hoped the officer assigned to drive me home would let me keep the blanket for the night. I considered it an old, warm friend at this point.

The door swung open, and there stood Edward. Edward Bailey. DCI Bray assigned Bailey to drive me home.

Despite my heart doing a little dance when I saw him, one glance let me know that this was not an errand he had volunteered for. His face was immobile, stuck in a scowl, his body tense.

He nodded once, pivoted, and marched away.

I shuffled along awkwardly, losing my left shoe twice.

"Is it still raining?" I asked, hoping a conversation would open a chance for me to apologize.

Nothing. Not even a head shake acknowledged my question.

If at first you don't succeed, continue to babble. "Because I don't have my umbrella. I left it in…" Bad idea. Leaving anything in Simon's car was not something I wanted to admit.

As it turned out, the weather didn't matter too much as Edward's police car was stationed in a parking garage.

Stepping to his side rather than following along like a stray cat, I glided to the shotgun seat. I rested my hand on the door handle. He couldn't ignore me if I sat right next to him.

Only, we were in England, and it wasn't the passenger seat. It was the drivers. He opened the door directly behind and stood aside, looking stoically across the hood.

I slunk around him, plopping in the back seat. I slid to the middle, so he'd have to make eye contact in the rearview mirror, but as I felt around and I found there wasn't a seat belt for the center, so I scooted all the way to the left. From there, I could at least see his profile.

His breathing sounded pinched, like he was forcing too much air out of his nose. He would have been more courteous to a bag of flour.

"I wasn't on a date with Simon, you know."

No reaction. What if that hadn't been Edward in the bar, and I admitted to being out with another boy? I was desperate for him to understand.

"I'd forgotten to eat, and it was raining, so he, Simon, offered me a ride home. He set me up. He wanted me away from the museum so that he could have me arrested."

Edward's steady gaze remained trained on the road. He carefully signaled for a right turn.

"That whole episode was his idea. The arresting thing. Believe me, I didn't know that my father donated money to the Baths or Sir Henry."

I did know that I didn't meet the minimum qualifications for the internship, but that didn't seem like a big deal at the moment. And now I knew why I'd gotten the post without being a senior. My dad had made a donation. He paid to get me accepted because he didn't think I was good enough to do this on my own. Maybe I couldn't, but now I'd never know.

"It was my dad," I insisted. "I would have stopped him if he'd asked." I waited for a beat. "He probably thought he was helping."

Edward lifted his hand in greeting to a pedestrian in a crosswalk.

"Oh, come on, Edward!" Apologies can only last so long. "You try going to a foreign country and discovering a body and see how well you do!"

Of course, as a cop, he'd probably do fine, but that was beside the point.

He pulled in front of the garden gate at Ash Tree Cottage and stopped the car. Opening my door, he avoided any indication that he had heard anything I'd said.

Until I got out. Edward slammed the door so hard the car rocked. Stiff legged, he marched to the gate and opened it. He stared above my head.

"Goodnight," I offered, lifting onto my toes. "I miss you."

Still nothing.

I sighed and turned to the path to the house. The soft click of the gate latch made me turn back, but I was alone.

Making a detour, I went to Roddy's hutch and peeked in. The bunny slept, his little pink nose tucked in his paws. I wanted to stroke his fur for comfort, but his cuteness was too cozy to disturb. Alone, I shuffled through the garden, ignoring its fairytale beauty.

After peeling off my wet, dirt-packed clothes, I took a hot, steamy bath. It fueled my steamy mood.

I mean, what was wrong with Edward? He did not show one bit of kindness to me, even when I apologized.

Then it hit me. I'd never said I was sorry. I blamed my dad and Simon and fed him excuses for my behavior. Like every guilty person everywhere.

Chapter Twenty-Four: The Apology

I awoke with an urgent need to hear a friendly voice. I called my mom. Her cell went straight to voicemail because it was still the middle of the night in Arizona. I disconnected without leaving a message. A voicemail was no way to tell her that I had failed. Or that I hadn't won the internship on my own merit. That I would never make it as an archeologist.

I shook myself.

There was a chance that Tori would still be awake. I logged in and connected, ready to hear her advice on my whole weird, awful day.

"Hey, you!" Her voice sounded too enthusiastic, and she hadn't activated the video window.

"Hey to you, too. You won't believe the day I had yesterday."

Muffled voices in the background came through, like the last time we talked. "It's Maddie. Okay?" Like she was asking permission.

Scott was with her again.

After a few more seconds of rustling, Tori returned. "Hey. Sorry about that. He's been trying to protect me from my frenemies. He's getting a little carried away, though."

As much as I wanted to talk about me, her voice held a sadness that had to be addressed. "Is it okay? Are you lonely?"

The pause before she answered was too long. "Yeah. Scott's been great. He's here, like, all the time now, so I'm not lonely at all."

"But?"

"But nothing!" She practically shouted at me.

I backpedaled. "Okay. That's great. I'm happy for you."

Another pause with more rustling. "It's just that," Tori whispered. "Sometimes I'd like a girls' night. You know?"

"Totally. Like right now. Last night I—"

From far away, Scott called Tori's name.

"Just a second!" She called back. To me, she said, "I have to go. But, hey, I thought of a solution for you and Edward. You should make a scavenger hunt for him that leads to an apology. You know, like your mom used to do for your birthday presents?"

"Tori!" Scott's voice was sharp.

"Gotta go! Love ya, girl!"

With a snap, she was gone.

I considered calling my dorm mate in Chicago. But she would drop everything to help me, and I knew she was dealing with family stuff. Lily's ready smile came to mind, and I wished for information about her.

Without anyone else to keep me company, I pulled on shoes and padded downstairs. Looking at the rain-soaked landscape, I pictured the Wellies I'd borrowed sitting in the Oversight office at the Baths. I'd forgotten all about them.

Buying a new pair to replace Mr. Priestly's seemed like a much better idea than returning to the Baths. At this point, I never wanted to see a Roman artifact again.

Rummaging through the bench in the mudroom, I searched in vain for women's Wellies I could borrow. No luck. Kids' sizes and a large pair of galoshes dominated the space.

The larger shoes were definitely men's, but I didn't want to fight to pull them on over my tennies, so I put them on with just socks. They flopped like clown shoes as I trudged through the sodden grass to Roddy's hutch.

"Good morning, Roderick. Would you like to spend the day inside with me?"

He hopped and let me scoop him into my arms. I hurried across the garden, oversized shoes slapping the stepping stones.

My toe caught the edge of the threshold of the front door, and I tripped, pitching forward. Dropping Roddy, I landed hard on my wrists. Crawling on my hands and knees, I went to him.

"Roddy, bunny, are you okay?"

I ran my hands over his limbs, checking to see if anything was broken. However, he seemed stronger than ever and kicked away from my arm with his powerful hind legs. My shirtsleeve tore, and a scratch welled up with blood.

"Ouch! Dammit, Roderick, I was trying to help!"

He hopped away to the kitchen.

"Fine," I told him. "Be that way."

I followed, ready to blame the shoes for the accident. Instead, I opened the door to the kitchen, allowing him to hop in.

The kettle sat on the counter, waiting to be plugged in for tea.

"Okay, so maybe I'm not the best at apologies," I admitted, stabbing the plug into the outlet. "I've had to endure a lot since I've gotten to this stupid country." Slamming a mug onto the counter with more force than necessary, I complained to the rabbit.

"The first of which was, I might add, found by you."

I glared around the kitchen, my eyes landing on the French press in the corner. I tossed packages out of the way, searching for coffee. Laying like buried treasure, hidden away in the pantry, vacuumed sealed, was a perfect bag of beans.

The second the scissors bit into the foil, the beans released a whiff of dark roasted delight.

I continued to rant at Roddy. "Hear me out." My voice's tempo increased. "If you hadn't nibbled that box open and found the ear, I wouldn't have met Edward, and I wouldn't—"

An image of Edward standing by the stove, cooking dinner, struck me so hard that I almost dropped the coffee.

He was intelligent and kind, and I'd ruined any chance at us being friends. A tear leaked out of my eye. I sank to the floor and cried.

All the stress from yesterday came out in five minutes of heart-wrenching sobs. "I don't know anyone else. And Edward's adorable and sweet, and I'm stuck talking to a rabbit because my only friend got hit by a bus, and I'm in a foreign country. And I spent half the night in jail."

At this, the rabbit in question hopped to me and crawled into my lap. "I'm sorry I dropped you."

My tears subsided as I stroked his long silky ears.

After a gentle hug, I set Roddy aside and stood. "I think I've had enough of a pity party, don't you? Yes. Quite right." My failed English accent did not impress the rabbit, but he was kind enough not to react.

As the coffee bathed in hot water, the scent filled the kitchen like a comforting quilt. Multigrain toast with butter and a fried egg completed my breakfast.

"Well, Roddy. Today is for you and me." I didn't want to admit to him that I lost my internship. My breathing hitched as my hands clenched into fists. No, I thought. No more pity.

"Maybe Tori's right," I said brightly. "I should make a treasure map apology for Edward."

For every birthday I remembered, my mom made a scavenger hunt for my presents. Her riddles would lead me to a landmark in our neighborhood where the next clue could be found. I hadn't visited enough places in England to make a city map, except maybe at the Baths, where I was never going again.

The carving of Lucifer at the Abbey popped into my head. The church had plenty of features that I could use. It was worth a try.

I opened the Abbey's website and scanned for artifacts I might be able to use as clues. There were gravestones. Creepy, but effective. The organ pipes were my favorite, so he would find me there.

My enthusiasm faded as the details of the plan presented themselves. Edward hadn't responded to my texts since the swing incident when he found that picture of Sir Henry's coded thank you note on my phone. Which I also hadn't apologized for. Texting him a riddle of my own might remind him of that indiscretion, even if it ended in "sorry."

Both hands went to my face, and I rubbed. "This is hard."

Digging out my phone, I texted, "Can we talk, please?" to Edward.

The phone sat silently.

A drop of blood smeared across the screen.

"What the heck?" The scratch Roddy gave me was still bleeding. Spots of blood decorated counter and floor.

My eyes lifted skyward.

After wrapping a kitchen towel around my arm, I scrubbed the area and returned to the Abbey website. Clicking from link to link, I wondered if I still had the brochure Ella had given me. I could mark it and leave it at Edward's desk.

Nope. Nix that. I was never going to the police station again, either.

Mail. I could mail the scavenger hunt. And that would take forever to get to him, a cowardly part of me whispered.

Setting aside thoughts of possible rejection, I roamed the house looking for a distraction. Blankets by the fire and a good book would do. Sometimes the heft of pages and scent of old paper were necessary.

My arm throbbed. A band-aid was in order, too.

In the second-floor bathroom, I searched for band-aids. I found a long piece of gauze and wrapped my arm. After rinsing the bloody kitchen towel with cold water, I hung it over the side of the bathtub.

Looking for a replacement cloth in the linen cabinet, I uncovered a cache of books. I pulled out the first couple. The Bible.

Not exactly light reading.

When I read the title of the second volume, I dropped it. *The Memoirs of Sherlock Holmes*.

I poked at the book with my toe. "Like I haven't had enough of those stories."

Pawing through the rest of the books, I found nothing but mysteries, including a collection of Agatha Christie shorts. I nodded my approval, and as I turned to go, I kicked the Holmes book.

"Oops." I picked it up and flipped through the table of contents. This volume contained both the severed ear story and the skip code adventure. Maybe the universe was telling me something.

Tucking both books in the crook of my arm, I went downstairs and deposited the Christie and the Doyle in the living room. In the kitchen, I refilled the French Press and whisked hot cocoa. Finding an extra-large cup, I combined the coffee and drinking chocolate into a rich, creamy, chocolatey elixir and carried the heavy mug to the table near the fire.

I settled under the pink afghan, read two Christie stories, realized my mug was empty, and concocted a second steamy mocha. Facing a different direction on the couch, I selected a Holmes tale at random. *The Adventure of the Musgrave Ritual.*

As I read, it became clear that the tale was perfect for the elaborate apology I was creating for Edward. The ritual in question wasn't a ritual at all but a set of directions to a treasure.

Inspired to plot out more of my Abbey scavenger hunt, I pictured the Abbey as I padded upstairs to my tower room. Plopping onto my bed, I started my laptop, opened the Abbey website again, and asked my brain to be smart.

I could start the hunt at the Green Man. Tori would be proud.

Not bad. I had an opening and closing spot at the organ pipes. An actual hunt would require at least two more clues.

My eyes drifted closed, laptop balanced on my stomach.

I awoke stiff and felt hungover. How I managed to sleep with that much caffeine in my system was a mystery.

As I stretched, the scratch on my arm pulled open.

"Arg," I groaned.

I carefully picked my way back to the kitchen, unsteady on my feet.

After tossing the carafe of soured coffee, I made more hot cocoa. Laying out cheese, crackers, and a veggie board for lunch, I cut a few carrots for Roddy. As I munched, I visualized Edward's reaction to my treasure map.

He might decide that I was bright and charming. Or, I was meddling in the investigation by making a coded message like the evidence he found on my phone. Or, he could wonder why I didn't simply say, 'I'm sorry.'

As I twisted a strand of hair through my fingers, I thought about the best approach. When my finger started to turn blue because I wrapped the tress around it too tightly, I decided that tomorrow I'd go to the Abbey and count steps, like in the story.

Despite my unexpected afternoon nap and loads of coffee, I was exhausted by 9:00 p.m. After putting Roddy in his hutch, I took an extra hot shower and then crawled into bed.

The quiet nagging of my inner voice told me I shouldn't bother with the scavenger hunt and just apologize. But if Edward didn't forgive me, every aspect of my trip would officially be a failure. The more elaborate my apology, the better my chances.

Chapter Twenty-Five: A Mysterious Call

I ran through the overly bright airport, bumping into people in business suits and knocking into small children. The plane waited at the gate, doors still open. I'd made it!

Panting, I slapped my first-class ticket on the counter.

The desk attendant looked at it and shook her bleached curls. "No. I don't think so," she said with a heavy Bronx accent.

"What?" Confusion surfaced. "The plane is still here." I pointed to the window. "I made it in time."

She smacked her gum, then blew a bubble at me. Her eyes raked over me, scathing. The bubble popped. "We can't let you on the plane dressed like that." She pointed at me, and everyone at the gate guffawed.

My jeans were torn and filthy. Instead of a shirt, I wore a burlap sack with holes cut for my head and arms.

As my hands came into view, my eyes popped open.

I sat upright in bed, heart still thundering. "What the hell?"

It took a few seconds to orient myself. "I'm still in England." Talking grounded me in reality, chasing away the hold of the nightmare.

What I wanted was to call my mom. She'd do anything if she knew I was in trouble. Like, bring down the whole British government kind of anything.

She'd take me to her condo, install me in the guest bedroom, and call in every academic favor she had to find me a new internship. She would cook me breakfast and make us caramel lattes in the morning. All of those things sounded so wonderful right now.

But I couldn't call her without confessing what a disaster my first trip alone had been. If I let her fix this mess, there would be nothing to keep my dad from insisting I take an internship in sales with his giant conglomerate.

Again, I considered calling my college roommates. They were great, but I didn't want to recount my failures, especially after they were so excited for me when I got the internship. Same with my old high school crowd.

Which left me with Tori. Maybe if I called now, Scott wouldn't be there.

Connecting my laptop, I dragged my fingers through my hair over and over. Sometimes it took forever for the computer to load.

"New updates are available for your operating system. Would you like to download them now?" my computer asked.

"No," I told it. "I want to call Tori."

Which I did.

After multiple rings, a male voice answered. "Tori's computer."

My heart sank. "Scott?"

"Obviously." He was so snarky. Always. No wonder Tori's friends wanted him gone.

"Where's Tori?" As in, have you caged her away so that no one else can ever talk to her?

"Not here."

It was like dealing with an American Simon.

"Okay." I could be short, too. Except, I needed something from him. "Will you tell her I called? It's important that I talk to her."

"Yeah."

"Thanks," I offered, but he'd already cut me off.

I blew air out of my lips, making a horse sound. I did it again because it was fun. Scott would tell me I was childish. I stuck my tongue out at the computer.

Well, there was nothing for it but to get dressed and go to the Abbey to work on my scavenger hunt for Edward. Even if I was a failure at my internship, if I left England with at least one friend, it wouldn't be a total disaster.

"But..." I said aloud. The thought of running into someone from the museum stopped me dead. Then again, I had to do something after my day of reading yesterday.

The square formed by the Abbey on one side and the Roman Baths next to it offered no place to hide. If I went around the back of the church, I could avoid walking by the museum. Nodding, I confirmed the path in my head.

I pulled on my favorite pair of worn jeans, a class rock t-shirt and drew my hair in a high ponytail. I reached the front porch when my phone rang with a number I didn't recognize.

Hoping beyond hope that it was Edward, I answered immediately. "Hello? Yes? This is Maddie."

"Miss Madeline McGuirc?" a cultured woman's voice inquired.

Uh oh.

"Yes? This is she."

"This is Vivian Pacok. Why aren't you at work at the Baths?" she demanded.

"Um." Eloquent, that's me.

"No matter. My car is at your door. Use it."

The countess was gone without waiting to see if I agreed.

Because, duh, who wouldn't?

Running upstairs, I quick-changed into my khaki slacks and a blue shirt, the standard uniform for the Baths. Taking my hair down left it a frizzy mess. I braided it down one shoulder.

I raced outside, looking for a sleek town car with tinted windows. Something worthy of a countess. I instead found a red Citroen sedan idling at the curb.

Peering into the front windshield, the scenario from *Taken* ran through my mind again. Was I actually going to climb into a strange car just because a faceless voice on the phone told me to?

A window opened, and a little old man poked his head out. "Miss Madeline?" His accent was thick and disarming.

This was apparently enough to get me into a car with a stranger. Add a bit of a British accent, and I'm putty in a kidnapper's hands. It was a good thing to know about myself.

Sliding across the back seat, it occurred to me to confirm his employer. "You're from the countess?"

"Yes, miss. Rivers."

I assumed that was his name, but he didn't give me a chance to clarify.

"She instructed me to deliver you to the Baths as quickly as possible." He accelerated through the quiet narrow streets at an alarming speed.

I struggled with my seatbelt.

His voice continued in a calm, conversational tone. "They are quite behind with the dig, and the tours need tending."

"Why isn't Simon—?" My inquiry was cut short as we turned a corner, and the G-Force took ahold of my body, smashing me against the door. I clicked the buckle before being thrown the other direction.

My questions would have to wait until we reached a stop sign.

We slammed to a halt. "Coordinating—?" I was thrown to the back of the seat when he jolted forward. Okay. He won. No talking.

Rivers flew to the front entrance of the Baths, stopped on a dime, and reached back to unlock and open my door for me.

I jumped out. "Um, thanks."

"Of course, miss. My pleasure."

He sped away, using the momentum to pull my door shut.

Head whirling with questions and motion sickness, I approached the museum with caution. Somehow there seemed to be more steps to the door than I remembered. They stretched before me, each one harder to take than the last.

I hadn't been inside more than ten seconds before I heard her. "Ah," the countess's imperious voice sounded. "There you are." She said it like I'd been dawdling by the riverside, drinking lemonade instead of attending to my duties.

Earlier that morning, I thought I didn't have duties.

The countess was dressed in a pink tweed suit with an ankle-length skirt.

"This way." She glided to the Oversight office with me trailing behind.

Bits and pieces of questions popped around my brain, yet I couldn't say anything. I opted for staring straight ahead.

"Here is the tour schedule for the day." She handed me a piece of paper. "Before you get started, go and check on the volunteers at the dig site."

"Yes, ma'am."

Speed-walking to the elevator, I took out my phone, put it in airplane mode to save the battery, and stuffed it in my bag. Pulling it immediately out, I turned data back on and texted Edward. "I'm going into the Undercroft. Out of range for a bit," before returning it to the airplane setting.

I descended. I was all the way to the bottom floor and out of the elevator before my first question adequately formed. What, exactly, was I checking on?

Bewildered, I went to the site. The damp scent of mildew had worsened. Skirting the signs cordoning off the restricted area, I touched a putlog by the sealed room I'd first seen when Simon showed me the tessare at the dig site.

The stone sealing the chamber wasn't seated squarely. Simon had insisted that no one used the block-and-tackle system that sat by the door to move the stone, but it appeared that someone had been working in there. The moldy stench seeped out, causing my nose to wrinkle. Still, I would give anything to work in this area.

Further along the hallway, Dr. Daniels and three volunteers brushed at the mosaic beyond the passage entry.

"Hi," I offered.

Dr. Daniels grunted, but one of the volunteers remembered me from when I had been sifting what felt like a lifetime ago. She stood. "Hello. Do you think you'll have a free moment to fetch us tea today?"

Glancing over the tour schedule the countess had given me, I nodded. "I'll have a long enough break between 1:00 and 2:30. What would you like?"

I took the order, using my phone to make notes. "Okay."

They had all gone back to their brushes, unaware that I lingered. For someone who had sworn off the Roman Baths only yesterday, I sure wanted to be back on the team.

At least I was in the building. I silently made it a goal to get the archeologist to know my name. If my luck held, I could survive a whole day without Simon sabotaging me. My parents would never need to know that I was almost sent home in disgrace.

By the time I got upstairs, a group of tourists had gathered around the Grand Bath, awaiting a guide.

"Welcome to the Roman Baths," I announced.

As I led the tour, I returned my phone to normal. "Back up," I texted Edward. Technically, he had asked me to send these notifications. I was simply obliging.

And for consistency, I texted him again when I went back to the dig site to deliver tea to the team.

My phone charge held steady at seventy percent. Tomorrow I'd tell Edward he was wise in the ways of batteries. That is if I managed to make things right between us. I hadn't heard a word since he closed the gate at Ash Tree cottage.

* * *

After the last tour of the day, my feet ached, and my voice had gone hoarse. It felt wonderful. So much so that I would have loved to find Simon that exact moment because he had some explaining to do. I mean, honestly, how could he think I had anything to do with Sir Henry?

I marched to the Oversight office and barged in. The room was empty but comfortingly well-lit. A note perched on the edge of the desk, my name below the fold.

In impeccable cursive, it read, "The keys are in the top drawer. Please lock the museum and be here early tomorrow to reopen. – Lady Vivian."

Lifting the simple ring holding two disappointingly ordinary-looking keys, I stared in disbelief. Leaving the keys to a national museum in the hands of the new intern? What was she thinking?

The first of the two keys didn't fit in the lock of the Oversight office, but the second one turned with a satisfying click. Right. The first must go to the front doors.

Emergency light glowed red at the entrance. It cast such little light I had to put my hand on the cold stones to guide me. When I got to the lock, I shined my phone light. No way either key in my hand fitted into that.

I turned the flashlight off and waited for my eyes to adjust.

"Lost, miss?" A voice sounded in the gloom.

"Ahhhh!" I flat out screamed.

A penlight shined in my face, and I pawed the air at it, hyperventilating. The light moved to the floor in front of a man in a guard's uniform. He started walking. "The employee exit is this way," he said, ignoring my embarrassment.

I followed meekly. Of course, the countess and Simon hadn't left the keys to the museum with me. Although, I have to admit that now that I knew they hadn't, a bit of disappointment crept in. Thinking I had the keys to a national treasure boosted my frame of mind a lot.

"I always leave when the museum is still open," I explained to my mysterious guide. After a moment of silence, I added, "Sam never showed me the employee entrance."

"Heh," he grunted. "I sit there when I'm not on my rounds." He took his hat off and rubbed his bald head. In the half-light, a glimmer of a smile appeared on his face. "I miss the old girl."

Old girl? How is that even a thing?

"Two more weeks," he muttered cryptically.

"Till what?" I asked, curious.

Was Sam coming back? Simon said she'd been fired. I think. Maybe he implied it, and I misinterpreted his words. Or he said it in a way to confuse me. Who knows what a guy who's willing to have a girl arrested for nothing will do?

"Here we are," the guard announced and held the door open to the night.

This time, curiosity did not win out. Staying even later in the creepy museum at night wasn't worth finding out what it was two weeks till.

Chapter Twenty-Six: Sticking Plaster

Pain pulsated in my arm, sending alarms to my sleeping brain. I opened one eye.

The filtered sun poked through fluffy clouds. The other eye came open, and I rolled off my side, struggling to remember what had awoken me.

"Hmm," I sighed happily. A little sunshine brightened my mood. Arizona averages 360 days of sunshine a year. The clouds and rain I'd been experiencing was a pleasant change, but I needed the sun to feel normal.

With a jaw-cracking yawn, I reached for the sky in a full-body stretch.

"Ouch!" My arm throbbed.

Checking the gauze, I discovered an explosion of fresh blood.

"Jeez, Roddy," I complained through the wall in the direction of his hutch. "You did a number on me."

There was nothing for it but to find band-aids.

After picking my way down my stairs, I conducted a more thorough check of the bathroom medicine cabinet. I unearthed something called 'sticking plaster," which I'd discounted at first because of the name. I didn't need a plaster on anything, but the picture showed the right thing. After opening the package, I discovered what I had been looking for.

The gauze came off quickly enough, but I hadn't disinfected the scratch properly when I first wrapped it. After searching a bit more, I found a single tube of antibiotic cream. I checked the expiration date. Three years prior.

"Nope." I replaced the cream on the shelf. Soap and water would have to do.

Cleaned, I thought my wound would pass my mom's inspection, but her voice niggled at me anyway. "Bacteria lurk, fester, and ulcerate." Because Heather McGuire never said anything simply when complex would do.

The bottle of thieve's oil spray was still buried in my purse. The essential oils were supposed to have antibiotic properties. Retrieving the oil, I gave the scratch a couple of squirts. It stung, which I took to mean it worked.

While the area dried, I returned to the bandages. Every arrangement of sticking plaster on my arm required at least five band-aids to cover the wound. I looked ridiculous. The gauze was overkill but more effective, so I removed the band-aids and rewrapped the injury in a fresh piece of fabric.

After making tea, I headed to my room to call Tori. She still didn't know that I had been arrested. Or that Edward had seen me with Simon at dinner, or that I'd almost lost my job, or that I'd gotten my job back, or the discovery of a new passageway.

Stupid Scott. When I opened my laptop, there was an email from Tori waiting for me. "Scott's spending the full day with me. I'll call when I get a chance."

Fine. We'd known each other long enough that we could handle being temporarily rejected for the sake of a guy. I only wished her guy wasn't Scott. Tori deserved the best.

As I scanned my inbox, another email from Tori popped up.

"Dear Madeline," the email began, and my heart sank. Tori never called me by my full name. Only Scott did.

"Scott and I have been talking, and we think that it would be better for you if we didn't talk so often while you're in England. It would be in your best interest to branch out and make new friends while you're abroad. Tori"

"Tori? Tori!?! Tori didn't write this email, you meddling jackass!" I yelled at the computer. "And pardon me if my first and only friend here was hit by a bus!

"Screw that." I closed the email and opened our phone app.

"Hi, Maddie," Tori's voice, only flat. "I sent you an email you should probably read."

"Yeah, that. Look, Tori, turn on your camera."

A couple of clicks, and her face came into view. I almost cried in relief at the sight of her. A knot formed in my throat.

"Nice hair," she teased, sounding like herself again.

Okay. This would be okay. "I—"

"Maddie, listen. I miss you tons, but you'd probably make more friends if you didn't rely on me so much. I want you to be happy there."

She sounded so sincere that I think she believed her rejection would help me. But that wasn't the point right now. She had been brainwashed.

I arranged my face to neutral. "I'll work on that. Look, Tori, when was the last time you went out with friends?"

"Scott's my best friend. You know that."

"Okay, first off, ouch. Second—"

She rolled her eyes. "You know what I mean. And stop looking like the world is coming to an end."

So much for my poker face.

"I'm serious. Who have you talked to other than me this week?"

Her eyes dropped. "My other friends are so mean about Scott. Hanging out with them is too annoying to deal with."

"Tori, you know I've never said anything against Scott, right?"

She nodded, looking sad. The screen froze for a second, glitching.

"Tori?"

The screen went blank.

"Tori?"

"Still here," her voice came through thick with tears.

She was crying.

"He's getting out of hand," I added gently.

"No! Not you, too!"

"Honestly, he is. I've always got your back, but this whole thing is a form of abuse. He's isolating you so he can control you. You need to break it off now."

"I'm not about to take advice from someone who hasn't had a relationship that lasted more than three months. How dare you try to understand what we have!"

191

The connection went dead.

I burst into tears. Anger at Scott, fear for Tori, and sadness for myself came out as gasping breaths.

"Fine!" I smacked my laptop shut and stood. "Be an idiot! See if I care!" Swiping at my own tears, I stomped to the stairs, shouting.

"Why does she like him? And why are boys so stupid?" I slammed the bathroom door so violently my toothbrush fell off the sink. "So stupid," I whispered, tears still leaking across my cheeks.

I turned the water on and splashed my face, hoping the coolness would make me look less like a pinched tomato. After a couple of slurps out of the faucet to soothe my throat, I felt stable.

Without bothering with shoes or even a bathrobe, I ran to Roddy's hutch in the garden. He was already awake, and as soon as I opened the door, he hopped from flower to flower in the sunshine.

"Hey, Sir Roderick. You want to come in for a bit?"

His nose twitched at me, but he went back to nibbling.

"Yeah." The scene couldn't have been more bucolic, but my mood didn't lighten. "I don't blame you."

You've hit a new low when not even your rabbit wants to hang out with you, I thought as I dragged myself inside.

As I finished getting ready, I remembered that I had the keys to the office and needed to get to work early. If I was fortunate and everything went according to plan, I might see Edward tonight. Despite my rush to dress, I picked my one and only sexy bra to wear under my plain work clothes. Its black lace covered solid bright red silk, and it gave me a burst of confidence every time I wore it. I threw on everything else without a second glance.

I ran down the stairs stuffing things into my purse and hoping I didn't forget anything. Detouring to the kitchen, I grabbed a dusty power bar from in the larder. I stuffed it into my bag along with a half-liter of bottled water. I wouldn't be lured into dinner or closets again without preparation.

Hurrying along the road from Ash Tree Cottage, I almost walked right in front of one of those light blue sedans that seemed to have it out for me. As I stared after it, another one, although red, rocketed into view.

This one I recognized. The countess's driver, Rivers, was flying toward my house.

"Nope," I said as the car nearly rounded a corner on two wheels. "Not today. I've had enough excitement."

The long path that switch-backed through the park allowed me to avoid the sedan's carnage. Speed Racer would have to take the far way around to catch me. Even if he hadn't been sent to retrieve me, I was safer on a different road.

I hurried along to the town center as fast as my feet would carry me. Rivers screeched to a halt in front of the Museum as I entered the plaza. I waved to him cheerily.

The Citroen window opened, and a hand popped out to return the greeting. Rivers reversed and zoomed out of sight.

Tilting my head to the side in disbelief, I watched him go. "Dodged that bullet."

The warm, damp air of the museum greeted me as I opened the door. Making my way to the Oversight office, I braced myself for a Simon encounter. I couldn't imagine his reaction to me being trusted with keys.

My head snaked around the wall, eyes scanning. The coast was clear.

The key unlocked the office door with no problem. At every turn, I expected something to happen. Simon waiting, the police coming for me, a deportation notice, an archeologist yelling in distress. Fortunately, the morning carried on without incident.

I needed to relax.

Since I had time before my first tour, I went to check on the dig site. I copied my Undercroft message from yesterday and texted it to Edward before putting my phone in airplane mode.

After finding Dr. Daniels, I greeted him and asked if he'd like the same tea order as the previous day.

A blank expression greeted me. "I'm sorry. Who are you?"

After a brief moment of disappointment at being that forgettable, I rallied. "Madeline McGuire." I stuck out my hand. "I'm interning in archaeology from America, and I'm honored to be working with you."

His hand shook mine absently as he turned his attention back to the mosaic. "Of course," he said, apparently forgetting what I had asked him.

"Tea?" I prompted. "And a ploughman's with Stilton?"

"No, thank you. I expect I'll have that for lunch."

I smiled brightly and vowed to make myself more memorable. In Dr. Daniels' eyes, at least.

"I'll bring that at lunch."

He'd already hunched back over his work.

I couldn't blame him. I'd give anything to be working back on the dig itself. Grateful as I was for the countess bringing me in, tours seemed tepid after sifting dirt for hidden treasures.

Which brought me back to Simon. How long was he planning to avoid me? Because he wasn't here, he wasn't working in the office, and I needed answers. *Maybe, just maybe, he felt badly and was avoiding me out of guilt,* I contemplated.

Sighing, I shook my head, not believing it.

The office was occupied when I got back, but not by Simon. Countess Vivian perched regally behind the solid oak desk.

"Good morning." I stood tall, avoiding my tendency to shift my weight on one foot. "I've checked on the team, and my first tour is in thirty minutes."

"Excellent." She used a tone that didn't encourage chit-chat.

But Simon wasn't here, and she was.

"Your Ladyship?"

Her imperious glare almost dissuaded me. I needed to get an intimidating stare like that. I plowed ahead.

"Do you think I'll be able to rejoin the dig team at some point?" I bit off the urge to add, *"please."*

Her velvety eyes blinked once, like a cat's. "Perhaps when Ms. Niven returns from her research trip."

"Sam's coming back?" I blurted out like an excited parakeet. "I thought she, um...." I trailed off, not wanting to admit that I thought she'd been fired.

The countess nodded. Once.

Very economical in her reactions, the countess. A lot like Edward.

I knew I shouldn't pester her, but my curiosity got the better of me. I continued questioning. "What about Simon? Won't he be, um, annoyed?"

The countess put the pen she had been holding back on the desk and tilted her chin.

I was pretty sure she thought I was impertinent.

Nevertheless, she answered. "Simon works here specifically to learn from Ms. Niven. She is quite accomplished."

"But she—" I almost blurted out that I'd seen her application, and she wasn't as qualified as Simon, but I caught myself and stopped.

"But what?" The countess was having none of it, whatever she perceived "it" as being.

My eyes darted around the office while I thought of something to tell her. *The office.*

"Simon rearranged the office and redid her filing. Won't she be annoyed?"

Lady Vivian picked the pen up again, turning her attention to the checklist.

After a moment, she said, "Ms. Niven's fieldwork and research are unparalleled. However, she isn't always the tidiest of people, and Simon's administrative background is quite good. She will appreciate his efforts."

I nodded, happy to be done with the conversation.

As I backed out of the room, she asked, "Have you seen him today?"

I stopped. "Simon? Not yet."

"Send him to me if you do. He's been distinctly unreliable these past couple of days. Rather like that Cliff person, actually."

Halfway out the door, I stopped and tilted my head. "Cliff?"

The pen lowered again, and her deep blue eyes bored into my soul. "The intern."

"Oh, yeah. Yes, I mean." It was like having your grade school principal watch you take a test. I wanted so badly to match her propriety, but I couldn't manage to maintain it. "Yes. I started my internship early because he left to work at Stonehenge."

She sniffed in a disapproving type of way. "Everyone must do what they think best, even if they are wrong. I had expected more from him than to simply disappear." Her eyes drifted around the office. "And of my nephew. Do send him here when you see him."

"Yes, ma'am."

Which would be better? Not to see Simon at all or to find him and send him to his aunt? Something vindictive did a happy jig inside me, and I hoped I'd run into him first thing. I had a feeling that being summoned by the countess would be more horrific for Simon than jail had been for me.

As I went to conduct my tour, I kept alert for a sign of him.

Chapter Twenty-Seven: The Scavenger Hunt

W
ith a two-hour gap between tours, I fetched tea and biscuits for the dig team on my break. No sign of Simon in the Undercroft. I couldn't blame him for avoiding me because I kind of wanted to kill him. Well, in a not dead-in-a-Roman-bath sort of way, but in a how-dare-you-be-so-devious-and-mean way. Every hour that I didn't get to yell at him or send him to the countess for punishment increased my annoyance. He would pay for the way he treated me, one way or another.

But, if the guy didn't want to be found, there was only so much I could do. At lunch, I took myself to the Abbey to make my apology map for Edward.

I was so engrossed checking the kiosk for a brochure of the layout that I didn't hear Ella's approach. The thump of her cane on the stone floor caused me to turn around.

"Oh, hi, Ella. You startled me."

"Hello, Maddie," she said, resting her gloved hands on the cane. "Can I answer a question for you?" She indicated the brochure in my hand.

Even though she was a bit intense and rather old, I felt like Ella was the only person I could talk to in England. Tori was mad at me. Edward was mad at me. Simon was avoiding me, which I was a little grateful for, but I also missed him in an annoying sibling kind of way.

"Perhaps you can help me? I want to make a sort of treasure map for my friend."

Blinking rapidly, she leaned closer to me as if trying to read my soul. "In the Abbey?"

"Well, no. Yes. I mean." A momentary panic that I had offended the only person still talking to me tied my tongue in knots. "Have you ever read the Musgrave Ritual?" I asked, hoping she had.

Ella smiled angelically. "You mean the Conan Doyle story?"

"No, Sherlock—"

I cut myself off when her eyebrows shot all the way up her forehead to her curly white hair. Sherlock Holmes was written by Arthur Conan Doyle. I knew that. Everyone knew that. I'd had a rough week.

"Yeah. That one." *Lame.*

Ella's brows returned to their normal position above her eyes but drew together into a scowl. "How exactly are you using the Anglican rituals?"

It was a question, but the tone of her voice made the correct answer completely clear.

"I'm not! I don't even want to use a ritual. I want to count off steps to various landmarks that lead to the organ pipes." My voice ran words together in a galloping panic. "I hoped that you could help me with the landmarks."

Nodding, she gripped her cane and turned. I took it to mean I should follow her.

Ella's first stop was a memorial marker for the wife of a doctor. Above the phrase, "In Memory of Elizabeth Grieve, wife of James Grieve, MD, physician to Empress Elizabeth of Russia," was a bas-relief with four figures. One was of a woman, presumably Elizabeth. The second was of a man reading a book who was perhaps the doctor. The last two were a man holding off a skeleton. I wondered if the man was the doctor, and the other was the grim reaper.

The overall impression was disturbing but very identifiable, so the perfect landmark.

We moved on to the stained glass of St. George defeating the dragon. The dragon was more like a baby winged lizard than the fire-breathing giant I'd been expecting. St. George boasted a bright blue cape, and the Kelly green of the dragon made for a picturesque stopping point on my apology map.

Deacon Michael appeared out of a side door and beckoned Ella away. I set to counting out the steps for the scavenger hunt.

From the gift shop door, walk thirty-seven steps forward to arrive at the Green Man's pew.

Turn East and go ten paces to the St. George stained glass.

Turn around. Walk ten steps and turn left.

Take twenty-six steps and turn right, then go thirty-two steps. This was the physician's gravestone.

Turn right and go thirty paces near six angels in flight, and there are the organ pipes where I would be waiting.

Tonight.

Maybe.

The more I thought about it, the more I hoped the distance to the police station would be a factor. If I didn't deliver my map, I would be guaranteed no rejection for tonight.

I wrote the instructions and folded them into the Abbey brochure.

Opening maps on my phone, I searched for directions to the constabulary, hoping it would be far away. The app blinked, "One-minute walk."

That was not how I remembered my nightmare trip from the other night.

Staring suspiciously at the screen, I followed the route. One minute, spot on. I wondered if the Bridgewater facility had been in a different town than Bath.

At the entrance, I double-checked my phone to make sure I was in the right place.

One Stop Shop, the building advertised.

"Huh?" I stepped closer and read the sign. "Public services - all under one roof... Okay." Avon & Somerset Police were first on the list. I gave myself a pep-talk before going in. "You can do it," I whispered. An unpleasant image bounced around my mind of a stony-faced guard dragging me to a dungeon.

"Don't be a coward," I said to myself, much louder than I intended. An elderly man scowled in my direction, pulling his cap down and hunching protectively over a packet of greasy newspapers that smelled of fried fish.

I was making a scene in front of a police station. *Great.*

Now I had to go in, if only to avoid the fish and chips gentleman. I pushed through the front door.

The station was well-lit. No one pointed and yelled, "Get her!" I wrapped my jacket tighter around myself.

The lobby was filled with kiosks and round information desks. The first one I saw boasted walking and boat tours. This was definitely not the same station I'd been hauled into the other night. I hoped they'd know where to find Edward.

I approached a large man in the middle of a donut-shaped desk. "I'm looking for Constable Bailey?"

He pointed to my right. "Over there, miss."

In the corner was a white-walled window with a sign advertising "Somerset and Avon Police." Two female constables sorted photos around a map. There were two chairs in front of them, so I slid into one.

"Yes, miss?" the dark-haired woman asked.

"Could you give this to Edward Bailey, please?" I set the brochure and my map on the counter.

"Of course, miss," she confirmed, not asking what it was.

The whole transaction was a lot easier than I pictured, and I wasn't sure what to do next. "Um, thank you," I mumbled. Even though I wanted to run when I turned to leave, I maintained a stately pace.

Once outside, the fresh air kept my panic from rising. My stomach flitted around, confirming how much I hoped Edward would come tonight. If he did, I would apologize the right way. I would swear not to pry into the investigation or break any more rules. Well, at least the rules involving police work. I learned that lesson the hard way.

I hoped I hadn't set myself up for more rejection, more pain.

Chapter Twenty-Eight: An Ice Cream Social

An afternoon of tours distracted me sufficiently from going down a rabbit hole of "what ifs." Each time my mind suggested that Edward might very well come just to tell me not to text him anymore, a tourist would ask if they could drink the green water in the Baths. Relieved at the distraction, I would direct them to the fountain by the gift shop.

Simon appeared only once in my peripheral vision. Unfortunately, he disappeared around a display as I backed my way into *Balneum* hall, pointing out features of the Immersion Pool. Tempted as I was to chase him, I restrained myself. Also, I wasn't 100 percent sure it was him, but the near-sighting served to stoke my desire for revenge. He would answer to his aunt, and I was convinced that would be hell for him.

The last tour of the day kept me so on my toes I almost forgot about the fact that Edward could reject me, again, soon.

The tour group included a large family of very young children, and also the intimidating deacon Michael from the Abbey joined us as well. I cringed under his steely gaze, but I couldn't tell if he recognized me from the infamous -in my mind- Green Man event. To be fair, his down-turned mouth always looked set in disapproval.

After a curt nod from the deacon at the tour's end, he smiled briefly.

My eyes widened with astonishment. Deacon Michael had liked the tour. It was everything I could do to keep myself from pumping a victory fist in the air.

Instead, I gave a slight bow and said, in what I hoped was a demure tone, "Thank you for coming, Father."

He mumbled something in reply that I couldn't hear and was therefore free to interpret as high praise.

I did one more check on Dr. Daniels and the dig site, scanning all the while for the elusive Simon.

I texted Edward going in and out of the cell-killing Undercroft, adding that I'd left him something at the station. My disappointment at not having a return message from him coiled in my throat like a rattlesnake, threatening to strike me if I moved unexpectedly.

"Come on, Edward," I pleaded in a quiet, quiet voice. "Talk to me."

I stuffed my phone away, composed my features, and set myself to encounter Countess Vivian. But the Oversight office sat empty. I left the museum a bit before closing and heading to the organ pipes to wait.

And wait.

I checked my phone, but there was no word from Edward.

My arm started to itch under the tightly wrapped bandage. I worked at the gauze underneath the cuff of my denim jacket and peeked at the scab. The scratch Roddy inflicted was healing infection-free. With nothing else to do, I folded back my sleeve with the intent of removing the gauze. I stopped when a man sat next to me and tented his hands in prayer.

Church, right. Behave yourself. I hung my head and surreptitiously put my shirt sleeve back in place.

Edward wasn't coming.

We hadn't known each other that long, but I liked him. A lot. He was kind and funny. And he had cooked me dinner. Plus, he liked my rabbit. I really wanted this scavenger hunt to work.

Pulling out my phone, I read my instructions for finding the organ pipe location. After tamping down yet another pang of sadness that Edward hadn't texted, I double-checked what I had written.

Left with little else to do, I decided to walk through the directions again, hoping we might run into each other. Scanning every dark, wavy-haired man in the Abbey, I followed the instructions counting out thirty-seven steps from the gift shop door to the Green Man.

"So far, so good," I allowed, reading, "Ten steps East." The clue here led to the stained-glass pane of St. George, foot on a red dragon. It didn't look exactly like I'd remembered it. Shrugging, I followed the other clues and didn't arrive anywhere near the organ pipes. I turned in a circle. The Abbey simply wasn't that big.

Instead of finishing the hunt by the organ, I was near the information center. I saw Ella setting up for the ice cream social.

"Hello," Ella greeted me. "You made it." Her cane lay on the table, and she struggled with a large, black, and silver bag.

My head wobbled in a non-committal way. "Kind of. I got lost reading my own map. Is there more than one stained glass of St. George?"

"No. But St. Michael also has a dragon."

That explained a lot. I'd found the wrong saint.

"Do you need help with that?" I offered.

She stepped back, letting me carry the load. The label read twenty pounds of rock salt. She must have an old-fashioned homemade ice cream maker. "Do you have someone to work the crank on the maker?" I asked.

Her little head bobbed. "The crank machine is for the children. We made the rest with electrical machines in the freezer."

I stowed the bag under the table, catching a flap that ripped into the sack. Salt trickled out of the tear.

The crystals weren't the walnut-sized ones from the ice cream block parties of my childhood. They looked like the salt that Roddy found on my second day in England. Like severed human ear packing salt.

I stared, reliving the horror of finding a body part on my doorstep.

"Why are you following it?"

"What?" I snapped to attention.

"The Musgrave Ritual?" Ella prompted loudly, stomping behind me, cane now in hand.

I forced myself to blink, allowing my gaze to break away from the salt. This bag was still sealed. This particular bag couldn't have been used to preserve a severed human ear.

I squeezed my eyes shut and shook away the memory before turning to face Ella. Her gloves were adorned with lace tonight, presumably extra fancy for the fundraiser.

"Yeah, the map I made. I don't know if I wrote the directions wrong or followed it incorrectly. Honestly, with my luck with maps, it could be both. He'll never find me."

"Who?" she asked.

"Who?" I repeated before remembering that she hadn't known the reason for the map. I wasn't positive she'd approve that it was to win over a boy. I made a feeble attempt to change the subject. "Um, hey. Who bought this salt?"

Her head tilted to the side. "Deacon Michael, of course. He has a stash here, actually. Why do you ask?"

My mind ran through calculations. I remembered we only used one bag at my neighborhood block party back home.

"Why does he have so much?"

Ella pulled her petite frame to her full height. My curiosity was bordering on intrusive. "The reverend has his reasons, and it is not our place to question them."

I backpedaled. I couldn't afford to lose another friend this week. "Um, yes." Not the best response, but I hoped I sounded pleasant. I plunged ahead. "Speaking of Deacon Michael, he came to the Baths today."

Ella's hand fluttered near her neck, the movement coquettish. "Did he really?"

Her eyes drifted toward an archway marked Private. I assumed the father's office lay that way.

"Yes," I nodded in rapid jerks and stopped when I realized I was trying too hard. "He seemed to like it."

Ella's brow furrowed. "You say he came to the Baths?"

"Yeah." Sometimes I forget to talk like a grownup. "Um, yes," I corrected, kinda. "He did." Nailed it.

She took my arm in her small, surprisingly strong hand and steered me out the entrance, across the square to the Baths. Partly holding on to me for balance, Ella hurried us along. Her cane kept a steady thump, thump by her side.

Ella's iron grip reminded me of Tori's abuela. The elderly have been gripping to life for so long that their fingers turned to steel. While marveling at this mystery, I forgot to ask what we were doing.

"Um." Eloquence defined. "Ella? What are we doing?"

"The museum hasn't quite closed yet." She sputtered. "I'll just need a bit of time."

"Time?"

As we approached, a guard secured the first of the two double doors. Ella changed our trajectory, and we aimed for the employee entrance.

"Time?" She sounded distracted. "What? Yes, of course. Deacon Michael lost his lapel pin and asked me to look for it."

Realization dawned on me. "Do you think it might have fallen off during the tour?"

We slipped in through the side door, which was propped open while the night guard locked the main entrance.

She blinked at me in the dim light. "Don't you?"

"I suppose. But the tour lasts for forty-five minutes. We don't have time to cover everything before the museum closes. And I don't want to get in trouble."

"Trouble? No. There's no trouble. Come along."

The countess wasn't even a match for the way Ella commanded the situation. I found myself tagging along after her like a lost puppy, happy to have a master. Ella needed me. She needed my knowledge of the Roman ruins and was relying on my position as an intern. I would be there for her.

She made a beeline for the elevator to the Undercroft, and my pace faltered. "No, wait. My tours don't go to the public explore zones."

"Of course not," she agreed, pushing the down button.

I narrowed my eyes quizzically at her. "But?"

Patting my arm, her gloved hand made a soft thwacking sound. "This morning, I told him about an off-piste hallway, and he may have gone there.

We can duck in and have a quick peek round." She squeezed my arm, and the moment of affectionate human contact surged through me.

I hated to admit it, but maybe Scott was right. I needed to make more friends in this town.

Once out of the elevator, Ella unerringly pointed us toward the hallway stationed by the new dig site. It was roped off to the public, and a signsaid, "Notice No Entry."

"Ella." I stopped short. "We can't go in there. How do you even know about this place?" A memory of Ella scowling thunderously when I told her about my internship surfaced. "I thought you didn't even like the Baths because they disturbed the tranquility of the Abbey."

She took my hand and smiled at me. "Your little tour was so informative. I've come back to explore many times since. A nice young man even showed me how a delicate person like myself could move that large stone."

I spoke about the system of pulleys on one of my tours, but I couldn't remember if Ella had been in attendance. I nodded. "It's a block-and-tackle. People have used them for centuries. Millennia almost. The first one was mentioned by a historian in year ten. Most people have seen them on ships, but the pulley system is beneficial for anything heavy. In college, one of my professors had me use one to lift a football player. I think he picked me because I'm so thin."

As I'd been trying to impress her with my extensive knowledge, she took us not to the dig but to the sealed storage room that Simon refused to give me answers about.

"Was the, what did you call it, block-and-tackle anything like this one?" Ella asked.

"In many ways, yes," My hand reached to turn the double-sided block rigged with two pulleys on each side. A thick rope threaded between them.

"Remind me again how the contraption operates?" Ella asked, eyes dancing with curiosity.

If my dad could see me being the tour guide for this inquisitive woman, he would understand why I loved it so much. As long as I succeeded at this job, I could deal with everything else.

"That other young man didn't explain things nearly as well as you do," she continued.

Securing the fist-sized metal hook to the receiving eye in the stone, I showed her the contraption. "See these four pulleys?" I pointed to each one. "By separating the rope this way, you create a mechanical advantage." I tugged, and the rock shifted an inch.

The mildew stench that I'd detected earlier worsened.

"Ugh!" I complained.

Ella produced a white handkerchief with lace trim out of a delicate pocket and held it to her nose. "Perhaps the room needs to be aired out a bit."

My eyebrows rose in disbelief. Giant fans running for days to clear the stench would probably be more effective.

"What did you call it?" she prodded. "A mechanical advantage? What exactly does that entail?"

There was a formula associated with block-and-tackle. When I did calculations, I saw ropes and weights in my head, flowing together. "The more pulleys you have, each one carries a larger portion of the weight."

I wanted her to understand, but I didn't know how to explain it any better.

"Why don't you show me." She pointed to the stone and appealed to me with a set of watery, expectant eyes.

"I don't think I should," I offered, giving the rope a fond tug. "I need this internship."

Bustling about me, the little woman ignored my protests. "Surely, this wouldn't get you in trouble. Really, that young man who also does tours opened it for me once. I'm quite sure he would have shown Deacon Michael, as well. I need to find Michael's pin, and it may be in there. You will help me, won't you?" She tugged uselessly at the rope, apparently having spent all of her strength in getting me here.

"Wait. Simon opened this chamber for you? And for other tourists? And not—?"

I cut myself off before I made this about me. But come on. Simon always treated the Undercroft like his own private dig site, never letting me do anything more than sit in a stairwell to sift dirt. I asked explicitly about this chamber a couple of times, and he made it seem like no one ever used it or that it was sealed for a reason above my pay grade, as Edward would say.

But Simon goes and opens it for Ella. Who isn't even the biggest fan of the Baths, in the first place. I am. Did I get to see this room? No. Was there a good reason I haven't? No. There was a malicious reason. Simon.

I blamed Simon that I caught the task of opening the chamber for Ella.

I guess part of the sting was that I wasn't one of the lucky few he wanted to show. Despite everything, I'd hoped he had a begrudging respect for me. For my tenacity, if nothing else. Because, dammit all, he managed the place well, and I wanted to learn from him.

But no. Simon had to exclude me.

"Twit!" I shouted as I yanked on the rope. The stone swung open so quickly I gaped, open-mouthed.

My jaw snapped shut as the stench of the room nearly plowed me over. This smell was not mildew but something far worse. Slapping my hand across my mouth, I fought the vomit curdling in the back of my throat.

"Ew, Ella," I choked out. "I don't think the deacon would have stayed here long enough to drop anything."

The moldy smell of a crypt was masked only by the odor of something fetid.

Ella's head was in the opening as she leaned forward, craning her neck to look around.

"Wait, Ella," I said, putting a steadying hand on her arm. "There's something wrong in there. It may not be safe."

She lurched further in, ignoring me. "I think I see something." Her arm pulled away from my grasp as she reached into the space. "I'm nearly there."

There is only so much a person can watch a tiny, elderly woman do before stepping in. The fear of Ella tumbling in and hurting herself far outweighed my repulsion of the stink.

I put both my hands on her shoulders and pulled her back. "Here, please. Let me. You'll hurt yourself."

Tilting my body into the entrance, I couldn't see a thing in the darkness. The last time I poked around an exhibit I shouldn't have, I found a floating body.

Which got me thinking. What if Deacon Michael had been here not only today but also when Sir Henry died. That formidable man was the kind of priest I pictured taking his religious beliefs to the zealot level. He would purge the world of anyone who disagreed with his vision.

Sir Henry's message came back to me. *Supporters of the Baths didn't love God.* No one took my interpretation of the skip code seriously, so I forgot about it. But this was close, and I was onto something.

I needed to talk to Tori about this. If I called her directly instead of using the computer, maybe Scott wouldn't interfere. Deacon Michael might be a real breakthrough in the case. We never had a suspect with a real motive before.

Every piece fit. The father was familiar with the ruins, and he worked nearby. Was that means or opportunity? Maybe both. When I mentioned the Green Man, he didn't like it, so anything outside his belief system counted as evil. Plus, the ancient Romans pulled a sizable amount of funding and attention away from the Abbey.

A picture of Edward's patient but stern expression came to me. I was doing it again. Constructing pillars of logic that weren't stable, which he wouldn't find impressive.

Besides, Deacon Michael had been attentive during my tour. In his own way, he seemed to thank me at the end of it.

My flurry of argument faltered. Old Tori would have helped me figure this out. Brain-washed Tori would tell me I was grasping at straws that were none of my business. I probably would conclude that anyway, but figuring problems out with Old Tori would have been much more fun.

It was still worth a try.

Turning to suck in a breath of fresher air, my mind raced to find a way to explain to Ella that there was no way I was crawling into that stench.

Ella stood right behind me, still trying to peer into the chamber.

I started a little at her nearness, my feet shuffling closer to the opening. She pointed. "There. Don't you see it?"

I blew out a breath of air, pulled my shirt over my nose, and told her, "No.

I couldn't see anything in the dark."

A whisper of sound floated out of the opening.

I stiffened, my blood running cold. "Did you hear that?"

Ella stood still, stubbornly pointing into the hole.

Gazing into the stinking storage room one more time, I reached into my bag to pull out my phone, so I could use the flashlight, but couldn't feel it.

Eyes trained inside my purse, hands fumbling, I felt Ella move around me.

Pain shot into the bruise on my shin, and I pitched forward into the darkness, my bag flying ahead of me. My hands flailed toward my feet, trying to clear them of whatever I'd tripped on. Making contact with a stick, I grabbed hold, tumbling to the stones below.

My feet hit the floor hard, jarring my knees. "Umph." The landing must have been four feet from the threshold of the storage room's door.

Face-forward to the room, I forced my elbow over the base of the opening and focused on boosting myself out. Digging into my years of experience hoisting myself out of backyard pools, I placed the palm of each hand behind me on the ledge, bent my knees, and jumped up and back.

My butt briefly scraped the edge of the opening before slipping again.

"Dammit!" Dust and the sharp smell stung my eyes. I refused to take a deep breath for my next try. I was sure Ella couldn't lift me, but a steadying hand could help. "Can you—"

As I turned my head toward the light, I found Ella standing at the rope of the block-and-tackle. A simple tug got the stone moving. She guided the block with her dainty, gloved hand.

"Ella?" I asked rather stupidly.

Panic electrified my limbs, and I hooked my hands around the door frame, pulling myself partway out. I had even less strength moving in this direction. I couldn't get my torso across the threshold before the stone swung dangerously close to my head. I jumped back, yanking my fingers away.

A thin wedge of light played around the edges of the passage before the stone settled into place, plunging me into total blackness.

"Arrrg!!! Ella!" I screamed, pounding the solid rock with my fist. "Ow!"

The second hit hurt.

Frantically, my fingers scraped around the edges of the rock, searching for any break. I found a single divot on the right side and dug. The nail on my left middle finger caught on the lip and tore back.

Pain shot through my arm and into the center of my chest, pulsating. Pulling the wounded hand in, I cradled it. I squeezed the finger, hoping to keep the nail from falling off completely.

Not that it mattered.

No one would ever find me. I hadn't even texted Edward that I'd be in the Undercroft.

"Help!" I shouted, the sound sharp in the enclosed space. "Help. Please, help me."

Tears leaked from my eyes. I clamped them shut.

"Don't cry. It's feckless." Echoing my mom's words grounded me. Her vocabulary defined her. I didn't understand what she meant until I looked it up as a teenager.

Sniffling, I rubbed my eyes with the heels of my hands. The movement caused the loose fingernail to jab hot pokers into my nerves.

Pounding both hands against the stones, I screamed again. "Ella!"

The jarring pain in my finger was making my hand go numb. "What do I do?" I asked. The pity in my voice snapped something in me. "One step at a time," I ordered myself. I needed to wrap my nail. That was it. Nothing else.

The gauze around my arm from Roddy's scratch was overkill for a finger. The only other loose bit of cloth I had was on my shoes. With deliberate slowness, I reached my right hand to my shoe. Untying the laces, I worked each string through the grommets.

"What's the end of a shoelace called?" I asked myself. "That's important because if you don't distract yourself...." I didn't want to finish the thought. Couldn't.

I'd been so proud when I was a kid and learned what grommets were. Then my mom, of course, asked me about the hard-plastic bits at the end of the laces. I'd never been able to impress her with my vocabulary because hers was so immense. Now I never could. She wouldn't even know to start looking for me for another week or two.

My mom had been brave about me being overseas. She promised not to call every night and to only email once a week. I knew it was killing her. Still, she wanted me to transition into adulthood and hopefully come to the conclusion that I needed a more practical major. When I didn't respond to her weekly message, she'd bury the hurt she felt and say something pretentious like, "To thine own self be true. She'll call when she's ready."

No one would come for me.

After another week, she'd bite the bullet and call my dad to see if he had heard. He'd probably tell her she was silly.

And here I would rot.

When she couldn't take it anymore when her heart would literally burst—

"Not literally, Maddie. For goodness sake," her voice chided in my mind.

When her heart couldn't take my being away for one more second, she'd call the museum.

What would they tell her? That I'd quit without notice, like Cliff, the intern before me? That my police record made it impossible for me to continue at the museum? That the lie I recorded on my application got me kicked out of the country?

Simon would probably be the one to talk to her. He wouldn't soften the blow at all. He'd be a jerk about it, gloating in my failure.

And her heart would break.

A sob shattered my body, doubling me over. My mom would never find me, never know what happened. I rocked toe to heel, curled in on myself. Horrifying gasps came from my chest that I couldn't stop.

My mom's voice came to me. "What's the biggest word in your extensive brain?" She used to quiz me when I was a little kid to bring me back during a tantrum.

"Aglet!" I shouted, lifting my head. "The plastic bit at the end of a shoelace is called an aglet."

I took a breath, muttering, "Three point one four one five nine two six five." I continued the sequence to Pi, chanting it like a mantra.

Pulling the shoelace free of the shoe, I braced myself and wrapped the lace around the loose fingernail. Each layer brought a wave of sickening pain. I twisted the last layer around itself to hold it in place.

The finger throbbed but not as severely. Accomplishing something gave me an anchor. I could do more.

My mouth opened to take in air, but the rotten stench of spoiled meat gagged me. Coughing, I pulled my shirt over my nose and took a breath, concentrating.

What would Holmes do? Something brilliant that I couldn't think of. Besides, I'd left the mystery behind to live in a real-life Edgar Allen Poe nightmare.

Images from stories ran like a slideshow in my head. *Tell-Tale Heart, The Black Cat, Berenice*. Peopled buried alive, claw marks on walls and coffin lids. Trapped with no hope.

"No!" I screamed.

Scratching my way out wasn't going to work. I needed a tool.

My hand traveled along the wall, locating the crack that sealed me in. Leaning my back against it, so I knew my exit, I slid to the floor and searched for my purse.

My right hand explored every inch within two feet of me. When my left took over patting the ground, it tormented me with every movement, but I finally connected with a hard, smooth stick.

Pulling my newfound treasure to me, I examined it blindly. Cylindrical, three feet long, a thin metal piece with a rubberized tip at one end and solid metal at the other.

Ella's cane.

The silver top fit into the palm of her hand. My fingers lightly touched the intricate design and felt a raised circle.

Suddenly, I flashed to the police photograph of the bruise on Sir Henry's head. His injury matched the one on my shin, and we both had the impression of a circle. I held the murder weapon in my hands.

I dropped it like it stung.

Ella. How could I have been so wrong about her? I thought it was Deacon

Michael for a few minutes, but never her. Not this petite, elderly woman who made ice cream for children. With rock salt.

It didn't make sense. How could she have known to send an ear to me?

I thought back to our first meeting. Ella's friendliness made me chatty. I remembered mentioning my internship but not my address.

My head thudded against the wall as I recalled our conversation. "Ash Tree Cottage. I told her how much I liked the name," I recollected, feeling idiotic.

With nothing to see, I closed my eyes and reconstructed her motivations. "I'm this sweet lady who loves the church. I think I'll start killing people."

I shook my head. Even with first-hand proof, I couldn't believe it. No one else would, either. She could keep doing this kind of stuff for years without anyone the wiser.

The gross smell in the chamber reminded me that we'd never discovered where the ear had come from. Violent shaking racked me as I considered the possibilities. It smelled terrible in here. "Really, rather, quite bad, actually," I said, my voice shrill and unrecognizable. Fast, shallow breaths were making me light-headed.

To keep from losing it, I pinched my covered fingernail. "Garg!" I screamed, but my brain focused.

Blinking, I peered into the inky darkness. Squeezing my eyes shut and opening them again produced temporary white dots, but nothing real.

"There better not be an earless body in here." I thought saying it out loud would banish the specter, but instead, my stomach flip-flopped. "Please don't be," I begged.

A small whimper escaped me, and I remembered an image of my dad slipping a comforting arm around me after I watched a horror movie against his wishes. "None of it's real, Pumpkin," he'd said to me. "All that blood is raspberry jam."

I recalled the hope that bloomed in my chest at his words.

"I bet the actors all make toast and have breakfast after they finish filming!"

Goofball best described my dad. After my parents divorced, he managed to keep silliness in my life, even from a distance. He had this picture on his phone of my best friend and me when we were eight years old, our heads wrapped in turbans of underwear. I tried to delete it so many times, but he insisted he was keeping that photo for my wedding day.

Tears leaked across my cheeks. Poor dad. He'd never get to walk me down the aisle. Would he become serious and withdrawn when he learned I disappeared? Would he still make friends with everyone he met? Or would he not be able to stop himself from telling anyone who would listen that his only child was gone without a trace?

Pathetic weeping took over.

After I cried myself out, I rested my head on the wall and closed my eyes. At least, I think they were closed. It didn't look any different. I was enveloped in darkness either way.

Chapter Twenty-Nine: The Chamber

I must have dozed off because I woke myself with a snore.

How long had I been asleep? Ten minutes? Twelve hours? There was no way to tell, no clues. Was that part of Ella's plan? To drive me insane to atone for my sins?

"I gotta get out of here." My voice sounded hollow, and for a split second, I questioned whether it was mine. If going nuts was part of Ella's plan, I was on my way.

A plan. Plans were good. I should have one. Right about now.

"Okay," I told myself. "I'm not totally deprived. I can hear. Hearing is good." My voice sounded fuller, more like me.

"Take inventory."

I felt in the pockets of my jean jacket, which revealed nothing but lint. "Probably not helpful," I said, putting it back. Patting over the rest of my clothes didn't expose much, but I took stock of everything anyway.

"A denim jacket. Denim is a strong fabric, so that could be a..." I paused. "A thing," I concluded before continuing my inventory. "A cotton polo shirt. Khaki slacks, a ridiculously attractive bra, my second shoestring, and the gauze around my arm.

"Now, my environment." Covering my nose with my hand, I took a breath, steadying myself. I felt around to find Ella's cane.

"One murder weapon," I added to my list. "Sturdy, with a metal cap. Maybe I could use it for tapping." I put my idea into practice and smacked the silver head against the stone wall.

Tap, tap, tap.

216

"Tapping, tap, tapping at my chamber door. Quoth the raven, nevermore," I quoted. Finally, a Poe story that didn't involve being buried alive.

Cane in hand, I gently thumped the floor, starting on my left side, where the rod had fallen. With any luck, my purse would have landed nearby.

"Because you're one lucky girl, you are."

Sarcasm wasn't always as charming as I thought it was.

Methodically, I extended my arm to its fullest and, starting at the wall, worked my way to my feet. Switching the cane to my right hand, I worked my way back to the wall. Gritty, stone floor lined my path.

I had to move away from the door if I was to find my purse. The exit with its enormous stone sealing me in. The door solidified my prison, but if I was ever going to get out, I'd need to go through it. It was my foothold. I couldn't lose it.

Paralyzed with indecision, I sat with my right hand reaching overhead to feel the bottom edge of the sealed opening.

Time stopped.

Darkness and silence surrounded me. The only sensation reminding me I was alive was the throbbing of my pulse in my torn fingernail.

"Do something." So soft, the sound barely registered in my ears.

Building my courage, I dug in my heels, bent my knees, and scooted forward a foot or so. The cane explored, working an inch at a time around my left side. I didn't find anything.

What if I ran out of oxygen? I was entombed. Would I die of starvation, thirst, or asphyxiation?

I gulped in another breath, and the stench hit me again.

Something was spoiling in here. And spoiling required air.

Shaking my head, I scooted forward, continuing to explore with the cane.

Tap, tap, tap, whack.

Whack?

I closed my eyes, needing to concentrate. Aiming the cane, I let it fall again.

Whack. I'd discovered something soft.

Swallowing hard, I extended the cane to the yielding surface, steadied it with both hands, and pulled. The object in question moved about a foot in my direction. I repeated the process, hoping the lump was my purse.

Visions of a giant rat shook my nerves, but I continued. If a rat could sustain itself in this prison, I could survive, too. But my bag would be preferable to a rodent. A lot better.

After the third try with the cane, I leaned forward until I was clasping onto genuine fake leather. Even though it was unzipped, the contents felt like they were in place.

"Thank you," I croaked to the powers that be. "Thank you, thank you, thank you."

I scooted back to what I thought was the wall but stopped mid-movement, disoriented.

The sealed door had to be behind me, but was it straight back or a little to the right? Or left?

Gathering my purse, I swept the cane around me.

Thunk.

I hit something large and solid but soft.

The vision of the rat came back, this time rotting. I poked the object in question.

It groaned.

The screech that emitted from me echoed through the chamber.

Total panic galloped back in full force. I stood too fast and dropped the cane.

Crouching to the floor, I felt around with both hands, searching for the staff.

Another groan penetrated my consciousness, which I answered in kind with another ear-splitting scream.

"Shhh," the groaning form urged, sounding miffed.

My mouth fell open, and the stench reasserted itself into my nose. Snapping my jaw shut, I spoke to the phantom. "Did you just shush me?"

"Water," it whispered.

"Um. I found my purse. Let me see."

Making sure my bag was upright, I slipped my hand in. I remembered grabbing a small water bottle from the pantry at Ash Tree Cottage.

"I have some," I offered, feeling like I'd conjured it by magic. "Just a second."

I unscrewed the top and took a small sip. Being from the desert, I knew you shouldn't ration water. It was better to drink your fill and keep your body functioning so that you could get rescued rather than taking a bit at a time. However, I figured whoever was in here needed liquid more than me. "Where's your mouth?"

Silence.

"Hello?"

Had I imagined it? Was my mind playing tricks on me because I couldn't deal with the isolation? This void was winning the battle waged against my sanity.

"Say something!" I gasped, listening. "Fine. I'm coming to you."

First, I screwed the lid of the water on tight and placed it in my bag. I carefully laid the cane on the floor, pointing in what I hoped was the direction of the stone door.

Finally, I reached my foot out as a feeler. When it brushed against an unidentifiable lump, I realized a shoe was a lousy detection device. Instead, I left my foot near the figure and followed along with the rest of me.

Huddled into a ball around my knees, I reached out to touch the phantom shusher. My hand hesitated over it. Each time I told myself to lower my arm, a force field popped up. At last, I decided a finger would do.

Index finger extended, I was met with clammy, sticky flesh.

It groaned.

I screamed. "Just, just, just." I paused, not knowing what I wanted. "Just hold on a sec. I'm not sure what to do here. Who are you? How did you get in here? Are you always coated in slime?"

Whomever it was mumbled something that sounded for all the world like, "Do be quiet, would you?"

I processed what these words meant. Only one person would say something so insufferable under these circumstances.

"*Simon?*"

My index finger poked at him again, which produced a groan. He apparently spent the last of his energy telling me off. Definitely Simon.

The grin that took hold of me couldn't be seen, but it was there. I had an ally in this mess.

"How long have you been in here?"

No response, but that wasn't surprising. I didn't know how long I had been trapped either. Thinking back, Simon hadn't been around to make my life miserable for two days. Had he been in here this whole time?

No matter, he needed help.

Without thinking, I reached my left hand into my purse for the water and bumped my nail. The pain went straight to my stomach, and I dry-wretched. Steadying myself, I turned to my coworker.

My other hand patted around Simon's head until I found his neck. Slipping my forearm underneath, I lifted his head and scooted under him so that he had my thigh as a pillow. If he had a back injury, I shouldn't have moved him, but I reasoned water was more important at this point.

"Slowly," I ordered, pulling out the bottle. Twisting open the lid, I patted around Simon's face until I felt his mouth and poured a dollop of water in.

His hand flew to the bottle, and I had to fight to keep it from spilling.

"Whoa," I chastised. "Easy there. You need to go slow. One more sip, then we're going to make sure you don't get sick. Okay?"

Simon didn't argue, so I carried out my plan. After he had finished, I shook the dangerously light bottle. There were probably only two sips left.

"I'm getting my phone next. But I'll stay right here. You're not alone."

The reassurance was more for me than him.

Feeling around the inside of the bag, I continued my inventory. Keys, the bottle of natural disinfectant spray, wallet with credit cards, and cash. Maybe I could use the credit card to dig around the door?

Who was I kidding? That entrance had been sealed shut for 2000 years. A little bit of plastic wasn't going to make it budge. I continued counting my mental list of tools.

Lip balm, ponytail holders, nail clippers, nail file, and a mirror all sat on top of my phone.

Trying to control the relief that the cell was still with me, I moved everything to one side and continued my hunt. The crinkle of plastic stopped me. With the utmost care, I felt the dimensions of the plastic-covered rectangle. I had found the emergency power bar. That name took on a whole new meaning today. Tonight. Whatever.

The purse was now my lifeline. Removing my cell, I zipped my bag, then tucked it into my lap. After a moment of thought, I undid my other shoestring. Lace in hand, I looped it through the handle of my bag and to a belt loop and tied it, ensuring I wouldn't lose the purse again.

"Okay. I think I'm getting the hang of this," I informed Simon.

He emitted a low wheeze.

"Simon? I'm going to unlock my cell. Close your eyes."

Brushing my hand over both sides to find the face of my phone, I angled it toward the dirt floor before hitting the Home button.

Even face down, light burst into the room, invading my eyes and exposing a nightmare. Slamming my eyes shut, I stuffed the cell inside my jacket pocket. Enough light escaped through the material for me to see.

Simon's blood-soaked face was miserable. "Simon," I whispered, my fingers dancing over his swollen eye.

The phone went to sleep. I desperately wanted to turn the light back on, but I couldn't risk the battery. Besides, I knew what I needed to do. Simon's head was bleeding.

Opening my purse, I searched for the disinfectant spray. Once in hand, I delicately probed the wound on Simon's forehead and gave it a couple of squirts.

He twitched and grunted in protest. His hand flailed at me, connecting with my arm and jostling the bottle.

"Stop that this instant." I gave him one more spray for good measure.

"Do you have any idea how bad you smell?" I complained.

What he grunted sounded like, "Not me." He'd probably never been covered in grime in his entire life.

Ignoring him, I scrolled through my mental inventory for something that would work to bind Simon's head wound.

My jacket would be too bulky, but my shirt was thin enough. Nodding, I gingerly tugged the arm of my coat, brushing against the bandage on my arm. The eye roll I gave myself was epic.

"Or, you could use the big piece of gauze that's sitting uselessly on your arm."

Unsurprisingly, self-deprecation awoke Simon's interest. "What?"

"I'm going to bandage your head. We need to stop the bleeding."

"Right," he agreed.

Unsnapping my jacket cuff, I unbuttoned the shirt sleeve. I tugged the gauze out, unwrapping it a bit at a time.

When the last section pulled free, I risked pressing the Home button on my phone again from inside my jacket pocket.

Simon's face had not improved. Cleaning off the excess gore would waste water, so I wiped at his cheek with my shirt.

I wrapped the bandage tightly around his head. There was enough for two circles and a secure tie-off before we were plunged into darkness again.

"That should help," I was aiming for encouraging, but I think it came out sort of demented. "I'm sorry I don't have anything for your eye."

"It was…" His pause stretched for so long I thought he'd fallen asleep. "An old woman," he finished.

Head bobbing, I said, "Me too. Her name is Ella."

"You know her?" Simon's outburst caused him to cough in a feeble gurgle. "Water?"

Without telling him how little liquid we had, I retrieved the bottle and opened it. I hit Home again and used the light to find his mouth.

"One sip," I warned.

"Cow," he grumbled.

"I'm here giving you my last sip of water, and you're calling me a cow. I should leave you here. What would you think about that? Huh?"

A hint of a smile crossed his face before the light went out. Half dead, and we were finally starting to be friends.

"Clearly, you're feeling better." Now for the real sacrifice. "Do you think you could handle food? How's your stomach?"

His nodding head rubbed against my leg.

"I'll take that as a yes. I have a power bar. I don't know how old it is or what flavor. I'm going to give you most of it because you've been here longer, but I'm keeping a bite for myself."

The movement changed directions. Simon was shaking his head no.

"No? Look, I need something," I started.

His hand lifted to pat my ankle. "No, Maddie. Take it all. Keep strength."

I couldn't tell if he was trying to be chivalrous. Perhaps he thought he was going to die no matter what.

The thing is, my first impulse had been to keep the whole thing for myself and not tell him I had food. Deep down, I thought I was a better person than that. It took a lot for me to offer the food. I felt terrible about my initial reaction.

"You've lost your pronouns, so I'm going to ignore your gibberish."

Now that the offer was out there for me to take it all, I didn't want it. "I don't want to be in here without you. So, we're going to split the power bar, and you're going to help me find a way out."

Simon gurgled.

Locating the bar by touch, I snapped it in half, opened the package, and pulled out a section.

Breaking that half apart into four pieces, I took one and poked Simon.

He groaned.

"Come on. Wake up enough to eat."

"You take the food." The pathetic resignation in his voice was heartbreaking, even for Simon.

"What happened to "stiff upper lip" and all that? What would Aunt Vivian say?"

At the name, he startled.

He pushed himself backward, which had the effect of raising his head onto my leg more.

"Okay. Ready?"

Slow nod.

I dropped a morsel into his mouth. He chewed.

"That is disgusting," he let me know.

I grinned, despite everything. It probably was. "You're welcome. Another?"

"Yes," he said and waited for a beat. "Please."

Handing him the next piece, I told him, "I'm going to look around the room now."

"Don't," he recommended, chewing. "Your battery will die."

As soon as he said it, I knew that I hadn't set Airplane mode. The battery was merrily draining away, looking for service. "Wait, I need to turn off the wifi and roaming."

Still in my jacket pocket, I turned on the cell. "Close your eyes." I pulled it out, and garish light filled the chamber, illuminating a large lump in the corner.

I squinted toward the object.

"Don't," Simon said again.

Ignoring him, I shone the light in the direction of the pile. Clothing resolved, then an arm. "Oh my god," I whispered as the final picture clicked into place.

The image of an earless face, covered in blood, eyes frozen in horror, stared back at me.

Chapter Thirty: Yet Another Discovery

I screamed. Again.

"Maddie—" Simon started.

I cut him off with another screech.

I never considered myself to be a screaming, squeamish girl, but you learn a lot about yourself when you're trapped in a dark dungeon with a decaying body.

Simon awkwardly patted my leg in an attempt to console me. "Maddie, chin up. He can't hurt you."

The absurdity of his statement stopped me. "Well, duh," I replied. "I didn't think he could." Boys can be dense sometimes.

"Then why on earth are you screaming?"

I sputtered, "Because of the dead body, that's why."

"You've seen one before," he pointed out.

I gaped. Was I supposed to get used to this? "That one," I gestured. "Is particularly grotesque. You handle this kind of thing way better than you should, by the way. A loud screech is entirely forgivable."

"One, perhaps. But you've been rather emphatic about it, actually."

I wasted an excellent glare at him, but Simon's distraction had worked. I didn't feel nearly as shaky as when I first saw it. Him. It. Jeez, this did not ever get easier.

"Who is it? Did you recognize it?"

Simon reached a hand to the top of my shoe and patted awkwardly.

"Cliff Whitely," Simon told me. "Your predecessor."

Buzzing roared in my ears, and I lifted both hands to cover my face.

I remembered to hold out my left middle finger to protect it from the movement, but the nail still ached.

"I thought," I said through my hands, "that he got a job at Stonehenge."

Simon continued his version of comfort, which happened to work on me. "Yes, well. Apparently, that was a ruse."

I blinked at him in the darkness. "A ruse? I've never heard a real person use that word in a real conversation. You sound like my mother."

His hand stopped. "With the greatest respect, I don't think that's important."

The way he emphasized "respect" gave me the feeling that he thought I was an idiot.

"Let me get this straight."

Simon sighed.

"No. I'm trying to figure this out."

"Your phone?" he reminded me.

"Oh, yeah." The cell was still in my hand. I faced it toward the ground, pressed on, and unlocked it. Slowly I uncovered the home screen, allowing my eyes to adjust to the assault of light. The signal blinked zero bars, which wasn't surprising. In Settings, I switched it to airplane mode. "The battery is at twenty-two percent."

The time was 6:00 p.m. I'd been entombed for almost twenty-four hours. "Quite good."

I realized, belatedly, that a lot of what Simon said meant the opposite.

"So," I ventured on. "I got to England, met an unassuming old woman at a local church, and she promptly sent me the ear of a guy she had dumped at a dig site. That sounds normal."

"Very interesting," he commented, not sounding the least bit interested. "But we have more pressing matters at hand. Have you eaten?"

"It smells awful in here," I grimaced. "And there's a dead person. Which smells. Especially bad. I'm not hungry."

"Miss McGuire."

All he said was my name. Like I was a misbehaving student or something.

Slowing reaching into the purse, I pulled out a bit of power bar and popped it into my mouth. I gagged. "Bleck."

"It's a bit disappointing," Simon admitted. "But effective. Swallow."

I did so, wondering how he had managed to take the role of the boss when I was the rescuer.

"Is there more water?" he asked.

He sounded so much more vital that I didn't want to disappoint him, but I couldn't pretend otherwise. Except... My survival tactic from when Simon had left me locked in a closet clicked into place.

I felt around for a small pebble on the floor and rubbed it on my jacket sleeve. Moving quickly, I retrieved the disinfectant spray and gave the rock a couple of squirts.

"We're out of the water. However, Native Americans who lived in the desert had a trick for thirst. You put this stone in your mouth, roll it around your tongue, and it'll create saliva and keep your mouth from getting dry."

Silence.

"Simon?"

"Were these the same people who lived in teepees while we built cathedrals?"

I punched his non-injured shoulder.

"Sorry," he mumbled.

"Come on," I insisted. "Try it."

His hand flopped onto my leg. I set the stone in the center of his palm. "I disinfected it."

He sniffed.

"Okay, so, what did Cliff do to turn Ella into a murderer?"

"Again," Simon said with his teeth clenched. "We have more pressing issues."

The sound of his jaw working carried. Despite his complaints, he was trying the rock trick.

Pressing issues like what? I thought to myself. My cell phone had zero signal, so it wasn't like we could call anyone for rescue.

But that kind of thinking was the dusty road to death, as my mom would say. There was a way in, so there had to be a way out. Recognizing, of course, that block-and-tackle doesn't work two directionally. Still.

An audible swallow came from Simon.

"Is it working?" I wanted to know.

"Actually, yes," he admitted.

Huh. "Of course it does."

I mused aloud. "I can't access the block-and-tackle system from this side."

Simon's head moved. "No?" He managed to sound like he doubted my conclusion.

"I love architecture," I informed him in a huff. "Just because I haven't finished my archaeology degree doesn't mean I'm useless."

He snorted, though he wasn't in any position to belittle me.

"I'm checking the door."

"The stone is immovable."

"Try to be more encouraging," I suggested.

He chose not to respond.

"Thank you," I said. I readied the phone. "Close your eyes."

Turning the phone on, I tore my gaze away from Cliff's body and to the door. The wall was blank, the stone fitting snugly into its opening. Something was wrong, but I couldn't figure out what.

I shut the phone off.

"We're going to move to the wall."

Simon moaned in protest.

"It'll be okay." Double-checking that my purse was still tied to my khakis, I secured the cell in my jacket pocket. Reaching back to feel the cane, I oriented myself.

"I'm going to reach under your arm and pull you up to sit. Can you help at all?"

"Right, then." The confidence in his ability rang in his voice. If I'd asked him to levitate, he would have if only to show me how British he was.

Repositioning Simon was more difficult than I had anticipated. Using only my right hand didn't give him enough leverage. I had to jam my left hand under his other arm and pull. The lace protecting my ravaged fingernail shifted, and my stomach turned in pain.

228

I inhaled deeply through my nose. Cliff's decomposing body invaded me. Bile rose in my throat, but I swallowed it.

Simon sat upright, supported by my torso.

"Good," I grunted. "Let's wait a bit before we move back. To give you a break."

"I'm fine," he assured me, although his breath had become short and raspy.

I rewrapped my finger without dry heaving. I could do this.

Gripping the cane, I gave Simon directions. "We're going to move back by bending our knees, then pushing. Can you do that?"

"Yes."

Nothing more.

"Ready? On three. One, bend your knees. Two. Three and go." The action was a little awkward, but we were on track. "Two more times, and we'll be golden."

Once we connected with the wall, I reached to find the threshold of the doorway. I wanted to cheer.

The problem was, we were still trapped.

Chapter Thirty-One: Putlogs

"Excellent." If I said it out loud enough times, I might believe it. The move had exhausted me.

A strangled sound escaped from Simon. The situation must have been worse for him.

"Here," I said, shifting. "Lie down." He was still propped against the wall. I thought it might be too strenuous for him, what with the bleeding and starving and darkness and all.

He slumped onto my shoulder.

"Simon?" My hand shot to him, feeling for his neck and a pulse. I missed my target and smacked him in the face.

"Bloody hell," he scoffed.

"Sorry!" I paused. "I'm glad you're not dead."

I couldn't remember why it was vital that we move to the wall. Resting my head on Simon's, I closed my eyes and became aware of my heartbeat. Slow but loud. Every pump jarred my body.

It felt very, very wrong. They'd find my body here in 1000 years and conclude that people of my generation died of heart attacks at age twenty.

I'd never felt like this before. Every beat panicked me a little more.

"Madeline," Simon whispered.

"What?" I startled.

"Food," he suggested.

He was back to single-word sentences. The few bites he had eaten earlier gave him a ton of energy.

"Right," I answered in one word.

Resting a hand on my bag, I allowed my head to recline against the wall.

With a jerk, I awoke, not knowing how long I was out. Seconds? Hours? My heart pounded.

Simon poked me.

What now? I thought, unable to spit the words out.

"Bar?" he asked.

Bar? What was that supposed to mean?

The lightheadedness that had set in kept me from thinking straight. I shrugged him off.

He shook me, dislodging my grip on my purse. I slapped his hand away.

Rations. Bar. Power bar.

"Oh," I croaked. "One second."

Hands shaking, I dug in and found the wrapper with the half a bar left. Lifting it the wrong way, the food tumbled out of the package. Frantic, I clawed through the bag but couldn't find the pieces.

As I opened the bag to dump it out, Simon caught my hand.

"Carefully," he reprimanded, handing me the half of the power bar I'd dropped.

My eyes strained, and I forced myself to shut them.

I broke the remaining half apart and handed a piece to Simon.

"You," he murmured, pushing my hand toward my face.

I took it. The stale protein disintegrated in my mouth. Without thinking, I popped another morsel in my mouth.

"Oh no," I muttered.

Resting my head against Simon's, I closed my lids, exhausted.

A persistent jab in my side startled me awake. My eyes flew open. Darkness, everywhere. For a moment, I didn't know where I was. Scrunching up my face, everything clicked into place. Trapped with Simon, who continued to poke me urgently.

"Sorry. I dozed off." What was left of the power bar was still clutched in my fist. Uncurling my fingers, I took a chunk for Simon. "Here."

I felt his head move back and forth in disagreement.

"Are you arguing with me?"

"You," he said in a pathetic whisper.

It dawned on me that he was trying to be chivalrous again. Well, screw that. I'd rather have company.

"Take this bite of food and swallow it. I am not sitting here with two dead bodies. Okay?"

After a drawn-out pause, his hand flopped across my leg. I dropped another piece into his palm. "Eat."

When the sound of swallowing finished, I extended the last of our food to him.

"No," he insisted. "You."

I hesitated. "I'll save it. Okay?"

His head shifted, which I took as a nod of agreement.

My stomach moaned, but my heart was no longer pounding out of my chest.

"Why did my heart freak out?"

The question had been rhetorical, but Simon answered anyway. "Sensory deprivation. Everything else is working harder since you don't have your eyes, so you need more energy."

It was true. A little food went a long way for both of us. My thoughts were clear enough to continue musing.

I returned my focus to the wall with the door. Something hadn't looked right. "I need to turn the light on again," I informed him.

"Why?"

"Because no one knows we're here, so we have to figure this out ourselves."

"Maddie," he said, sadness tinging his voice.

"Oh no, you don't," I warned. "We're getting out of here." My voice held the strength of conviction I didn't realize I had. I was starting to believe it. I just needed to figure out the puzzle. "Close your eyes."

Twisting around, I dislodged Simon to unlock my cell. The wall appeared blank, hiding its secret.

"Something's not right," I insisted. Shutting the phone off, I pictured the hallway and the block-and-tackle system, weighted so delicately that a tiny old lady could operate it. This nightmare would never make sense.

I'd been so happy to be in England, to communicate with the past. The feel of the venerable stone under my fingers had seemed like magic. The wooden putlogs that held the scaffolding were still intact despite the damp and the years. The Roman builders had thought of everything.

Putlogs. I'd touched the putlogs around the opening of this room when I walked by with Simon. Why weren't there any on this side?

I turned my phone on again, ignoring Simon's groan of protest. The putlogs had been mudded over to finish the inside walls. Maybe I could locate one.

Taking a breath, I realized I had gotten used to the stench permeating the room, but only when I was careful.

After covering my nose and inhaling through my shirt a few times, I lifted my hands above my head and found the threshold of the door four feet above me.

Touching the side of the doorframe, I moved out a few inches.

The texture was different. I stood on wobbly legs.

"What's happening?" Simon asked, but it barely registered.

Laying my palm on the antique stucco, I let my fingers explore. *There.* The slight depression of a rough circle. I located the center and went up hand over hand, about eighteen inches. Another one. The putlogs.

A ghost of an idea formed.

Chapter Thirty-Two: An Act of Vandalism

"Where's the cane?"

Keeping my left hand on the depressed area of the wall, I moved my foot as gingerly as possible in an arc. A slight resistance alerted me I'd found the walking stick. Spreading both arms, I pivoted to the floor and picked it up.

"What cane?" Simon asked a few beats behind the program.

I rocked back and found my place again.

"The one that bashed your head in. Don't worry, I got it."

"Evidence, you know."

I cut my eyes to him in the dark, shaking my head.

Flipping the cane so that the silver head faced the plaster, I held it like a javelin. With the fingers of one hand splayed around the depression, I aimed as best I could and smashed the cane into the wall.

Simon yelped.

Grinning, I cracked the silver head into the wall again.

"Stop it!" He sounded horrified.

"Simon, I'm—"

"You can't deface the Baths!"

All it took was ruining a national treasure to get him to wake up.

"Look," I began, but he was having none of it.

"These ruins have been here for two millennia."

"I know." I whacked again. "I do tours."

"You can't—"

This time I interrupted him. "Simon. You know what else ruins a dig site? Three twenty-first century corpses."

Smack, and the aged cement shifted. I'd broken through.

Using my intact fingernails, I picked the pieces of mortar out. The wood of the putlog felt cool and pliable.

Crouching, I dug through my purse for nail clippers and a file. I snatched the little rasp and stood, my bag dangling from my belt loop.

Puffing out a breath, I started digging. There were at least six inches of rotted log to burrow through. I grimaced.

The surface resisted my efforts. "Come on," I encouraged the wall to give way. "Come on."

Scratch, scratch, scratch. The image of rat claws resurfaced.

Brushing away the tiny amount of sawdust I'd created, a thick splinter fell out. I'd gotten through the hardened surface to the decaying wood inside.

Encouraged, I stabbed, sawed, and clawed at it. Little chunks of wood tumbled off until I had created a hole two inches across at the mouth.

I panted with the effort, grit coating the inside of my mouth. "Come on," I muttered again.

Simon hit my leg.

"Plan?" he asked, hopeful.

"My plan? Dig through this putlog and yell for help."

He patted my leg again. "Eat the rest of the food."

I was about to protest, but then it hit me. Simon had faith in me. He thought this would work. I took his advice and ate more of the power bar, saving for one nibble for him.

Digging with renewed vigor, I made my way through another inch of rotted wood. Halfway. Progress celebrations were cut short when I stuck the file into the hole and didn't connect with anything. I hollowed out as far as the make-shift tool could.

"Dammit," I whispered, not wanting to discourage Simon.

He heard me, though, and mumbled. "Hmm?"

"My file is too short to reach any further," I said, sinking to the ground.

I felt Simon's hand flailing about next to me, and I wanted to reassure him. "It's okay. I'm sure I have something."

Except I knew I didn't. My earlier inventory had no other useful items for digging.

"Describe the cane," he requested.

"Why? Too big for the hole I've made, that's for sure."

"Humor me."

I closed my eyes, picturing the cane. "Black stained wood, metal tip with an intricately carved silver head. There's a band around it with a small round protrusion."

"Give." His hand flopped across my lap, and I handed him the murder weapon.

Snick.

It sounded exactly like a sword being unsheathed.

"What was that?" I asked, alarmed.

Simon took my hand and placed a thin metal item in it.

"Um," I expressed artfully as I felt it. Long, pointed, with a sharp edge and small, metal handle. Head. Pommel. Whatever. "Did you just pull Excalibur out of a stone?"

"Sword in the cane," his thin voice offered. "Dig."

It took a moment for my shaking hands to wedge the sword into the indentation I had started. But once there, I worked quickly.

I got into a rhythm, circling the blade round and round. The edge was razor-sharp, and I wondered if it had been used to remove Cliff's ear. If so, I was definitely destroying evidence. I'd be happy to face punishment as long as my prison had electricity and plumbing.

My hand suddenly shot forward, knuckles colliding with the wall.

Lowering my mouth to the work area, I blew hard to clear away the debris. Gasping, I saw a pinprick of light.

It was so tiny I couldn't tell if it was a trick of the darkness.

Stab, stab, stab.

I squinted. Light. Honest to God light.

"Simon," I whispered. "I'm through." I kept digging, widening until a diffused beam shone into our prison.

"Help," I whispered. Barely audible. I'd spent every ounce of energy on the hole, and now that I had it, I didn't have the voice to call for help.

Also, I didn't know what time it was. Why yell in the middle of the night? This passage of the Baths had very little traffic. A shout, even if I managed one, would go unnoticed unless someone stood right by the door.

My strength failed me, and I collapsed to the floor.

I gently whacked Simon with the back of my hand. "Do you think someone will notice it?" I asked. "The hole?"

No response.

"Would you?" I prompted.

Simon lay stock-still. He wouldn't last much longer.

I considered using my phone light. Shining it through the hole would attract attention. The battery was so low already that I wouldn't get many chances.

I needed something to hang out of the opening that anyone would find. Something that wouldn't require me standing there, listening.

Leaning my head against the wall, I recalled the brief glimpse I had gotten of Simon's clothes. Dark blue and tan just like me. Everything we were wearing blended in with the limestone of the Baths or the shadows.

Cliff might be dressed differently, but I didn't think I could face him.

What do I have left?

A ponytail holder wouldn't be bright or big enough to attract attention. Gum would probably plug the hole I'd worked so hard to create. Did I have gum? I couldn't remember.

So that was it. In a few days, someone would notice the hole, the stink of decaying bodies, or both. They'd open the chamber and find the three of us oozing. The medical examiner would wonder why I had such a colorful lace bra under my drab work clothes.

"Wait." It came out as a croak.

My ridiculously. Sexy. Bra. Red with black lace. A bright, eye-catching candy red.

"Don't peek," I instructed Simon's quiet form. Sitting tall, I scooted

237

forward. The jacket came off first, the shirt next, then the bra.

The cold air made my skin prickle, and I replaced my shirt and denim jacket as fast as my fingers could button.

When I was dressed, I wrapped the bra strap around my wrist. Twisting the other strap around the end of the sword, I poked it into the hole.

The bra went in about halfway before catching on the cup. "Stupid underwire," I complained as I yanked it back out. Sitting flat again, I employed my nail clippers.

I clipped at the area near the support wire until a big enough tear had formed. The wire slid out. I stored it in my purse, mentally adding wire to my inventory. I did the same to the other side.

I smushed, twisted, and flattened the bra as much as possible. It remained bulky.

Why couldn't any part of this escape be easy?

"Alright. Here goes." My voice was raspy.

I snipped through one strap as close to the cup as I could. I pulled off the plastic length adjusters. Stretching the strap to its full length, I estimated it measured eight or nine inches.

Standing, I reattached the shredded bra to the blade and fed it into the hole in the putlog.

The tiny bit of ambient light that filtered in became obstructed, and my throat tightened. I wasn't sure how long I could take total darkness again. "It's okay," I reassured myself and Simon, in case he was listening.

I jabbed until the strap poked through the other side.

"Okay," I sighed as my knees buckled. The adrenaline that had kept me going fled.

You're not finished, my brain informed me.

Fine.

I retrieved one of the underwires and tied it to the strap that dangled free on our side. Using a ponytail holder, I piled my hair on top of my head in a ballerina bun. Finally, I wove the underwire strap contraption into my hair.

I closed my eyes to the darkness.

Chapter Thirty-Three: The Lord

Someone pulled my hair.

"Ow." My tongue was too big in my mouth, causing the sound to come out muffled.

Tug. Little hairs pulled and snapped.

My hand flew to the top of my head. "Stop." The hoarse rasp had no effect.

After forcing my eyes open, I remembered where I was.

Someone had found my breadcrumb trail.

Twisting to face the wall, I clawed my way to the hole I'd made.

"Help," I mouthed as I untangled the lifeline in my hair. "Help," a bit louder.

"What, what?" A voice came.

I pounded my fist on the rock. Useless. "Helllllpppp." A long whisper.

"I rather think someone is in there. I say, Dr. Daniels." The voice moved away.

"No!" I yelped, not willing to let my savior go. The voice didn't return. I sank to my knees, unable to produce the tears to cry. The bra strap had let go, the wire remained tangled in my hair.

An eternity later, or maybe a couple of minutes, sounds of people gathering came through the opening. An indignant voice complained of vandalism. Dr. Daniels, I assumed.

A brilliant beam of light raked across the room. They were looking.

Forcing my knees to straighten, I walked my hands up the wall for support.

The light that hit me in the face felt like a physical blow. My hand flew to cover my eyes.

A cacophony exploded. Shouts, scraping, wheels creaking. They must have been moving the block-and-tackle into place.

"Simon," I croaked. My foot nudged his side. "Almost home." I gently touched him again when he didn't respond. "Simon," I whimpered, wispy and weak.

At that moment, a crash echoed into the chamber. I put my eye to the opening and saw the peeved profile of Dr. Daniels.

"Bloody vandals!" His outrage was aimed not at me but at the ground.

The beam from a flashlight blinded my eye. "Block-and-tackle crashed. This may take a bit of time."

Ella. Tiny and frail, yet I had no doubt she had removed a pin that caused this accident. She didn't want anyone to find us for years.

The thought of staying in here one more minute pressed in on me. And Simon needed help.

"Water," I shout-whispered.

"What?" He leaned his ear to the hole.

I repeated the request.

"Right, right." He stepped away, and I heard, "Get water."

A couple of minutes later, the first voice returned. "Here we go! Water, sir."

"Perfect. How will I push the bottle through, then?"

The gopher must have thought the water was for his boss.

"Straw." My tongue was so swollen and heavy against my teeth that the word came out with a lisp. I repeated, "Long straw."

"What? Straw? Quite."

This time it took longer for the runner to return. Eventually, a straw extended into the hole. It only cleared the wall by half an inch, causing me to smush my face against the stone as I sipped.

Nectar. Relief. Life.

I wanted to drink an ocean's worth, but I remembered my advice to Simon. The hardest thing in the world was to step away from the fount, but I did.

After a couple of calming swallows, I tested my voice. "There are two of us," I reported. "He's unconscious."

"There's a bit of a complication," Daniels said in the understatement of the year.

I had to carry water to Simon, if only to wet his lips. Mine were cracked, and he'd been here a day longer.

"Straw?" I requested, and the water returned to me. I took a small sip, trying to think. Cupping my hands wouldn't work. I was filthy, and most of the water would spill.

An image from my childhood popped into my mind. My dad sinking a straw into a can of soda, placing his finger on top, and moving the straw to me. With my mom none the wiser, the milk in front of my childhood feast had remained wholesome and untouched.

I sucked at the straw, quickly covered it with my finger, and tugged. It didn't budge. "I need the straw," I said, my voice sounding almost normal. It released, and I carried the water-filled straw to Simon. In the dusty light, I could make out his features. His face, still covered with blood, painted a horrific scene. Thankfully, his chest moved steadily. "Hey, Simon. Come on." I released a few droplets onto his closed mouth. Then more. After the third, his lips parted.

Finally, his mouth opened.

I stood too quickly, black spots dancing in front of my eyes. "Whoa." Steadying myself, I moved toward the weak stream of light and stuck the straw through the wall.

"More water?"

I felt a tug on the other end. "Ready," someone called.

I began to repeat the move with Simon when I remembered that he had a pebble in his mouth. It would be like him to choke on it right when I was saving his life.

"Um, sorry," I said, fishing my fingers into his mouth to retrieve the little stone. "Here." Water released to him.

"Mhrg," he said.

"Almost a word! I knew you could do it." He wasn't coherent, but he also wasn't in a coma.

241

I returned to the putlog and our rescue team. "Any progress?" I asked. I mean, I didn't want to be pushy, but it'd been a rough day.

"Sorry, but I don't see how we can get this done today." Daniels spoke to the other rescuers, probably not realizing I was listening.

Pressing my eye against the hole, I watched the guy with the water bottle nod. Before he got a chance to repeat this depressing bit of news, I cut him off. Simon needed help. Urgently. "Could you tell Lady Vivian that Simon is in here and needs a doctor?"

I heard the thunk of a water bottle dropping to the stone floor.

"I say, what did you say?"

He didn't give me time to respond and instead strode out of my limited view. The next thing I heard was Daniels exclaiming, "Good God, we've found the lord."

The statement made zero sense to me.

"Stay," Daniels directed to someone. I could make out the water runner returning to the hole.

"Food?" I suggested, although I was tapped out on ideas of how to deliver it to us. I didn't know if the British had Slim Jims.

"One tic," the assistant chirped and zoomed off.

True to his word, he returned in a jiffy, stuffed a long, off-white package through the narrow opening. It wiggled in far enough for me to grab with two fingertips and pull. "Milkybar Wowsomes," I read and smiled. I'm not a big sweets person, but I tore into this sticky, manufactured mess like... well, like I hadn't eaten in days. The sweetness of the white chocolate was offset with crispy bits. The sugar zinged through my system instantly.

"Thank you," I said gratefully to my new friend. I was about to ask his name when a new face appeared.

"I'll take it from here," a formal, familiar voice notified him.

"Edward?" My voice went up an octave when I glimpsed his profile.

He turned. "Maddie?" He sounded shocked.

"Didn't you come for me?" Okay. In my defense, I was starving, and I had been deprived of light for longer than any sane person would like. Was it too much to hope for a knight in shining armor?

242

"I was on the property when a call came in for all available men to assist in the Undercroft. I really should have guessed you were involved."

"Look," I huffed, both hands on my hips. "I don't go looking for trouble. Every time I turn around in this country, someone is trying to run me over, scare me away, or, it turns out, kill me. Have you ever been attacked, Mr. Constable?" I saw him nodding, but I carried on. "Not only was I tripped by a homicidal old woman, thrown into a room with a wounded man, AND another murder victim him, it was in complete darkness. And I'm talking zero light here. Dunnest smoke of hell kind of dark. This chaos finds me, not the other way around. I don't want to be involved!"

The whites of Edward's eye, the one I could see, became visible around the brown and gold-flecked iris.

"Did you say, "Murder victim?" To Edward's credit, he asked calmly.

My throat tightened, a tear leaking over my cheek. I nodded, which I knew he couldn't see. "Yes," I admitted in a small voice.

"Do you know who?" His gentle tone made me regret my outburst.

"Cliff Whitely," I told him. "He was the intern before me. Everyone thought he left for another job."

His nodding head offered weird flashes of different parts of his face. I had to step back to keep from getting motion sickness.

"I'm going to make a phone call. I'll be right here."

"Okay,"

I eavesdropped on his conversation. "DCI Bray, please. Constable Bailey. Yes, I'm at the scene of Lord Pacok's rescue, sir. I believe it was attempted murder. There's another body on location. The information came from the American woman. Yes, the same one who discovered Sir Henry."

This was followed by a series of "yes sirs." I rolled my eyes when he faced away from the wall so that I couldn't hear as well.

"I was on sight looking for a friend."

During the ensuing pause, I wondered if I was the friend in question.

"She works here at the Baths, you see."

I softened.

He stepped a pace away, and I strained to listen.

"Her phone was off, and she hadn't texted to let me know." Edward's shoulders caved in around his chest. "Yes, sir. My friend is the American woman."

"Yes!" My voice was back, but I whispered this.

Edward disconnected and came back to me. "Horrible clachen dubh you've found there. Rough day?"

"I've had better," I said. "What's that mean?"

Scowling, he translated. "Dark place, not one I'd want to be in, my brave lassie."

A mountain of emotions crashed around me at his words. Then he ruined it by holding up his hand, a dirty, mutilated, but still sexy bra dangling from his fingers. "Effective lure," he commented.

"Um, well, I was hoping for a date." *Stupid brain! What are you thinking?*

He must have felt my embarrassment because he stiffly replied, "Proper help is on the way."

"Called for the cavalry, did you?"

His head tilted to the side, thinking.

"You must have cavalry," I insisted. "Warriors on horses?"

"Knights?" he suggested.

Oh, yeah. "Knights will work."

"Our cavalry escorts the Queen."

"Ah." I couldn't think of a response, considering America has no counterpart. Still, it was a relief to talk to Edward again. I was almost happy.

He ran a hand over his hair. "I have news of your friend, Lily."

From his expression, it couldn't be good. My heart sank. "Is she..." I couldn't bring myself to ask if she was dead. Not with Simon hanging by a thread right next to me.

Edward shook his head. "She's still in the ICU. They put her in a light coma to give her body a chance to heal. Her vitals are strong, and they have every confidence she'll recover."

Stepping away from the light, I covered my face and let the tears fall. Some good news.

"Did you say an old woman assaulted you?" Edward's voice interrupted my relief, grounding me.

I rolled my eyes. "Well, when you say it like that, it sounds ridiculous."

His head shook back and forth. "Not at all. Crazy old people strength."

My bark of laughter burst into the room. Hysteria wasn't far off.

"I say," the voice of the water runner sounded next to Edward. "Is she quite alright?"

If I wasn't mistaken, Edward rolled his eyes before his professional mask snapped into place. "Not really. No." He offered no other explanation, letting my situation speak for itself.

After a long pause, which I assumed was pretty awkward, the voice said. "Yes. No. Quite right." A beat. "Dr. Daniels found a simple peg had been removed from the machine here."

I assumed he meant the block-and-tackle. Ancient peoples would have considered it a machine. The mechanism that got me into this stupid room hadn't been Roman, but it wasn't modern by any stretch. All wood and stone construction, it may have been on hand as an example of nineteenth-century excavation.

"When can the machine be repaired?" Edward asked.

An embarrassed cough, followed by, "The problem, you see, is not for weeks."

Edward's form flew away from my sightline. "What?" His voice low and menacing.

"We've ordered a modern one." The man was trying to control himself, but his voice turned into a squeak. "It should arrive in a few hours."

"Hours? She's been through an ordeal! Break the stone if you need to!" Edward roared, his Scottish burr adding violence to the words.

"Hours." I didn't want to stay here for hours.

More pressingly, I didn't think Simon would survive much longer. I bent toward him. "Simon?"

It took a moment, but he groaned. "Hang in there. It shouldn't be too much longer. Okay?"

Nothing.

"Do you need water?"

When he didn't answer, I popped to the opening and overheard, "Of course, when we heard the lord was trapped, we were all hands."

"May we have more water, please?"

"Right," the water gopher said and came into view, looking a bit shaken. He extended the straw to me. I took a little, then did the finger on the end trick and dripped water onto Simon's mouth. His face moved in response, but he didn't come fully awake.

"We're almost free," I encouraged him.

Despite the horror of ruining an ancient dig site, I hoped Edward could get them to break the stone door.

As I was about to voice my opinion to the group gathered outside, a racket ensued.

"Where is she?" an imperious voice demanded.

"Here, your ladyship," Edward said, his calm official persona sliding back in place. Neutral accent and so professional that no one would suspect the coiled anger boiling below the surface.

The countess stepped into view. "How is my nephew?"

I used words from the medical TV shows I watched during summer break to sound more credible. "He's responsive but not conscious. He suffered a head wound and blood loss before we were able to bandage it. He's dehydrated, but I've gotten a little water in him. We split a power bar, so he's not starving, but he's frail."

"And you, my dear. How are you?"

The unexpected kindness threatened to crumble any composure I pretended to have. "I'm fine," I choked out.

"I'll have you out in just a moment," she proclaimed. I believed her.

While I swiped at my eyes, the stone sealing us in shifted. *Wow. If something needs to get done, call Lady Vivian.*

Five minutes later, the rock slid free, seeming to float above the ground.

The light pouring into the chamber assaulted my eyes, and I buried my face in my hands.

"Come on out, my dear," the countess called to me.

I shook my head and pointed to Simon. "Simon first. I can wait." I stepped back.

Two medical personnel climbed in and were handed a stretcher. They loaded Simon on and lifted him out. By the time I made it to the door, he was out of sight.

My eyes adjusted slowly. I could see if I squinted. Reaching for the threshold, I prepared to pull myself out.

Four hands, two on each side, lifted me out and set me on a gurney.

Edward hovered beside me as someone took my pulse. In an evidence bag, he held my bra. My bright red, lacy, ultra-sexy bra. I'm sure I blushed, but when I looked at Edward, I panicked, not wanting him to think I wore it for him. Even if maybe I had.

His smile fell away, and his face blanched. "Madeline," he dropped the evidence bag to the ground. Folding my hand into his, he repeated my name.

How bad did I look?

"Who did this to you?"

Pretty bad.

A young, wiry medical technician stepped between us. "Sorry, mate," he told Edward in a thick cockney accent. I was wheeled away and to the elevator before I could tell anyone about Ella.

I caught a glimpse of myself in the reflection of the ambulance window. My hair stuck out from the ponytail holder in every possible direction. An underwire hung by my ear. My face was smeared with gore on it, probably from dealing with Simon's wound. In addition to smudges of dirt everywhere, my lips were cracked and bleeding. All in all, I looked more like a Neanderthal than a girl.

Excellent.

Chapter Thirty-Four: An Overheard Conversation

I jolted awake, dim light flooding into my eyes. I thanked the powers that be. I never wanted to be in a dark room again. Getting a nightlight was the first item on my To-Do list.

Scanning my surroundings, I searched for what had startled me awake. White blinds covered a closed window. The plain cabinet with an oak top didn't have anything on it. I cranked my head around, searching behind the bed expecting to be attached to a pulse-measuring machine, but my only hookup was to an IV. The room looked so much like the hospital I was in when I broke my wrist horseback riding that I panicked that I'd been deported.

Voices sounding in the hallway caught my attention. Definitely English accents, so I was still in the UK. My skin prickled. I held my breath and listened.

A quavering voice insisted on seeing Simon.

I recognized it. Ella was in the hospital, and it sounded like she was winning the argument to get in to visit her intended victim.

Frantic, I rummaged for a call button.

The talking in the hall stopped.

"Hey!" I croaked, but my weak voice didn't carry.

Finally, my fingers landed on a remote, and I repeatedly pressed the red call button. The television blared on.

"Help!" This time my yell was drowned out by the local news.

Kicking my legs loose from the confines of the pale blue coverlet, I dropped my bare feet to the white floor and took a faltering step. I was yanked back by the IV in the back of my hand. It hurt.

Examining the contraption, I found two pieces. A shunt stuck into the vein of my hand, and a needle from the IV bag connected to it. Rather than messing with the part inserted into my body, I pulled the IV bag free and stumbled to the hallway.

The door opened out so quickly that I fell into the linoleum of the hallway with a thud.

The noise attracted the attention of a constable three doors away. The smart move would have been to ask who he was guarding and establish my credibility as a key witness. Instead, I screeched, "Where's the old lady?" Which had the effect of making me sound crazy.

His face registered shock at my sudden appearance. "Are you quite alright, miss?"

I put one foot under me, stood, and realized my pink hospital gown was not closed all the way in the back. Shaking my head, I staggered toward the constable. "She's the murderer," I explained, keeping us on track.

He backed away from me, apparently thinking my insanity was contagious.

"Kill," I panted.

Being sealed into a chamber for a day takes a lot out of a girl.

On the way to the hospital, DI Parikh jotted notes as I told him about Ella, but not much else. He'd removed his glasses and pinched the bridge of this nose. I wondered if I'd made myself clear before the medical staff allowed me to close my eyes. Why had the constable let Ella into Simon's room?

"Kill, Simon," I wheezed.

To my surprise, he pulled a club from his utility belt and brandished it at me.

At me? Honestly?

Leaning against a wall, I struggled for coherence. "The old woman. I heard her voice."

He lowered the club but didn't put it away.

"Miss, I'm sorry, but I think you should be back in your bed."

"She's trying to kill Simon. We have to stop her."

His expression changed from wary to offended. "Rubbish. She had a note from the countess to see the lord." He reattached the club to his belt.

The lord. People kept saying that. The phrase that got everyone moving came back to me. I attempted something similar. "Good God, she's trying to kill the lord!"

The officer straightened and quickly opened the door he'd been guarding. A hypodermic needle sunk into his arm, and he collapsed.

Faltering, I tumbled into the room and over his inert form.

Ella, in white lace, picture-perfect sweet. So much so that I almost doubted my own memories. No way this woman could do anyone harm.

The constable groaned, reminding me of everything she had done.

"Ella!"

She paused, a second hypodermic needle poised next to Simon's IV bag.

"How could you?" I scolded her. "What would God think?"

Fortunately, my outburst distracted her, and she turned her attention to me.

A fevered light came into her eyes. Her hands dropped to her side, and she took a step in my direction, away from Simon.

"God always used his angels." A beautiful smile came across her face. "Raphael punished the sinners. I was born for it. My calling."

Another step. Ella's head swiveled back and forth as if she remembered what she was supposed to be doing. She turned toward the IV.

I managed a shaky stride to the end of the bed. I fell across the foot of it, hoping I didn't hurt Simon in the process.

"Ella, don't do this."

Her beatific face morphed into something twisted and vengeful.

"Don't do this? God's work? You should be grateful to face my wrath and not His!"

"But why? What did we do?" I actually wanted to know.

"What did you do?" Spittle dripped from her lips. "All of you! Encouraging people to knock down the Abbey. How dare you?"

I tilted my head, flabbergasted. "It was a joke!"

"A joke?" The words came out of her mouth like an explosion of sound. "Joke about the house of God?" She turned her full anger at me, holding the hypo over her head, ready to strike it into me.

Okay, so I got her away from Simon. Mission accomplished. But jeez!

I rolled onto the floor. Battered as I was, I could still move faster than Ella's frail bones.

She scurried around the bed, aiming her weapon at me. Who knew what was in the needle?

I rolled away and collided with the officer. He was awake but completely stunned.

As I turned around on the floor, I felt like a turtle on its back. I maneuvered onto my knees, ready to fend Ella off. Only she'd returned her attention to Simon.

Reaching a hand toward her, I said, "Logically, isn't the sanctity of life the most important of God's covenants?" I thought Tori's abuela would be proud of that argument. If I survived, I'd tell her.

Unfortunately, it didn't work.

"How dare you mention His name! You're not worthy."

About a billion counterarguments came into my head, but none of them were helpful in this situation.

Looking to the fallen constable for help, my eye fell on the club he'd pulled on me. Inching toward him, I waved a hand to attract Ella's attention.

"What did Sherlock Holmes have to do with this?" Holmes never struck me as particularly religious.

"What?" Her face went lax as she narrowed her eyes at me, concentrating.

The Case of the Cardboard Box had a severed ear."

"Did it?" She seemed genuinely curious.

"Yeah, it did," I confirmed, side-stepping on my knees toward the fallen cop. "In the story, the ear was in a box packed in salt, like the one you sent me."

A horrific thought struck me that perhaps someone else mailed the body part to me.

Fortunately, she nodded her confirmation, lost in thought.

"The salt from the ice cream social," I prompted.

"Yes." She beamed. "Deacon Michael went to the hardware store for me and brought it all back to the Abbey. He's such a kind man. Devoted."

Uh oh. We needed to stay away from religion.

"And there's a Sherlock adventure with a skip code, too," I continued.

Her lips pursed, still focused. "No, there's not," she insisted but sounded unsure.

"Sure, there is!" I said it too enthusiastically and broke her musing. She renewed her attention to Simon.

The name of the story teased on the tip of my tongue. *What was it?*

I crabbed over another few inches.

"Don't move," she ordered. She left Simon and aimed her crazy at me.

"*The Gloria Scott!*" *Thank you, brain.* "*The Gloria Scott* is the story with a skip code. A man comes to town to claim his share of ill-gotten goods from his comrades."

She stopped again, concentration drawing her eyes away from me. I took advantage by lowering my hips to my heels, settling my grip around the club.

"I've read them all, you know," she nodded. "Dr. Watson is the true hero, of course. Holmes had too many vices. Watson survives."

Tugging, I felt it catch on a safety hook. My fingers fidgeted with the clasp, but I didn't dare look away from Ella.

"The skip code was shrewd," I told her. "The police didn't figure it out."

The serene smile returned to her face. It was even scarier than the vengeful one.

"I heard the words in a dream. Raphael spoke them to me."

"Had Sir Henry insulted you?"

Her glare flashed at me. "That money belonged to the Abbey!"

"How so?" I asked, mustering a matter of fact tone.

The club slid free from the constable's belt. My fingers tightened around it.

"Deacon Michael told me that Sir Henry had promised that money to us. At the last minute, he said he'd be presenting it at the Baths fundraiser instead. More press coverage, don't you know. I showed him my little note. Guided him to the right room. I knew a man with an ego like that wouldn't be able to resist more attention."

Her breathing had become fast, her eyes glazed, remembering. "He walked in and stooped over the bath. It was easy to push him in. When he tried to climb out, a little whack was all it took. He slipped under."

"I placed the paper into the donations. I wanted them to discover my clue."

Her face softened. She seemed to be enjoying the memory. Suddenly she pointed at me. "And it should have worked for you, too."

"Me?" I almost dropped the club in surprise. My heart constricted. *Lily.* "Did you try and push me in front of a bus?" Indignation fueled my words. "My friend is in a coma because of—"

"Of course not." she laughed.

Weird.

"The way you walked into traffic without looking, I wouldn't have needed to."

Good point. But what did she mean? Shifting on my knees caused the bruise on my shin to flare in pain. The bruise from my fall in Wookey Hole. The one that matched Sir Henry's and the head of Ella's cane.

Her finger dropped, and she turned back to Simon's IV.

"The cane," I said.

"A beautiful replica, don't you think?" She sounded like her docent self now.

"A replica of what?" I asked to keep her talking. The hypodermic needle still hovered near Simon's IV.

"Dr. Watson's cane." She said like I was a stupid child. "Victorian motif with a sword built-in." Her hand flexed as if remembering its feel. "I have missed it."

Her eyes laser-focused on me again. "It's your fault I lost my cane!"

"My fault? You bludgeoned me with it and tried to kill me! God's will took it from you for using it for evil!"

That got her attention. She flew at me with the needle, her arm swiping.

I swung at her hand with the officer's club. Even though she had tried to kill me and Simon and was probably trying to kill me now, I felt awful when the wood connected with her bird-like hand.

The hypo narrowly avoided me as it fell and rolled under the bed out of reach.

The sudden exertion took everything out of me. I face-planted onto the floor. Thinking that Ella couldn't do any more damage, I turned my head to the side, resting my ear on the tile. Ella was poised over me, a scalpel in her hand.

The scalpel came at my back.

A sense of duty must have triggered the catatonic constable because he launched himself on top of me. Then passed out.

Pushing with one arm, I attempted to dislodge him. He didn't budge.

Twisting my head around, I watched for Ella's impending attack.

Ella yanked the scalpel out of my rescuer's back. Blood dripped onto my face, the coppery smell reminding me of being trapped with Cliff's body.

The club was still in my hand. I couldn't block her advances, but I could do damage. Every breath took effort with the weight of the constable across my back. Scooting my arm under me, I lifted an inch and took in a bunch of air.

Readying my attack, I winced. I couldn't intentionally hurt Ella again. She was so fragile. How could I?

Another drip of blood landed on my cheek.

On the other hand, she was perfectly willing to scalpel me to death. I readied the club and pre-screamed to give me courage. "Ahhhhh!" I landed a smash on the toe of her shoe. "Ahhhhh!"

The scalpel clattered to the ground.

At last, the door flew open. A nurse came in complaining about the racket.

"She attacked me!" Ella screamed as she scurried out.

I closed my eyes and inhaled in a gasping sort of way.

I couldn't tell what the nurse was thinking, but I heard her run out of the room at full speed. Reinforcement came a couple of minutes later.

From my limited vantage, I could make out shoes. A pair entered that appeared to be part of a uniform.

Polished black boots stopped in front of me. The owner bent forward, and Edward's face came into view.

"Hello, love." He winked.

My brain cataloged my current situation. Blood on my face. IV shunt in my hand. Hospital gown probably opened in the back. A strange man passed out across me.

Enchanting.

Also, at the moment, unimportant. "Ella's getting away," I gasped.

"DI Parikh is coordinating the search. Unfortunately, it's easy for an old person to hide in plain sight in a hospital. She slipped into the elevator before the nurse sounded the alarm."

"Um," I struggled under the weight of the officer. "A little help here?" I pointed a finger at the man crushing me.

"Right," he said. Raising about halfway, Edward cradled the unconscious man and deadlifted him off of me.

My hand immediately shot to my exposed backside, where I pulled my gown closed. I rolled so that I could see more, and the world could see less.

More policemen came in, including Parikh. Edward respectfully asked, "Did you apprehend Raphaella Thomas?"

Parikh shook his head, looking pained.

Two orderlies entered and carried off the man who'd been guarding the room. An additional pair came for me.

I was disappointed. Gown and all, I hoped that Edward would gather me in his arms and carry me back to my room. Instead, a skinny man and burly woman lifted me onto a stretcher and wheeled me through the hall.

Simon stayed asleep through the whole ordeal.

Chapter Thirty-Five: The Hunt

Exhausted as I was, I summoned the energy to stumble to the bathroom and brush my hair. My belongings were considered evidence in a homicide investigation, including my purse. The hospital provided me with a brush and a toothbrush, for which I was grateful, but I needed more.

I limped to the door and stopped a passing nurse. "This is silly, but I don't have anything but the hospital-issued toiletries. Do you happen to have lip gloss?"

She arched an eyebrow, and I thought for sure she'd lecture me about priorities. Instead, she said conspiratorially, "Making yourself presentable for that constable, are ya?"

"Is it that obvious?"

"He watches you when you're not looking." She squeezed my arm. "Let me see what we can do. You lie back down, dearie."

She scurried off, presumably to the nurses' station, and I tumbled onto the bed. The pillow cradled my head in soft, deep comfort, and I drifted off.

When I awoke, a pile of cosmetics on my nightstand greeted me. A note said, "We took up a collection."

The kind nurses found concealer, a pale pink lip balm, and mineral powder foundation. It was more makeup than I normally wear. Still, I usually haven't been clubbed, stuck in a hole, or attacked with a medical instrument. I needed the extra help.

I picked up the lip balm and applied it as a start. That little movement encouraged me to sit upright. From my new vantage, I noticed a compact mirror sitting on the nightstand that I'd missed before. Nurses. They're like life-saving fairy godmothers.

Covering the worst of the bruises on my face, I at least looked human. Unlike the last two times Edward had seen me. Not that I needed his approval, but I'm not crazy about looking like a troll.

My eyes drifted toward the ceiling as I went through the last day or two in my mind. I hadn't heard about the officer who took a scalpel in the back for me. Or what he'd been injected with.

I also hadn't heard any reports on finding Ella. A tiny woman with a hurt hand and broken toes sounded like an easy target to me. But as Edward said, there were a lot of elderly patients in the hospital. Knowing Ella, she could talk herself into getting treatment without causing suspicion. Or she walked right out the door undetected and got on a bus.

I figured she couldn't go to a doctor because the police would look for that. It hurt my head to think about.

Finally, my thoughts drifted to Simon. Lord Pacok. I desperately needed to talk to him.

A tap on my door snapped me from my thoughts. Edward leaned on the door jam, dressed in his leather jacket and jeans. I made a mental note to send the nurses a thank you present for the makeup they'd provided.

"Hey," I said.

Without taking his eyes off mine, he strode toward the bed and sat, facing me. "How are ya, lassie?"

My brain melted. "I'm so sorry I took pictures of evidence. I wasn't trying to meddle. I wanted to help. But you asked me not to, and I should have listened, and I should have apologized. I'm sorry." Since I hadn't a lot of experience with apologies, I included it one more time. "Sorry."

To his credit, he didn't gloat or pretend like he wasn't interested. Instead, he took my hand. The one that wasn't bruised and taped. The doctor had decided I'd had enough fluids and removed the needle shunt from my vein.

"Why didn't you wait for me at the organ pipes?" he asked.

My face lit up. "You followed my map?" I wanted confirmation. And to know that I'd written it correctly.

"How could I say no to a girl wearing a red and black lace bra?"

I let go of his hand and shoved his shoulder. "Look," I explained. All the melty, squishy feelings got pushed aside as I made my intentions clear. "That bra didn't mean anything. I got tired of dressing like Indiana Jones, is all. Attractive undergarments are about me and how I feel. Not invitations. Got it?"

His chuckling made me cross my arms and release a humphing sound.

Leaning forward, he kissed my forehead. "I'm glad to see you back to normal."

I relented, dropping my arms and letting my hand fall next to him. He took the hint and put his hand over mine.

"How is the constable that Ella attacked?" I asked.

His smile reassured me that the man in question was okay. "Jones? He'll be fine. The scalpel didn't go in far. It created a clean cut that the surgeons stitched easily. His own fault. He was told the suspect was an old woman."

"Well, he saved me. She wouldn't have stopped if... you know."

Edward squeezed my hand.

I asked, "What was in the hypodermic needles?"

"Morphine in both."

I wrinkled my nose in thought. "Why? That wouldn't have killed Simon."

"From the information we've gathered, it seemed as though she walked by an open door, blindly grabbed the needles, and continued on. No one thought to question a patient getting exercise."

"Why did Jones collapse? Was it a dangerous amount?"

Edward's expression twitched with humor. "Fear of needles. Apparently, the man faints every time the doctors draw blood. I don't know what Ms. Thomas thought it would do."

"Maybe she was going to introduce bubbles into the bloodstream."

Edward's eyebrows shot up in surprise. "You're a morbid thing, aren't you?"

"Have you forgotten everything that's happened since I got to town? Thoughts of death have been forced onto me. Besides, the only books at Ash Tree Cottage are mysteries."

We lapsed into a companionable silence, which I was unable to hold for long. "Have you caught Ella yet?"

He wasn't one to talk about police work with civilians, and I didn't expect much but the standard press release answer. He shocked me by responding with details.

"Not yet. We've got all hospitals and doctors on alert, describing the wounds you inflicted."

I winced. "The sound it made when I hit her, I'll never forget it."

Squeezing my hand, he reached across my shoulder and gave me a reassuring pat. "You were brilliant. Absolutely.

"We've also covered public transportation, but there are quite a few pensioners in Bath."

My head bobbed in agreement. "It's like looking for a needle in a haystack."

He continued, "The Abbey has been warned, naturally. Deacon Michael was suitably horrified and sends his apologies. The Baths are on high alert, as well."

Edward considered me. "What else do you want to know?"

"Really?"

Nodding, he told me, "DCI Bray has given you full access. You've made quite an impression, lassie."

All my questions fled my brain except for one. "When can I get out of here?"

Edward's endearing lopsided grin appeared. "Right now. I'll drive."

Chapter Thirty-Six: Yet Another Citroen

The check-out process was surprisingly easy. I didn't know if that was due to my being under police protection or National Health, but I appreciated it.

Once at Ash Tree Cottage, Edward played host. He settled me onto the comfy living room couch, ushered Roddy inside, and brought me strong, milky tea.

I took an appreciative sip, but at the moment, I craved a caramel macchiato.

"Do you know how to make coffee?" I asked Edward.

"I'm to take on barista duties, am I?"

I smiled, hoping to look, well, hopeful. "With caramel? Or chocolate?"

He gave the top of my head a platonic kiss and strode back into the kitchen.

"It's your own fault, you know," I called after him. "You proved you could cook. In that very kitchen."

A few minutes later, he returned with a frothy, sweet brew.

"How did you froth the milk?" I hadn't found anything that resembled espresso gear.

"Scottish magic."

I laughed but said, "My mom teaches Shakespeare, remember? The only Scottish magic I know is "Boil, boil, toil, and trouble."

"Fire burn, and cauldron bubble," he added with his accent, making the words even creepier.

I pointed at him. "That," I explained, "is too scary for me right now."

Sitting next to me, he took my tea as his own. "Warm the milk in the microwave. Put it in a jar and shake. Foam."

My eyes crinkled in delight. "Since it involves a microwave, I'll count it as magic."

Sweet and aromatic, he had the proportions so perfect that when I closed my eyes, I pictured my mom sitting next to me.

I still didn't know what I would say to her when I told her about my ordeal. A part of me, a large part, wanted her to swoop in, fix everything, and take care of me for the rest of the semester. But what would I do for the rest of my life?

The sunset cast a pink glow across the white walls, bringing with it a chill.

Then there was my dad. How could I break the news that his incredibly generous gift had almost ruined chances at a career? I still didn't know if remaining in England was an option. The countess had only called me in because Simon had disappeared. Now that everything was under control, would they send me home?

"Could you light the fire?" I asked, a shiver taking hold of me.

I snuggled under my blanket and held my hand out for Roddy. He hopped to me and settled by the couch.

I hoped the Priestlys didn't find out that he was now used to having free rein of the house. I wouldn't tell if he didn't.

A giant yawn practically dislocated my jaw.

"You need sleep," Edward pointed out.

I nodded, but instead of closing my eyes, I broached the subject I had avoided so far.

"This may sound like an odd request." That got his attention. "Can you stay the night?"

"I assume you mean for protection and not," he paused long enough for me to feel the blush rising to my face. "Other activities."

"No. Although I think I've proven I can take care of myself," I asserted.

He shook his head. "No one, lassie. I repeat, no one would accuse you of being a damsel in distress."

I sat a little taller. "Thank you."

"But while a murderer who knows your address is on the loose, a police presence is in order. Do you want to stay here or upstairs?"

I pondered and picked the room with a cozy fire over a regular bed. "Here, I think."

Standing, he said, "Right. I'll be back."

He shot out of the room and returned moments later with an extra pillow and the quilted bedspread from my bed.

After arranging everything around me like a cocoon, he draped the thick, cable-knit afghan across the chair and pulled a coffee table in front of it. Placing a pillow on the table, he kicked off his shoes and propped his feet up. "I'll be right here when you wake up," he assured me.

As my eyelids grew heavy, Edward got a phone call and left the room.

Eavesdropping, I heard only the words "airport" and "train." I fell asleep wondering if a dragnet extended past the city.

* * *

My dreams startled me awake, filled with images I'd rather forget.

Instead, I focused on Edward, asleep in the armchair. What was it about sleeping guys that made them so adorable?

It was time I faced the day. The sun was out, so at least I'd slept through the night. Tentatively, I stretched, feeling for aches and bruises. Not bad, considering.

The need for coffee asserted itself, and I plodded into the kitchen.

Edward had washed and put away the dishes we'd used the previous evening. What was I supposed to do about him?

Instead of answering myself, I made coffee. Straight black, like my dad taught me. I missed meeting him for lunches where he'd tell his goofy jokes to every waiter in earshot.

Returning to my university in Chicago held appeal. I was sure my dad could make a deal to get me into a dorm mid-semester. But the more I depended on his arrangements, the more he would assume I needed them or that I couldn't take care of myself.

Coffee in hand, I climbed upstairs and got dressed. Opening the window,

I stepped through onto the roof and took in the vast, open sky. There were plenty of archaeology sites above ground. I'd aim for those in the future, whatever that held for me.

Sitting on the sill with my feet propped on the roof, I considered my options.

Stay in England, go home to Arizona and my mom, or go back to college near my dad. Each option's pros and cons shifted depending on my mood. I needed to straighten out my feelings before I talked to either parent. Or I'd wind up doing whatever they encouraged. Which would not include archaeology or my independence.

Lifting my mug for another sip of coffee, I found it empty. A short stroll would clear my head more than a second cup. Walking one block along the street should be safe enough. Or better yet, I could go to the park across the way.

I left a note for Edward telling him my plan and reminding him that I didn't have a phone. On impulse, I gave him a peck on the cheek.

Blushing, I went out the door, up the flower-lined path, and through the gate. The second the latch fell into place behind me, a light blue Citroen appeared on the street.

"Ubiquitous," as my mother would say. Knowing how peppy the engines and careless the drivers were, I flattened myself against the stone wall that guarded the house, waiting for it to pass.

As the car neared, the driver accelerated. The car jumped the curb onto the sidewalk and aimed straight at me.

Paralyzed for a moment, I couldn't process what was happening. Right until I saw Ella's crazed expression behind the wheel.

Frankly, it pissed me off. I'd had enough of this and of her. I took two steps to my right. She overcorrected to follow as I switched directions. Stumbling, I caught myself with one hand on the ground and the other on the wall. I tugged at the gate latch.

The car stopped. Gears screeched as it came at me in reverse.

I fell through the open gate.

Edward appeared out of nowhere, jumped over me, and onto the roof of the car. They sped back up the lane.

On hands and knees, I army-crawled back inside. Using the landline, I called the emergency number I memorized on my second day in town, thanks to Ella.

"Please state your emergency."

"Hi. I'm Maddie McGuire," I began out of habit. I couldn't think of where to start.

"Do you have an emergency?" the voice asked patiently.

"Yeah." Rather than starting at the beginning, I jumped to the matter at hand.

"A blue Citroen tried to run me down. Constable Edward Bailey pursued on foot, and last I saw, he was on top of the car."

"I'm sorry, I'm sure I misheard. What was that last part?"

"He leaped on top. He was clinging to the roof of the speeding car. I have his badge or collar number. 16941."

In case the operator thought this a crank call, I added. "The woman driving is wanted for murder. Ella Thomas. The police are looking for her."

That statement stirred a lot of action.

I wanted to hang up and see what was happening on the street. The voice insisted I stay on the line.

At that moment, I realized the phone wasn't even cordless. The receiver was tethered to the base of the phone, which sat on a table attached to a cord that went into the wall. How did people survive with landlines? I couldn't even leave the dining room.

Rummaging through the phone stand drawer, I grabbed a pad of paper and a pencil. I considered making a list of pros and cons for my next move but instead doodled nervously. I missed my cell. And I didn't know how to use a landline to make an international call to my dad to get a new one. Or how much that would cost. My doodles turned into dollar signs.

Finally, after fifteen minutes, the dispatcher returned. "Sorry, but did you say Constable Bailey?"

My attention snapped back to the phone. "Yes! Is he okay?"

Please let him be okay. Please, please.

"Did you say your name was Madeline McGuire?"

"Yes. Is Constable Bailey okay?" I repeated, possibly a little impatiently.

"He has a message for you."

I refrained from reaching through the phone line and throttling the operator. "And?" I prompted.

"Let's see."

I held the phone in front of my face and looked at it like, *Are you flippin' kidding me?*

I said nothing for about five seconds. I couldn't take any more. "Yes?"

"He's fine, and...."

The phone dropped from my hand in relief. *Thank you.* "I'm sorry, totally my fault, I'm sure," I said, channeling Simon. "What was that last part?"

"Ms. Thomas has been apprehended."

"You're kidding," I said, feeling a weight lift away from me.

"Actually, not. Good news."

I could have kissed the voice at the other end of the line. "Great news. Thank you so much. Are we done? Can I hang up now?"

"An officer should be at your door, momentarily."

My doorbell rang at that same instant.

"They're here. Do you want to talk to the officer?"

"Yes."

"Okay," I said, excited. "One sec."

I ran to the door, the receiver in hand, pulling the rest of the phone onto the floor. Picking up the receiver, I apologized. "Sorry. You still there?"

The voice affirmed, and I set the receiver on the floor.

A female constable opened the front door before I got there, and Detective Inspector Parikh followed her in. "Hello, miss. You've been busy."

I beamed. "Never a dull moment. How's Edward?"

"Constable Bailey is fine, and the suspect is in custody."

I nodded like a bobblehead and said, "I know. The emergency operator told me."

Something about that phrase was important. Then it hit me. "Oh! They want to talk to you." I pointed at the dining room door to guide him to the phone. "On the floor."

Parikh's step hesitated for a moment at the last statement, but he graciously said nothing before continuing to the call.

Once he had finished, the DI sat me on the couch, which still showed signs of my nesting, and interviewed me. Again. I'd seen more than my fair share of police on this trip.

As Parikh stood to leave, another constable arrived. Not Edward, though, who was the only one I wanted to see. First and foremost, because he'd caught Ella. Second, because I wanted to make sure he wasn't mad at me for going for an unsupervised walk. I finally gave him a genuine apology and promptly broke his trust again by sneaking out.

Not that I snuck. I left a note. Which he obviously found.

I sighed, realizing my rationalization. Maybe Tori was right. I had no idea how a real relationship worked. I didn't understand Scott, but she did.

With the thought of my friend, a fresh wave of homesickness crashed around me. If I could see her face to face, I could fix this rift between us. I'd even be pleasant to stupid Scott. And possibly consider not calling him stupid.

"Hello, miss," a male voice said.

I turned to find a vaguely familiar face, but I couldn't place him.

He held out his hand. "Jones," he said.

The guard from Simon's room. I didn't see much of him when he was draped across my back. "Oh, hello! You're at work already?" Obviously.

"The wound wasn't deep," he explained. "Only two stitches. All cleared for light duty."

"Thank you for taking that scalpel for me. She would have slashed me to pieces."

He coughed into his hand and avoided eye contact with me. What had I done this time? I would never understand how to get along in this country.

"Would you mind terribly if I started the kettle for a spot of tea?"

I shrugged. "Sure."

"Would you like a cuppa?"

A hot beverage sounded delicious, but I wasn't in the mood for tea. "No, thank you. I'll make coffee."

He shook his head at this statement, muttering, "Americans," under his breath.

"Hey," I called in a very American way. "Can you contact Edward Bailey for me?"

Jones looked down his nose at me. This action took some doing as we were about the same height.

I needed to talk to Edward before I called my parents and made plans.

I smiled. Brightly.

"Constable Bailey is occupied with other matters at the moment."

"My phone is in evidence. I don't have his number. Could you text him for me? Please?"

His dramatic sigh didn't stop him from pulling out his phone. "Yes, miss?"

"Tell him I don't have my phone, and I need his number so I can call from the landline."

Jones' eyebrows furrowed. "All that?"

My overly enthusiastic grin returned. "I can type it for you," I offered.

He typed, then slipped his cell into his pocket and left to the kitchen without giving me Edward's number.

I followed, using the coffee grinder before talking. "Edward's number?" I inquired.

He blinked a couple of times blankly before reaching into his pocket and glancing at the screen. "Right." He read the number.

I held up a finger. "One second." The junk drawer had a pad and pencil. I confirmed the number with him as I made the notation.

"Thank you, Constable Jones. I appreciate it."

Pointing to the tin of Tips tea on the counter, I left the kitchen and strode into the dining room.

Parikh had replaced the phone onto its stand. I dragged a chair next to it and dialed Edward.

"Hello, love."

How come all it took was two words from him to derail all the plans I had considered?

"Hi. I don't even know the number of this phone. Did it display for you?"
Frowning, I asked, "How did you know it was me?"

He chuckled, and I pictured him, crooked smile in place.

"I've got you," he said in a way that made me smile into the receiver.

"How much longer do you have to work?"

"I'm off work."

If he wasn't doing police stuff, why hadn't he come over? He didn't sound
mad about me leaving and almost getting hit by a car, but he hadn't given
Jones a message for me.

Was liking someone worth the aggravation? I wasn't sure.

"I'm on a secret mission," he whispered, and I heard giggling in the
background. Distinctly feminine giggling.

What was happening?

"Edward," I said firmly. "I'd like to see you. I'll be calling my parents this
evening and—"

"I'll be there in less than an hour," he interrupted. "With a surprise."

Enigmatic as a cat.

"I hate surprises," I informed him seriously.

He chuckled. "Everyone loves surprises."

"Not Jane Austen," I insisted. "'The pleasure is rarely enhanced and the
inconvenience considerable,' she wrote. I agree wholeheartedly."

"*Emma?*" he asked for confirmation.

My like-meter rose another notch. Edward knew Jane Austen. That was
the kind of surprise I could live with.

Hanging up, I left the dining room and climbed the stairs to my tower,
contemplating. Less than an hour was an unusual amount of time. *Had I
heard giggling?*

I checked the time. 4:00 p.m. Maybe my surprise was food. Did he drive
to another town to get me an American dinner? Was there good Mexican
food in England?

The questions swirling around in my head confirmed my dislike of the
unknown and unexpected. I decided to take a shower to kill time and make
myself feel better.

First, I called downstairs to Jones.

"Yes, Miss McGuire?"

"Do you need me at all? Anymore? Can I, you know, um…" 'Ignore you,' came to mind, but I didn't think I should say it like that.

"Of course," he said, understanding my intent. "We're wrapping up now. I'll lock the door on my way out."

"Thank you!" I called.

I let the steam of the shower distract me from whatever was coming my way.

Chapter Thirty-Seven: A Surprise

As promised, Edward strolled along the garden path to my front door within the hour. I was clean, comfortable, and clear-headed. Once he left, I knew what I'd ask my parents for when I called them.

As I opened the front door of the house, Edward entered the mudroom. He did actually surprise me by swooping me into his arms and twirling me. Although a bit awkwardly, because he could barely lift me off the ground as we were the same height.

I had no idea how to take that. He'd been so reserved since we met, and this action seemed beyond friendship. It felt nice.

"You were supposed to stay inside," he gently scolded.

"Well, you probably weren't supposed to jump on top of a moving vehicle," I said in response. "You could have been killed."

He kissed me on top of the head in an entirely non-passionate and unfortunately familiar way. "Got her, though, didn't I?"

I gave him a peck on the cheek. Daring, considering he was awake this time. "Congratulations. And thank you."

He squeezed me, lingered a moment, stepped away, and gestured me into the living room. "I was beginning to think every Citroen driver was a madman. Turns out it was her."

"We saw the car at Wookey Hole," he acknowledged.

"Yes." I appreciated the admission so much I didn't know what else to say.

"She's the one who tripped you. With that wicked cane."

I nodded. "I still can't figure out how. I didn't see anyone."

He shrugged. "There are all sorts of off-piste places. I saw a couple of schoolboys hiding when we were there."

To change the subject, I said. "Simon drives the same kind of car. And you know who a real madman behind the wheel is? The countess…"

I trailed off because after I sat, he didn't join me. In fact, he went back to the door.

"Hey," I complained.

"Stay here. Your surprise awaits."

That again. "Can't we talk? It's important."

He winked. "After," he promised and bolted into the mud or boot room. The porch door slammed shut.

A minute later, he reappeared with the goofiest grin I've ever seen. On anyone. Ever.

Then I saw it. There was a person behind his back. A sinking feeling descended on me. If he was about to introduce me to his fiancé, I didn't want to hear it.

Tori Gonzalez pushed him aside and ran to me. "No more preamble," she insisted. "Maddie hates surprises."

The long, thick black hair that hung down her back before I left was cut short, framing her round face. But the almond-shaped eyes over her elegant nose still held their mischievous twinkle.

My hand covered my mouth, and my whole body shook. Tears of sheer joy streamed down my cheeks as her arms flew around my waist. She was almost short enough for me to rest my head on top of hers.

"Except this one!" I sobbed, throwing my arms around her in return. "How did you get here? You're like, I don't know." I was at a total loss for words.

"A light in the darkness?" she offered.

I laughed, which helped to get my other emotions under control. "You've been filled in on my ordeal, I take it."

Squeezing each other again, we plopped onto the couch in unison.

"What can I say? Other than, it's you!" I exclaimed.

"Right? I have a million things to say, but my brain has been in a blender."

She reached and squeezed my leg. "I'm sorry," she said with such grace and sincerity that I sniffled again.

"It doesn't matter," I told her. "You came."

"Yeah," she said, a little teary herself. After another sniffle, she said, "I'm awesome."

That was it. I didn't need any more explanations because Tori was here.

Edward cleared his throat. "I'll leave you to it then. Call me later. Or if you hear a funny ringing in the dining room, pick up the phone."

I sprang from the couch and wrapped my arms around him. "Thank you," I said, holding him close.

He kissed my temple and left.

Tori said, "He's charming, isn't he?"

I nodded. "I know. But you're right. I don't know how to relationship."

"He may be worth figuring it out," she advised. "He drove all the way to the airport to drive me here."

"What?"

She nodded, a conspiratorial grin on her face. "When I got off the plane, and a man in a leather jacket held a sign saying, 'Tori Gonzalez.' I thought it was a mistake, but you know, I thought I'd ask. I went to him, and without any preamble, he said, "Maddie's friend?""

"Wow. I'm kinda, I don't know. I didn't think we were a couple. But, friends do things like that for friends. I mean, you came all the way here."

Tori brought her knees up, crossed her arms across them, and rested her chin on her petite hands. She was going for wise, I think.

"He really likes you," she said. "You drive him nuts, but he likes you. Like, like-like, ya know?"

"Like-like? Really?" My excitement was cut short, and I groaned. "That complicates things," I told her. "I'm calling my parents tonight."

"Of course you are, but you're staying here."

Her total confidence made me realize I was missing several pieces of the Tori at my doorstep puzzle.

"Wait. What? Tori, I don't think I can. It's all—"

Her head plopped onto the back of the couch. "Jetlag sucks," she groaned.

I sighed, not knowing how to finish my thought. "Completely. Come on," and took her into the kitchen.

Tori boosted herself onto the tiled counter as I fixed her toast and drinking chocolate. After a moment of consideration, I also started coffee in the French press for a mocha. The hospital doctors had wrapped a regular bandage around my hanging fingernail so I could move it around like normal.

"Okay, first things first," Tori began while munching. "This is delicious, by the way."

"First things, first?" I prompted.

"When they found you, Edward called your parents, and Heather called me."

"Of course," I said. The scenario made sense. My mom would want Tori to know, and Mom wasn't aware that we were in a fight.

"Scott answered my phone, trying to protect me from my frenemies."

"Of which I should not be included," I threw in.

"And," she continued, ignoring me. "Because it was your mom, Scott thought you were trying to get to me. He told her he'd give me the message." Tori arched an eyebrow. "Heather let loose on him."

My eyes popped. "What?"

"You know how your mom is about women and support systems. She went off. Full-on lecture mode, professor voice and all. I heard her from across the room. He tried interrupting for the first few minutes but eventually gave up. Then he started to look scared."

I wasn't sure if I should apologize for my mother's behavior or cheer. I searched Tori's face for a clue as to how to respond.

"We're okay. Scott needed it. I did, too. We'd gotten to an unhealthy place."

It seemed safe to ask, "Are you still, um…"

"Together? Yes. We have stuff to work out, but yeah. I think we can do it." Her expression was too complicated to read. Nostalgia, mixed with love and sadness. Until she held out her cup for more chocolate. That face I could understand.

"I didn't think we liked hot cocoa," she said as I refilled her mug.

"We didn't. But we do now. You want to mocha it?" I indicated the coffee left in the press.

Shaking her head no, she hopped off the counter and made herself another piece of toast. Once the refreshments were taken care of, we each sat on a countertop, just like home.

"He sends his deepest apologies to you," she told me, her face hopeful.

It wasn't the time to point out her boyfriend's various faults. "He was kinda right. I do need to make more friends," I admitted.

Her head bobbled in a noncommittal way. "And to show he meant it, he bought my plane ticket here."

The bit of bread that was on its way to my mouth missed and tumbled to the floor.

"He has his issues, but he is sweet. He's afraid people will take advantage of him if he shows it too much."

"This counts. It was super duper sweet. Thank you, Scott!" I shouted.

A little twang of sadness tugged at me. Tori was here, but my mom wasn't.

"What," she asked, reading my expression. "Wondering why your mom didn't come?"

The great thing about a best friend is that words aren't necessary. "I know I said I wanted to be independent, but..."

"Well, the answer is, she will. In two weeks, during fall break. I went to her condo, which still feels weird, by the way. You should be my neighbor. I can't get used to it."

"Tell me about it," I agreed, missing my old house. I'd redecorated my bedroom every year. Pink and brown dots one season, light purple the next, sophisticated blue jacquard bedspread the year after. I'd get a whim, and my mom would haul out the ladder to paint, and we'd find new curtains and comforters together. I sighed.

"Anyway, Heather was already packed and searching for flights when I got there. I told her I was coming. Of course, she asked about my midterms, so I told her I could turn them in online. I suggested we stagger your visitors so you're not alone. Plus, it'll give you time to readjust. At that point, she admitted that she planned to stuff you into her carry-on and never let you out of her sight again."

That was what I needed. The warm mother-bear hug from a continent away. "My mom." I felt her love from the top of my head to my toes.

Tori nodded. "I know. Anyway, she's giving you space. And I'm here so you can rant."

I put my hand on my chest, mock offended. "Moi? Rant? I don't have any idea what you mean."

She threw a crust of bread at me.

"I also talked to your dad. He'll be here next week, the day after I leave. He'll stay till your mom gets here. He wants to meet Edward."

Little shivers ran through me at the thought. My dad had never met one of my boyfriends, even in high school.

Tori took our mugs to the sink and rinsed them out. "Can I shower?"

"No," I joked. "There's no water in England."

She left the kitchen, exploring on her own. Her suitcase sat at the top of the staircase. Scottish magic, I assumed.

I didn't feel comfortable taking over one of the Priestly's rooms, so we carried her bag up one more flight to my room and settled her in. Tours of the house and visiting could wait.

In the morning, we would decide my future.

Chapter Thirty-Eight: A Hospital Visit

I awoke to the sound of the landline ringing. Slipping down the two flights of stairs, I raced to the phone and checked the caller ID. Which, of course, the phone didn't have. I'd been plunged into Medieval times. "Hello?"

"Miss McGuire?" an unfamiliar male voice inquired.

"Yes?" I groaned.

"Lady Vivian is sending a car. Please meet Rivers on the street in thirty minutes."

Thirty minutes? I could pull it together in that time, but Tori couldn't. "Thirty?"

"Very good, then." Click.

I raced upstairs and shook my sleeping friend. "Tori." Pause, staring intently. "Tori!"

"Go away," she mumbled and scrunched further into her blanket.

Incentives needed to be offered. "I'm going to visit a real live countess. Wanna come?"

No movement.

"Tori."

She flopped the blanket covering her face and opened one brown eye. "Will there be coffee?"

I waggled my head in a wishy-washy way. "No guarantee."

Her face went back into hiding. "Take pictures," she mumbled.

"You sure? They're sending a car."

Her eye reemerged. "Is it a Rolls Royce?"

My gaze dropped to the floor, thinking about Rivers and the red Citroen. She knew what the look meant. "Bye."

I gave her a squeeze and rushed to get ready.

In thirty-five minutes, I made it to the curb.

The countess's driver, Rivers, leaned against the car. "Good morning." He opened the door for me.

With the terror I'd experienced in the past few days, I didn't know if I could deal with his break-neck speeding. I stared at the car, not moving.

"Come along, miss. Lady Vivian awaits."

I clenched my fists and bolted into the car, moving quickly so I wouldn't chicken out. I wanted to click my seatbelt before he put the car in Drive.

To my total shock, he drove like a functioning member of society. Full stops, signals, and appropriate speeds. I wondered if I warranted extra care after helping Simon.

I expected to be carried out of town to a manor house, but instead, we arrived at the Royal Crescents. "Are you kidding me?"

I couldn't believe my luck. I was going to see the inside of one of the famed Royal Crescent houses. There were thirty of them in all, curving in front of an extensive garden of immaculately tended grass.

I had my seatbelt unbuckled and my hand on the handle before I saw her ladyship glide to the car. Rivers bounded out and held the passenger door open for her.

"Thank you, Rivers," she said, all the while ignoring me.

Still driving at a stately pace, Rivers took us to the hospital. The car doors were opened by workers who suddenly appeared. Once inside, we were escorted to a private room. It sat in the corner of the building with windows on either side, allowing sunshine to flood in. Not surprisingly, Simon lounged in an armchair, bathed in light.

There he sat. The lord. I wanted to giggle at the thought, but his appearance checked me. Dressed in jeans and a tee, he looked thin. Dark circles hung under his eyes, and stubble covered his chin. The hair on one side of his head had been shaved, and gauze covered the wound.

"You look awful," I informed him.

"Ta," he responded. He nodded to the chair next to him. "Please, sit." He rose, standing tall but moving in slow motion, and pulled out a seat for his aunt.

"Aunt Vivian. So good of you to come."

She sat in the proffered chair. "Thank you, Simon. Let's begin, shall we?" Without waiting for us to agree or for me to ask what was going on, she continued. "So far, I've kept the press off, but if we don't tell Jeffrey from the newspaper *something*, he'll speculate. We can't have that."

"Of course," Simon agreed.

Wisely, I stayed quiet.

"I'll need a list of facts I can feed to the odious little man without seeming to. Simon, how did you get yourself into this mess? I'd think you'd have had more common sense."

So, we were going in with a stiff upper lip on this matter.

Simon wiped a hand over his face, closing his eyes. He seemed to clear his thoughts before turning to his aunt.

She pulled out a little pad of paper. The delightful scent of rose emitted from it as she flipped to an empty page. She had a half-sized, gold mechanical pencil poised to take notes.

"I'd finished dinner at The Boater and returned to the Baths to do my final walkthrough."

He failed to mention that he'd had me arrested during this dinner, but I supposed that fact shouldn't go into the tabloids, so I let it slide.

Simon went on, "When I arrived at the dig site, a frail, elderly woman stood in the roped-off hallway, crying. The silly cow had gotten her shawl wedged into the opening with the pulley system. My first thought was to call the police and have her in for trespassing."

Vivian crossed her arms, clearly agreeing with Simon's disdain.

"But I couldn't leave her there," Simon admitted.

Chivalry won out over justice. Point for Simon.

"Of course not," the countess responded.

"The woman told me Cliff Whitely had shown her how to use the block-and-tackle, so she tried it herself. I'd never seen the stone moved and was furious at his indiscretion. Eager to finish with her, I pulled the stone away to free her shawl." He shrugged. "She struck me on the head."

Nodding, I finally felt like I had something to contribute. "Exactly the same thing happened to me. Although she lured me there, telling me that the deacon lost something inside. And that Simon had opened it for her."

"The reason," Vivian scolded us in an imperious tone, "the room is sealed is because it holds no artifacts. It shouldn't be polluted, but it holds little interest."

"Turns out it held a dead intern," I volunteered.

Her velvet blue eyes cut to me. I shrank back in my chair, unable to help myself.

"Be that as it may." She glanced at Simon. "I assume you took control of the situation. At what point did you discover the putlog as a means of escape?"

My jaw snapped shut as I ground my teeth together. Clenching my fists into tight little balls, I glared at Simon.

He didn't need my encouragement, though.

His head shook no, and he held up his hand to stop his aunt from writing her version of the story. "No, Vivian. We need to be clear about this." He looked directly into my eyes, a gesture I realized he usually avoided. "Miss McGuire saved my life several times."

Lady Vivian's glance returned to me. "How so?" Although her eyes remained on me, she still addressed Simon.

"The first I remember was after Maddie had forced some bite of food on me. Ghastly stuff but brought me back from the brink."

The steadiness of her gaze directed at my face became uncomfortable. I laced my fingers together in my lap.

"Is this true?" For some reason, she sounded perturbed.

I shrugged, all self-deprecation now that the truth was out there. "Yep." She blinked slowly.

I took it as a sign to continue. "Ella missed hitting my head—"

"I'm sorry. You knew her?" Lady Vivian's expression was incredulous.

I nodded. "She worked at the Abbey." I wanted to point out that she'd been the only companionable person I knew other than Sam and Lily. And now Sam was gone, and I didn't want to think about poor Lily. But I didn't think it was appropriate to point out. I continued, "She tangled my feet with her cane. I managed to grab it as I fell. I landed on my feet, but she maneuvered the stone in place before I could crawl out.

"I found Simon while I was looking for my purse, and I bandaged his head to stop the bleeding. When I located my bag, I split the power bar and a bottle of water. It took me a while to discover the putlogs."

She blinked again.

This time I stayed quiet, waiting.

After a drawn-out pause, she spoke. "As you may know, I have no children of my own. When my husband died, Simon inherited his title. You, Miss McGuire, have saved a peer of the realm." She snapped the little notebook closed, slipped the pencil into its side pocket, and stowed it in her clutch. "Whatever I can do for you, at any point, you need only ask."

Chills traveled across my arms at her words. "Thank you," I choked out.

The countess stood. "I'll leave you for now." She declined to share her plans regarding the press.

When the door closed, I burst out laughing. It was a relief to release all my pent-up tension. Simon stared at me for a minute, then joined in.

"You're a lord," I told him.

He nodded. "Indeed. Rather ridiculous, isn't it?"

"Rather," I agreed, giggling. "So, when I told the rescuers you were with me, and one of them said, 'Good God, we've found the lord.'" I snorted with laughter. "I thought it was an English phrase like OMG."

Simon's face grew somber. "Thank you, Maddie."

I shrugged. "You would have done the same for me. You did actually make me take the last bites of food."

An uncomfortable silence fell between us. Despite everything, we weren't there yet. To break the awkwardness, I said, "I'm totally mentioning this every time you're a jerk to me."

He grinned. "Aristocracy are never jerks. Haven't you learned anything?"

My smile matched his. "We had a revolution against that nonsense."

"Indeed." His expression turned serious again. "You'll need to hold the fort for a couple of days. You're up for it, I assume."

The pit of my stomach fell away. Tori and I hadn't had a chance to talk about my future yet. Staying. Remaining in a place where someone almost succeeded in killing me. Was the stress worth the experience?

Last night and even this morning, the answer was *no*.

But now. Now Simon was on my side. An honest to goodness countess, too. Tori was here, and my parents were coming.

And Edward.

What about Edward? That was too much to think about.

Simon's coughing came from far away. He was doing that polite English thing of getting my attention without pointing out that I'd lost focus.

"Huh? Oh. Sorry."

"Not today, of course. Aunt Vivian can schedule tours while we're out. But everything will go pear-shaped if we're both away for too long."

Standing, I paced around the spacious room, thinking. Finally, I stopped in front of Simon and hooked my hands on my hips. "How can I possibly be invaluable when you've done everything you could to keep me from learning anything? Not to mention that you had me arrested. I mean, literally."

He chortled softly at this point, but I kept going.

"Suddenly, you need me? I haven't spent one day in this country without something horrible happening to me. Why would I stay? What special skills do I have that you need?" All of the sneering I'd endured since I got there came flooding back to me. "What was your problem with me in the first place? And how did you get Edward to the pub that night?" The humiliation of my arrest still stung.

"Your little constable? Posh accent, no money, that one." He chuckled until a cough shook him.

"And why the heck take me to dinner before having me arrested? What kind of psycho does that?" I quit ranting and poured him water out of a crystal decanter.

"Well?" I demanded once his breathing returned to normal.

He raised his eyebrows. "Well, what?" he asked, smiling to himself.

"Answer all those questions." I sat. "Now."

"I didn't know Edward would be there." He took a sip of water before continuing. "Your tours are a hit. You've proven your extensive knowledge of Roman architecture." He shrugged. "Dr. Daniels likes you."

My mouth fell open. I sniffed bull. "Daniels doesn't know I'm alive. I've checked."

"As the person who brings him lunch, no. As the person who sifted, he's asked for you by name. The white stone you set aside showed your diligence."

Several things shifted in my chest.

Stubbornly, I insisted he tell me. "Why take me to dinner?"

With a shrug, he said, "The same reason I let you sift. I wanted you to have a good day. All the way from America wouldn't be a disaster if you had a real experience." He paused, taking another sip. "It's not like I thought you actually had anything to do with it. But procedures must be followed."

Simon stood, a graceful movement despite his weakened state. "No need to worry about tours today. Give Rivers a call. He'll drive you in tomorrow."

I wanted to argue or hear more about Daniels. But Simon obviously needed rest.

"Okay." I wasn't agreeing, but I didn't say *no*, either.

Chapter Thirty-Nine: The Mind Of A Psychopath

As I walked to the car, I saw Rivers there alone. I wanted to ask where the countess was, but I figured it was none of my business. I sat quietly while we zoomed through the city.

Once inside Ash Tree Cottage, I smelled food. In the kitchen, Tori had several pans going at once. The mouthwatering scents of toast, eggs, and coffee made my stomach rumble.

"There you are," she said.

"Am I?"

"Pretty sure." She pointed to the electric kettle. "I almost put that thing on the stove burner. Luckily, I saw the cord."

I spit laughter, going to Tori and hugging her. "I don't know how I survived without you," I told her.

"A struggle, I know. but you managed."

"Barely."

"Beautifully!" She flicked the switch to the kettle back on. "I figured out your French press. I'll have coffee *in uno momento.*"

She handed me a small box with a cell phone logo on it. "This came for you. I think your dad worked one of his deals."

Tearing it open, I found a fully charged phone. I turned the cell on, and all of my contacts blinked to life. "Wow." I stroked the phone like a lost pet that had miraculously returned home.

Striding over to the pantry, I pulled out a tin of tea. "I'm actually in the mood for a cuppa today, ya know?"

We took breakfast in the dining room.

I sighed, aiming for as dramatic as possible.

Tori raised an eyebrow but said, "I've been doing research."

"Of course you have."

"Anyway." She drew out the word with a bit of drama on her part. "Neither Arthur Conan Doyle nor the character of Sherlock Holmes nor Dr. Watson was religious in any way."

"Right?" I agreed. "I asked Ella about that, and she got strange. When I told her about the similarities of her crimes to the stories, she didn't realize she'd done it. She seemed wistful or something."

Tori nodded. "Very odd. How'd she chop the guy's ear off, anyway?"

A shudder ran through me at the memory. "Cliff," I told her. "My predecessor. She used the sword in her cane."

"A sword-cane?" Tori sounded in awe.

The cane was always clutched in her hands. I'd never thought anything of it, even though she never seemed to need it. "You have to picture her," I told Tori. "She's fun-sized, like you."

"Thanks." Tori glared at me affectionately.

"She always wore gloves." I continued. "They're probably isn't a fingerprint anywhere in the Baths. I thought she was classy. Crafty old bird."

I poured a dollop of milk from the glass jar into my tea, watching it blossom. "Ella must have conned Cliff into opening the area with the block-and-tackle system and whacked him on the head. If he fell outside the hole, she could have cut off his ear before rolling him in."

"Yeah, but why did she cut off his ear in the first place?"

I shook my head. "Dunno. Souvenir?"

Tori tilted her head to the side. "Well, if that was the case, why did she send it to you."

I scrunched my eyes, thinking. All I came up with was "Crazy?"

The expression on Tori's face displayed evident disappointment in my deductive powers.

"Fine." I tried a different avenue. "Ella sent it to me because I told her I was Cliff's replacement. And I mentioned Ash Tree Cottage." I tilted my chin. "Motivation. Plus, she had Sherlock Holmes stories whirling in her mind. I think she was trying to warn me away." Another shudder wracked me. "It almost worked."

Tori's nod of agreement gave me courage for the change of subject I hadn't wanted to mention. "Simon asked me to run the tour office while he's recovering."

I expected a big reaction to this news, but instead, Tori nodded. "Okay, that makes sense, though, because her real motivation was the name."

I shook my head no. "The angel Raphael. She told me."

"Si. He threw sinners into a pit in the desert."

"Great. Why did she attach herself to that one? Why not pick a benevolent angel?"

Tori made a face at me, a sure sign I was missing something. "Her name."

"Ella?"

"What? I've been here less than twenty-four hours, and even I know her name is Raphaella. How did you miss that?"

The heel of my hand flew up to bonk myself on the forehead. "I have no idea. I knew her as Ella. To be fair, I've been under a little pressure here."

Tori gathered our dishes and took them into the kitchen.

I showed her to the garden to meet Roderick.

As she stroked Roddy's soft fur, Tori asked, "Why don't we have bunnies at home?"

"I know. He's wonderful. I don't think I would have made it past my first day without him. Although he did, you know, discover the ear."

She sat, and Roddy hopped into her lap. "Who's a clever bunny? Hmm? Did you discover a clue? Yes, you did."

"He finds your baby-talk undignified."

Shrugging, Tori turned to face me, "Maddie, listen. There's a reason your mom won't be here for two weeks. No one wants you to make a decision about leaving until you've had enough time to think."

"A madwoman tried to kill me!" I protested. "No amount of time will ever make that go away."

The shrill ring of the landline inside the house cut short the rest of my declaration. I held out a finger to indicate to Tori that we were not done with this subject and scampered to the console table, holding the phone.

"Priestly residence," I answered.

"Madeline? Is that you?" A woman whose English accent I didn't recognize shouted through a crackling connection.

"Yes?" My mind went blank. I couldn't think of anyone who would be calling me.

"We've got her," I heard her muffled voice say to someone else. The mystery woman redirected her talking back to me. "It's Meryl, dear. Meryl Priestly."

I sank to the floor, the receiver clutched to my ear. How could I possibly explain everything that had happened to me since I arrived at the Priestly's home? I settled for "Hello!"

"We arrived in Skopelos with instructions to call Constable Bailey. I don't know how he found us, quite frankly. He filled us in on everything you've been going through. You poor thing. We abandoned you, and look what's happened."

"No, I'm okay," I assured her.

"You must be simply traumatized, poor dear." Her motherly concern came through the line like a comforting hug.

Tori came into the room, handed me a cup of tea, and sat beside me.

I mouthed, "Thank you," at her.

Tori. My eyes popped. I had invited another person into the Priestly's home without permission.

"I'm okay," I let Meryl know. "But um." She sounded so lovely that I didn't want to hear the disappointment in her voice when I told her about Tori. "I'm sorry I didn't email you, but my best friend is here," I said in a rush.

"Thank goodness, she is," Meryl replied. "Constable Bailey told us about your visitors."

My head flopped back with relief.

"And of course, we're working with the cruise line to catch a flight home

286

as quickly as possible so we can help to take care of you," she said.

Tears sprang to my eyes at the unexpected support. "You don't have to do that," I offered, only half meaning it. "My dad will be here, then my mom. I'll be okay. Don't ruin your vacation."

"Well, it's hardly a vacation if we're worried sick over your well-being. We'll be home as soon as we can. In the meantime, put your guests in the bedroom closest to your stairs. There's quite a lovely bed and an en-suite sink."

"I can't thank you enough," I told her.

"Don't you think twice, dear. I must ring off. See you very soon."

She was gone, but her calming presence lingered.

"They're coming home," I informed Tori.

She hugged me, and we sat like that for a moment.

Neither of us wanted to admit it, but sometimes it's nice to have an adult to lean on.

"What were we talking about?" I took a sip of the tea.

"About your staying on. Which you will do."

I set my cup on the table, suddenly wishing it was coffee. "A homicidal maniac," I reminded my friend. "Tried to kill me."

"I know." She snaked an arm around my shoulders again. "And you handled it. If you can do that, you can do anything." Releasing me, she added, "Besides, I won't be available at your beck and call next semester."

"What?"

"Washington, DC. I got the internship."

"You've been sitting on that news? Tori, that's incredible!"

Her eyes flicked away, and she hid a shy smile. "Well, my news didn't rate, considering all...." Her hand made a continuing motion to cover the extent of, well, everything.

"What's Scott think?"

"He fussed at first, but he got out his calendar and planned weekends when I could come home and visit."

"Is he going to visit you?" I blurted out before thinking.

Bristling at first, she shook it off. "One step at a time. If he doesn't come,

I'll send him to your mom to set him straight."

Having Tori with me was like a soft pillow. Everything felt better. While Scott had a point about me making more friends, I'd never let anyone distance me from Tori again.

A text dinged on my new phone. I glanced at it, then looked at Tori, eyebrows raised.

"Well?" she asked.

"Edward wants to see me."

Chapter Forty: The Decision

The strange part was that Edward wanted to meet at the Baths. Did I need that kind of reminder so soon? No, no, I did not.

"How about Sally Lunn's?" I suggested, hopefully, as an alternative.

Tori and I got ready together, discussing food, British politics, and the royals.

I played tour guide on our walk into town.

"I love these clouds," she commented.

"Right? Everyone here apologizes about the lack of sunshine, but I love it."

I pointed out the Devonshire Arms. "The bus drops you here to get to the cottage. It goes around back." I said this with such confidence that even I believed I knew what I was doing.

"The Sally Lunn house is one of the oldest in Bath. The bunns, or bunnies, are delicious."

As I explained more landmarks, my love for the city tapped on my heartstrings. Beautiful, rich in history, and home to a constable who was currently standing in front of the cafe, Bath had its charms.

"He's kinda cute," Tori commented with her eyes on Edward, whose leather jacket was thrown over one shoulder.

"Sigh," I said, still not knowing what to do about him.

We all hugged, and I opened the door for us to go in. Tori did, but Edward handed me a bunn and steered me to the Baths. "We'll be back," he told her.

"Hey!" I complained, indignant on my friend's behalf. "That was rude."

"She'll be alright. Ten minutes."

I stopped, channeling my fear of going to the museum into anger at being tricked and bossed around. "You're not in charge of what I do. My friend flew all the way from Arizona, and I'd like to visit with her." I shoved the bunn back at him and stomped into the shop.

He followed me all the way in this time. I found Tori chatting happily with an elderly gentleman in a plaid cap and matching scarf. It was the same man who had told me about the hanging tree days earlier.

"Oh! Here she is," Tori exclaimed as I walked toward her. "This is Fred," Tori introduced us. "He's keeping me company while you go to the Baths."

Staring at her, I turned to Edward. "Are you coercing my friend behind my back?"

He screwed his face up. "When you put it like that, it sounds bad."

Fred discretely turned back to his own table.

"Well, it is bad. Talk to me. I'm right here. No surprises, remember?"

Edward pulled out a chair for me, and we sat. I couldn't decide on what to drink, so I picked at the bunn instead.

"My last surprise worked out okay," Edward insisted.

I cut my eyes to him.

He raised his hands. "Okay, okay. No more." He changed the subject. "Coffee or tea?"

Neither sounded appetizing, so I shrugged. "Tell me what's going on." I glared from one of them to the other.

Tori spoke first. "Edward texted and asked if I could get you to the museum. I agreed that you need to face your fears."

"So, tricking me is the answer?"

"He's right. When you say it like that, it doesn't seem as sympathetic as we meant it."

"Why do I need to go to the museum? Tell me. Straightforward."

Edward grinned. "Samantha Niven has returned and wants to see you."

My face beamed with happiness. "Sam? Why didn't you say so?" I stood, hugged Tori, and skipped out of the restaurant.

Edward followed. "You're right. You really don't like surprises."

"Simon made it seem like she'd been fired. Later, I found out that she was doing research on a job he found for her."

We stopped in front of the double doors, and I went cold.

I breathed in and out a few times.

Edward gave my shoulders an encouraging squeeze.

I nodded, ready to talk with Sam. As I turned toward the Oversight office, Edward pulled me into him.

"I apologize." He sounded sincere, and my stomach flip-flopped.

I waited for an explanation. His hand tucked a strand of hair behind my ear.

After what seemed a very long time, he said. "You don't need to be tricked or coerced. You are the bravest person I've ever met."

To keep the sudden surge of emotion from overwhelming me, I said, "I bet your cop friends wouldn't agree."

He grinned. "I don't know. Parikh was impressed. Jones is definitely afraid of you."

I laughed, then threw my arms around him. All in all, it was a massive display of public affection in front of a British landmark. Shocking.

Letting go, I indicated that he should stay back. I strode inside.

Sam stood in the center of the Oversight office, hands on her hips. She pivoted slowly and stopped when she saw me. "Would you look at what he's done?" she demanded, indicating the office's new configuration.

I nodded. "Simon had everything changed within an hour, I think."

She leaned against the desk. "It's better, though, isn't it?"

Agreeing, I came in and sat. I didn't understand why I was so attached to her. I'd only worked with her a few days, but relief washed over me now that she was back.

"He does this, you know," she informed me. "Simon. He finds a brilliant opportunity for me, gets me out of the way, and reorganizes everything."

Incredulous, I asked, "He's done this before?"

"I admit to being a bit of a mess," she answered. "The part that annoys me is that he always hides a flask." She moved around and checked a file cabinet drawer. "I can't find it this time."

I stared. "The flask is Simon's?"

"No, of course, it's mine. Simon's idea of a joke on my being Irish and all. I keep honey in it for my tea."

Once finished with the filing cabinet, she rummaged through the desk drawers. "I've heard you dug a hole in my perfectly preserved Roman museum.," she continued.

I couldn't detect any displeasure at my vandalism, so I kept my answer light. "I thought it would be better than polluting the site with a pile of dead bodies." My tone darkened as I lowered my voice. "I felt awful doing it, but I couldn't think of another way out."

"It'll probably bring in more tourists than the Romans do. At least for a few months. Lady Vivian has offered to help with the restoration of the area." Rifling through more drawers, she said, "Simon tells me you're in charge of the tours until he's back. Can you be in first thing in the morning?"

"Yes, of course." The answer came out before I had time to think, but it felt right. I'd stay. Of course, I would. What budding archeologist would give up an opportunity like this?

Sam found what she was looking for at the back of the bottom desk drawer; a silver flask with her initials engraved across its face. She turned it over a few times, a crease between her eyebrows.

"What's wrong?" I asked.

She held out the flask. "It's lovely. But not mine."

I pointed out her monogram. "Maybe Simon got you a new one?"

She grinned. "Just like him. Buy me a gift, then hide it." She unscrewed the cap and inhaled deeply. "Fine Irish whiskey." She shook her head. "I'll bring it back with honey tomorrow."

She patted my shoulder. "See you in the morning, then."

Impulsively, I hugged her. As I turned and scurried out of the office, I heard her say, "You're flying it, alright."

Back at Sally's, I joined Edward, Tori, and their new companion Fred. He stood when I entered and offered me his seat.

"I'll see you around," Fred promised me with a wink as he left.

"Tea or coffee?" Edward asked again as I sat.

I knew the question was about more than beverages. I'd made up my mind. "Tea," I answered. "Definitely tea."

After an hour of the three of us talking nonstop about nothing, Edward turned his Scottish burr on Tori. "If you don't mind, lass, I'd like to speak to Maddie alone."

She answered, "If you asked me with that accent, I'd go stand in traffic."

"Don't," he gave her that lopsided smile. "Too much paperwork for me." He stood and held his hand out to me.

We left the cafe still holding hands and walked to a stone arch alcove draped in vines. My heart fluttered in anticipation of what he'd say next. He'd gone through an awful lot of trouble to make me feel secure these past two days.

"I want to be completely honest here," he began, and heat traveled to my face in waves. Tori said he liked me but hearing it from him was different.

"DCI Bray asked me to make sure you didn't leave the country."

I blinked. That confession was not what I was expecting. I opened my mouth, then snapped it shut. "What?"

"For the conviction to go smoothly, we need you here for the inquest. You're not a suspect, so we can't take your passport, but it's important to the case that you stay."

Okay, that made sense. I was sure there was more. "But?"

His eyes held mine, causing little butterflies to flurry in my stomach. "But what?" His voice took on a quiet, intimate tone that made my fingers tingle.

"Or better, and?" I insisted.

He leaned in and whispered into my ear. "And what?"

No. I wanted to hear the words. No assumptions. I put my hand on Edward's chest and pushed him gently away.

"And what about you?" I demanded. "And don't ask 'what' again."

He pulled me in for a hug. Stepping back, he searched the sky. "If you were an English bird, I wouldn't have needed to say more. I'm not used to you Americans. You're so...."

"Straightforward," I provided.

"Pushy, I'd say. Bleedin' annoying, it is."

"Honest," I offered, beaming.

"Assertive."

"Forthright." I took his arm.

He slipped his other hand into mine. "Obnoxious."

"Delightful."

"Mmmm," he sighed contentedly but said, "That's not the same thing."

"No, but it's true."

He turned to me, eyes half-closed, lips parted, and I whispered, "You didn't drive my best friend from the airport on police time."

He laughed, dropping his head, shaking it. I let go of him. Taking a deep breath, he cupped my face in his hands and said, "Alright. I want you to stay. Will that do?"

Yes, that would do. I kissed him. Electricity shot through the length of my body, causing explosions of fireworks as my eyes fluttered closed.

Until I remembered we were on a public street. It took some effort to pull away.

"I was sure I wanted to leave, except for you," I confessed.

He nodded, a small smile playing around his lips. "Have you ever heard of the Cotswold Way?" he asked.

"No. Why?"

"We'll go on a hike and a picnic. A straightforward, regular date."

I squeezed his hand. "It sounds wonderful."

We embraced again and then strolled to Sally Lunn's.

"You'll love it," he assured me. "I guarantee you won't find a body in a bath."

I nodded my approval. "Good. I could do without that."

He pulled me in close. "And you'll discover a bit of real magic."

I already had.

Acknowledgements

The Roman Baths and the Bath Abby are incredible historical sites that should be visited on any trip to England. To my knowledge, neither has ever been the hotbed of violence depicted in this work. On the contrary, the personnel and guides at both institutions are helpful, kind, and knowledgeable. I would also like to acknowledge the Blackbird Writers for their invaluable support and wealth of experience.

About the Author

Sharon Lynn was raised in Arizona, but it was living in England as a teenager and every return trip since that inspired the setting of her first novel. As a professor of theater, film, and writing she coaches and mentors aspiring artists. Her short stories can be found in anthologies from Malice Domestic and Desert Sleuths. She is a member of the Mystery Writers of America, Sisters in Crime, and the Author's Guild. Please sign up for her newsletter at www.blackbirdwriters.com and www.sharonlwrites.com.

SOCIAL MEDIA HANDLES:

@sharonlwrites on Twitter, Instagram, Pinterest, Tumbler and Facebook page.

AUTHOR WEBSITES:

www.sharonlwrites.com and www.blackbirdwriters.com

Also by Sharon Lynn

"Final Curtain" (2020) in Malice Domestic's *Mystery Most Theatrical*; *"Carne Diem"* (2019) in the Anthony Award-winning *Malice Domestic 14: Mystery Most Edible*; *"Death on Tap"* (2017) in Sisters in Crime's Desert Sleuths anthology *SoWest: Killer Nights*. *"The Professor's Lesson"* was published in *Malice Domestic 16* in 2022. Recipes and writing tips included in *Recipes to Kill For*.

Death on Tap and *Carne Diem* are available as standalone short stories on Kindle.

CPSIA information can be obtained
at www.ICGtesting.com
Printed in the USA
BVHW081809301222
655313BV00001B/126